Forged in Fire

"Don't stand there gawking like a sea bass—*fight!*" Lieutenant Destine shouted, then shook off her panicked captors and snatched her sword from one's belt. Whipping it overhead, both hands on the pommel, Belinda Destine sank the sharp blade to the hilt in an octopus limb."

One Who Swims With Sekolah

Between heartbeats Iakhovas's right arm blurred, becoming something edged and sharp, something that somehow looked more right on him. The razor edge sliced the captured sea elf's throat. Blood sprayed into the water, drifting into a fine mist.

The Crystal Reef

Then the sharks came.

There were only a few at first, slashing through the red water, snapping and chomping and devouring anything they touched. The battle continued until only three skiffs remained, their crews rowing madly for the relative safety of the outer reef. A large tiger shark wriggled into the sinking boat and chased the inhabitants into the arms of waiting locathah. . . .

THE THREAT FROM THE SEA

Rising Tide
THE THREAT FROM THE SEA: BOOK I
MEL ODOM

Under Fallen Stars
THE THREAT FROM THE SEA: BOOK II
MEL ODOM

Realms of the Deep
THE THREAT FROM THE SEA
EDITED BY PHILIP ATHANS

The Sea Devil's Eye
THE THREAT FROM THE SEA: BOOK III
MEL ODOM

May 2000

THE THREAT FROM THE SEA

REALMS OF THE DEEP

EDITED BY
PHILIP ATHANS

REALMS OF THE DEEP
The Threat from the Sea

Cover art by Don Maitz
Interior art by Sam Wood
First Printing: March 2000
Library of Congress Catalog Card Number: 99-65607

9 8 7 6 5 4 3 2 1

ISBN: 0-7869-1568-4

T21568-620

U.S., CANADA,	EUROPEAN HEADQUARTERS
ASIA, PACIFIC, & LATIN AMERICA	Wizards of the Coast, Belgium
Wizards of the Coast, Inc.	P.B. 2031
P.O. Box 707	2600 Berchem
Renton, WA 98057-0707	Belgium
+1-800-324-6496	+32-70-233277

Visit our web site at **www.wizards.com**

CONTENTS

Hard Choices

Lynn Abbey

19 Ches, the Year of the Gauntlet

"What happened here?" the gray-bearded merman asked.

"Sahuagin," Shemsen replied.

Yesterday there had been twenty-two sentry posts out where the Waterdeep outflow channels cut through the sea shelf. Today there were twenty-one.

The merman frowned, all shifty shadows in the soft, greenish light of the living lanterns he and his companions strung from the reins of their seahorse mounts. Forty fathoms up, through wisps of plankton, the moon danced on a becalmed sea. It had been different at dawn.

"They came riding a squall," Shemsen explained. A sea elf refugee from warmer water, he'd been swimming Waterdeep for a decade, long enough to master the local underwater dialect. "We looked up, and there they were."

Sahuagin weren't the only sea-folk who hid in the heavy water that fell from the sky. Any hunter with wits swam with the rain: merfolk, sea elves, selkie, dolphins. Though the sahuagin were, perhaps, the best at hiding their stench in freshwater torrents.

"We were outnumbered from the start."

The merman's frown consumed his face. "You survived."

It wasn't something a man liked to admit, but one-on-one, sahuagin over matched both mermen and sea elves. If Shemsen's patrol had been ambushed *and* outnumbered, there should have been no survivors.

Gashes in Shemsen's silvery green flesh winked blood as he shrugged. "What happened, happened." Fatalism was bred in salt water. "They were in a hurry, bent on destroying the beacon. They didn't stay to feed."

The gray-beard's second levered his trident against a mauled sea elf corpse. Shemsen closed his eyes, remembering how Peshhet, trailing his own blood and gore, had come between him and death. Shemsen turned away before reopening his eyes and found himself facing the charred remains of the outpost beacon.

"We heard it shatter," the merman said, guessing Shemsen's thoughts. "It will be a tenday before the Waterdeep mage-guild enchants a new one—more than a tenday with Fleetswake on the tide. There'll be a blind spot now, till it's replaced. Not a big one, but a gap in Waterdeep's defenses all the same. And sahuagin! What are *they* doing so far north?"

2

Shemsen turned; they faced each other. A vagrant current—an underwater breeze thick with plankton—passed between them. Krill swam with the plankton, a school of young menhaden swam after the krill. Conversation stopped as Shemsen and the mermen each snatched a menhaden meal.

Umberlee's will: Only a fool ignored what She provided.

"Can anyone of us claim to understand the sahuagin mind?" Shemsen asked afterward.

"Well said, sea elf," the merman second said. "Eadro watches!" He touched the blood-coral amulet of his private god. "We thought Waterdeep was beyond their reach."

Shemsen didn't know the four mermen. If they'd all been in their native water—their balmy, crystal clear southern seas—they'd have swum around each other's wakes. Instead sea elves and mermen alike had been driven north by shadowy enemies that were not sahuagin, or not exclusively sahuagin.

"Who's to say they weren't fleeing something larger and darker themselves?"

The second clutched his coral amulet in his fist, but the gray-beard was carved from stouter stuff. "Let them try Waterdeep Harbor. One eye blind, and they'll still meet their match. Outnumbered, you say, but they took a loss and you survived. Let them tell *that* to the sharks, if they dare."

The gray-beard swept out an arm to clap Shemsen on the shoulder. Through his wounds, Shemsen braced for the blow. His heart rate doubled and his muscles relaxed, even so he flinched as it fell.

"I have salve," the gray-beard said as one of the two juniors swam over with a wax-sealed shell.

3

Shemsen shrugged off the merman's hand and offer. "I'll tend myself when I get to the harbor."

"You can swim, then, and not fall behind?"

"I'll keep up or fall behind. I've swum alone before. I waited here only until you or someone else came to investigate and relieve me. This was my post for Waterdeep. I'd not have it said that I abandoned it."

The gray-beard shook his head. Mermen kept their own customs. They were brave enough, when riled, and dutiful, but no two pairs of eyes saw honor the same way in air or water.

"Call for a mount, if you need one," the gray-beard said from his seahorse, "or latch onto the dorsal."

All four mermen rose from the silt.

"You're leaving no one behind?"

"The beacon's gone, sea elf. A dark spot, true, but a small one. If the sahuagin are clever enough to return without catching another beacon's eye, then let them try the inner defenses. Until after Fleetswake, any one posted here is as isolated as he'd be in Umberlee's Cache. I'll not leave men where they can do no good."

Cold water surged over Shemsen's gills as he sighed. Only a fool refused what Umberlee provided.

* * * * *

There were no reefs in Waterdeep harbor, no kelp forests or gardens, and despite the concerted efforts of all those living above and below the waterline, an unpleasant taste or texture wasn't uncommon. Shemsen never forgot he was a refugee. Even his home-quarters reminded him. When sea elves first sought sanctuary here, the mage-guild had carved straight-lined niches into the cliffs that gave the harbor its name. A woven

4

net was fastened over the niche, lest the scouring tides steal what little he'd accumulated during his ten-year exile.

Shemsen shared the niche with another sea elf. Eshono had been shark-mauled during their long retreat to Waterdeep. Their surviving healer had done her best, but what Eshono had needed most, a month's rest and regular meals, were beyond provision. Eshono's leg had withered. He got around well enough in the harbor, but he couldn't handle the long patrols that the refugees claimed as both right and obligation. Instead, he'd trained himself as an advocate who labored on the lubber's dry ground, mediating the disputes and confusions that plagued the sea elf refugees in their safe, but utterly strange, sanctuary.

They were an odd pair, Shemsen and Eshono, with little in common but a destroyed village and a harrowing journey to cold water. These days, though, that was enough.

"To Peshhet," Eshono said, saluting the dead sea elf with a paste-filled shell. "While we live, we remember him."

He swallowed the paste. Shemsen mirrored the other sea elf's movements.

"I tell you, my friend, you must take a wife before there's no one left to remember us," Shemsen joked bleakly.

Him, Shemsen the Drifter, telling jokes! His gill slits fluttered in disbelief. Against all odds, he'd come to think of crippled Eshono as a friend.

"When you do," Eshono replied, scooping another portion of paste from the bowl floating between them. "And not a day sooner."

"Too old."

"How old? Four hundred? Five?"

"I feel older," Shemsen replied honestly.

"All the more reason. Take a wife. Make a family before it's too late."

Shemsen lowered his head, a gesture most refugees understood. All carried scars and secrets and guilt for surviving what so many others had not. Shemsen had more than most. His friendship, such as it was, with Eshono survived because the other man had a keen understanding of where the uncrossable boundary lay.

"I have salve," Eshono said, changing the subject. He retrieved a pot from beneath his hammock. "I got it from one of the lubber temples. It's not as good as Auld Dessinha made, but it seals you up. This one's almost empty. Take what's left, if you wish."

Eshono had lost so much meat to the shark that his wound would never quite heal. His over-taut skin seeped and cracked whenever he exerted himself. He went through pots of salve and had become a connoisseur of priests, healers, and potions.

Shemsen, who'd been slashed to the bone in several places, accepted the fist-sized pot. "I'm going out."

"So soon? Your body needs rest—"

"My mind needs it more. I'll be back when I'm back." Shemsen took up his trident and kicked toward the open corner of the netting. He was halfway through before turning back to say, "Thanks for the salve. You're a good man, Eshono. Don't follow me."

"I wouldn't ever," Eshono assured him, a look of boyish anxiety across his face. "Be careful, Shemsen. We're so few now. Everyone's precious."

Shemsen kicked free of the niche. His thoughts were heavy, and he sank down and down, until he passed the deepest of the niches. Here, a man needed a lantern to see past his own feet, unless his eyes weren't his only navigation senses. Of course, such a man who didn't rely on his eyes, even though he might look exactly like a sea elf, couldn't possibly be a sea elf.

Shemsen daubed a bit of Eshono's paste on the least of his gouges. A man who wasn't a sea elf couldn't tolerate Auld Dessinha's salves. But a lubber's salve—a pitchy salve that stung but didn't burn—wouldn't harm him if it didn't harm Eshono. Shemsen slathered his wounds and let the emptied jar sink to the harbor bottom. When the sting was gone, he swam away.

Ships cast shadows through the water. Shemsen hid in darkness until he reached the main channel. Stealth, even deception, was habit with his kind. No one, including Eshono, suspected him. Entering Waterdeep for the first time, he'd been touched by one of Faerûn's mighty mages—all the refugees were before they were granted sanctuary. He'd raised his heartbeat, relaxed his skin, and expected to die, but the mage had passed him through.

And why not? In the water and above, most folk didn't believe his kind could exist. A sahuagin shaped like a sea elf? That was a cautionary tale for disobedient children. Among sahuagin, the elf-shaped malenti were tolerated, rarely, because sahuagin needed spies. Even among sahuagin the elf shape was accounted a curse rather than a blessing. Hatchlings were swum through the gardens where malenti quartered and trained.

Give glory to Sekolah that He provides all that His worshipers need to serve Him. Give thanks to Sekolah that He did not shape me *malenti.*

7

The word itself meant "grotesque" and Sekolah in His wisdom, if not His mercy, understood that malenti torment should not endure for long. The elf-shape was lethal. By the measure of sun and tide, Shemsen was younger than Eshono, yet Eshono was counted a youth and Shemsen for a man nearing the end of his prime. In his bones, Shemsen felt older still.

Merfolk appeared overhead. Pilots, it was their job to guide the ships through the channel to open water. Shemsen dived to avoid the eddies as the rudder beat against the estuary current. Safe below the roiled water, he swam toward Deepwater Isle, and the underwater lighthouse that marked the rift called Umberlee's Cache.

With Fleetswake scarcely a tenday away, folk of all types were making preparations for the moment when Waterdeep made its annual gift to Umberlee, Goddess of the Sea. Twenty barges, maybe more, had been lashed and anchored into a ring above the lighthouse. Already they rode low in the water, laden with offerings from landlubbers and sailors, guilds and shops, wizards and priests.

It was no different below. Most of the sea folk passed their tokens up to the barges or tied them to the great funnel net being strung even now below the hulls. On Fleetswake Eve, when the offerings were cast into the water, every sea-dweller would swim to the net and make sure nothing drifted free. There was no worse omen than a gift meant for Umberlee not falling into Her Cache.

Lubbers arranged their pantheon in alliances and tried—for the sake of their fears—to bind Umberlee in a controllable place. Those who dwelt in the sea knew better. No sea-dweller worshiped the Queen of the

Oceans. She was the oceans personified, and She always triumphed.

Net weavers hailed Shemsen as he approached. Did he know where he was? Was he lost? Inebriated? Bent on self-destruction? He told them, in words gleaned from the rough edges of the harbor, to tend their own affairs. A few responded in kind. A sea elf—a woman he didn't know—hauled the funnel net aside, allowing him to swim through an as-yet-unsewn seam.

"Peace to you," she called from above. "Peace for your pain."

The words were not a traditional sea elf greeting. Shemsen was impervious to those. By the time he'd left the sahuagin garden to steal a place in a sea elf village, he'd known all their traditions and despised them without exception. For almost a century he'd lived among them, his malaise and nausea relieved only when he slipped away to drop a cunningly knotted string where another sahuagin might find it. He wore his orders around his neck and the sea elves— the thrice-damned fools—admired his treachery so much they'd ask him to fashion similar ornaments for them.

Then, on a moonless night when the sea had been too quiet, miasma, like ink from all the cuttlefish that had ever swum, had descended on the village. It clung to gills and nostrils alike. Suffocation wasn't the worst part. The miasma had talons, or teeth, or knives— Shemsen never knew which. He never saw what slashed at him. He'd assumed it was some new boon the sahuagin priestesses had sought from Sekolah. Certainly, he'd survived because he was sahuagin, tougher than any sea elf and blessed with true senses beneath his malenti skin.

Shemsen had expected to find sahuagin beyond the miasma, but there were only sharks so wrought with blood frenzy that no malenti could hope to dominate them. It had taken Shemsen's remaining strength to resist their call as they tore through the sea elf survivors. He couldn't say, then or now, why he'd resisted, except that however much Shemsen had despised his neighbors, he hadn't wanted to be anyone's last living vision.

Exhausted from his private battle, he'd fallen to the sea floor in a stupor. When he'd opened his eyes again the miasma was gone and he was neither alone nor among sahuagin. A handful of villagers had survived. They were numb and aimless with grief. Shemsen had easily made himself their leader and led them west with the prevailing current, toward the sahuagin village he hadn't seen in decades. He anticipated the honor that would fall around his shoulders when he, a malenti, finished what the miasma and sharks had left undone.

Ten days later, they swam above deserted, ruined coral gardens. A year, at least, had passed since Shemsen's kin had swum through their ancient home and he, suddenly more alone than he'd imagined possible, did not tell his look-alike companions what had happened. True, there had been no entwined instructions waiting for him the previous spring, but that hadn't been unusual. In Shemsen's centuries of spying on the sea elves, he'd often gone four years, even five or six without contact. He'd never considered that something might be wrong.

He'd never know what happened to his kin. If there'd been survivors, none had thought to leave him a message. Shemsen didn't think there had been survivors. Knowing what had been there, he saw the scars of violence and destruction. Sahuagin did war against each other, for the glory of Sekolah, who decreed that only the best, the strongest and boldest, were meant to survive, but in none of the many tales Shemsen knew by heart did sahuagin abandon what they'd won or lay it to waste.

It had seemed possible that both villages, sahuagin and sea elf, had fallen to an unknown enemy, a shared enemy. A mortal mind did not want to imagine an enemy that was shared by sahuagin and sea elves.

Shemsen hadn't embraced the sea elves that day above the ruined sahuagin village. Neither compassion nor mourning were part of the sahuagin nature, which was Shemsen's nature, if not his shape. Still, a sahuagin alone was nothing and faced with a choice between nothing and sea elves, Shemsen chose the elves. He made them his own, his sacred cause, and led them north, to fabled Waterdeep. By the time they arrived, his loathing had been transformed into something that approached friendship.

So he rolled over in the water and called, "And peace with you, for your pain," to the woman before making himself heavy in the water.

Shemsen had heard that as recently as sixteen years ago, the Cache was a maelstrom that spewed or sucked, depending on the tide, and chewed up any ship unfortunate enough to blunder across it. Then the merfolk had arrived in Waterdeep. In the name of safety, their shamans had gotten rid of the maelstrom and poked a ship-sized hole in a goddess's bedchamber.

That was the merfolk. Half human, half fish, half mad. Except they, too, were refugees with tales of

11

black water and annihilation weighing their memories. Perhaps they'd known exactly what they were doing.

Shemsen sank until the water changed. Heavy, cold, yet tangy with salt, it was the richest water he'd ever drawn across his gills. He knew that had there been light, he would have been able to see to the bottom. If there had been light. . . .

The darkness within Umberlee's Cache went beyond an absence of light. There was silence, too, in Shemsen's ears and in those sensitive places along his flanks. He couldn't tell if he was drifting up, down, or sideways.

Malenti!

A woman's voice, beautiful and deadly, surrounded Shemsen, and checked his movement through the water.

Malenti, why are you here? Why do you disturb me? Does the Shark not hear your feeble prayers?

Shemsen gathered his wits, but the Sea Queen didn't need his words. She flowed into his mind and took answers from his memory.

Shemsen had told the truth to the mermen two days earlier, just not all of it. Sahuagin had ambushed his patrol. The sea elves were outnumbered and they were doomed, yet Shemsen fought with them until it was just him and two sahuagin left. It had been a better showing than he'd expected from the likes of Peshhet. One of the remaining sahuagin was a yellow-tailed priestess.

When she gave him her full attention, she knew. By Sekolah's grace, the priestess had recognized Shemsen for what he was.

Malenti!

12

She had the god-given power to compel him and, because he'd rather die a free-willed man than a priestess's plaything, Shemsen had thrown down his weapon.

Why had he fought them, she'd demanded, and Shemsen had answered defiantly that she was not from his village, his baron, or his prince. He owed more to the enemies he lived among than to a stranger. She demanded the name of his village. Shemsen spat it out along with the names of his baron and prince.

"Prince Kreenuuar chose poorly," the priestess had said. "He became meat and all those who followed him became meat. You serve Prince Iakhovas now."

Shemsen hadn't recognized the name, which meant little, except that Iakhovas wasn't a sahuagin name, not even a malenti name. He couldn't easily imagine a prince with such an unseemly name, until he thought about Prince Kreenuuar's fate and the black cloud.

"Choose wisely, malenti!" the priestess had said, threatening Shemsen with the shark's tooth amulet she wore against her chest.

Had he truly believed he'd escape his malenti fate? Sekolah had called up the sahuagin to magnify His glory. He'd called up the malenti to magnify the sahuagin. Shemsen could serve this new Prince Iakhovas and his priestess freely . . . or he would serve as a spell-blinded thrall. Pride that only another malenti might understand had raised Shemsen's elven chin, exposing his soft, unscaled throat as he clasped his hands behind his back in submission.

The priestess accepted Shemsen's wise choice, adding only slightly to the wounds he'd already borne. She'd reminded him that he was a spy, then asked

13

what he knew about Waterdeep.

"Prince Iakhovas comes to teach those who dwell on the land a lesson about the sea. We are charged with finding a safe passage for a single surface ship and fliers. How do we counter these defenses?"

The priestess had pointed at the shimmering beacon and with no further persuasion Shemsen had told her how the power she wielded with Sekolah's blessing could destroy it. Shemsen did not add that one surface ship and all the sahuagin-crewed fliers in the sea would not be enough against the might of Waterdeep. He doubted the priestess would have believed him. One of the few traits sea elves and sahuagin shared was a bred-in-the-bone disdain toward magic, and it was magic that fueled Waterdeep's greatest defenses.

Shemsen thought he'd done well, serving the unknown prince without truly betraying the cold water harbor that had become his most unlikely home, but the priestess hadn't finished.

"The ship and the fliers aren't all. Prince Iakhovas commands a second army . . ."

Many years had passed since Shemsen's survival had depended on his ability to read emotions from a sahuagin's rigid face, still he would swear—even to the goddess as She ransacked his memories—that the priestess feared the new prince's second army, and feared the prince even more. He'd begun to wonder what he'd do if she'd demanded that he swim away with her. Death, he'd thought, might be a wiser choice than serving a prince who put that kind of fear in a yellow-tailed priestess.

In the end, she hadn't asked him to make that choice.

"Prince Iakhovas commands the attack in eleven days' passing. There will have been a festival?"

Shemsen had nodded, and wondered how many other malenti were spying in Waterdeep. "The Eve of Fleetswake. The harbor will be thronged and drunk. A good time for a surprise attack."

"Of course," the priestess had countered, reminding Shemsen of the contempt properly shaped sahuagin directed at malenti. "I will wait for you here as the sun sets after this Fleetswake, and you will guide the second army into the harbor. Fail me, and Sekolah will find you—in death. He will find you and bring you to Prince Iakhovas."

The memory echoed in Shemsen's mind, overriding the scenes that followed: the destruction of the beacon, the feast on fallen comrades. He'd been gone too long. His gut rebelled against the taste of sentient flesh. He'd chosen to die rather than serve Prince Iakhovas. Yet Shemsen had not told the whole truth to the mermen, nor spilled his conscience to the harbor guard. With the priestess's dire threats swirling in his memory, Shemsen had come here, to Umberlee.

Umberlee showed no mercy. With blinding, numbing speed She unraveled the strands of Shemsen's life back to the hatchling pools and the garden where he'd learned what it meant to be malenti. She compelled him to relive the black-cloud night in such detail that he cried out and lost consciousness. He recovered with the strange name, Iakhovas, vibrating in his skull and a thumb-size conch shell hung before his eyes, glowing with its own light.

Take it.

Shemsen needed both hands to grasp the goddess's token, but as soon as its warmth was against his flesh the darkness was lifted. He saw himself in a chamber of wonders: of gold and gems enough to sate the greediest pirate, of weapons to stir the blood of any warrior, and magic of the most potent sort. In the corners of his eyes, Shemsen saw life, men and women stripped naked and helpless. He closed his eyes, but the images lingered.

Ask no questions, the goddess warned. *You will do as Sekolah expects. You may guide the priestess, her prince, and his army to the harbor's heart with My blessing. Fear not, you will know the moment to reveal My gift. You will lead them to Me, and I will reward them.*

Then come to Me yourself, malenti, for your own reward.

Return to me.

A man's mind was never meant to hold the voice of a goddess, much less Her mirth. The insensate blackness returned. Shemsen awoke in his own niche, his own hammock. Eshono hovered beside him, a lantern in one hand and a wad of kelp in the other.

"Shemsen? Shemsen? You've given us all a scare. Tell me you know me."

"I know you, Eshono," Shemsen whispered. He tried to rise, but lacked the strength. "How long?" he asked. "How did I get here?" His last clear memory was of the Cache and Umberlee's voice in his head. Seizing Eshono's wrists, Shemsen hauled himself out of the hammock. "What day is it?"

"The harbor guard found you days ago, drifting near the docks."

"Days!" Shemsen shivered, and not because of the cold, outgoing tide flowing past their niche. "What day is it?"

16

"You've lain here like the dead for six days, and you'd been missing five days—"

"The *day*, man! Tell me what day it is. Have I missed Fleetswake?"

Eshono tried to pull away, but Shemsen's strength was already returning.

"It's Fleetswake morning, Shemsen. The offerings were made last night. Umberlee is placated for another year and Waterdeep is drunk with celebration."

"It's not too late . . . I must go." He released the sea elf and realized, belatedly, that he was naked. "My garb! Eshono, was I like this when you found me?"

"I didn't find you, friend,"

"Was I empty-handed? Pray to all your gods, Eshono, that I was not found empty-handed."

The sea elf's eyes widened dangerously. "You were fully garbed when the guards brought you here, but your hands were empty. There was a bag, though . . ." Eshono gave a kick to the slatted crates where they kept their belongings. "I didn't open it."

Shemsen snatched the small sack from the crate, tore the knot, and shook the contents out. The small conch shell, Umberlee's gift, drifted toward the net. He caught it. Unnaturally warm in his hand, the shell rejuvenated Shemsen completely.

And just as well, the ruined beacon was a day's swim away, even with the tide on his heels. He dressed quickly in eel skin leathers, ignoring Eshono's pleas that he needed rest, food, and a visit to the healers. When he'd strung the small sack to his belt and snugged his belt around his waist, Shemsen took up his trident.

"Wait!" the sea elf protested.

Shemsen brought the tines level with Eshono's heart.

17

"Listen to me, Shemsen, you're not well. Come with me. We'll go to the temple."

Shemsen shook his head slowly, "Move aside, Eshono. I don't want to hurt you, but I have to leave."

Eshono made a wise choice and drifted to the other interior corner. Two kicks and Shemsen was outside the net, which he drew up and hooked over the pegs. It was a strictly symbolic act. The net was meant to confine objects, not elves, but the meaning wasn't lost on the pale, wide-eyed Eshono.

"Whatever happens tonight," Shemsen said earnestly, "know that I have come to think of you as a friend, as I had never imagined I would have a friend, and I would be angry—unhappy—if I thought something happened to you. Stay here. Lie low, and be safe."

"What are you talking about?" Eshono shouted after him, but Shemsen had found the estuary current and was headed for open water.

The conch shell restored Shemsen whenever his strength faltered, and he used it often. Remembering what the priestess had said about the sahuagin plans, Shemsen took a longer route that steered him clear of both ship channels and long-range patrols.

The sun was setting when he emerged from a shortcut rift. Its light turned the overhead surface into a dazzling mirror pocked with dark splotches. Shemsen was heaving too hard—drawing too much water over his labored gills—to focus his eyes clearly. He dug out the shell and clutched it against his heart. Calmed and restored, he looked up again.

One ship, yes—a wallowing pentekonter with a gaping hole amidships where its sahuagin crew could arrive and depart without breathing air. Behind the pentekonter, a single file of oval, wooden fliers, each capable of holding several hundred warriors. Shemsen did the arithmetic. Waterdeep would survive—he'd seen demonstrations of what the lords of the city could bring to a battle—but the harbor would run red first.

And this, if Shemsen believed the priestess, was only the first army. He shaped a prayer to the Sea Queen and breathed it into the conch shell.

Then, what? He could have swum to a working beacon and told them that several thousand sahuagin were headed up the main channel. Assuming he was believed, the beacons could give Waterdeep a few hours to prepare. What could even Khelben Blackstaff, his Lady, Maskar Wands, Piergeiron Paladinson, and all their ilk do to forestall the sahuagin attack, Shemsen asked himself. Notions leaped to his mind, but none stronger than the memory of Umberlee's voice.

You will do as Sekolah expects . . .

Shemsen rose from the seaweed and swam toward the outpost. The yellow-tailed priestess was waiting. She berated him for being late. Between his kind and hers, it was usually wisest to answer contempt with contempt. He snarled that he saw no signs of a second army.

There were others, the priestess admitted, leading the second force across open water. They weren't expected until twilight. Then they'd await a signal from Prince Iakhovas.

The conch shell weighed like iron against Shemsen's hip. *You will know the moment . . .* Did Umberlee expect him to intercept the prince's signal? No. *You will lead them to me . . .*

The priestess—she gave her name as Quaanteel—

19

offered Shemsen meat. He declined and settled against the same stones where he'd waited for the mermen. With a final, reddish flash, the day ended. Night gloom settled quickly as clouds massed above to block the moon and stars. Sekolah's power did not reach above the waves, but Umberlee could summon a storm, if She chose.

And so could any great mage of Waterdeep.

Shemsen nestled deeper into his lair. The sea was cold and full of shadows. Every slight change in the water brought them all to attention. The priestess invariably looked to the southwest, so Shemsen chose a different stone and spotted the army himself.

The shapes Shemsen watched were wrong for surface ships or fliers. They didn't seem to be on or near the surface, either. It was almost as if Prince Iakhovas' second army were a school of giant fish. Sahuagin kept sharks, and some good-sized sharks at that, but not giants and not this far north. The only giants that swam in these cold waters were whales. If the prince had persuaded *whales* to swim against Waterdeep then, perhaps, the city was in trouble.

Quaanteel leaped up. She funneled her webbed hands around her mouth and emitted a series of chirps and clicks, less than words or language, but enough to reach the vanguard of the second army and bring it to a halt before she led Shemsen and several other sahuagin out to meet it.

Three priestesses of considerable rank swam out to meet them. Quaanteel engaged the largest of them in an animated, private conversation that, from Shemsen's distance, did not seem to go well on either side. He had an idea why they might be arguing. The shapes weren't ships or fliers. As best he could make out, the second army was composed of abyssal beasts. He counted aboleths and dragon turtles near the front and had a bad feeling there was worse swimming in the rear.

Fierce as they were, sahuagin steered clear of the abyssals and none of the abyssals were known to school together. Their combined presence implied that a power greater than, or at least significantly different from Sekolah was involved in this attack. That, in turn, implied a few things about Prince Iakhovas, things no self-respecting priestess would accept without an argument.

The men who'd swum with Quaanteel stayed well away from the quarreling priestesses. Those who'd swum with the second army did likewise. There weren't many times when being malenti brought advantages, but this was one of them. Shemsen frog-kicked his way into their conversation. Eight angry, silver eyes focused on his elflike face.

"Go away," Quaanteel commanded.

"Impossible. You named me your guide to Water-deep harbor. If I'm to succeed—for the glory of Seko-lah—I must know what I'm meant to guide through the channel currents. I seek only to serve you well, most favored one."

There was a chance Quaanteel was unfamiliar with sarcasm, and there was a chance she understood it perfectly and meant to put it to her own use. Either way, she flashed her teeth before turning to the larger priestesses.

"The malenti speaks the truth. A guide must know what he is guiding. Show him," she demanded.

If he lived past midnight, which he very much doubted, Shemsen knew he'd never forget swimming among the abyssals. It wasn't just the aboleths, dragon turtles, great crabs and seawolves, eyes of the deep, sea snakes and giant squids massed in one small space, though that was eerie and unnerving in itself. At every heartbeat, Shemsen expected them to come alive with a viciousness that would put blood frenzy to shame, but the beasts were oblivious to their neighbors and surroundings, enthralled by Prince Iakhovas, or so the large priestess explained in an anxious whisper.

"Our orders were to herd them here and wait for his signal."

Shemsen didn't know Khelben Blackstaff personally. Harbor rumor said the man was among the most powerful wizards on the land, and his consort, Lady Laeral, nearly so. Shemsen doubted that even the two of them together could hold so many beasts in thrall.

"And that signal will be?" Quaanteel asked, her fins flared in irritation.

"Prince Iakhovas said we would know it when it came."

That sounded uncomfortably like Umberlee's instructions to him! "I cannot guide these beasts once they awaken," Shemsen protested. "Begging mercy . . . no one could. All we can do is swim toward Waterdeep harbor until we are overtaken."

Quaanteel nodded. "That, undoubtedly, is the prince's plan. For the glory of Sekolah!" Her fist shot above her head. "The land-dwellers shall know fear as they have never known it before. Waterdeep shall be ours!"

Not *ours*, Shemsen thought as he sculled backward, easing his way slowly out of the uncanny school. We are bait, not even meat.

22

They'd all reached the same conclusion, though no one spoke aloud. The priestesses fussed with their amulets while the men stropped their weapons on the sea stone. Shemsen thought of Umberlee's conch and the insignificance of any one man's life. He settled in the silt, both eyes on the somnambulant beasts— morbid curiosity. He wanted to know what would eat him.

An hour passed, then another and another. If they'd successfully ridden the tide all the way in—and Shemsen had no reason to think they hadn't—the pentekonter and fliers should be near the harbor. They should have been noticed, but a wizard who could enthrall an army of abyssal beasts could delude a few pilots and guards, especially the night after Fleetswake. Shemsen wasn't worried, not any longer, not about anything. His arms grew heavy, his vision clouded.

He was suffocating in unnaturally calm water. A malenti's gill slits were relatively small. They relied on currents to speed water over their gills, or they made currents with their hands, or—when all else failed—they used the last of their strength to breach the surface. Shemsen breached like a shark-chased dolphin and gulped air like a drowning lubber.

Except for his thrashing, the air above was as calm as the water below, and just as dark. Shemsen couldn't see the storm clouds, but he felt them pressing down on the air and the ocean. There were no waves. The surface was a midnight mirror, flat and quiet. In all his life, Shemsen had never experienced the surface without a ripple.

His companions appeared nearby, ready to mock his malenti weakness but they weren't fools. They knew

23

wizard weather when they felt it. The priestesses clutched their amulets, invoking Sekolah. Green lightning flashed in the northeast, over Waterdeep.

"Below!" the large priestess shouted.

They needed no second warning as clouds and beasts both came to life.

"Come," a smooth, cruel voice sang as the sea rose. "Obey my words and destroy my enemies. Unite with We Who Eat in our labors."

Lightning struck the surface, drawing up a wave that waited for the wind that surged out of Waterdeep. It buffeted the beasts, enraging them. One of the men struck a sea snake and disappeared. Shemsen cast aside his trident and swam against the surge. At full strength, he slid backward, into a dragon turtle's shadow.

The cruel voice—Prince Iakhovas' voice—energized the ocean. It flowed over Shemsen's gills, seducing his senses. He saw his friend, Eshono, with a gash across his belly and his innards trailing red in clear water. It was an invitation to feast.

You will know the moment . . . You will know the moment . . .

Umberlee's voice came to Shemsen from the depths of his spirit, and from the southwest, on a wind that calmed the wizard weather. While others, beast and sahuagin, cast about in confusion, Shemsen withdrew the conch shell, held it against his lips, and blew.

The eyes of an evil army placed Shemsen at the center of their vision. His strength faltered. He'd hoped for a different sort of miracle, but malenti were used to disappointment. He found a rhythm—water drawn over his gills, air blown into the shell—that left little room for consciousness. His memories of

Umberlee's Cache broke free. Flowing from the conch shell, they mixed uneasily with Prince Iakhovas's commands.

"Obey my words!" the wizard's voice echoed through the sea.

Return to me . . . for your reward . . .

Images of wealth, power, and prey danced among the beasts, caressing their hot minds. The sea crackled with its own lightning as greed warred against obedience. Another moment and blood frenzy would have consumed them all, but the tide changed and, with the southwest wind behind it, rolled toward Waterdeep in a single, wall-like wave.

No choices were required. The abyssal beasts and their puny sahuagin escort rode the tidal surge while Shemsen poured his spirit into Umberlee's shell. Faster than any fish could swim, they raced up the channel, catching the last of the sahuagin fliers as they entered the harbor. The wave rose higher—too high—and began to crest.

"Destroy my enemies!" the wizard's command swirled within the wave.

Return to me . . . for your reward . . .

Shemsen's work wasn't done. When the tumbling wave had drawn even with Deepwater Isle, he blew till his innards bled. With his dying strength, Shemsen dived down, through wave, air, and harbor water, straight into Umberlee's Cache.

* * * * *

Cold shock ripped the shell from the malenti's grasp. His hands were numb, bloodless. The abyssals—not all of them and only a few of the sahuagin—had followed him. Enough, he thought, to insure that Waterdeep would emerge from this battle with its substantial strength intact.

Return to me . . .

Umberlee welcomed Shemsen with glimpses of wealth beyond measure and Her minions reaching out to the abyssals to tear them apart. He fell away from the carnage. There was a woman swimming toward him. Through fading vision, Shemsen knew her instantly.

Return for your reward.

She took Shemsen's weakening body gently in her arms. His heart stopped. There was darkness and, at the end, there was peace for one malenti.

Fire is Fire

Elaine Cunningham

30 Ches, the Year of the Gauntlet

What did you do when the Sea Devils attacked, Grandsire?

Oh, how I savored that question! I could hear it in my mind even as I ran toward the battle. The words were as real to me as the stench of smoke that writhed in the sky above the West Gate, and they rang as loudly in my mind's ear as the boom and crash of wooden beams giving way under wizard fire. No matter that the question would be many, many years in coming. A wizard's apprentice learns that all things must first be conjured in the mind.

As I ran, I conjured apace. Wouldn't the little lad's

face be expectant, his eyes bright with the pride that comes of a hero's bloodline? Wouldn't the bards leave off their strumming and gather near, eager to hear once again the tale of the great wizard—that would be me—who'd fought at Khelben Arunsun's side?

That's what it would come down to, of course. That would be the first question to come to everyone's lips: What did Khelben Arunsun do during the battle? How many monsters fell to the Blackstaff's might? What spells were employed?

I must admit, I myself was most anxious to know the end of this tale.

"Above you, Sydon!"

Panic infused my companion's voice, lifting it into the range normally reserved for elf maidens and small, yapping dogs. Without breaking pace, I followed the line indicated by Hughmont's pointing finger.

The threat was naught but a goodwife at the upper window of the building ahead. She was about to empty a basin of night water out into the back street—a minor hazard of city life that did not abate even during times of conflict. Hughmont was at best a nervous sort. Clearly, he was not at his best, but he was my training partner nonetheless, so I snagged his arm and spun him out of the way. He tripped over a pile of wooden crates and sprawled, but if his landing was hard at least it brought him beyond reach of the fetid splash.

A word from me sent the tumbled crates jostling into line like soldiers who'd overslept reveille. They hustled into formation, then leaped and stacked until a four-step staircase was born. I whispered the trigger word of a cantrip as I raced up the stairs, then I leaped into the air, flinging out my arms as I floated free. My exuberant laughter rang through the clamor of the city's rising panic, and why should it not? What a day this was, and what a tale it would make!

Hughmont hauled himself upright and trotted doggedly westward, coming abreast of me just as my boots touched cobblestone. The look he sent me was sour enough to curdle new cream. "You'd best not waste spells on fripperies and foolishness. You'll be needing all you've got, and more."

"Spoken like the archmage himself!" I scoffed lightly. "That bit of excitement is more danger than you'll face at the West Gate, I'll warrant."

Hugh's only response was to cast another worried glance toward the harbor. Smoke rose into the sky over southern Waterdeep, visible even in the darkness, and it carried with it the unsavory scent of charred meat and burning sailcloth. "How many ships fuel that blaze?" he wondered aloud. "The harbor itself must be aboil!"

"A dismal caldron to be sure, but no doubt many sahuagin flavored the chowder," I retorted.

Not even Hughmont could dispute this excellent logic, and we hurried along in mutual silence—his no doubt filled with dire contemplation, but mine as joyfully expectant as a child on midwinterfest morn.

I will confess that I am vastly fond of magic. My lord father paid good coin to secure me a position at Blackstaff Tower, and I have learned much under the tutelage of the archmage and his lady consort, the wondrous Laeral Silverhand. But not until this night did I fully understand how impatient I'd become with Lord Arunsun's cautions and lectures and endless small diplomacies. By all reports, the archmage hoarded enough power in his staff alone to drop the entire city of Luskan into the sea, yet I knew few men who could bear witness to any significant casting. The spells Khelben Arunsun used in the daily course of things were nothing more than any competent but uninspired mage might command. Mystra forgive me, I was beginning to view the archmage's famed power in the same light as I might a courtesan of reputed beauty and unassailable virtue: of what practical use was either one?

Then we rounded the last corner before West Wall Street, and the sight before me swept away any disgruntled thoughts. The Walking Statue was at long last making good on its name!

Each footfall shook the ground as the behemoth strode down the northernmost slope of Mount Waterdeep. My spirits soared. No one but Khelben could create a stone golem ninety feet tall, fashioned of solid granite with an expression as stolidly impassive as that of the archmage himself.

But the statue faltered at Jultoon Street, stopping in the back courtyard of a low-lying carriage house as if made uncertain by the swirling chaos of the panicked crowd. After a moment the great statue crouched, arms flung back and knees bent for the spring. People fled shrieking as the golem launched itself into the air. It cleared house and street and landed with a thunderous crack on the far side of Jultoon. Shattered cobblestone flew like grapeshot, and more than a few people fell to the ground, bloody and screaming, or worse, silent.

A flash of blue light darted from the gate tower, and the Walking Statue jolted to a stop. The golem glanced up at the tower and shuffled its massive feet like an enormous, chastened urchin. In apparent response to an order only it could perceive, the statue turned toward the sea. Its stone eyes gazed fixedly upon the cliffs below.

"I wonder what it sees," murmured Hughmont.

I had no such thoughts, nor eyes for anything but the source of that arcane lighting. It came from the West Gate, a massive wooden barricade that soared fully three stories high, surrounded on three sides by a stone lintel fancifully carved into the face of an enormous, snarling stone dragon. Atop this gate was a walkway with crenellations and towers contrived to look like a crown upon the dragon king's head. Wizards lined the walkway, flaming like torches with magical fire. Brightest of all burned my master, the great archmage.

I broke into a run, no longer caring whether Hughmont kept pace or not. My only thought was to take my place with the other battle wizards, and in the tales that would be written of this night.

* * * * *

These shores stank of magic. I could smell it even before I broke clear of the water. The scent of it was bitter, and the taste so metallic and harsh that my tongue clove to the roof of my mouth. I did not remark on this to any of my sahuagin brothers. Though I called the source of my discomfort "magic," they might name my response by another, even more despised word: *fear*. To me, the two were one.

I broke the surface. My inner eyelids slid closed, but not before a bright light burst against the endless dome of sky. Half blinded, I waded toward the shore.

Hundreds of sahuagin were on the sand, and scores of them already lay in smoking piles. We expected this.

31

We had trained for it. Avoid magic-users, storm the gate, breach the walls.

Good words, bravely spoken. They had sounded plausible when spoken under the waves, but what was not easier underwater? I felt heavy on land, dangerously slow and awkward. Even as the thought formed, my foot claws caught on a fallen sahuagin's harness and I tripped and fell to my knees.

It was a most fortunate error, for just then a bolt of magic fire sizzled over my head and seared along my back fin. I threw back my head and shrieked in agony, and none of my dying brothers seemed to think the less of me. Perhaps no one noticed. In the thin air sound lingered close and then dissipated into silence. How, then, could there be so much noise? If a hundred sharks and twice a hundred sahuagin entered blood frenzy amidst a pod of shrieking whales, the clamor might rival the din of this battle.

It took all the strength in my four arms to push myself to my feet. I stumbled toward the place where the baron, our warleader, stood tall with his trident defiantly planted as if to lay claim to this shore. Two paces more, and I saw the truth of the matter. A large, smoking hole had opened and emptied the baron's chest, and through this window I could see the writhing bodies of three more of my dying clan. One of them clutched at my leg as I passed. His mouth moved, and the sound that came forth was thin and weak without water to carry it.

"Meat is meat," he pleaded, obviously fearing that his body would be left unused on this shore.

I was hungry after the relentless journey to this city—desperately so—but the stench of burning flesh stole any thought of feeding. Meat is meat, but even good sahuagin flesh is rendered inedible by the touch of fire.

I kicked aside his clinging hand and looked around for my patrol. None had survived. All around me lay the carrion that had been sahuagin. Their once proud fins were tattered and their beautiful scales were already turning dull and soft. Meat is meat, but there were not enough sahuagin in the north seas to eat this feast. Our leaders had promised a great conquest, but there was nothing to be gained from this, not even the strength to be had from the bodies of our fallen kin.

Anger rose in me like a dark tide. Orders were orders, but instinct prompted me to turn back to the sea, to flee to the relative safety of the waves. As my eyes focused upon the black waters, what I saw drew another shriek from me. This time, the sound was triumphant.

The pounding waves stopped short of the sand, piling upon each other and building up into a massive creature born of the cold sea and magic new to Sekolah's priestesses. A water elemental, they called it. Like a great watery sahuagin it rose, and as it waded to shore each pace of its legs sent waves surging onto the black and crimson sand. The sahuagin yet in the water took heart from this. Some of them rode the waves to shore and hit the sand running. They, too, died in fire and smoke.

The water elemental came steadily on. Blue light— endless, punishing, hellish light—poured from the flaming wizards. A searing hiss filled the air as the elemental began to melt into steam. The magic that bound it faltered, and the watery body fell apart with a great splash. It sank back into the waves, and where it had stood the waters churned with heat.

For a moment I was again tempted by retreat, but there was no safety in the sea, not when steam rose from it. So I lifted one of my hands to shield my eyes from the blinding light, and I studied the gate tower.

There were many, many wizards—far more than our barons had led us to expect. In the very center stood a dark-bearded human, tall by the measure of humankind and strongly built even to my eyes. If he were a sahuagin, he would be a leader, and so he seemed to be among the humans. All the wizards threw fire, and the dark circles on the smoking sand were all about the same size—ten feet or so, the length of a sahuagin prince from head fin to tail tip. All fire killed, but the fire thrown by the tall wizard turned sahuagin into fetid steam, and melted the sand beneath them into oil-slicked glass.

I turned tail and padded northward toward those wizards who merely killed. Great piles of stinking, smoking corpses were beginning to rise. Soon they would reach the wall, and those who survived would swarm over them and into the city beyond. That part of the plan, at least, was going as expected.

As planned, no sahuagin approached the great gate. No corpses added their weight to the wall of wood. As I began to climb the mountain of carrion, I prayed to almighty Sekolah that none of the humans would fathom the reason for this.

Just then a new wizard took his place along the wall and hurried northward toward the spot I planned to breach. Judging from his size he was young. He was as small and thin as a hatchling and lacked utterly the hair that so disfigured the other humans. I was close enough now to see his face, his eyes. Despite the strangeness of his appearance, his eagerness was apparent to me. This one regarded battle with the joy of a hungry shark. A worthy foe, if any human could be so named.

Ignoring the searing pain of my burned fins, I readied myself for battle.

* * * * *

I raced up the winding stairs and onto the ramparts, smoothing my hand over my head to tame the curly red locks before I remembered that my head was newly shaved—I had grown tired of the taunts that had dogged me since childhood. A bald pate, which I contemplated decorating with tattoos as did the infamous Red Wizards, was more befitting a man of magic.

But the sight before me drove such trivial thoughts from my mind, freezing me in place as surely and as suddenly as an ice dragon's breath.

The sea roiled, the sand steamed, and enormous green-scaled creatures advanced relentlessly through a scene of incredible horror.

"Sydon, to me!"

Khelben Arunsun's terse command snapped my attention back to the task at hand. I edged along behind the spell-casting wizards to the archmage's side.

Before he could speak, the largest elemental I have ever seen burst from the waves like a breaching whale. Up, up it rose, until it was taller by half than even the great Walking Statue. Its shape was vaguely human in such matters as the number and placement of limbs, but never have I seen so terrifying a creature. Its wide, shark-toothed mouth was big enough to swallow a frigate. Translucent, watery fins unfurled along its arms, back, and head like great sails.

"Sweet Mystra," I breathed in awe. "Wondrous mystery, that mortals can wield such power!"

"Save it for your journal," Khelben snapped. "Hugh, mind the gate."

Hughmont hurried to the center of the dragon head rampart. He was not an accomplished mage, and his fire spells were as limited as festival fireworks—all flash and sparkle, but little substance. Even so, I had to admit that the effects he achieved were quite good. His first spell burst in the sky with rose-colored light— a titanic meadow flower budding, blooming, and casting off sparkling seed, all in the blink of an eye. It was most impressive. A few of the sea devils hesitated, and I took the opportunity to pick several of them off with small fireballs.

A spear hissed through the air. Instinctively I ducked, though it would not have hit me regardless, nor the man next to me. The man next to *him* was less fortunate. He jolted as the spear took him through the chest. The blow spun him around, and he lost his footing and toppled over the guard wall. He was falling still when the sea devils began tearing at him with ravenous hands.

Khelben pointed his staff at the grim tableau and shouted a phrase I'd never heard used in any magical context—though it was no doubt very common during tavern brawls. Before I recovered from this surprise, a second, greater wonder rocked me back on my heels. The dead man's wizardly robes turned crimson—no longer were they spun of silk, but fire. The flames did not seem to touch the fallen wizard, but they seared the creatures that dared lay hand on him. The sea devils blackened and almost melted, like hideous candles tossed into a smithy's forge.

The archmage seized my arm and pointed to the burning robe. "Fire arrows," he commanded, then he turned his attention to the next attack.

This was my moment, my spell—a new spell I had painstakingly committed to memory but had never had occasion to cast. I dipped into my spell bag for a handful of sand and flint pebbles, spat into it, and blew the mixture toward the sea. Excitement raced through my veins and mingled with the gathering magic—so potent a brew!—as I rushed through the chant and gestures.

The fire that enrobed the unfortunate mage exploded into a myriad of gleaming arrows, each as orange as an autumn moon and many times as bright. These flaming darts streaked out it all directions. Sea devils shrieked and writhed and died. It was quite wonderful to behold. This, then, was how my grandson's tale would start, with a partnership between the great archmage and myself to cast a devastating feint and thrust.

Before I could fully celebrate this victory, an enormous tentacle rose from the waves and slapped down on the beach. My eyes widened as my disbelieving mind tried to guess the measure of the creature heralded by that writhing limb.

Such mental feats were not required of me. Before I could expel the air gathered by my gasp of astonishment, another tentacle followed, then a third and a fourth. With heart-numbing speed the entire creature worked its way from the water. I had never seen such a thing, but I knew what it must be: a kraken, a titanic, squid-like creature reputed to possess more cunning than a gem merchant and thrice the intelligence.

The creature humped and slithered its way toward the gate. Khelben thrust his staff into my hands and began a series of rapid, fluid gestures I did not recognize and could not begin to duplicate. Silver motes sparkled in the air before us, then shot out in either direction and formed into a long, slim, solid column.

I could not keep the grin from my face. This was the Silver Lance—one of Lady Laeral's fanciful spells.

Khelben reached out and closed his fist on empty air. He drew back his hand and pantomimed a toss. The enormous weapon followed each movement, as if it were in fact grasped by the great wizard's hand. He proved to be a credible marksman, for the lance hurtled forward with great force and all but disappeared into one of the kraken's bulbous eyes.

The creature let out a silent scream that tore through my mind in a white-hot swath of pain. Dimly I heard the shrieks of my fellow wizards, saw them fall to their knees with their hands clasped to their ears. Dimly I realized that I, too, had fallen.

Not so the archmage. Khelben snatched the Blackstaff from my slack hand and whistled it through the air as if writing runes. I could see the pattern twice— once, as my eyes perceived it, then again in the cool dark easing of the pain that gripped my mind.

The silent scream stopped, and the pain was gone. Where it had gone was apparent. The kraken thrashed wildly in an agony I understood all too well. Somehow Khelben had gathered the force of that foul mind spell and turned it back upon the creature.

The kraken seemed confused by its great pain. It began to drag itself along the sand in a hasty retreat to the sea, yet one of its flailing tentacles probed about as if seeking something important. The tentacle suddenly reared up high, then slammed straight toward the gate. I caught a glimpse of thousands of suction cups, most at least the size of a dinner plate and some larger than a northman's battle targe, and then a great length of the sinuous arm slammed against the wooden door and held firm. The kraken did not seem to notice this impediment to its own escape. It sank into the sea, still holding its grip on the door. Wood shrieked as the gate bulged outward.

I took this as happenstance, but my master was more versed in the ways of battle. His brow knit in consternation as he divined the invaders' strategy.

"Brilliant," muttered Lord Arunsun. "The gate is thick and well barred—no ram or fuselage could shatter it. But perhaps it can be pulled outward."

He gestured toward the Walking Statue. The golem vaulted over the city wall, and its feet sank deep into a pile of sea devil corpses. Lady Mystra grant that someday the sound of that landing will fade from my ears!

With a noise distressingly like a thousand boots pulling free of mud, the golem extricated itself and strode to the shore. Huge stone fingers dug into the kraken's stretched and straining tentacle. The golem set its feet wide and began to pull, trying to rip the tentacle free of the gate—or the kraken. Terrible popping sounds filled the air as one by one the suction cups tore free of the wooden door. Then the flesh of the tentacle itself began to tear, and enormous bubbles churned the water in explosive bursts as the submerged and possibly dying kraken struggled to complete its task. The gate bulged and pulsed in time with the creature's frantic efforts. I did not know which would yield first: the gate or the kraken.

A splintering crash thrummed out, blanketing the sounds of battle much as a dragon's roar might diminish birdsong. Great, jagged fissures snaked up the massive wooden planks of the gate. The statue redoubled its efforts. Stone arms corded as the golem strove to either break the creature's hold or rend it in twain.

Finally the kraken could bear no more. The tentacle came loose suddenly, abandoning the gate to wrap snake-like around the golem's stone face. The Walking Statue struggled mightily and dug in its heels, but it was slowly drawn out into the water, leaving deep furrows behind in the sand. The water roiled and heaved as their battle raged. Great stone arms tangled with thrashing kraken limbs for many long moments before both sank beneath the silent waves.

Lord Arunsun did not look pleased by this victory. "We are winning," I ventured.

"When there is so much death no one wins," he muttered. "Too much corruption in the harbor . . . this sort of victory could destroy the city."

A terrible scream sliced through the air. Somehow I knew the voice, though I had never heard it raised in such fear and pain. I spun toward the sound. Finella Chandler, a lovely wench who was nearly my equal in the art of creating fire, had apparently grown too tired to control her own magic. A fireball had exploded in her hand, and she flamed like a candle. She rolled wildly down the slope of the inner wall and ran shrieking through the streets, too maddened by pain to realize that her best hope was among her fellow wizards.

A second shriek, equally impassioned, rang out from a young fellow I knew only as Tomas. He was a shy lad, and I had not known that he loved Finella. There was no doubting it now. The youth spent his magic hurling quenching spells after his dying love, but her frantic haste and his made a poor match. I shuddered as I watched Finella's last light fade from sight.

Khelben gave me an ungentle push. "To the north! The sahuagin have nearly broken through."

For a moment I stood amazed. This possibility had not once occurred to me. I had no idea how I would fight sea devils in the streets of Waterdeep. The gods had gifted me with a nimble mind and a talent for the Art, but I was not a large man and I was unskilled in weapons. My fire spells would not serve in the city. Old timbers and thatched roofs blazed like seasoned kindling, and as Finella had learned to her sorrow, fires were far easier to start than to quench.

New urgency quickened my steps, and with new seriousness I reviewed the spells remaining to me. I prayed they would suffice. The sea devils had to be stopped now, here.

I ran past Hughmont and seized his arm. "Come with me," I said. "Frighten them with your sparkles and purchase me time."

He came along, but his hand went to his sword belt rather than his spell bag. I was alone in the possession of magic, and I spent my spells freely as we pushed northward. I tried not to contemplate what I might do when my purse was emptied.

When we reached my assigned post two dire things occurred in one breath. Just as exhaustion dwindled my last fireball into harmless smoke, two enormous, webbed, green-black hands slapped onto the rim of the guard wall directly before me.

Six fingers, I thought numbly. The sea devils have six fingers. The malformed hands flexed, and the creature hoisted itself up to eye level.

I forgot everything else as I stared into the blackness of those hideous eyes. They were empty, endless, merciless, and darker than a moonless night.

41

So this is what death looks like, I mused, then all thought melted as mindless screams tore from my throat.

* * * * *

The hairless wizard began the undulating chant of a spell. It was a fearsome noise—more ringingly powerful than I would have thought possible without water to carry it. For a moment fear froze me.

A moment of weakness, no more, but the wizards were quick to exploit it. A second wizard, this one pale as a fish's underbelly, ran forward with upraised sword. This was a battle I could understand.

My first impulse was to spring onto the parapet, but I remembered that none of the humans seemed to carry my particular mutation. They all had but a single pair of arms. I held my place until the fighting wizard was almost upon me, but with my unseen hands I reached for two small weapons hooked to my harness.

He came in hard, confident. I lifted a knife to catch his descending blade. The appearance of a third arm startled him and stole some of the force from his attack. It was an easy thing to throw his sword arm high, so simple to slash in with a small, curved sickle and open his belly.

The sweet, heavy, enticing scent of blood washed over me in waves. I heaved myself up and lunged for the proffered meal. Strictly speaking, this was still an enemy and not food, but that was easily resolved. I thrust one hand deep into the human's body and tore loose a handful of entrails. Life left him instantly, and I tossed the food into my mouth.

"Meat is meat," I grunted between gulps.

Blessed silence fell as the hairless wizard ceased his keening chant. He began to back slowly away. His eyes bulged and ripples undulated through his chest and throat. A moment passed before I recognized this strange spellcasting for what it was: sickness, horror, *fear*. In that moment, my personal battle was as good as won.

Nor was I alone. Other sahuagin had breached the walls and were fighting hand-to-hand with the humans on the wall. Some wizards still hurled weapons of magic and flame, but most of them seemed to have emptied their quivers.

Triumph turned my fear into a shameful memory. I gulped air and forced it into my air bladder to fuel speech. "Where is your magic fire, little wizard? It is gone, and soon you will be meat."

The wizard—now nothing but a human—turned and fled like a startled minnow. For a moment I hesitated, frozen with surprise that any warrior would turn tail in so craven a fashion. This was what their magic-wielders came down to in the end. They were as weak and as soft as any other human. This pathetic coward was the monster I had feared?

The irony of it bubbled up into laughter. Great, gulping, hissing laughter rolled up across my belly in waves and shook my shoulders. I chuckled still as I followed the cowardly not-wizard as he half ran, half fell down a winding flight of stairs.

Despite my mirth, my purpose was set. I would eat my fear, and thus regain my honor.

* * * * *

Sweet Mystra, what a sound! Next to that hideous laughter, everything else about the battle cacophony was as sweet music. I ran from that sound, ran from the death in the sea devil's soulless black eyes, and from the memory of brave Hughmont's heart impaled upon a sea devil's fangs.

In the end, all who fought and fell at West Gate would find the same end, the same grim and lowly fate. Be he shopkeeper or nobleman wizard, human or sahuagin, in the end there was little difference.

Behind me the sounds of booming thunder rolled across the sands. I sensed the flash of arcane lighting, the distinctive shriek of a fire elemental, but I no longer cared what magical wonders Khelben Arunsun might conjure. I no longer *thought*. I was animal, meat still living, and I was following animal instinct and running from death.

Death followed me through the city, running as swiftly as the sea devil behind me. The cataclysm of defensive spells had sparked more than one blaze. To my right a corduroy street caught fire, and flames licked swiftly down the row of tightly-packed logs. On the other side of the street a mansion blazed. There would be nothing of it come morning but a blackened shell, and the charred bones of the aged noblewoman who leaned out of the upper floor window, her face frantic and her hands stretched out imploringly. These things I saw, and more—more horrors than I could fit into a hundred grim tales. I noted them with the sort of wordless, mindless awareness that a rabbit might use to guide its path through a thicket as it flees the fox. Screams filled the city streets, and the scent of death, and the crackle of fire.

Fire.

For some reason, a measure of reason returned to me as my benumbed mind took note of the rising flames. I remembered all I knew of sea devils, and how it was said that they feared fire and magic above all things. That was why I had been chosen for the West Gate, why I had been summoned to the walls to fight beside the archmage. I possessed a number of fire spells. There was still one remaining to me, encased in a magic ring I always wore but had in my fear forgotten.

But where to use it? There was fire enough in the streets of my city. Ah, there was the answer. The building beside me already blazed—I could not harm it more. I tore up a set of stairs that led to a roof garden, and I could feel the heat through my boots as I ran. The sea devil followed me, its breath coming in labored, panting little hisses.

When I reached the roof I whirled to face the sahuagin. It came at me, mindlessly kicking aside blackened stone pots draped with heat-withered flowers. All four of its massive green hands curved into grasping claws. Its jaws were parted, and blood-tinged drool dripped from its expectant fangs.

I would not run. Hughmont—the man whom I had regarded so smugly and falsely—had stood and fought when he had no magic at all remaining. I tore the small ring from my finger and hurled it at the sea devil.

A circle of green fire burst from the ring, surrounding the creature and casting a hellish sheen over its scales. From now until the day I die, I will always picture the creatures of the Abyss bathed in verdant light. The sea devil let out a fearful, sibilant cry and dropped, rolling frantically in an attempt to put out the arcane flames.

I looked about for a weapon to finish the task. There was a fire pit on the roof, and beside it several long iron skewers for roasting gobbets of meat. They would suffice.

Never had I attacked a living creature with weapons of steel or iron. That is another tale that will remain untold, but by the third skewer the task seemed easier. With the fourth I was nearly frantic in my haste to kill. The sahuagin still lived, but the green fire was dying.

Suddenly I was aware of a rumbling beneath my feet, of a dull roar growing louder. The roof began to sink and I instinctively leaped away—

Right into the sahuagin's waiting arms.

The sea devil rolled again, first tumbling me over it and then crushing me beneath it as it went, but never letting go. Frantic as the sahuagin was to escape the fire, it clearly intended that I should end my days as Hughmont had.

Though the creature was quick, the crumbling building outpaced its escape. The roof gave way and fell with an enormous crash to the floor far below. I felt the sudden blaze of heat, the sickening fall . . . and the painful jerk as we came to a stop.

Two of the sea devil's hands clasped me tightly, but the other two clung to the edge of the gaping hole. The creature's vast muscles flexed—in a moment it would haul us both away from the blaze.

It was over. No magic remained to me. I was no longer a wizard—I was meat.

My hands fell in limp surrender to my sides, and one of them brushed hard metal. It was the sickle blade that had torn Hughmont.

I grasped it, and it did not feel as strange in my

46

hands as I'd expected. The sahuagin saw the blade too late. I thought I saw a flicker of something like respect in its black eyes as I twisted in its grasp and slashed with all my strength at the hands that grasped the ledge. I had no more fire spells, but it mattered not.

"Fire is fire," I screamed as we plunged together toward the waiting flames.

Somehow, I survived that fall, those flames. The terrible pain of the days and months that followed is also something that will never be told to my admiring descendents. The man Sydon survived, but the great wizard I meant to be died in that fire. Even my passion for magic is gone.

No, that is not strictly true. Not gone, but tempered. A healing potion fanned the tiny spark of life in me, and gave a measure of movement back to my charred hands. Khelben Arunsun visited me often in my convalescence, and I learned more of the truth behind the great archmage in those quiet talks than I witnessed upon the flaming ramparts of the West Gate. With his encouragement, now I work at the making of potions and simples—magic meant to undo the ravages of magic. While there are wizards, where there is war, there will always be need for such men as I. Fire is fire, and it burns all that it touches.

Grandsire, please—what did you do when the sea devils attacked?

Someday I might have sons, and their sons will ask me for the story. Their eyes will be bright with expectation of heroic deeds and wondrous feats of magic.

They will be children of this land, born of blood and magic, and such tales are their birthright.

But Lady Mystra, I do not know what I shall tell them.

Messenger to Serôs

Peter Archer

10 Tarsakh, the Year of the Gauntlet

Shafts of golden sunlight drove down through the blue-green water, sparkling and flickering. Fish darted in and out, between and through them, their scales gleaming, then turning dark. Along the clean, sandy bottom, a manta glided, stirring a soft cloud of silt in its wake. Above a red and yellow coral bed, a grouper lazed in the afternoon sun, while smaller fish hovered in its shade.

The sea currents bent and changed, and the grouper started from its place and ponderously swam around the coral. A large school of glistening silverfins swayed and parted like a curtain as the merman darted through, his long, blue hair streaming behind him, his tail flicking back and forth, propelling him on. Streams of tiny bubbles flowed back from his arms and upper body. He scythed through the water and was gone. After a few moments the grouper returned to its original position, and all was as it had been.

The merman darted on. In his mind, he could hear the commands of Narros as clearly as they'd reached his ears.

"You must travel to Serôs," the shaman told him. "Warn our people there of the peril of the sahuagin invasion. Tell them of the disasters that have befallen us in Waterdeep. Your message *must* reach them—and in a timely fashion. Otherelse they may come here only to find a sea of the dead."

"But, Narros, how can I travel there in time to do any good? Serôs is hundreds of miles inland, and we are sundered from our kindred there. Even if I reached there in time, and even if they were willing to listen to me, would they really send aid?"

"They must," the shaman said grimly. "This is no mere skirmish with the sea devils this time. This time it is an age-old prophecy that rises from the depths of the sea against us. If it triumphs, all Faerûn is in peril."

Narros took Thraxos's arm and guided him to the edge of the chamber. Beyond the door, seaweed eddied and swirled with the currents.

"It has been long rumored among our people that to the south of Waterdeep, in the depths of the cliffs that line the shores, there may be found passages that join in some waterway leading beneath the land. Perhaps in one of those passages you may find a dimensional gate to our brethren in the Sea of Fallen Stars. You must do the best you can. We are depending on you."

Thraxos's mouth twisted. *Depending*. Thraxos was nothing if not dependable. Not heroic. Not dashing. Not brilliant. Just . . . dependable.

And now, to be sent by Narros on this hopeless mission . . .

After traveling south from Waterdeep, Thraxos had scoured the coastal cliffs for two days. For two solid days he had swum back and forth, probing caverns, exploring crannies, hoping each would be the one to lead him to the underwater way to Serôs.

All had proved false.

He had begun to think that the old legends were but garbled tales of a far-off past in which perhaps such a passage *had* existed, only to be destroyed in some gargantuan upheaval that tossed about sea and land alike.

Now the rocks beneath the sea's edge loomed up before him again, black and forbidding. They reared themselves into a great cliff, fifty feet high. About halfway up was a black spot.

Another cave.

With a sigh, Thraxos shot upward. The cave door was roughly ten feet wide, worn smooth by the passage of the tides. Its sides were cloaked in mossy growth that wavered in the pale light that shone about the entrance from the sunlight streaming from above. Thraxos entered, his body adjusting to the sudden chill of the waters around him. The passage was pitch black, and Thraxos felt his way cautiously along its sides, which were rough and irregular. Once or twice he felt an empty space on one side or another, as if the main passage had intersected with smaller ways, but he continued to follow the large tunnel.

The tunnel bent sharply to the right, and Thraxos, bending with it, encountered a cold surface in front of him. Rock. Another dead end.

He almost wept with anger and despair. In a rage, he slammed his hand against the side of the passage.

Something gave way under the blow. The blocking wall, on which he had rested one hand, fell back, and the water around him leaped forward into the narrow tunnel beyond. Thraxos had barely time to put his hands above his head and make himself as thin as possible before the current swept him into the opening.

The water propelled him along the tunnel with increasing speed. He could feel the rush of movement all around him, yet he was helpless to control his progress. Instinctively he knew that the way had widened somewhat. The water carrying him grew faster and rougher, and several times he was banged against the walls of the passage. He smelled blood in the water and knew it was his own. Once or twice his head struck against the walls of the passage. He felt as if he had lost consciousness, but he could not be sure. When he opened his eyes, everything was exactly the same as it had been: the same hurtling motion, the same blur of water and walls around him.

Faster and faster. Now he had no conception of the speed at which he was traveling. His body felt as if it were being stretched before and behind, as if he were being pulled to an infinite thinness that could only end with him shattering into a myriad of pieces.

From ahead of him came a dim light that grew stronger. Suddenly the rocky walls fell away, and space and light surrounded him.

He looked behind him. A shaft in the dark wall was slowly closing by some unseen mechanism. In a moment the edges ground together with a resounding boom, and the rocky wall looked as impervious as the barrier he'd encountered on the other side of the passage.

How far have I come, he wondered, and where in all Faerûn *am* I?

As far as a preliminary look could tell him, he was in a shallow lake of some sort. Twenty or thirty feet above, the surface was flooded with light, almost blinding to him after the darkness of the passageway. He rose toward it, and in a moment his head burst above the water.

Nearby was the shore against which soft waves were lapping, while dark firs ringed the water. Their tops whispered softly together and made a kind of accompaniment to the sound of weeping.

Thraxos looked about. Some ten yards beyond the water's edge was an overturned caravan. Smoke smoldered from the ashes of a nearby campfire, while various bags and bundles were scattered roughly about the ground. They had been torn open and the contents plundered—by human robbers, Thraxos suspected. In his travels along the shores of the Sword Coast he'd seen enough to realize the extent of human barbarity practiced against other humans. But where was the crying coming from?

A young girl, scarcely more than eight or nine, her golden hair twisted around a tear-stained face, sat next to two of the bundles. They were bigger and more compact than the others, and it took Thraxos a moment to realize they weren't bundles after all but bodies. From where he floated on the water's surface, he could see the rivulets of red that ran along the stony ground from beneath them and found their meandering way to the waters of the lake.

Thraxos had little interest in the details of the affair, but he urgently needed to know where his unexpected journey had brought him.

"Hey," he called softly.

The crying did not cease, so he tried again. "Hey, there!"

Now the girl lifted her face from her hands and looked about wildly, fear suffusing her face. Thraxos flipped his tail and glided up against the rocks that ringed the lake.

"Girl . . . where am I?"

She stared at him, her eyes wide, then a fresh storm of sorrow seized her. She threw herself on the mossy ground, kicking her heels, screaming and wailing.

"Stop it!" Thraxos yelled. "Stop it at once, do you hear?"

His voice, which contained every ounce of force he could put into it, seemed to shock her back to some semblance of calm. She sat up and rubbed her eyes with grubby fists.

"Where am I?" Thraxos asked again.

"Mummy and Daddy are . . ." Her voice trailed off, and she looked as if she might burst into tears again.

Thraxos's scales itched with impatience, but he tried to keep his voice even. "Yes. I'm sorry. Were you attacked?"

She bobbed her head. "Robbers. Mummy told me to hide under the bed in the wagon. I did, and I heard Daddy yelling. Then Mummy screamed, and then the robbers were laughing, and then the wagon fell over and I was under the bed. I almost couldn't breathe. I don't remember anything else for a while. Then I crawled out, and Mummy and Daddy . . ." She began sobbing again, punctuated by hiccups.

Some part of Thraxos's mind noted that being knocked unconscious had probably saved the girl's life. The robbers had evidently been in too much of a hurry to search the caravan thoroughly. They'd ransacked what they could easily find and fled, leaving the bodies of their victims for whatever scavengers prowled this land.

The girl had finished her crying and was now looking at him more calmly. "Are you a ghost?"

"What?"

"Are you a ghost?" Her tone was matter of fact. "Mummy told me this grove and this lake were haunted. We wanted to get through here quickly, but our horse went away and we had to wait before getting a new one."

Thraxos realized that she had no idea of his true nature. All she saw was the head and shoulders of a man protruding above the water. He shook his head. "No, child, I am no ghost. I do not even know where I am. Can you tell me?"

"This is the Frahalish Grove."

The name meant nothing to Thraxos. "How far are we from Serôs?"

She said nothing, but looked puzzled. Clearly the name meant nothing to her.

Thraxos remembered Narros calling the sea by some other name, the name the surface dwellers in Waterdeep had used. What was it?

"The . . . Sea of . . . Falling . . . *Fallen* Stars. That's it. How far from here?"

"A long way." She shook her tresses briskly. "A long, long, long way. We were going to Cormyr. Daddy told me we wouldn't get there for days and days and days."

55

Thraxos looked around him. The lake was really not much more than an extended pond. The far shore, rocky and looking very much like that against which he leaned, was not more than a mile away. He sighed inwardly and tried again.

"How far are we from the Sword Coast?"

She considered gravely. "Ever so far. My Uncle Aelias lives in Waterdeep, and we never see him because Daddy says it's too far away to travel."

Thraxos's heart sank. The passage he'd been through, though evidently not a gate in the precise meaning of the word, had deposited him at incredible speed in this lake in the middle of—nowhere. He was trapped here as surely as if he'd swum into a fisherman's net. The passage behind him was blocked. There might, of course, be an exit elsewhere in the lake, but the gods only knew where it would take him.

The girl was watching him with solemn eyes. "Why don't you come out of the water?" she asked abruptly.

Thraxos ignored the question, and she asked it again more loudly. He turned back to her with a sigh. "Because I cannot. I am a merman."

Her mouth fell open, and several high-pitched squeaks emerged before she got her voice.

"Really? I've never seen a merman. My Uncle Aelias says there are mermen who live near Waterdeep and who help protect it. My friend Andriana says that if you catch a merman by his tail he'll give you three wishes, but I don't think I believe that. I mean, if you caught a merman by the tail you'd have to swim faster than him, and no one can do that, because everyone knows that merfolk swim faster than anything, even than fishes, but I don't know about that because I had a pet fish once, its name was Berf—"

"Silence, child!" Thraxos roared. His head was splitting. The little girl stared at him in astonishment for a moment, then burst into tears again.

"Oh, for Tyre's sake!" Thraxos flipped his tail impatiently. "Child, I did not mean to be angry, but you must understand, I have an urgent message to be delivered to the ruler of our people in the Sea of Fallen Stars. The fate of all Faerûn may easily depend upon it, but now I do not see how I am to accomplish this mission."

Bile rose in his throat. "They *trusted* me! They *depended* on me. I have let them down. That is what they will say of me! They will say 'Thraxos was given an important task, and he failed miserably. No one ever even found his body. He was lost somewhere in the distant waters of—' "

"Wait!"

The little girl had stopped crying and was looking at him again, her eyes large. "Why don't we take a mount?"

Thraxos shook his head. The pounding behind his eyes grew stronger. He plunged his head beneath the surface, drawing a deep breath of water before returning to the surface. "What do you mean, child? I have no mount, and even had I the fastest dolphin in existence, it could no more get out of this lake than I can. No, the matter is lost. I shall linger here, despairing, while songs are sung up and down the Sword Coast of my sad fate, and—"

The girl, whose eyes had been wandering about the lake during this peroration, suddenly interrupted. "Why don't you ride a horse?"

Thraxos stared at her, dumfounded by her stupidity. Then, in the voice he might use to address a simpleton, he said patiently, "I cannot ride a horse. I have told you, I am a merman. How would I mount? Besides, a horse would travel far too slowly. I must be in water every hour or so, or I will die. Breathing is difficult for me after even a few minutes. You see—"

The girl shook her head impatiently. "No, no. Not a regular horse—a *flying* horse. They travel much faster, and you could see lakes from the air. You could take a bath in them and feel ever so much better."

Thraxos snorted. "And where, pray tell, would I get a flying horse?"

The girl nodded solemnly. "Wait there a minute." She dashed over to the wreckage of the wagon, dived beneath a jutting spar of wood, and rummaged energetically.

Thraxos remained where he was, grumbling quietly to himself. An unnatural rustling in the leaves a hundred yards away startled him, and he wondered if the robbers might have come back.

The girl returned, something long and slender clutched in her chubby fist. "It's Daddy's magic rod," she said calmly. "He used it to make a horse when ours died."

Thraxos glanced at the wagon where the corpse of a slaughtered animal lay between the traces. The girl followed his gaze and shook her head. "Oh, no, not that one. We bought that one in town a long, long time ago. Last tenday, I think. But it wasn't a *magical* horse."

In spite of himself, Thraxos was impressed. "What happened to the magic horse?" he asked.

"It went away, but I can make another one."

"Was your other magical horse a pegasus?" He saw her brow wrinkle in puzzlement and amended hastily, "A flying horse?"

"No, but watch."

She took the rod between both hands and pointed

the end toward a clear spot of grass nearby. Thraxos saw that the rod was smooth, wooden, and had some sort of metal wire binding both ends. The girl closed her eyes and bowed her head in concentration. After a moment, Thraxos fancied he saw the end of the rod begin to glow. In another moment he was sure of it.

With a startling suddenness a beam of white light shot from the end of the rod and spread across the grass. It brightened to an intense flash, and Thraxos blinked, spots swimming before his eyes.

When he blinked, the spots went away. In their place was an enormous hedgehog, standing on the grass with an expression of vague surprise. From its shoulders sprouted two slender wings. They resembled those of an emaciated bat and were obviously inadequate to bear the animal's considerable weight. The hedgehog stretched its snout over its shoulder and subjected its unusual appendages to a prolonged snuffle. Having exhausted whatever interest they held, the creature examined its surroundings, grunted cynically, and set off for the woods at a gentle, though earth-shaking trot.

Thraxos looked at the little girl in exasperation. "For goodness sakes, child, be careful. Objects like this usually have a limited number of charges. We cannot afford to waste any on foolish mistakes."

She stared back, her lower lip thrust out in a pout.

"Well, it's not *my* fault," she said. "I've never used it." She turned her back on him.

The merman put out a hand. "Never mind. Better give it to me. Perhaps I'll have better luck with it."

"No! It's mine! It belonged to my daddy." He could hear tears trembling at the edge of her voice.

Thraxos made a careful effort to keep his voice calm.

" Did your dadd—father tell you how many charges the rod contained?"

She thought a moment, then said, "Three. That was it. He said we could use it three more times."

Thraxos winced. "Very well, but you've already used one, so only two remain. Try again, and please try to get it right this time."

She nodded and held the rod out before her again. This time Thraxos turned his head away as the light emanating from the rod grew brighter. When he turned back to the patch of grass, a magnificent white horse stood on it, quietly champing at the meadow. Folded along its back were a pair of the finest wings the merman had ever seen, surpassing even those of the pegasi that occasionally dipped and swooped above the skyline of the City of Splendors.

The girl approached the animal without any trace of fear. It watched her with liquid eyes and bent its graceful neck toward her. She stroked it, patted its mane, and whispered softly in its ear. Then she looked at the merman.

"Well, come on."

He asked, amazed, "How do you know what to say to it?"

She looked puzzled for a moment, then replied, "Whoever summons the creature controls it. That's what my daddy said." Daddy was evidently an oracle whose words were unquestioned.

All the elation Thraxos had felt at seeing the magical appearance of this mount dissolved in an instant. He shook his locks despairingly. "How can I mount? How could I hold on for such a flight?"

She considered the question gravely, then went back to the rubbish around the wagon, dived into a pile, and

came up with a length of rope. With fingers remark-
ably sure in one so young, she twisted it into a rough
halter, which she cast about the unresisting pegasus.
She led the animal next to the rocks on which Thraxos
rested his arms, and handed him the end of the rope.

"Catch hold of that and hang on."

Before the merman had time to reply, she slapped
the animal's rump. It backed suddenly and Thraxos
was drawn in an instant from the water and lay flopping absurdly on the dry, hard ground.

The girl laughed, and Thraxos felt the blood rising
to his cheeks. No merman feels more helpless than on
dry land, and Thraxos was no exception.

"What are you doing?" he shouted irritably at the
child. Raising himself on his arms, he began struggling
painfully back toward the inviting, cool waters of the
lake.

"No, no!" The girl caught him by the shoulder.
"Wait."

She looked at him critically, from his majestically
muscled torso, to his long, brilliantly scaled tail. Turning back to the pegasus she busied herself with the
rope, hiding what she was doing with her body.

Thraxos felt his lungs contract painfully. The sun
scaled his tail, used to the cooling waters. He flicked it
across the dry ground and marveled that humans and
others could manage to exist on anything so unpleasant.

"There!"

The girl stood back, and Thraxos could see she had
fashioned a kind of rough harness that was suspended
across the beast's side. He felt a sinking sensation in
his stomach as he asked, "What is that for?"

"For you, silly!" In obedience to the girl's command,
the flying horse trotted over to Thraxos and knelt

beside him. "Now," said the girl, "catch hold of that rope"—she touched a dangling line—"and Freyala will pull you up. I'll bind the harness around you so you won't slip, and we'll be off."

There were so many objections to this scheme that Thraxos had no time to voice them. The girl placed his fingers firmly around the rope. The pegasus—when had she *named* the damned thing, Thraxos wondered—rose, and Thraxos felt the lines of the harness gather around him, supporting him. The girl pulled another rope and the harness tightened around him.

"There," she said triumphantly. "Comfy?"

It was hardly the word Thraxos would have used. He had never been caught in a fisherman's net, but he imagined the sensation was similar.

The girl ignored his growls of discomfort. She walked over to the bodies of her parents and tenderly drew blankets over them. Then, without further ado, she picked up a lantern, opened it, and poured the oil over the corpses. She searched until she found flint and tinder, struck a spark, and stood back as the fire took hold. Watching the flames for a moment, she gave a keening cry in some language Thraxos did not understand. Then, resolutely turning her back on the pyre, she climbed nimbly up the side of the horse and grasped the improvised reins.

"Let's go," she said. Without further command the horse sprang into the air, spread its wings, and soared away.

* * * * *

Thraxos concluded very quickly that travel by air was at least as uncomfortable as he imagined travel by land must be. The wind whistled continually in his ears, making conversation all but impossible, and the rushing air dried out his scales and skin until they stung as if a thousand needles were being pressed into them. At the end of an hour, he could stand it no more. The girl, who had given him an occasional glance, understood and ordered the pegasus to swoop lower. She half rose in her seat, looking over the beast's shoulder, then she pointed ahead and down.

"There!"

The pegasus dived, and Thraxos heard the wind's cry rise in a deafening crescendo. In a moment he realized it was his own shrieking voice.

They landed with a bump, and the horse folded its wings and trotted smoothly for some dozen yards. Every step painfully jarred Thraxos, and the ropes dug into his skin with agonizing force.

The girl dismounted easily, and the pegasus trotted forward. Thraxos was about to ask what was going on, when he realized the horse was walking through water that was steadily rising around them. In another moment he was immersed in a clear, cold mountain pool.

The relief was overwhelming. Thraxos breathed in great gulps, thrashed his tail to and fro, and let the blessed cool sink in around him and over him. Looking around he could see the sides of the pool nearby. It was scarcely more than a magnified puddle, perhaps five feet deep and twenty across. The water was fresh and felt as if it had come from melting snow. At another time Thraxos might have found it too cold, but now it seemed an oasis of peace.

He was still constrained by the harness, and he could feel the gentle rise and fall of the pegasus's

63

breathing as he pressed against the creature's side. It felt so real it was hard to believe it was the product of magical conjuration.

The animal shook its head and trotted briskly out of the pool until the water rose only to its chest and Thraxos was still partially immersed. He felt refreshed and laughed aloud with pleasure.

The girl, sitting idly by the water's side, laughed with him. He looked at her with new respect and asked, "What's your name, girl?"

"Ariella. What's yours?"

"Thraxos, of the merfolk of Waterdeep."

She nodded, absorbing this information.

"How far have we come, Ariella?"

She shook her head briskly and said, "I don't know. Before we came down I saw a big forest . . . over there." She gestured vaguely to the right. "I don't know how far away it is. I think we've come an awfully long way, but not as far as we need to go because I haven't seen the sea anywhere, but if I look behind us I can't see the sea either so there must be a lot of land between the sea and the sea, don't you think?"

Thraxos's headache, which had disappeared while he was beneath the water, showed signs of reappearing. He twisted around in the harness and splashed water on his face and shoulders. The girl chattered heedlessly on for a few more minutes before suddenly turning businesslike.

"Well, we'd better go on."

Once again they rose into the air and soared over Faerûn. Thraxos found that time did not reconcile him to the experience of being out of water. Again, after an hour or so they descended, this time on the shore of a small lake. This time Thraxos insisted the girl release him from the harness, and for half an hour he swam around in the water, loosening his stiffened limbs. The girl seemed oddly impatient, and at times seemed almost frantic when Thraxos delayed as long as possible resuming his position in the restraining harness.

The odd group continued their journey in the same manner, rising and falling with the air currents. The sun, which had been rising in the east when they began their traveling together, reached its zenith, then set slowly in the west. They set down about every hour, though once or twice they flew longer. On these occasions Thraxos felt sick and dizzy and spent longer in the pools of water in order to recover.

Night fell, and they flew in utter darkness. They had traveled for about an hour and Thraxos felt the familiar sinking in his stomach that told of descent. His discomfort was, as usual, mixed with anticipation for the water, though the travails of the journey had eased somewhat since sunset.

Lower and lower they drifted, and the wings of the pegasus seemed to beat more gently against the soft night breezes. Then, suddenly, Thraxos felt the familiar warmth of the horse's flank vanish. The next moment he realized he was tumbling end over end through the air. He had a moment of gut-wrenching panic before he plunged into water.

The pool was extremely shallow, more so than any they'd encountered. Fortunately, Thraxos had fallen only a dozen feet, but even so the sudden impact knocked his breath from him. He rolled in the mud at the bottom of the pool, breathing in the life-restoring water, then surfaced quickly.

"Ariella!" he called.

There was silence, broken by a rustling, then a small voice called out, "Thraxos?"

"I'm here. What happened?"

More rustling, then by the dim starlight he saw a tiny figure emerge from the bushes into which it had fallen. The girl's face was dirtier than ever, and there seemed to be several long scratches along her forehead, but Thraxos saw with a surge of relief that startled him with its intensity that she seemed otherwise unhurt.

"What happened?" he asked.

She snuffled a few moments, then replied, "Freyala went away."

"Went away? What do you mean? How could she fly away from under us?"

"She didn't *fly* away," Ariella said impatiently. "She just *went* away. They all do."

Thraxos shook his head in an effort to clear it. "What do you mean?"

"They all go away after a day."

Thraxos sighed. Things had obviously been going too well to last. He should have realized that a magical mount would have only a limited span of existence.

"Can you conjure her back?" he asked.

She nodded. "Yes, but let's rest a while here. Besides, I'm hungry. I'm going to look for some food."

Thraxos glanced around. As far as he could tell they were on some sort of plateau. Before them the land fell away to an unguessable depth. The forest lands had given way to bare rock and scrub, with little shelter.

"What sort of things do you expect to find here?" he asked.

"I don't know," she answered. "I think there might be some wild strawberries back there. I smelled something like that when I fell in the bushes." She giggled

66

despite herself.

Thraxos shook his head. "I don't think you should go wandering around in the dark. We're better off continuing the journey."

"I'm hungry." Her voice turned sulky and petulant. She rose from where she had crouched to converse with the merman and walked back into the shadows.

"Ariella!" Thraxos shouted. "Don't do that! I . . . I forbid it! It's dangerous. . . ."

There was no reply.

"Ariella!"

Still silence. Thraxos cursed softly to himself. Human children were obviously no easier to deal with than the children of merfolk.

A sudden squeal rent the stillness of the night, and a bright torch suddenly flared. Thraxos shielded his eyes from the vision-obscuring flame. When he dared glance in its direction, he saw Ariella scampering toward him. Behind her, over a low crest, came three hulking figures. One carried a flaming brand, and all three wielded clubs. They were clad in ragged garments, and their faces, low-browed and brutal, were crisscrossed with scars. Drool dripped in streams from yellowing tusks.

Ogres.

Ariella dodged behind the pool that sheltered Thraxos, while the ogres stared greedily at her. They charged forward. Two skirted the pool, chasing her around it. The third stalked straight into the water. None of them seemed to notice Thraxos, his head alone protruding from the water.

The brute in the pool was allowing his club to drag in the water. Thraxos reached up unseen as the creature passed and snatched the club from its hands.

"Urgh?"

The ogre stared vaguely up in the air and all around, evidently convinced its weapon had been taken by some spirit of the air. Thraxos rose as high as possible and swung the club against the creature's knee with all his strength.

The ogre dropped into the pool with an enormous splash and thrashed about, howling and clutching its broken kneecap. Thraxos struck again at its head, but only grazed it. The monster seized the merman by the throat and squeezed, pain giving force to its grip.

The world swam before Thraxos. The night filled with colors, and he heard a loud roaring. Before his eyes he saw the horrid face of the ogre fade in and out of focus. In desperation, he brought up the slender end of the club and jabbed it at the monster's eye.

The ogre dropped the merman and fell back shrieking, covering its face with its hands. Streams of blood ran down its body and flowed into the pool. Thraxos swung the club again, and the screams stopped abruptly. The ogre fell, half in and half out of the pool.

Thraxos looked around for Ariella. She had taken shelter behind a small scrubby tree and was dodging around it as the two monsters slowly pursued her. Her slight build and speed had saved her thus far, but Thraxos knew the chase could only end in one way.

He cast desperately about for a plan. He shouted, hoping to attract the attention of the ogres, but they ignored him, intent on their smaller, more vulnerable prey. If they had seen their companion fall, they gave no sign of caring.

One of them caught Ariella's ragged dress. The girl screamed and twisted away, the cloth tearing. The ogre gave a horrid laugh and raised its club.

Groping about on the side of the pond in which he was imprisoned, Thraxos's hand touched something long and slender. The magic rod. He lifted it, and something Ariella had said earlier during the first part of their journey came back to him. The animal conjured is under the control of whoever conjures it. Without further thought, he pointed the rod and concentrated.

For a long moment nothing happened, and a thought flickered in the back of his mind that the rod was out of charges. Then the tip glowed and flared brilliantly. The ogres, distracted by this unusual sight, looked at the merman, growling. Then another growl, louder and angrier, added itself to theirs.

A tiger stood before them.

With a shriek, the largest ogre turned to flee. The tiger swept its clawed paw up and out, and the monster's head was torn from its shoulders. The other ogre ran, but the tiger ran faster. It leaped, there was a horrid tearing sound, and the death scream of the ogre echoed in the night air.

Ariella ran to Thraxos and flung herself into his arms, sobbing. He stroked her hair, surprised at how soft it was. After a while, her crying ceased, and she looked at him solemnly.

"Why did you do that?"

The merman shrugged. "It seemed the only thing to do. I couldn't get out of the water to attack them, and they were about to kill you." He looked at the tiger, who was calmly sitting at some distance, cleaning a paw. Thraxos almost fancied he could hear the big cat purring. The merman turned back to the girl. "We'll rest here and be on our way in the morning."

She looked away, and he sensed something wrong. "What is it?"

"That was the last charge in the rod."

Thraxos sank back into the pool and ducked beneath the surface. His mind was churning. There *had* to be a way. They could not have come this far, only to fail.

In a few moments he rose. The night was still black but in the far distance, where the land sank away, he could see a few tiny pinpricks of light. He pointed them out to Ariella and said, "You must go toward there. Take the tiger with you for protection. Nothing would dare attack you as long as the beast is beside you. When you arrive at a settlement, you must tell them your name and where you are from. Tell them you have a message to take to the kingdom of the merfolk in the Sea of Fallen Stars. Tell them Waterdeep has been attacked by armies of sahuagin, and they must prepare themselves for an assault from the sea devils. Tell them they must send whatever aid they can to the Sword Coast before it is overrun. Can you remember all that?"

The girl shook her head. Tears were close to the surface of her eyes. "You have to come too," she insisted. "I'll stay here with you. Somebody will come and find us. You'll see."

Thraxos shook his head. "No, Ariella. This is more important. When you've delivered the message, you can send someone back for me, but this word *must* get to the Sea of Fallen Stars. Now, repeat the message."

She had to repeat it many times before he was satisfied. All the while, he was conscious of the passing moments and of the expiring life span of the tiger she needed for protection. At last she was ready.

He pointed into the darkness. "There seems to be a trail along there leading downward. It probably goes

70

off the plateau into the valley. When you get to the bottom, strike due west and you should find the settlements. Hurry, now. I'm relying on you and . . ." He paused a moment, then brought out triumphantly, "Sheeraga."

"Sheeraga," she said thoughtfully, looking fondly at the great cat. "That's a nice name. Yes. I'll call you that. Come on, Sheeraga."

The tiger rose, walked over to Thraxos, licked his hair, then followed Ariella into the darkness.

Thraxos sank back into the pool and surveyed his surroundings. The body of the ogre, in falling, had splashed more of the water out of the pool and that which was left was an unpleasant compound of blood and mud, only a few feet deep.

The night passed slowly, and the sun rose, burning, in the east. The pool grew hot, and tiny wisps of steam rose from its surface. By noon it had shrunk to half its size. Thraxos's body lay half in the remaining water, but the pool grew steadily smaller. With a final effort, the merman rolled on his side and gazed out over the rolling hills of Faerûn. From where he lay, he could see, far in the distance, at the very edge of sight, a thin line of blue. The sea, he thought, the Sea of Fallen Stars.

He dreamed that he dived deep into the water, laughing, crying with joy, chasing fish in and out of reefs, clinging to dolphins as they skimmed along the surface. Above him, below him, all around him was his world. Slowly it faded, and Thraxos felt a great peace.

* * * * *

To the west, a little girl with a dirty face and a torn dress marched stalwartly up to a cottage door and

71

knocked. The stout peasant woman who opened the door stared at her in amazement as the girl said, "Hello. My name is Ariella. I have a message for the merfolk of the Sea of Fallen Stars. It's really quite urgent. Hadn't you better let me in? Then perhaps you can help me to get there."

Pausing, she looked behind her, where the setting sun turned the hills blood-red, and smiled.

The Place Where Guards Snore at Their Posts

Ed Greenwood

9 Kythorn, the Year of the Gauntlet

Their jaws were clamped shut, forefin muscles pulsing in the tightening that signified irritation or disapproval. The orders and judgment of Iakhovas evidently weren't good enough for these sahuagin. Bloody-minded idiots.

Sardinakh uncoiled his tentacles from the halberds and harpoons he'd been oh-so-absently caressing since their arrival, and settled himself a little closer to the map on the chartroom table. He did this slowly, to show the fish-heads just how little he feared them, and tapped the lord's seal on the dryland map of Mintarn—the seal of the sahuagin lord Rrakulnar—to remind them that their superiors, at least, respected the authority of a "mere squid."

"The orders I was *personally* given by Iakhovas," he said gently, driving the point home a little deeper, "were to blockade Mintarn, allowing nothing into, or more importantly, out of, its harbors. Taking the island would be a bold stroke—and I frankly find it an attractive one—but it cannot be our main concern. Before all else, we must prevent ships from leaving Mintarn to go to the aid of Waterdeep, Baldur's Gate, and the other coastal cities."

"And that isss bessst done," the larger and burlier of the sahuagin hissed, affecting the invented accent of Crowndeep, the fabled—and perhaps mythical—cradle-city of Sword Coast sahuagin, "by capturing the entire isle." He spoke as if explaining bald facts to a simple child, not his commanding officer.

Fleetingly, but not for the first time, Sardinakh wondered if Iakhovas derived some dark and private amusement from putting seafolk who hated each other together, one commanding the other. Perhaps it was merely to make treachery unlikely, but it certainly made for some sharp-toothed moments.

The tako slid a lazy tentacle across the map, to let the fish-heads know he was no more frightened now than when they'd begun drifting forward from the other side of the table to loom close in beside him, fingering their spears and daggers.

"We'll discuss this at greater length as the brightwater unfolds," he told them. "I see that Mlavverlath approaches."

The sunken ship that served Sardinakh as a headquarters lay canted at an angle on a reef that had grown over it, claimed it, and now held what was left of it together. Those remains did not include most of the landward side of the hull, which left the hulk open to the scouring currents—and provided a panoramic view of the gulf of dappled blue water across which Mlavverlath was swimming.

Mlav was impetuous and ambitious, more like the sahuagin than his own kind, and so ran straight into the jaws of his own reckless impatience far too often. Yet unlike the fish-heads menacingly crowding Sardinakh's office, his hide still wore the dappling of raw youth. Their overly bold ways were long years set, and a problem he was going to have to contend with.

Sharkblood, he was contending with it now! Like all tako, Sardinakh could dwell ashore or beneath the waves, though he preferred warmer waters than these. He knew Mintarn's worth. To drylanders it was an island strategic to Sword Coast shipping, offering an excellent natural harbor and independence from the shore realms' laws, feuds, and taxes. Sardinakh also knew he hated these two sahuagin officers even more than he hated all fish-heads, and must contrive to get them killed before they did as much for him. Unfortunately, they commanded a strong and able fighting force of their own kind that outnumbered all others here at Downfoam six to one, or more. His moment must be chosen with extreme care.

Thankfully, "extreme care" was a concept most tako embraced, and no sahuagin really understood. If only Mlav could be taught to use some measure of it before it was too late.

"Perhapsss we could now deliver our important re- portsss," the sahuagin Narardiir said, in a tone that made it clear he was neither requesting nor waiting for permission to do so.

Sardinakh carefully did not glance at Mlavverlath's approaching form as he said in a cool, almost flippant tone, "Why don't you?"

Both sahuagin hissed to show their displeasure at that, but when he neither looked at them or made any reaction, they were forced to move on. Their black eyes were staring, always staring. Ineffectual gogglers. He turned his back on them to show fish-heads held no fear for *this* wrinkled old tako.

"There is newsss both good and bad from our ssspiesss assshore," Narardiir began stiffly. "The dragon Hoondarrh, the one called 'the Red Rage of Mintarn,' has not long ago begun a Long Sssleep in his cave. Ssshould we invade, he won't intervene."

"The good news," Sardinakh agreed calmly, his eyes now on Mlavverlath as the tako passed over the outer-most sentries, regarded but unchallenged. "And the bad?"

The other sahuagin spoke this time—and, by the mercy of whatever god governed sea refuse, did so plainly. "Recent dryland pirate smuggling and slaving has driven the human Tarnheel Embuirhan, who styles himself the Tyrant of Mintarn and is the dry-land ruler of the isle, to hire a company of mercenaries to serve Mintarn as a harbor garrison. A human force, and highly-trained, by name the 'Black Buckler Band.' It is thought, and we concur, that they won't hesitate to wake the dragon if beset by foes who seem on the verge of victory."

"There isss little elssse to report," Narardiir added, "but—"

"That is a good thing," Sardinakh interrupted smoothly, "because Mlavverlath is here."

As he spoke, the younger tako flung out his tentacles

in all directions, to serve as a brake to his powerful journeying, and slid into Sardinakh's office with his tentacles rippling, water swirling around them, and grace hurled to the currents.

Befitting an underling in disgrace, Mlavverlath passed between the hissing sahuagin and Sardinakh's desk, and struck the far wall of the chamber with a solid thump. The old but coral-buttressed bulkhead scarcely quivered.

"Hail Sardinakh, master of all our voyages," Mlavverlath said hastily, venting many bubbles in his haste and nervousness. "This one salutes you and at the same time humbly beseeches your pardon at my lateness. This one has devised a cunning plan, as promised, and has come to unfold it before you."

He glanced at the two sahuagin and blushed a little in his nervousness. His purpling promptly deepened when the fish-heads hissed mockingly, "Cunning plan, cunning plan," and leaned forward to hear with exaggerated sculling of their webbed claws.

"My officers are somewhat excited," Sardinakh explained in dry tones, ignoring fish-head glares. "Ignore them, and speak freely. Keep me not waiting."

Mlavverlath jetted forth bubbles in a sigh, slid some tentacles around the nearest mast-pillar, more for the reassurance an anchor-point brought than for anything else, and said, "This one's plan should eliminate both the merfolk who dwell in the harbor, and the new dryland garrison of human mercenaries."

The sahuagin hissed loudly at the thought that their news was obviously old tidings elsewhere in Downfoam, and Sardinakh took care that the beak-fluttering that signified tako mirth was well hidden from his underling. Mlavverlath's tone of speech would have better matched the announcement: "This one has devised a plan that this one hopes will win this one back a place in good favor with Sardinakh."

"Please excuse this one's plain recitation of simple facts," Mlavverlath began haltingly. "It is intended as no insult, but to anchor the scheme. Thus, then; for some years, the merfolk of Mintarn have praised and hungrily devoured oysters brought from the Shining Sea nigh eastern Calimshan and the Border Kingdoms, where the waters are warmed by the outflow of the Lake of Steam. Suldolphans—the humans of the city whose dwellers harvest most of the oysters—like these oysters, which have somehow acquired the name 'Mabadann,' done in lemon. So, too, do the merfolk of Mintarn."

The two sahuagin showed their fangs in unison, then, in great yawns designed to display their boredom. Sardinakh ignored them, but Mlavverlath, obviously flustered, continued his speech in stammering haste. "I-in the friendship feasts th-they hosted to welcome the new garrison, whom after all they must trust and work with, the merfolk fed the human warriors these oysters."

In his quickening enthusiasm, the young tako forsook his anchor to flail the canted deck with his tentacles as he moved restlessly across the room, then back again. "The humans so dote on these oysters now that the water-filled barrels of live Mabadann oysters are the most eagerly awaited shipments into Mintarn. The drylanders have even taken to sneaking some shipments past the merfolk to get more for themselves."

The sahuagin were drifting a little closer now, their heads turning to hear better; a sure sign of interest.

Mlavverlath warmed to his telling. "Now, in coastal caves nigh Suldolphor dwells a malenti, Jilurgala Rluroon by name, who owes this one a debt. Long ago she perfected a magic that puts creatures into stasis— unbreathing, unseeing, as if dead—for short times, with set trigger conditions."

The tako's tentacles were almost dancing with excitement now. "If she can be induced to cast her spell on a hundred or so armed bullywugs," Mlavverlath added, his voice rising, "of those who dwell near at hand, on the Border Kingdoms coast, south of Yallasch—and Jilurgala sets its trigger to awaken them when their barrel is opened, they can be the next shipment of oysters smuggled past the merfolk and into the drylander kitchens of Mintarn."

It is rare for a tako's mirth to be loud, but Sardinakh's quivering, loud venting of raging bubbles was uproarious laughter. It drowned out the amused hooting of the sahuagin, and left the commander of Downfoam barely able to signal his approval to his flushed and quivering underling.

"To it, O Master of Oysters!" Sardinakh roared, tearing apart a waterlogged bench with a sudden surge of his tentacles. "Go, and come back victorious!"

* * * * *

"Truly," Brandor muttered, as two of the tallest, most muscular Black Buckler warriors minced out of his way, twirling their hands in mockeries of spellcasting and crying out as if in mortal fear as they rolled their eyes and grinned at him, "this *is* The Place Where Guards Snore At Their Posts."

He ignored their shouts of laughter and the

inevitable bruising of hilt-first daggers bouncing off his slender shoulders—insulting reminders that as a Black Buckler himself, Brandor had recently been publicly reminded by a senior warrior that he must be ready to do battle with his fingers and dagger, should his spells prove too pitiful. The apprentice pounded down the slippery steps that led to the kitchens . . . and his current punishment.

Brandor was forever collecting punishments. Since the arrival of the Bucklers on seawind-swept Mintarn, his daily acquisitions of reprimands and duty-tasks had reached a truly impressive rate, even for the youngest weakling ever to wear the Black Buckler badge.

It did not help that he was the sole apprentice of the accomplished but aging Druskin, supreme sorcerer of the Black Buckler Band. That made the other two band mages see "the little grinning fool Brandor" as a future rival, to be ridiculed and discredited at every opportunity. Most of the strapping Buckler warriors, he knew, saw him as a pitiful excuse for a man, to be made sport of until he fled into the sea and rid them of his face and his pranks.

Ah, yes, his pranks—his only source of fun, and his only weapons. Long ago he'd fallen into the habit of responding to bullying with his quick wits and nimble fingers. Those who pestered Brandor the Fool paid the price, be they ever so mighty—and their colleagues roared with laughter.

Mintarn was small and mostly bleak, its folk suspicious of armed outsiders and guarded in their deeds, slow to welcome curious wanderers—and slower still to welcome one who wore both the Black Buckler badge and the robes of a wizard. Boredom had led

Brandor to dub the island "The Place Where Guards Snore At Their Posts," and that arch observation had earned him no love among the Tyrant of Mintarn's own warriors.

It had done so just as Brandor's boredom was chased away forever by the sight of dark-eyed, darker-browed Shalara, her hair the hue of the sun as it kissed her slender shoulders and vanished down her beautiful back. He began to hurry down the steps at the thought of her. She often stopped to talk with Halger; she might be down there right now.

The Tyrant's daughter slipped around Mintarn's ramparts and windswept stairs like a shy shadow, free to wander at will. Folk said she was the image of her dead mother—who'd never had any use for brawn and bluster, but had admired a keen mind. Hence her voyage from far Suldolphor to the meager splendors of this lonely isle, despite the coughing chills that had finally claimed her.

The Tyrant was said to dote on Shalara, but Brandor was utterly smitten with her. He would wait on bone-chilling ramparts for hours just to catch a glimpse of her, and Halger had finally forbidden him the kitchens—save when he was working therein for punishment—after he'd lurked and loitered for the better part of a tenday, staring intently at Shalara whenever she poked her head in.

She'd obviously been reluctant to enter and speak freely with him swallowing and staring at her, and Halger had said so. Yet he'd have done anything—anything, even endured a public beating from the fists of the hairiest, most sneering of the brutish Buckler warriors, or foresworn his paltry magic—to have earned her smile and friendship.

Instead, he'd fallen back on the only way he had to get noticed. Pranks.

Brandor the Fool had staged a series of increasingly spectacular pranks to impress Shalara Embuirhan. He'd begun with guards' boots stealthily hook-spiked to the flagstones as they dozed at their posts, just to prove the fitness of the catch-phrase he'd coined, then he switched around all the garrison stores orders.

That had been followed by the switching of officers' undergarments, then the swapping of those same small-clothes with those of the haughtiest ladies of the Tyrant's castle. Then all of the shields hung on the castle walls had mysteriously begun changing places, and the castle chamberlain's usual feast welcoming speech had been hilariously rewritten, just on the night when the chamberlain had taken ill and the understew-ard had been called upon to read out the speech in his place, with the stern admonition to "change not a word."

Not a night later, the moaning ghost of Mintarn had been heard again, just outside the windows of the shuttered house near the docks where the Buckler warriors were wont to take their coins and their rest-lessness to the doors where plump and smiling lasses beckoned. Then someone had let out a paddock-full of mules to clatter and kick around the docks, and . . .

The inevitable results had come down upon Bran-dor's head. He'd seen kitchen duty and more kitchen duty, washing mountains of dishes, pickling jars upon jars of fish, and staggering down the long, spray-slip-pery path out of the castle, to dump slimy basket after slimy basket of kitchen-scraps in the breeding pools where the tiny silverfin boiled up like fists reaching out of the water, their miniature jaws agape, to greet his every visit.

All of these panting, sweaty tasks had been done under the watchful eye of the old cook of Castle Mintarn, and Halger was not a man to miss noticing or tolerate a single moment of prank-preparation or malingering. A fat-bellied, greasy ex-pirate whose left arm ended in a stump (which he usually fitted with a blackened, battered cooking-pot), Halger stumped and huffed around the lofty, smoke-filled hall that was his domain, somehow contriving to keep no less than three cooking-hearths alight and a steady stream of food going forth on dome-covered platters to feed the folk of the Castle, the Tyrant's guards, the Bucklers, and whomever was in port and at the Tyrant's guest table.

Down the years, Halger had also found the time to be Shalara's confidante, trusted confessor, and wise old guide to the wider world. He knew her secret thoughts and yearnings, and her judgments of the world around her and the people in it. The amused look in his eyes when they fell upon a mutely staring Brandor made the apprentice squirm and sometimes want to shriek in sheer frustration.

As he ducked through the dogleg of archways designed to keep gusting storm winds from blowing out the kitchen-hearths, Druskin's apprentice let out a sigh of relief. Someone had piled too much wood on the blaze in the corner hearth. The smoke and sparks were roaring up the tallest chimney, the one that soared up through the thick walls of the beacon tower for a long bow shot, into the skies. Halger was shouting and red-faced men were running hither and yon with fire-tongs and soot-blackened aprons, while the women bent grimly over their pots and waited for the tumult to blow over. The lofty, many-balconied kitchen was ruled by swirling smoke and chaos.

There among it all was his waiting pile of potatoes, blessedly bereft of the old pirate cook standing with arms folded across his mighty chest and a soft but razor-edged query as to the tardiness of a certain apprentice. Thankfully Brandor snatched up the peeling-knife Halger had left waiting on the stool, eyed the waiting bucket of similar knives that he was supposed to turn to whenever the knife he was using grew dull, and realized he was doomed.

The corner hearth had held leek-and-potato soup, almost certainly scorched down the insides of its caldrons and ruined. Halger was going to be striding over here all too soon, in his flopping sea boots, expecting to find thrice his own weight in fresh-peeled potatoes waiting. If a certain diligent apprentice worked in frantic, finger-cutting haste, he might—*might*—have six potatoes ready by then.

Brandor swallowed, sat down on the stool, and closed his eyes. If he changed the incantation of the dancing dagger spell just so, it should serve to cause the blade to cut in a curve. Add four . . . no, six would be better . . . such phrases to the casting chant, and the cuts should come around the surface of a single roughly spheroid object. Treble the crushed mosquitoes and the iron filings, and add the trebling phrase to the summation, and he should have four knives whirling in their own dance, peeling his potatoes for him. All he need do was stand back—with stool and bucket—out of harm's way, and watch for idiots blundering into the field of flight. A simple snap of his fingers would still cause the knives to fall to the floor in an instant. By Azuth, it couldn't fail!

Casting a quick look around at the subsiding chaos to make sure Halger wasn't watching, Brandor drew in a deep breath, then performed the spell in mumbling haste. He almost lost a finger when the knife in his hand tugged its way free to plunge into the waiting mound of potatoes, but it worked. By Mystra, it worked!

He was drawing breath for a satisfied laugh when he saw that the knives were whirling ever faster, and the brown, wet shavings they'd been strewing in all directions were now pale white. The air was full of wet slivers of potato! The—oh, *gods!*

He snapped his fingers, but the cloud of carving before him only whirled faster. Desperately he stammered the summation chant backward—and with a gasp of relief that was almost a sob, Brandor saw the knives plummet to the floor. Their landings made no clatter, because that floor was now knee-deep in fresh, wet potato hash.

Staring at this latest disaster, Brandor suddenly became aware that he was drenched—covered in slivers of cold, wet potato that were slowly slithering down his face, off the ends of his fingers, and past his ears— and that a vast and sudden silence had fallen in the kitchen.

He hardly dared lift his eyes to meet Halger's gaze, but there was no ducking away now. Shaking diced potato from his hands, Brandor reluctantly raised his head.

And found himself looking into the eyes of Shalara Embuirhan—eyes in which mirth was swiftly sliding into disgust.

"Uh, well met, Shalara," he mumbled, hope leaping within him when there should have been no hope. Gods, but his humiliation was complete.

"When are you ever going to grow up and stop

wasting your wits?" those sweet lips said cuttingly, anger making them thin. "Pranks are for children—grown men foolish enough to play pranks end up very swiftly dead."

No, he'd been wrong a moment ago. *Now* his humiliation was complete.

She stood staring at him with contempt for what seemed like an eternity before whirling away in a storm of fine gown and long, flared sleeves, storming back out of the kitchen.

Brandor hadn't managed to do anything more than blush as red as a boiled lobster and nod grimly at her words. He was still standing crestfallen, covered in wet slivers of potato, when the entire kitchen heard the dull boom of the door to the beacon tower stairs slamming. It was a crash that could only have been made by a young lady deep in the grip of anger.

Brandor looked down at his hands, and discovered they were shaking. A pair of all too familiar battered sea boots came into view as they stopped in front of him. He raised his eyes with no greater enthusiasm, this time.

Halger was standing with his hairy arms folded across his chest, and a twinkle in his eye. Of course. He met the miserable gaze of the apprentice, chuckled, then grunted, "Want to impress the ladies, do we? Peel yon mountain before we finish, and I'm sure she'll be impressed."

A familiar knife flashed out of his fist, spinning down to an easy catch. Brandor fielded it grimly, looked glumly at the mound of untouched potatoes beyond the slippery heap of hash, and made his sliding way across it, to set to work peeling—the old way.

* * * * *

"I've nothing of import to pass on to you, goodsirs," the Tyrant of Mintarn said quietly. "You know as well as I that no ships have called here, or even been sighted from atop the beacons, these six days past. It's as if the seas have swallowed every last ship, and given us—silence."

They reached for their goblets in grim unison: the white-bearded ruler of Mintarn; the robed, white-haired sorcerer Druskin; and the handsome, saturnine leader of the Black Bucklers, Oldivar Maerlin, who looked every inch an alert, dangerous battle commander.

It was Maerlin who lifted his eyebrow then, in a clear signal to the mage. Druskin cleared his throat, sipped his wine, and cleared it again before saying, "Spells give us some feeble means of piercing such silences, lord. Last night I worked an experimental magic, seeking to touch the mind of a night-flying seabird, and see through its eyes. The experiment was largely a failure. My probing confused the birds, and they tended to tumble out of the air and strike the waves, but I did snatch a temporary seat, undetected, in the aft cabin of a caravel running swiftly north out of Amn, bound for Neverwinter or, failing that, a safe harbor anywhere."

The Tyrant raised his head to fix the wizard with a hard stare. Those last words were clear talk of war.

"A seat at a table where sailors were discussing . . . ?" he prompted. His voice was as quiet as before, yet the room seemed suddenly as tense as the waiting moments before foes who are glaring at each other charge forward, and a melee begins.

87

"Dark tidings, but heard secondhand," Druskin replied. "There was an attack on the harbor at Waterdeep—an attack in force, by all manner of marine creatures. Ships were sunk, crews slaughtered fighting to defend their own decks . . . that sort of thing. Something similar befell at Baldur's Gate. The sailors spoke of ships putting out from there being 'sunk by the score' . . . in some cases being 'dragged down from below.' One of them had heard talk of merfolk communities along the coast being overwhelmed by sahuagin, with bodies drifting in the depths so thick that engorged sharks were dying of sheer weariness, sinking to rest on the bottom."

The wizard regarded the empty bottom of his goblet in mild surprise, and added, "How much of this is fancy remains to be seen, but it seems clear that forces from beneath the waves have struck at ships and settlements ashore up and down the Sword Coast, and perhaps elsewhere, too, as if all that live in the sea have risen up at once to slaughter those who breathe air and dwell up in the dry Realms."

A little silence fell after those words, as the three men traded glances. The Tyrant looked longest at Maerlin, who stirred and said grimly, "My duty to you and your people, lord, is to see to the best defense of Mintarn. We can no longer trust in the merfolk, it seems. Simple prudence demands we shift our garrison duties so as to keep watch for forces from the depths coming ashore unseen elsewhere in Mintarn, and attacking us here from unforeseen places and ways."

The Tyrant nodded. "So much I was thinking. Watches and ready arms, guarded food stores and water I know well . . . what of magic?"

The ruler and the commander both looked at

Druskin, who smiled faintly and replied, "Warning spells may well be needed, to watch where even trained warriors grow weary. I shall establish a web of such magics by next nightfall, and a duty watch rotation among all Buckler mages, myself and my, ah, wayward apprentice included."

The Tyrant reached to refill their goblets and said in dry tones, "Ah, yes, the valiant Brandor. My daughter has told me of some quite clever, but dangerous pranks that he's been pulling. Daring, for so young an apprentice."

"Daring? Perhaps, lord. I'd rather use the term 'foolish,'" said Druskin, his voice sharp with sudden anger. His hand came down on the table in a loud slap. "We dare not let him continue with such foolishness, when all our lives may be at stake. I should have curbed him, I own, long ago, but I must break him of these habits now. *Right* now."

He rose in a swirling of robes, refusing another goblet with an imperiously raised hand—only to turn in surprise, a stride short of the door, at the unmistakable sound of boots striding along firmly behind him. Two pairs of boots.

"My lords," Druskin protested, "it's customary for disciplinary dealings between master and 'prentice to be conducted in private."

The Tyrant smiled. "Nay, Sir Mage, I want to watch this little confrontation. After all, we starve for excitement . . . in this place where guards snore at their posts."

The senior mage of the Bucklers reddened. "You may be assured, lord, that I shall make Brandor apologize to you, on bended knee and as prettily as he knows how, for *that* little remark."

He turned again to the door, and in a swirling of robes, fine tunics, and ornate sleeves, they hastened out together.

* * * * *

The little green door in the darkest alcove of the kitchen opened, as he'd known it would, and Shalara came out, eyes bright and cheeks flushed. Her talks with Halger, and the wine that accompanied them, always left her emboldened. Brandor loved to talk with her then, when her mood made her tongue outrun her reserve and let her swift wit shine. They'd laughed together many a time, with Halger smiling his slow smile nearby.

He'd been awaiting this moment, knowing that Shalara would stop to look in on the potato-peeling miscreant on her way back to her own rooms. With the cook striding along in her wake, the Tyrant's daughter swept imperiously past the feasting-spits and the cutting tables to where Brandor should have been hard at his peeling—and came to an astonished halt. Her lips twisted.

The pile of potatoes stood almost untouched, very much as she remembered it. Brandor Pupil-of-Druskin was standing in front of that earth-caked mound wearing a satisfied smile, his arms folded across his chest in the manner of a conqueror.

Shalara put her hands on her slender hips, eyes snapping on the amused edge of anger. "And what by all the good gods, Sir 'Prentice, have *you* been up to?"

Brandor flung out a proud hand toward a long row of large barrels on the roll-rails behind him. "Lady fair, the latest shipment of the oysters we all love so much has just been delivered, and in the brief time 'twixt then and now, I've devised a spell to cook all of them inside the barrels."

Despite herself, Shalara was interested. She was always fascinated by new ways and ideas. "Oh? How so?"

Brandor caught up Halger's long tongs—heavy, man-length metal pincers used for raking coals and setting wood into the large hearth fires—and gestured at the stop-log that held the barrels in place.

"With yon spar removed," he explained, "the barrels will roll, prodded along with these tongs. My spell creates an enchanted space—or 'field'—of intense heat, but no flame to scorch the wood. We wait, the oysters cook, with luck the barrels don't burn, and—there we have it! I'm just about to try it on the first barrel now. Would you care to watch?"

The Tyrant's daughter shrugged and smiled. "I've no doubt you're going to pay dearly for this, Brandor," she said, as Halger looked at the apprentice over her shoulder, amusement warring with interest on his weathered face, "but the fiasco should be . . . entertaining."

"One barrel only, mind," Halger growled. "Ruin an entire shipment, lad, and they'll have me cooking *you* for evenfeast! And what good are barrels turned to ash? We reuse them, you know."

The cook's words rose like angry arrows to the ears of the Tyrant, the wizard Druskin, and the Buckler commander as they came out onto a balcony overlooking the mound of potatoes. The mage stiffened, but the Tyrant put a firm hand on his arm and murmured, "Hold peace and silence for now. Let us watch and learn for a bit."

91

Druskin gave him a glare of mingled astonishment and embarrassment, but clamped his lips together and turned his burning gaze to the scene below.

Brandor saw that movement, and glanced up. At the sight of the three most powerful men in all Mintarn looking back down at him, two faces coolly calm but his master quivering with suppressed rage, the apprentice went pale.

The Buckler commander—*his* commander—leaned forward and said calmly, "Pray proceed, Brandor. One last prank? Or a clever stratagem that can benefit us all? For your future, I hope 'tis the latter. The true value of a warrior is less often bold innovation than minstrels would have us believe. More often, 'tis in carrying out the drudge duties of potato peeling—or, yes, of watching at our posts *without* snoring—than in all the glorious charges and bloodily victorious attacks that all too many bards sing about . . . but I'm sure your master will have more pointed words to address to you in the near future. Cast your spell and redeem yourself, if you can."

Brandor trembled, managed a sickly smile, and stared down at his hands. What else could he do but cast the spell?

He drew in a deep breath, turned his back on them all, and raised his hands to work his latest magic.

His fingers were still poised, the casting not begun, when something moved inside the first barrel. It rolled forward—just an inch or so, shoving the heavy stop-log with it—and the faint reek of swamp water wafted to Brandor's nose. He swallowed, and turned to Shalara. "D-did you see . . . ?"

She nodded, face as pale as his own. Something that could move that barrel would have to be *big*. Not a thousand-odd oysters, but something very much larger. . . .

"Well, 'prentice?" Druskin's voice was as angry as his expression had suggested. He leaned over the balcony rail. "Is there a particular reason why you hesitate to carry out Commander Maerlin's order? Or is this yet another prank?"

Brandor tried not to shake nor look as pale as he felt as he looked up and blurted, "P-please, sir—the barrel *moved!* There's something alive in there."

"Well, of *course* there is, boy! Oysters aplenty, hmm? *Cast your spell!*"

Brandor looked helplessly at Shalara in the unhappy silence that followed, and she came to his rescue.

"Sir Mage," she said crisply, looking up, "Your apprentice speaks the truth, and I saw him fall from confidence to . . . *dread* in but a breath. I also saw why. The barrel moved. Something within is trying to get out."

Druskin's eyes narrowed, and he said softly, "Trying to play the hero and impress a lady again, lad? A spell of yours moved that barrel, I'll warrant. Have done. Stand away, cast no more spells, and take yourself to my quarters without delay. I shall have words to impart to you there."

In the silence that followed, the barrel gave a slight groan, then things happened very fast.

The end of the barrel bulged, then hissed open, coming slightly askew. A swampy reek rolled across the kitchens and before anyone could say or do anything, the end piece was sent flying.

A green torrent of stinking water poured forth. Brandor saw a glistening wet hide, staring froglike eyes, then a curve-bladed cutlass vying with a short spear for the pleasure of enthusiastically ending a certain apprentice's life. Something the color of an olive, that had the head of a giant frog, lumbered forth and stood upright on webbed feet. It was taller and broader of shoulders than any man Brandor had ever seen. Corded muscles rippled under glistening slime as it thrust viciously at Brandor with its spear. It wore armor made of the carapaces of sea turtles and a murderous expression. Its long red tongue lapped forth hungrily from between jagged-toothed jaws, and its breath stank.

"A-a *bullywug?*" Brandor asked Faerûn around him in utter astonishment.

As the cutlass whistled past his head, he ducked, raced three frantic paces to the long tongs, and spun around again—just in time to strike aside the spear and end up with the tongs wedged between them.

The bullywug towered over him, its fetid tongue slapping his face and hair. Shalara screamed. Brandor shrank back from a snapping bite, clung desperately to the tongs, and tried to set his feet on the wet, slippery floor. He could hear startled curses from Halger and from the balcony, and the slap of the cook's boots . . . running away.

Then he had no time to pay attention to anything else but staying alive. The bullywug was upon him, hacking and biting.

"Get *away* from it, boy!" Druskin shouted. "I can't cast a spell with you there."

Almost shoved off his feet by the bullywug's writhing and head-down charging, Brandor clenched his teeth and fought back, becoming suddenly and acutely aware that the only thing keeping the swamp monster from leaping around the kitchen to slay at will were his own hands on the long tongs, and whatever skills he might acquire in its use in, say, his next five panting breaths or so.

"Hold on, lad!" Halger shouted, his thundering boots now growing closer again. "I'll be right there!"

He wasn't strong enough to hold it. He was going to die. He was—

Abruptly the thing gave a roar of rage or disgust, and clawed Brandor sideways, sending him skidding helplessly on the wet flagstones. He fell hard on his behind, saw the cook sprinting across the kitchen with a harpoon in his hands, heard the men on the balcony strike alarm gongs with enthusiasm—and saw the bullywug pounce on Shalara.

She tried to run, slipped and fell, and screamed in utter terror. Up on the balcony, Druskin was cursing like a sailor, hands raised to unleash a spell he dared not cast.

Brandor scrambled up, swung the tongs with all his might, and rushed forward with his swing. The hearth girls chose that moment to scream.

He blundered clumsily into the bullywug's side, managed to make it hiss and stagger, then was flung free, losing his grip on the tongs, by one slap of a webbed hand.

The metal tongs bounced on the floor with a clang like a forge anvil, and the bullywug's hiss rose into a sort of a roar as it flung its spear, taking Halger in the shoulder and spinning him around. The harpoon that Brandor would barely be able to lift bounced away.

The apprentice gulped, found his feet again, and ran like he'd never run before in his life. The cutlass was already sweeping up. When it came down, Shalara's life would end.

The bullywug had fought men on pitching ship decks, beaches, and on wet, rock-strewn shores. It had faced down sharks in its time, and even slain sahuagin, but its experience of weak, clumsy, and recklessly stupid apprentices was limited. It chose to ignore the puny youth's charge as its blade swept down to lay open the she-thing.

That blade went wide, striking sparks from the flagstone floor, as Brandor lost his footing and crashed helplessly into the bullywug's legs. The frog-monster staggered, then turned to hack this persistent annoyance to pieces.

Brandor stared up into cold, goggling eyes, saw his death in them, and as he wriggled sideways in wetness, remembered slipping about in slivers of diced potato, and—of course! Mystra aid me, he thought. The *potato-peeling spell!*

"Get away, Shalara!" he cried, frantically rummaging in his robes for the components, and continuing to wriggle sideways on the floor, away from the Tyrant's sobbing daughter. The bullywug made a chuffing hiss that could only be laughter. Gods, he must look like a fish flapping out of water. Go on, goggle-eyes, laugh at me just a moment longer . . .

He snapped out the spell with haste but precision, as the cutlass swept up again, then rolled aside, throwing his hands up in front of his eyes. He doubted diced bullywug blood would be something he wanted to ingest.

The squalling, hissing, and wet slicing sounds were truly grisly, and the smell made him gag, but to Brandor they might have been a minstrels' symphony, embroidered with trumpets—well, one blast at least: the clang of the cutlass striking the floor.

He was drenched, he was rolling desperately, cold slime was everywhere . . . and it seemed an eternity of sweaty, desperate rolling before he ran into something lying on the floor that groaned at him. Halger.

"Easy, lad," the cook husked in a weak echo of his normal voice. Brandor stopped rolling and opened his eyes. He was looking up at a ring of angry faces: the Tyrant, Commander Maerlin, his master Druskin, and a growing army of men-at-arms with drawn swords in their hands.

"Your cooking spell," Druskin snapped, "and quickly!"

A dozen hands hauled Brandor to his feet before the apprentice could do more than blink. Druskin slapped a hand across Brandor's forehead to wipe away bully-wug blood and slime, no one let him look at what was spattered all over the floor, and the apprentice found himself frog-marched—if that wasn't too unfortunate an expression—across the chaos of the kitchen floor.

An army of hard-faced warriors in full armor was watching him. He was drenched and stinking with dead bullywug. Anger and fear glared forth at him from scores of tight, white faces. Oh, gods, he was in for it. They looked about two breaths away from executing an apprentice . . .

"The spell, lad," Druskin said flatly. "Now."

Brandor saw six gauntleted hands bring the long tongs up and hold them ready by his side. He let out a long, unhappy breath, swallowed, felt for the components he'd need, faced the empty space in front of the stop-log, and did his duty.

Warriors snatched the log aside and wrenched the empty barrel out of the way. The others began to roll. The tongs were handed wordlessly to Brandor, and he steadied the first full barrel squarely in the midst of the field only he could see.

Steam rose from its staves, and an evil smell. When he rolled the barrel along, warriors with axes hastened to break it open. A bullywug sagged out, dark and slimy, with steam pouring from its gaping mouth. It sagged to the stones even before their axes bit down in bloody unison. The smell made Brandor retch.

Commander Maerlin barked an order Brandor did not catch, and the armsmen surged forward. They swarmed up around the barrels, rolling them into Brandor's field and breaking them open with axes. Squalling bullywugs were pierced with spears and pinned in place to cook with brutal speed and efficiency. The slaughter went on and on, and more than one person in the kitchens was noisily sick. Several spewed in unison when Halger looked up from the priest tending to his shoulder and told the room gruffly, "No, I *don't* know any recipes for bullywug soup . . . but I'm willing to improvise."

Brandor rolled barrels into the heat with the heavy, unwieldy long tongs like a madman until someone—the Tyrant of Mintarn himself—took him by the shoulder and shouted at him to stop and stand easy.

When he let the long tongs fall, Brandor found that he was shaking with weariness. He looked across a kitchen that stank with carnage. Shalara, Druskin, and the other two Buckler mages were on their knees, white-faced and retching, and grim armsmen were clambering about knee-deep in wet, bloody bullywugs. Oh, he was going to catch it now . . .

Commander Maerlin was wading grimly through the remains toward him. Brandor closed his eyes and waited for the cold words that would end his Buckler career and direct him to a cell.

The hand that came down on his shoulder gripped warmly, and out of a dizzy fog Brandor heard Oldivar Maerlin say, "Well and bravely done, lad. My thanks."

From his other side came the sound of Druskin clearing his throat. The wizard sounded a little breathless as he said, "You'll teach us all both of those spells, I hope. I'll exchange four of comparable power for each of them, of course."

"Moreover, Mintarn you've saved," the Tyrant said from nearby, his voice rolling out to carry to every corner of the lofty room, "and Mintarn is in your debt. I see no reason that we cannot reward you fittingly in the days ahead."

Brandor lifted his head, then, to stare at the ruler of Mintarn in astonishment, but somehow his gaze was caught and held by the shining eyes of Shalara. They stared at each other for a long, wordless time, and suddenly the Tyrant's daughter raced across the space between them, heedless of heaped bullywug remains, and threw her arms around him.

Her kisses were warm and fiercely eager, and it was some time before she drew back, her eyes shining. It was longer still before Brandor could look at anything else but the look of adoration on her smiling face. The first thing he saw was the bullywug slime and gore that had soaked all down the front of her fine gown, and even its flared sleeves where she'd embraced him.

"I've . . . I've ruined your dress," he mumbled, reaching forth a tentative hand to brush away slime from her bodice, letting it fall without touching her.

Shalara glided up to him again, and murmured into his chest some words only he could hear: "Let it be the first of many of mine you ruin, lord of my heart," before whirling away from him.

It was about that time that Brandor became aware that the movement he'd been noticing out of the corner of his eye was a broad and knowing smile growing across the Tyrant's face.

Brandor's face flamed, and he looked down quickly. Then he bent, fished around in the gore at his feet, and came up with something that was small and bloody, but unmistakably a weapon.

"Hold hard!" said the Tyrant in alarm, stepping back. "What's that for?"

"The drudge duty of potato peeling," Brandor replied in a voice that quavered only a little. He waved with his knife at the mound of potatoes. "The true value of a warrior, sir."

A slow smile grew on the Tyrant's face. "Really?" he replied, "and here I thought it was doing guard duty . . . snoring at posts."

Shalara's high, tinkling laughter rose over the chorus of deep warriors' chuckles. Brandor, who was busily turning all shades of red as the Tyrant dealt him a friendly slap on the back, thought it was the most glorious sound he'd ever heard.

Lost Cause

Richard Lee Byers

17 Kythorn, the Year of the Gauntlet

Resplendent in his burnished plate armor, jaunty scarlet plume, and matching cape, Sir Hylas rode his roan destrier down the white sand beach. A dozen militiamen and I, their sergeant, trudged along after our new commander, each of us carrying one of the pickaxes we'd borrowed from the quarrymen. The young knight had sneered when he saw them, but we'd found them more useful than short swords against our current foe.

Gray on this overcast morning, the surf murmured, filling the air with the smells of seaweed and saltwater. Granite cliffs towered on our left, and, dead ahead, a colossal mass of rock extruded across the beach and into the waves.

The closer we got to the promontory, the edgier the men became. At last, Hylas reined in his steed.

"So that's it, is it," he said in his cultured baritone voice. "The castle of mine enemy."

"Yes," I said, "and you can see that it would be as difficult to take as any keep built by man. We certainly couldn't seize the place with fifty men-at-arms." In reality, we were already down to forty-two. Three were dead and five more too sorely wounded to serve.

"It might be impregnable if we were fighting other humans," Hylas said, "but surely these crabmen of yours are no better than beasts."

"That may not be true," I replied. "Even if it is, they're formidable beasts, and the caves are full of them."

The knight grimaced. "There has to be a way," he said, and at that moment, a crabman scuttled forth from one of the narrow fissures in the birdlime-spattered crags.

The creature was ten feet tall with an orange shell. Like all its kind, it walked on two legs, and held two sets of pincers before it, the greater above and the lesser below. The intricate mandibles comprising its mouth twitched, and its eyestalks swiveled back and forth.

Hylas grinned and couched his lance.

"No!" I cried. But Hylas was already charging, with never a thought to spare for directing his command. It fell to me to give the order the men were dreading: "Forward!"

* * * * *

The irony was that I'd prayed for a new officer to arrive. I'd been in charge since the crabmen killed Haeromos Dothwintyl, the previous First Captain, and I was sick of it. In my nigh unto thirty years as a mercenary, I'd occasionally borne the responsibility of command before, but never under such grim circumstances.

Still, as soon as I saw Hylas, I had misgivings. It was dusk, and I was sitting cross-legged atop a chunk of crumbling stonework, one of the few surviving traces of Port Llast's ancient walls, keeping watch. When the knight rode out of the twilight, I was struck by his youth and a certain hauteur in his expression.

"Sergeant Kendrack?" he asked

I slid down from my perch. "Sir."

"I'm Hylas of Elturel," he said, dismounting, "knight bachelor and a rider of Torm's Fury." A company of high-born cavaliers serving the Lords' Alliance, the riders of Torm's Fury were renowned for their prowess with lance and sword. "I've come to take command."

"Yes, sir. We've been expecting someone ever since we sent word of the First Captain's death." I hesitated. "It's quiet this evening. A company of armed men couldn't march into town without me hearing them."

"I came alone," he said. "I don't know how much news you get in this backwater." He gestured toward the low stone houses and narrow streets that made up the village of seven hundred souls. "The sahuagin have attacked Waterdeep itself. The Alliance needs every warrior it can muster to defend the great cities farther south."

"I gathered as much, since the lords pulled all their troops out of Port Llast, leaving us militiamen to hold on by ourselves."

"*I* am needed in the south as well, fighting the real war, and I have leave to rejoin the Fury as soon as I solve your little problem. I intend to do so expeditiously. Tell me exactly what you're facing."

"Well," I told him, "a bit more than a month ago a party of sahuagin, aided by some sort of huge sea monster no one's gotten a good look at, started waylaying fishing boats and merchants ships offshore. Eventually the sahuagin disappeared, seemingly leaving the other beast to carry on alone, and we took comfort in the thought that at least folk ashore were safe from attack.

"Alas, we'd reckoned without the colony of crabmen that dwell in a cave to the south. In times past, they'd never hurt anyone, and we had no reason to expect them to throw in with the sea devils, but a couple of tendays ago they assaulted the town. We only barely managed to drive them back, and not before the First Captain perished in the fighting. Since then we've been fending them off as best we can."

Hylas snorted. "No wonder the hamlet is still in peril. You can't simply allow the foe to attack repeatedly, then 'fend' him off. You have to carry the fight to him. We'll clean out this nest you spoke of."

"With respect, Captain, that might not be as easy as you think."

Hylas frowned. "And why is that?"

"Let me show you in the morning."

* * * * *

The men hesitated, and I feared they weren't going to follow me. They'd come to escort their new commander—who'd scarcely even bothered to greet them—on a scouting mission, not to follow as the crabs lured him into an ambuscade. They were good lads, though, and after only an acceptable hesitation they ran after me up the beach. The soft sand sucked at our boots.

Up ahead, Hylas closed with the crabman. His lance crunched into the creature's chest. The brute fell, wrenching the weapon from its attacker's steel gauntlet. Whooping, Hylas turned his war-horse and drew his sword, a curved blue blade that shimmered with enchantment.

Behind him, the cracks in the granite vomited crabmen, who clambered down toward the sand with terrible speed. In a heartbeat, the cliff face was crawling with them.

I rushed one of the first to reach the ground, intercepting it before it could attack Hylas from behind. It pivoted toward me, its serrated fighting pincers gaping. I avoided the creature's grab and swung my pick at its midsection. The point crunched through its carapace, and the crabman fell. I dealt it another blow that split its triangular head, then peered about to see how my comrades were faring.

We militiamen had prevented the crabs from overwhelming Hylas, who had just finished off another of the creatures. Smiling fiercely, guiding his destrier with his knees, he turned to ride at a third. Which is to say, he meant to stand and fight.

"Retreat!" I bellowed.

The militiamen did so hastily. Hylas shot me a glare, but, recognizing the impossibility of rallying the men now that they were in flight, he wheeled and galloped after us. Thanks be to Tempus, we eventually left the pursuing crabmen behind.

* * * * *

The barracks was a long hall with a pitched roof, smoke-darkened rafters, and a plank floor. It smelled of the lye soap we used to scrub it down. Rows of bunk beds flanked the aisle that ran from front to back. In happier times, the room had echoed with laughter and the clatter of dice. Since the advent of the sahuagin and their minions, it had become quieter, as the men glumly contemplated the likely outcome of the ongoing conflict. Now it buzzed like a hive of angry hornets, at least until I stepped through the door.

"Don't fall silent on my account," I said, setting my pickax on a scarred, rickety table. "If something wants discussing, let's chew it over together." No one spoke up, so I fixed my eye on the hulking, ruddy-faced fellow, who, of all of them, was least prone to hold his tongue. "Come on, Dandrios, what's wrong?"

"Well . . . you said that when the new captain came, he'd bring reinforcements."

"I thought he would. Evidently the lords have decided their other warriors are needed elsewhere."

"Better that no one had come than the one popinjay who did," muttered Vallam. A small, green-eyed fellow of about my own age, he'd grown to manhood as a slave in Luskan before escaping, and bore a fearsome collection of scars from the abuse he'd endured.

"He *is* a bit overdressed," I said. "The last time I saw so much scarlet and glitter, it was on a streetwalker in Neverwinter." The feeble jest elicited a laugh, momentarily breaking the tension. "But he must be fit to lead, else the Lords' Alliance wouldn't have sent him. He wields a lance and sword ably enough."

"Perhaps," Dandrios said, "but he nearly led us to

disaster on the beach today. It's a wonder we all made it back alive."

"Yet we did," I said, "and now that he's taken the measure of the crabmen, he'll be warier henceforth."

"I hope so," said Vallam glumly.

"By Tempus's bloody wounds," I snapped, "I've never heard such whining. Are you warriors or timid old women?" Startled, they stared at me. "Answer me, curse you!"

"Warriors," Dandrios growled.

"Then behave like it," said I. "Remember how we routed those hobgoblins two summers ago? We've beaten every foe we've ever faced, and we can handle the crabs, too, as long as we don't lose our nerve."

I continued for a while in the same vein, bucking them up as best I could. Afterward, and with a certain reluctance, I crossed the street and rapped on the door of the two-story house opposite the barracks. The maid, who, with her red, puffy eyes, looked as if she hadn't stopped weeping since the previous master of the household perished, ushered me into the First Captain's oak-paneled study. It seemed odd to behold Hylas sitting there, especially since Haeromos's collection of scrimshaw still cluttered the room.

I came to attention. Hylas kept me standing that way for several seconds before saying, "I imagine you know what I want to discuss."

"Yes, Captain. When we scouted the crabmen's lair, you were in command, but I ordered the retreat. I offer no excuse. I can only say that I actually have been in charge here for a while, and in the heat of the moment, I forgot myself."

He raised an eyebrow. "I expected you to argue that you were right and I was wrong."

"No, Captain," I said. "I assumed you were about to order a retreat yourself, considering it was obvious that the crabs would have slaughtered us if we'd stood our ground."

His mouth tightened. "If I'd had the rest of Torm's Fury riding beside me, we would have slaughtered them."

"But you didn't," I said, "and as long as you're here, you won't. You'll have to make do with militiamen, local boys mostly, trained as well as the previous First Captain and I could manage, but not the kind of elite warriors you're used to."

He grimaced. "You're telling me I can't trust them to fight?"

"No, sir. They're game enough. I'm saying you can't expect them to do everything that scores of knights could do. Also, I'm reminding you that you have only forty-two of them, with no one to replace them if they fall."

"Hence your strategy," Hylas said sourly. "Don't attack, simply repel the enemy when they make a foray."

"As you say."

"Had it occurred to you that the crabmen were simply going to whittle down your force a bit at a time until they overwhelmed you and massacred the towns-folk in the end?"

"I thought I was buying time until reinforcements could arrive," I said. "Even now, knowing they won't be coming, I can't see a sound alternative. If you can, I'd rejoice to hear it."

He scowled. "When I do, you will. Dismissed." As I turned away, I heard him murmur, "Curse this wretched place."

* * * * *

Hylas was taken aback when I led him to the window and showed him the line of folk waiting in the street.

"Petitioners," he said flatly, repeating what I'd told him a moment before.

"Yes, sir," I replied. "As First Captain, you hold authority in all matters, civil and military alike."

"I know that," the knight said irritably, "but isn't there a bailiff or reeve to attend to this sort of thing?"

There were, but I'd instructed them to make themselves scarce. "As you keep remarking," I said blandly, "Port Llast is a small town."

"Very well," he sighed. "Show them in one at a time.

The first supplicant, a young but careworn widow, smelled of blood and hobbled in with the aid of a crutch. A crabman had maimed her, and the wounds were slow to heal. Six children with pinched, hungry faces followed along in her wake.

When she stood before Hylas, she tried to curtsey, and nearly lost her balance. The knight sprang from his chair, darted around his desk, and took hold of her arm to steady her.

"That isn't necessary, mistress," he said. He looked at me. "Fetch a chair." I did, and we saw her safely seated. "Now, how can I help you?"

The widow swallowed. "It's the dole. We don't want to ask for more than our fair share, but it's never enough to see us through the tenday. I have so many little ones," she concluded apologetically.

"Now that the fishing boats can't go out, First Captain Dothwintyl thought it prudent to ration the food supply," I explained.

"Well, I want this woman and her family . . ." Hylas faltered as his head caught up with his heart. "Do we know exactly how much food there is, and how quickly the village is running through it?"

"I'll get the ledgers," I said.

My notion was that by rubbing Hylas's nose in the town's woes, I'd show him that the defense of Port Llast was a mission worthy of his talents. To some extent, it seemed to work. Over the course of the next few days, he received the villagers courteously, and did his best to ameliorate their difficulties.

Yet it was plain that he was still impatient to return south, where a dashing cavalier could win renown. Indeed, it was possible that my efforts only made him even more eager to crush the threat to the settlement quickly. I feared that, his previous experience notwithstanding, he'd eventually insist on assaulting the crabmen's lair, and the men shared my apprehension.

Instead, he hit on another plan. Alas, it was just as reckless.

* * * * *

The broad-beamed merchant cog was no warship, but at least it could carry more men than a fishing boat and was more maneuverable than a barge. As, sail cracking, timbers and rigging creaking, we put out to sea, the catapults on the cliffs looked down on us. The contraptions might well have annihilated a flotilla of pirates, but they were useless against the present foe.

I peered over the side, saw what I'd feared to see, and went to speak to Hylas. He stood at the bow, his red plume and cape fluttering in the wind, seemingly oblivious to the resentment in the faces of the men.

"Have you looked at the water?" I asked. "Yesterday's storm stirred up the bottom, just as I predicted. You can barely see below the surface."

"The murk may hide ordinary fish," he replied serenely, "but I'm sure we'll be able to spot a sea monster."

"Not necessarily," I said, "not soon enough. This is the wrong day for this venture."

"The town is hungry," he snapped. "We have to kill the creature so the fishermen can fish. You and I have already had this discussion."

"Yes, Captain." Then, wondering why I even bothered, I added, "At least take off your armor." I'd left my helmet and brigandine in the barracks and so had the other militiamen.

"This is how knights of the Fury go into battle," Hylas replied. "I'll be fine."

Very well, I thought. Whatever comes, it's on your head. Harpoon in hand, I returned to the gunwale and studied the gray-green, heaving surface of the ocean.

For the next hour, nothing happened, and I dared to hope that nothing would. Then we heard the scratching. When I went below to investigate, the ship had already begun to take on water. I scrambled back up the ladder and found Hylas waiting to hear my report.

"Something's clinging to the hull," I told him, "picking it apart."

"The leviathan?" he asked.

"I doubt it," I said. "As best as anyone could judge observing from shore, it attacks a ship ferociously, not surreptitiously. I think we have crabmen trying to scuttle us."

"I . . ." He hesitated, and I could see how he hated

111

acknowledging that, landlubber that he was, he didn't know what to do next. "What do you recommend?"

"I see only one way to deal with them as long as they're on the bottom of the boat. Some of us will to have to dive down and dislodge them."

He nodded. "See to it."

I picked three men to accompany me and gave instructions to the rest, then it was time to pull off my boots and slip over the side.

The frigid water shocked my flesh, and the salt stung my eyes. Clutching my harpoon, kicking, I impelled myself beneath the barnacle-studded hull, and my comrades trailed after me.

It was little easier to peer through the cloudy water now that I was immersed in it, but I eventually made out the crabmen dangling from the keel, ripping and prying at the caulked timbers. Grateful there were only two, I swam to the nearest and thrust with the harpoon.

The water stole some of the force from my attack, but I still pierced a joint in the crabman's natural armor. Caught by surprise, the creature twisted toward me, just in time for one of my companions to spear it in the mouth, whereupon it relinquished its grip on the hull.

Jabbing, relying on the length of our weapons to keep us clear of its claws, we drove the crab from beneath the ship, while the other militiamen did the same to its fellow. As soon as the beasts were in the open, harpoons showered down into the water, several finding their mark.

By now my chest ached with the need to breathe, but I didn't care to venture out into the rain of lances, so I turned to swim back under the boat. Just in time

to behold our true quarry streaking upward from the
•depths.

It was like a jellyfish with a soft, white, undulating
body half the size of our vessel. Scores of thin, translucent tentacles swirled around it. Even startled as I
was, I wondered that such a creature could be so cunning. How had it known to attack precisely when every
single member of the crew had his eyes turned in the
opposite direction? Then I noticed the crabman swimming along at the larger monster's side, and surmised
that it was directing the creature's efforts.

No sane man would care to swim closer to this duo,
but with my lungs ready to burst, I had no choice. I
kicked upward, and luck was with me. None of the jellyfish's arms flailed into me.

As I broke the surface, glistening tentacles did the
same. Shooting up into the air, they lashed back and
forth across the deck above me. From my vantage
point, I couldn't tell precisely what they were doing up
there, but I could tell from the screams that they were
wreaking havoc.

The next instant, a figure of shining steel and gaudy
scarlet tumbled over the rail, his glimmering sword
flying from his grasp when he struck the water.
Weighted by his armor, Hylas sank like an anvil.

If I balked, it was only for a second, then I dropped
the harpoon, drew a deep breath, and dived after him.

By rights Hylas should have plummeted all the way
to the bottom, but he managed to grab hold of a section
of one of the jellyfish's tentacles. Bubbles boiling from
his mouth, he clung with one arm and tore at his
armor with the other.

My ears aching from the pressure, I hovered at his
side, helping him, fumbling with the clasps and

113

buckles. The ornate regalia of Torm's Fury fell into the depths, one piece at a time. When it seemed we'd disposed of enough—and in any case, our air was all but gone—I half dragged him to the surface, then to the side of the boat. A line dangled in the water, and I put it in his hand.

To my relief, men were still fighting on deck. The jellyfish had wrapped some of its tentacles around the cog itself, and appeared well on its way to capsizing her or tearing her asunder.

"Hang on to the rope," I said.

Hylas tried to answer but could only cough. I drew my knife and swam away from the boat, weaving my way through a mesh of writhing tentacles.

As before, the jellyfish didn't molest me. Even the crabman didn't notice me at first. Perhaps the monsters were too intent on the destruction of the ship, or perhaps the cloudiness of the water, and the effort I made to come in on their flank, helped conceal my approach.

As I prepared to attack, the crab sensed my presence and turned, grabbing for me with its pincers. Somehow I twisted out of the way, then raked my knife across the soft orb at the end of one of its eyestalks.

The crab recoiled and fled into the depths, and the jellyfish broke off its assault on the cog. Realizing that the colossal beast would be all but indestructible, I'd hoped to deter it by disposing of its handler, and my tactic had paid off. Still, I'd accomplished very little. No doubt the jellyfish would resume its depredations soon enough.

When I paddled back to the cog, I learned that three militiamen had perished in the battle. Under the circumstances, that was fewer than we had any right to expect. The ship itself was crippled but capable of limping back to port. On the way in, Hylas's face was bleak. I wondered bitterly if he was grieving for our fallen comrades or his lost gear.

*   *   *   *   *

That night, when we were still exhausted and dispirited, the crabmen attacked the settlement. Four more warriors died, along with sixteen of the townsfolk.

I knew more or less what the men were going to say. It was clear from their conspiratorial air, to say nothing of the lookout posted at the barracks door, but I judged it wiser not to let on.

"Very well," I said, "what did you want to talk about?"

"Captain Hylas," Vallam said. Some trick of the wavering candlelight made the old scars on his face look raw and new. "You told us to give him a chance, and we did, but he isn't working out. These . . . *schemes* of his are killing us like flies."

"We lost a few men before he arrived, and we've lost a few since. Considering what we're up against, we could expect nothing better."

Dandrios shook his square-jawed head. "It's different now. That high-born lunatic doesn't care about lowly militiamen. He'd sacrifice us all to rejoin his precious Fury. Well, Talona wither me if I'll die for that. We want *you* to lead us, Sergeant. Hylas can disappear."

Vallam smirked. "We'll tell everyone the crabmen got him."

"No," I said. I'd seen mutiny before, and no matter how wretched the deposed officers had been, it was always a disaster. Once a company of warriors decided they had the option of pulling down their commander, discipline decayed until they were no longer an army but a rabble.

Vallam scowled. "Sergeant—"

"No!" I repeated. "Whatever mistakes the First Captain has made, he's our leader, and we'll follow him in accordance with our oath."

"I won't," Dandrios said. "If we can't get rid of Hylas, I'm leaving." He turned away, presumably to gather his belongings.

Wishing he weren't so much bigger than I, I yanked him back around. "No one's deserting, either. The town needs us."

"Bugger the town," he said.

"All right. If you've no backbone, it comes down to this. Run, and I'll hunt you down and make you wish the crabs *had* gotten you."

He snarled and swung at me, a haymaker fit to break my skull. Happily, a man has to wind up for a punch like that. I saw it coming and sidestepped. In any common brawl, I would then have kicked my opponent in the knee, but Dandrios wouldn't be able to serve if I lamed him. I hooked a blow into his belly, then a second into his kidney.

The punches didn't faze him. Spinning, he clipped my jaw with his elbow. My teeth clacked together, and I stumbled back into one of the bunks. He scrambled after me and grappled, immobilizing my arms. I butted him twice in the face, and his grip loosened. I twisted free, then kneed him in the stones.

He gasped and doubled over. I kicked him, laying him out on the floor, then, careful not to damage him too severely, went on kicking for a while. I didn't like playing the bully, but matters had reached such a pass that the only way to maintain order was to make the garrison more afraid of me than they were of the crabs.

When I finally stepped back from my victim, I judged from the militiamen's wide eyes and white faces that I'd made my point. But it was only a temporary remedy. Ere long they'd be talking of making *me* disappear, or simply start slipping away in the dark.

They might have been surprised to learn that afterward, as I wandered the benighted streets, trying to calm down, I flirted with the notion of desertion myself. I didn't want to die for a lost cause, either.

* * * * *

Musty-smelling books and scrolls littered the First Captain's desk, and Aquinder perched on a stool beside it. A gray-bearded old man with a nose like a sickle, clad in a ratty scholar's gown, he was Port Llast's closest approximation to a sage, and in truth, had considerable skill as a herbalist and chirurgeon.

He gave me his usual curt nod as I stepped through the door. Hylas greeted me with the constraint that had entered his manner since the battle on the water. I didn't know what the change portended, but I preferred it to the cocksure posturing of yore.

"Please, take a chair," the young knight said. "I've asked Master Aquinder to come and ponder with me, and it occurred to me that it would be worthwhile to hear your thoughts as well."

"If I can help," I said, "I will."

"As serious a problem as the jellyfish is," said Hylas, pacing restlessly about, "the crabmen are the greater threat. Unfortunately, as you warned me, they're too numerous to exterminate, but if we could figure out *why* they've allied themselves with the sahuagin, perhaps we could somehow sever the bond."

I cocked my head. "I confess, that tack never occurred to me."

"Sadly," said Aquinder, "those sages who've studied the crabmen agree that they're insular creatures, with no ties to any other race. None of the available texts provides the slightest insight into the local colony's anomalous behavior."

"So I hoped you might have an idea," Hylas said. He gazed at me with a hint of desperation in his eyes.

Wonderful, I thought. He finally wants my opinion, and I haven't got one. Then, however, a notion struck me. I suspected it was a stupid one, but I offered it anyway. "We have fresh carcasses from last night's skirmish. We could cut one up."

Aquinder's gray eyes narrowed. "You mean, dissect it?"

"If that's what you call it," I said. "I've heard that's what sages do when they want to learn about a creature."

Hylas and Aquinder exchanged glances. The scholar shrugged and said, "Why not?"

We dissected the carcass where it had fallen. Stripped to the waist, I used an axe, mallet, and chisel to break open the dead crabman's shell. His sleeves rolled to the elbow, Aquinder probed the creature's stringy gray flesh with a lancet and tongs. It wasn't long before both of us were spattered with reeking slime. Meanwhile Hylas looked on anxiously.

None of us knew what we were searching for, nor did we actually expect to find anything. Yet when it appeared, it was unmistakable. A coin-like disk of polished red coral, wedged between two of the chitinous plates that armored the crabman's head.

Aquinder wiped it clean with a linen kerchief, then inspected it with a magnifying lens. He grunted, and Hylas asked what he'd found. Ignoring him, the old man extracted a pink quartz crystal from his pouch and touched it to the disk. The crystal glowed like a hot coal.

Having seen Aquinder perform the same test before, I knew what the light meant. "Magic," I said.

The scholar nodded. "The faces of the medallion are graven with glyphs of subjugation devised to turn a creature into some magic-wielding entity's willing thrall. I daresay all the crabmen have been enslaved in the same way."

"But how could a handful of sahuagin force scores, perhaps hundreds, of such powerful beasts to submit to such a thing?" I wondered aloud.

"If the brutes have a chieftain," Hylas said, "perhaps the sea devils captured and enslaved it, then bade it command the other crabmen to accept the talismans. At any rate, they managed somehow. I trust you see the implications."

"Yes," I said, though I didn't like them much.

* * * * *

I assembled the men on the training field, and Hylas explained the plan. "It would be impossible to invade the caves and slaughter all the crabmen," he said, "but Sergeant Kendrack and I believe that, if someone else created a diversion, a small force might be able to slip inside, locate the magic-wielding creature controlling the crabs, and kill it."

119

Not that we actually knew for certain that the slave driver in question was even in the tunnels, but it seemed likely.

"Here's what we'll do," Hylas continued. "The majority of you will march to the headland and entice the crabmen out. Once they appear, you'll make a fighting withdrawal, endangering yourselves no more than necessary, but luring the creatures after you. Meanwhile, the rest of you, Kendrack, and I will slip into the caves from the other side.

"Both tasks will be perilous, but infiltrating the tunnels, particularly so, and I won't compel anyone to go. Instead I ask for volunteers."

The men stood still and silent. My heart sinking, I stepped forward to harangue them, but Hylas lifted his hand to forestall me.

"I don't blame you for declining," he said to the men. "Since I arrived, I've blundered repeatedly. I led you recklessly, stupidly, and good men died as a result. I regret that more than I can say. Though I've finally learned the error of my ways, I don't ask you to follow me on that account. I've forfeited any claim on your loyalty, but Port Llast hasn't. Many of you were born here. You all have kin or friends here. I beg you, don't let your home perish when we still have one final chance to save it."

For several seconds, none of them responded, then Dandrios, of all people, his face bruised from the beating I'd given him, stepped from the ranks. "I'll come," he rumbled. "What the hells."

Vallam and six others followed his example.

* * * * *

Giving the crabmen's promontory a wide berth, we circled around to the other side of it, hid in some brush, and settled down to wait. After a quarter of an hour, we heard our comrades shouting and generally raising a commotion on the other side of the rock. Then came the long, wavering bleat of a trumpet to tell us the enemy had taken the bait.

On our side of the headland, the largest and thus most promising entrance to the caves opened offshore in the foaming surf. On Hylas's command, we ran toward the shadowy archway, our dash becoming a laborious floundering once we entered the waves.

Finally we made it into the cavern. The first granite vault seemed empty. If a lookout had ever been stationed here, it had evidently forsaken its post to join the battle our diversionary force had started.

I looked at the walls, hoping to find a ledge we could use as a path, but in this chamber at least, the wet rock surfaces were too steep, jagged, and generally treacherous for a human being to negotiate, though I suspected the crabs could manage nicely.

"We'll have to keep wading," said Hylas, echoing my thought.

Vallam nodded. "At least—" he began, then something snatched him down into the water. His hand flailed above the surface for an instant, then disappeared again.

I hurried toward him and the others did the same. Suddenly, I too plunged downward. For one panicky instant, I imagined that something had pulled me under, then realized I'd stepped in a hole. Fortunately, none of us was wearing armor this time, and, despite the encumbrance of my pickax and lantern, I clambered out without too much difficulty.

I was virtually on top of Vallam before I finally made out what was attacking him. When I did, I cursed in shock, for he was squirming amid a tangle of writhing dark green seaweed. I'd heard traveler's tales of man-eating plants, but never dreamed I'd be unlucky enough to encounter such myself.

Beneath the water, slimy fronds sought to slip around my limbs and torso. I dropped the objects in my hands, drew my short sword, and began hacking and sawing at them.

The fronds could draw as tight as a strangler's noose, and it seemed that for every one I severed, two more slithered forth to take its place. Finally the weed yanked my legs from under me, and, as I splashed down into the water, slapped another length of itself around my neck. I groped behind my back, but couldn't find the member that was crushing my throat.

The plant let me go. When I found my feet and looked at the panting warriors around me, it was plain that it had released everyone. Evidently, working together, we'd finally done enough damage to persuade it to abandon the fight.

But alas, we hadn't done so quickly enough to save everyone. Somehow, Vallam himself had survived, but the weed had broken another lad's back.

When it was clear that nothing could be done for him, Hylas murmured a terse prayer to Torm, then turned to Vallam. The scarred little man was a mass of scrapes and bruises, and his eyes were wild. Hylas gripped his shoulder. "Are you fit to go on?" he asked, holding the militiaman's gaze. "I hope so, for we need every hand."

Vallam grimaced and gave a jerky nod. "Yes, Captain," he croaked, "I'll stick."

"Good man," Hylas said. He pivoted toward the others. "Is everyone else all right?" The militiamen indicated they were. "Then let's keep moving."

Those of us who had dropped pieces of gear recovered what we could, and we slogged on.

I won't recount every moment of our trek through the caves. Suffice it to say, it was hellish. We felt we had to use the hooded lanterns sparingly, lest they give our presence away. A bit of light leaked in through chinks in the rock, but we still crept through gloom at the best of times and near absolute darkness at the worst. Moreover, only occasionally did we find a dry track to walk on. Often we waded in cold, murky water, while currents and uneven places on the bottom strove to dunk us. The crash of the surf outside echoed ceaselessly, deafening us to the stirrings of hostile creatures.

And such menaces abounded. Evidently the diversion had worked, and most of the crabmen were busy fighting on the beach, but they hadn't all departed, and sometimes one would pounce out of the darkness. So would other threats, like gray lizards that blended with the rock, leeches the length of a man's forearm, and sea urchins that hurled their venomous spines like darts.

We slew or evaded the beasts as best we could, but the most demoralizing thing was the mazelike nature of the passages. We kept running into dead ends, or realizing we'd inadvertently returned to some spot we'd visited before. The men began to whisper that we'd never find the puppeteer before the crabs returned. Some even worried that we were so completely lost we wouldn't even be able to find our way out.

Hylas and I did our best to brace them, speaking with a matter-of-fact confidence, harshly, or jocularly as the moment demanded. Meanwhile, I wrestled with my own unspoken fear.

Finally Hylas came up to me and murmured, too softly for the men to hear, "We've explored everywhere, haven't we?"

"So it seems to me," I replied. "Perhaps the master really isn't here, but out in the ocean somewhere."

Hylas shook his head. "If so, Port Llast is doomed, so we must assume it is here. So why can't we find it? This is a cavern, not a manmade fortress. It shouldn't have hidden doors or secret passages."

"True." Then a notion struck me. "Curse us all for a troop of idiots!"

"What is it?" Hylas asked. The men clustered around us.

"Of course a sea cave can have hidden passages," I said, "if the entrances are under the water."

"You're right," Hylas agreed, then turned to the men. "We'll go through the tunnels again, searching for such a passage."

And so we did, peering and probing for something that might well have proved difficult to locate even in good light. Though I was reasonably sure we were on the right track, I very much doubted we were going to discover the opening before time ran out.

It was Dandrios who called, "I found it!"

We all hastened to join him where he stood waist deep in water by the left wall. Ducking down, I groped about and took the measure of a hole four feet high and twice as long. Large enough to admit even a crab if it didn't mind cramped quarters.

"Good work," said Hylas to Dandrios. "Of course, we don't know that this is the right opening. We'll need to send a scout in."

I said, "I'll do—"

A vast rustling sounded through the cavern. The rest of the crabmen were returning. The men cringed and gathered themselves to flee in the opposite direction.

"All right," Hylas said briskly. "Apparently we've no time for reconnaissance. Everyone through the opening. Quickly, before the crabs have a chance to spot us."

The men gaped at him. "But Captain," one of them quavered, "you said yourself, we don't know this is the right hole . . . or if there's even any air on the other side!"

"True enough," Hylas said. He wore a soaked, plainly tailored wool tunic and breeches like the rest of us, and the water had plastered his artfully barbered chestnut curls to his head. Somehow, at that moment he didn't need burnished armor or a magic sword to look like a cavalier. "We do know this is our last chance for victory. Our last chance to save the village. I'm not going to throw that chance away, and if you're the warriors I think you are, you won't either." He discarded his pick and lantern and disappeared beneath the water.

"You heard him," I said.

I dropped my own more cumbersome gear, followed my commander into the hole, and for the next while, wondered if any of the militiamen had been fool enough to come after me. In the lightless passage, I couldn't tell.

I swam on and on, periodically bumping my head or extremities against the rocky sides of the tunnel. My lungs soon burned with the need for another breath, and I had to fight a panicky urge to turn and swim in the opposite direction. Even had I been willing to turn tail, I'd already come too far to make it back alive.

After some time I could dimly make out Hylas, silhouetted against an oval of lesser darkness. He passed through the opening and swam upward. I did the same, and my head came up into air. Gasping, I peered about.

We'd emerged in a high-ceilinged chamber whose sloping sides formed a sort of natural amphitheater around the pool in the center. Part way up the rock perched an altar of crimson coral. Poised in front of it, green-black, scaly arms upraised, its delicate fins weirdly beautiful, a sahuagin was performing some sort of ritual. It seemed entranced with ecstasy or simple concentration.

Turning his head in my direction, Hylas pressed his finger to his lips, expressing his desire to take the creature by surprise. As silently as we could, we swam in its direction.

Alas, we'd forgotten that there might be other foes about, and if so, they were as likely to be lurking under the dark water as wandering about on the rocks. I suddenly sensed something rising at me and wrenched myself around to face it, but I was too slow. The crabman grabbed me by the leg and pulled me under. Kicking, I struggled to break free before it snipped off my limb or drowned me.

It convulsed and released me. When I got my head above water, I saw that Dandrios had stabbed it. He and the others had followed me.

Hylas bobbed up beside me, blood streaming from a gash on his jaw. "Get the sahuagin!" he panted to anyone who could hear.

We swam for the shore. Another crab darted at us, and Dandrios turned to intercept it and keep it off our backs. In the end, only Hylas and I managed to drag ourselves up onto the slope. Everyone else was busy fighting the creatures in the water.

By now the sahuagin was well aware of our intrusion, and so were two more crabs that scuttled down the rocks to meet us. Still starved for air, blinking the stinging salt water from my eyes, I scrambled up and yanked my short sword from its scabbard. I evaded the crab's first attack, stepped in, and thrust, wounding it in the flank. The monster hopped backward and poised its claws to threaten me anew.

I could see Hylas from the corner of my eye. He too had made it to his feet and was battling the other crab.

The beasts fought well. Still, I fancied that Hylas and I would prove a match for them. The sea devil, who'd remained before the altar, began to weave its webbed hands in mystic passes and chant in its sibilant, grunting, inhuman tongue.

Plainly, it was indeed the sorcerer-thing we'd come to slay, and if we didn't do so immediately, it was likely to strike us down with a spell. Hylas and I attacked our opponents fiercely, striving to kill them so we could rush their master before it completed its incantation. They, conversely, played for time, adopting a defensive posture that posed less of a threat but made them damnably hard to get at.

I dropped my guard, inviting an attack, and my crab couldn't resist the opportunity. It grabbed for me, and I recklessly dived under its pincers and plunged my sword into its belly.

The creature fell, and I charged up the incline—until a gigantic invisible hammer struck me down.

I felt as if a huge hand were squeezing me. It was all I could do simply to expand my chest and breathe, and

I feared the pressure would crush me to pulp in time.

The magic was assailing Hylas as well. He was staggering and seemed about to crumple. In no hurry now, his opponent reached for him.

Grunting with pain and effort, Hylas threw his short sword at the sea devil. The blade spun like a wheel, and the point plunged deep into the monster's globular eye. As the brute fell backward onto the altar, the power that gripped me faded away.

By that time, the crabman's claws were about to snap shut on Hylas. I shouted, and, startled, the creature faltered. Hylas scrambled back from the beast and we killed it together.

After that, aching and exhausted though we were, we had to aid the men still fighting in the water. In the end, our side prevailed. In fact, once we hauled ourselves up onto the shore, we determined we'd been lucky. Only two more men had died. Others were cut up pretty badly, but I thought they could recover with proper care.

Not that they were likely to receive it. A minute later, scores of crabmen began to surface in the pool.

"No," Vallam moaned. "It isn't fair!"

Clumsy with the pain of his gory wounds, Dandrios floundered around toward Hylas and me. "We killed the sahuagin that enslaved them," he said. "They aren't supposed to want to hurt us anymore."

"We're still intruders in their nest," said Hylas, rising. "I fear all we can do is sell our lives as dearly as possible."

We formed a circle to guard one another's backs, but though the crabs climbed up onto the slope, they kept their distance.

A particularly large specimen ascended to the altar,

picked up the dead sahuagin, and cast it aside, thus uncovering two red coral carvings I hadn't noticed before. One represented a crabman, the other a jellyfish. Evidently these were instruments of subjugation that worked in concert with the disks.

The crabman broke them in its pincers. Its fellows clacked their claws together in what seemed a frenzy of celebration, then the big one gestured to us, inviting us to make our way back to the pool.

"You were right," Hylas said to me, wonder in his voice. "They are more than animals. They understand that we liberated them, and they're letting us go."

"Apparently," I said, scarcely daring to believe it. "Let's get out of here before they change their minds."

* * * * *

After our escape, we learned that the majority of the diversionary force had survived their mission. Port Llast still had a functional garrison, if only barely so. Hylas spent another three days in town, long enough to make sure the jellyfish was truly gone. On the morning of his departure, we conferred in his study, attending to a few final pieces of business.

"It's strange," he said when we'd finished. "Now that it's time to go, a part of me wishes to linger. But you no longer need me." He grinned. "If you ever did."

I grinned back. "No common man-at-arms would ever admit to needing an officer, but you did come in handy once or twice."

"Thank you," he said, becoming serious. "For everything." We shook hands, then went out to review the men. He had a jest or a word of praise for each of them, and they gave him three cheers as he rode away.

Afterward I wondered when the Lords' Alliance would appoint a permanent First Captain, and what sort of master he'd prove to be. Finally a messenger brought the answer. Hylas had praised me to his superiors, and in consequence, they'd promoted me.

Forged in Fire

Clayton Emery

22 Kythorn, the Year of the Gauntlet

"Have at 'em, me hearties! Sweep 'em into the sea, me brave ones!"

Screaming, swinging cutlasses and scimitars, pirates boiled over the side. Bounding from the deck of their dromond onto the merchantmen's cog, bare feet slapping the deck, the pirates rushed the quarterdeck.

Clustered on the quarterdeck were a captain and first mate who shouted encouragement at a dozen sailors. Simple merchantmen, they looked reluctant to fight.

Clambering carefully over the foaming, gnashing space between the ships, came the corpulent pirate chief who urged on his cutthroats with a cyclone of words. Heart of a Lion no longer fought toe-to-toe with enemies, but kept to the rear to supervise. Someone had to watch the two ships lest they ran aground, after all.

"Take 'em, me fearsome children!" he hollered. "A swift attack brings a short battle!"

Howling, thirty pirates split into two packs like wolves and surged up the short companionways to the quarterdeck. With luck, terror would make the merchantmen drop their arms and surrender. Heart of a Lion noticed the merchant captain, a skinny black-bearded man, had been born with a scowl, and the first mate's face was tattooed like a desert nomad's. Too, the other companionway was guarded by a lean woman in bright pinks and yellows, and such people were always trouble.

Sure as taxes, he saw, the ship's officers offered the pirates straight-thrust steel.

A pirate swung his cutlass to bat the first mate's scimitar aside, but an arm like oak simply riposted. The pirate yelped and jumped, pinked in the thigh. Hampered by the narrow stairs, another pirate sliced his cutlass at the mate's ribs, but that blow too was deflected, and the mate drew blood from a forearm. Below, in the waist, Heart of a Lion hollered useless instructions. Why would his crew never listen at sword practice? The chief was glad to see a tall pirate finally reach past his fellows and ram hard with a boarding spear. The first mate dodged, but banged into his captain alongside. The spear split his throat. Gargling blood and spraying his enemies red, the first mate dropped.

Pirates hollered in triumph, and pushed across the

red-slick deck after the rangy captain. He bore a worn scimitar and a small round shield with a nasty spike. He swiped viciously to fend two pirates back, then lunged at a third. A fast chop cut a pirate's wrist to the bone. As blood fountained and the pirate screamed, a shipmate behind rammed him with a shoulder. The wounded pirate blundered into the merchant captain, tangling him. A boarding pike hooked the captain's leg. Tripped up, the captain crashed on his back. Quick as cats, two female pirates jammed blades in his belly and throat. With their officers dead, already the sailors were throwing down their rusty scimitars while the pirates hooted.

"Excellent! Your captain is proud!" yelled Heart of a Lion.

He swiftly marked the progress of the two ships. The pirate's dromond, a long, lean, lateen-rigged, many-oared vessel named *Shark's Fang*, was bound to the merchant's cog by stout ropes tipped with chains and iron grapnels. Locked, the two ships pitched and yawed in the lee of a big island to the south. Tharsult of the Shining Sea had many rocky clefts deep-shadowed by dawn, an excellent spot for ambushing the sea lanes. Waves burst into spray against a shore covered in seaweed. With a full day of bright sun burgeoning, the pirate chief exulted. They could loot this vessel's cargo and be hidden again by sundown.

Heart of a Lion carried no weapon, only a hollow tube of brass that he waved while exhorting his crew. "Press on, sons and daughters of seven devils! Conquer like kings! Drive—eh? Curse me for a camel boy!"

In a heartbeat, the second pack of pirates had run into a tigress.

Blocking the starboard companionway was the lean

woman in pinks and yellows—the colors of the Nallo-jal, the Navy of the Caleph of Calimshan. Her white cork helmet, wrapped with a purple turban and sporting a brass bill, identified her as a lieutenant of the Imperial Marines. She hefted a straight sword like some northerner, and fire flashed from her eyes as she hollered, "Glory to the Caleph!"

Down in the waist, Heart of a Lion groaned. He may need his brass tube, despite the danger of burning the ship to the waterline. Didn't anyone simply *surrender* anymore?

Charging the lieutenant came a huge pirate named Tasyn, famed for his brawling and swordplay. He leered as he feinted with his cutlass, relying on a trick to distract her. While the swordsman feinted, the lieutenant struck. Cruel as a dragon's claw, her straight-bladed sword skimmed his knuckles and chunked into a knee carelessly put forward. Tasyn's leg crumpled. As the big pirate tilted to the wounded side, the lieutenant slammed the side of his neck. Blood pinwheeled into the sky and striped the lieutenant's blouse and vest.

Another pirate, a woman, attacked as the lieutenant dispatched her first victim. The pirate squatted so low her hams brushed the deck, then she stabbed upward to spear the marine's groin. Fast as thought, the lieutenant's blade spanked the pirate's cutlass so hard the tip bit the deck, then the straight blade bounced back up. The female pirate saw the sword tip fly for her face like an arrow, then the point pierced her eye and brain.

Ducking herself, using the dropped bodies as a barrier, the lieutenant flicked her sword tip at pirates who suddenly hung back. She taunted, "Come closer, jackals. Taste the iron tongue of the Imperial Marines!"

"Ilmater made me to suffer," sighed Heart of a Lion. His pirates' attack had stalled, and might even fail if the sailors rallied around that devilish lieutenant. "But Sharess finds favor for those who love life."

Raising the brass tube in his hand, Heart of a Lion sighted down its hollow length at the ducking, weaving lieutenant, then stroked his fingers down the tube, invoking, "*As'tal rifa!*"

Like a wyrm's belch, from the tube billowed flame that coalesced into a sphere and sizzled through the air. Big as a fistful of flaming pitch, the fireball bounced off the lieutenant's turbaned helmet. Purple silk scorched and ignited, as did hanks of short blonde hair below her cork helmet. Panicked, the lieutenant flipped off her burning helmet, and was in turn slammed alongside the head by a cutlass blade. She dropped, face down in blood.

Yet Heart of a Lion's attack had worked too well. The fireball ricocheted from the sturdy cork helmet and lodged amidst tarred ropes and deadeyes in the standing rigging. Tar sputtered and flared like kindling. Paint on woodwork blistered and peeled, smoked and curled, and burst into flame. Within seconds the fire streaked up the rigging and set ablaze the mizzen sail.

"Fire aloft!" hollered a pirate.

Instantly seamen chopped at stays to bring the sail down. The merchant sailors joined in, a tacit surrender, because everyone afloat feared fire at sea. Slipping in blood, they loosed belaying pins to free the running rigging. Let go, pushed by the wind, the flapping, flaming sail flopped over the taffrail and hissed to extinction in the pitching waves. Pirates and sailors alike lowered buckets on ropes and sloshed the quarterdeck to douse stray sparks. Blood swirled with seawater and ran out the scuppers.

As the emergency passed, and sailors and pirates caught their breath, Heart of a Lion puffed his way up the short companionway. Graced with a glorious black beard combed and perfumed—and rubbed with soot to disguise gray hairs—the pirate chief wore a flowing red shirt that minimized his potbelly, blue trousers cut off at the knee, and a wide silk scarf of gold that matched a yellow turban.

Spreading his hands, he announced, "Gentlemen, ladies! Fellow Brethren of the Brine! The gods decreed we possess your worthy vessel, and so it came to pass. You should find no shame in surrender. Tell me, if you please, who among you is leader?"

With the captain and first mate dead, the worried sailors turned to a grizzled man with a salt-and-pepper beard and scarred cheek. Like most sailors, he wore patched baggy trousers and a plain sturdy shirt, but laced across his chest was a red leather vest wildly embroidered with slant-eyed dragons and doe-eyed maidens. Heart of the Lion noticed most of the sailors wore similar exotic vests. Obviously, this ship returned from far over the eastern horizon.

"I'm Bollus, esteemed sir, humble boatswain of *Eight Lightnings* out of Calimport. Two-hundred sixty-four days out of Kozakura. You shan't kill us, will you, honorable *rysal*? We were ordered to defend the ship, and hope we didn't offend."

"Eh? Oh, no, we shan't kill you." Heart of a Lion was distracted. Where under Father Sky lay, what had he called it? Koza-koonit? What kind of outlandish cargo would they carry? "In fact, we welcome new recruits, so you have a choice: join us or be put ashore. Take your time and think it over. In the mean, spruce up this mess, if you please. Flake those lines, dress the sails, holystone the decks. A busy man is a happy man."

Relieved to be spared, the sailors jumped to work. First to get pitched over the side were the bodies of fallen pirates and merchanters, once they'd been stripped of weapons, jewelry, and saleable clothing.

A surprised shout went up as the pirates discovered the marine lieutenant was still alive. She was dragged before the captain, head hanging and mouth drooling. Her cheek and neck were singed and wept a sticky fluid, and her hair was burned away on one side. Heart of a Lion noted her blond hair and fair skin under the dark tan. Probably born of foreign mercenaries, she was nevertheless a daughter of the desert. Typically Calishite, whose people were united in a mongrel heritage.

"Shall we cut her throat, captain?" asked a pirate. "She killed Tasyn and Nureh."

Heart of a Lion squinted, considering. "That's no big loss. Tasyn was a bully and Nureh cheated at cards. No, I believe we'll chain her to an oar. If she survives the row to port, we'll ransom her back to the navy."

Down in the waist, Harun, the pirates' first mate, had stripped the canvas covers off the hatches to scout the cargo. This merchant's cog was a general-purpose vessel with moveable bulkheads below, fat and beamy as a wooden shoe, with a wealth of square sail. *Eight Lightnings* could easily sail beyond Faerûn, and obviously had.

"Captain! You'd best see this!" bellowed Harun.

Broad-shouldered and brown, the first mate favored a black mustache curled with beeswax, perhaps because his pate was bald as a bollard. Being an authority on a notoriously undisciplined pirate ship, Harun always sounded disgusted, but especially bitter now. With a sigh over a captain's busy lot, Heart of a Lion plodded down the companionway.

"Cast your eyes on this filthy muck."

The gaping hold contained cask stacked upon cask. Crewmen hefted a dozen barrels up and plunked them on the deck, but they all held the same thing, to judge by the identical calligraphs branded on the ends. Harun pried out a bung with his iron knife and let liquid gurgle into his palm. It was clear and faintly golden, like the wines of Waterdeep.

Heart of a Lion dipped his finger and sniffed. The liquid smelled faintly like burnt honey mixed with turpentine or cedar resin. Gingerly the pirate chief touched his tongue: it burned like spicy pepper. "What is it?"

"Flog me like a dog if I know," Harun scowled, waving callused hands. "But we've got plenty of it. Three holds full. The master cabin has some raw silk and silver, and more of these frilly clothes and painted dishes, may Oghma take my sight. We can sell them for a small profit, but these casks . . . they're worthless."

Heart of a Lion waggled his brass tube for Bollus. Treading lightly, the captive boatswain shook his head.

"A thousand pardons, gracious sirs, and a hundred apologies, but we don't know what these barrels hold either. Our captain and mate kept it a secret. They were part owners in this vessel, which is why they fought so ferociously to defend her, while we simple sailors are paid by the day. They didn't trust us to know the cargo, and none of us could speak the language in Kozakura. I think the liquid is pressed from rice, or else juice of the sugar cane, or both. Our captain claimed he'd market it overnight in Cal- imshan, but how, we don't know."

"Where is your ship's log?"

"Again, ten score apologies, but the captain threw it overboard when you attacked. It had lead covers so t'would sink."

"A secret cargo from an unknown land . . ." Heart of a Lion smelled his fingertips again. "It's not lacquer, nor vinegar. 'Haps it's lamp oil, like the spermaceti they press from whale blubber at Luskan."

Pirates had gathered to gauge their luck, and now looked glum. Several dipped their fingers in the strange brew. One offered, "It's too thin for lamp oil." Another opined, "It might've spoiled in the hold, lost its body soaking up heat." "If it tastes putrid, it must be medicine." "Did you shake the cask? Perhaps it's sepa- rated, like unchurned camel milk." " 'Haps it's camel piss."

"This voyage is cursed," growled Harun. "Without the owners' connections in Calimport, we'll never sell this stuff. Who'd buy something the sellers can't even identify? What with having to lay in food and water casks and new sails, and these slim pickings, we won't win enough on this voyage to make our expenses. Some pirates. We can't even profit by stealin'!"

Silently, Heart of a Lion agreed. These past three months, ocean traffic had mysteriously thinned, so even the busy sea lane spanning Tharsult and Alm- raiven lay deserted. A couple more tendays of bad luck, the pirate chief knew, and his crew would grow restless and angry, and blame their captain for ill for- tune. Heart of a Lion would be voted out of his post— if he weren't forcibly retired over the side on a windy night.

Yes, he sighed, pirating was a dodgy business. Especially since Heart of a Lion no longer wielded a scimitar. A growing prosperity around his middle had slowed him as well. These days he preferred to exercise his brain, and to even experiment with mystical gewgaws. Hence the brass wand of fire-casting, which he'd acquired in the market of Memnon, a city besmitten by efreet. The tube was a handy weapon, though some of the crew thought magic-wielding was sissified, and hinted darkly that their captain might fare better in another profession. Like flower-drying, or fish-mongering. . . .

So, sighed Heart of a Lion, he better make some captainly decisions before the crew entertained doubts. Stumping around the deck, he checked the million details a mariner must attend at all times. The two ships were still linked by iron and hemp. The tide was flowing, so they drifted safely away from the rocks of Tharsult. The day was barely begun—his ample stomach growled for breakfast—so they had plenty of light to work by, but what to do next? Should he order some of these mysterious barrels transferred to *Shark's Fang*, or just jettison them? Without this heavy load, the weed-encrusted *Eight Lightnings* would ride higher. Perhaps by painting out the name and sailing her to Suldolphor, they could gain a quick profit that might satisfy the crew. Unless the ship had already visited Suldolphor, where it would be recognized—

"Ho, Captain! Our pardon, but the pink tiger demands to speak to you."

Braced by two brawny pirates, scorched, bloody, and dazed, the marine lieutenant was still undefeated. She snarled at the pirate chief like a rabid tiger. "Are you mad? Why are you fools doing this?"

Perplexed, Heart of a Lion asked, "Doing what?

140

Raiding ships? What do you expect pirates to do?"

"*Ptah!*" The lieutenant spat blood off a split lip. Having been clubbed upside the head, she strained to focus. "I am Lieutenant Belinda Destine of the Caleph's Imperial Marines. Are you really the pirates' captain? How can that be, a quivering tub of lard fat as a manatee?"

"Did you never hear of Heart of a Lion?" he asked with great dignity. "The boldest pirate of the Trackless Sea, fearless and feared up and down the Sword Coast? Who in the Year of the Shadows stole the Tethyrian tribute ship from under the Syl-Pasha's very nose? Who, during the Darkstalker Wars, looted the bottomless coffers of the Dark Dagger's stronghold, carrying off the Goblin King's crown before Ralan El Pesarkhal even knew it was gone?" Out of breath, the pirate chief paused, then patted his great girth. "Admittedly, those adventures occurred before you were born, but my mighty mind is ever-sharp and even today my name strikes terror—"

"Shut up, you blithering baboon!" The officer snarled in a parade ground voice. "Haven't you heard, you sheep-headed shearwater? We're at war!"

"Oh. Again?" Heart of a Lion shrugged, both hands in the air. "Someone's always at war, bless the dark dabbling of Shar. War is good. Pirates prosper when countries clash and supplies are shipped—"

"Not countries," she barked. "The kingdoms of the coast are at war with the deep! The swimming races vie against the speaking races. At every coast fish-men and water-harpies, whales and whatnot, spring from the waves and scuttle ships and massacre shore-dwellers. No village or city that touches water is safe from assault, nor any vessel."

141

All the pirates, and sailors too, had gathered to hear the news. Her head ringing, the lieutenant rasped on. "No one knows why they attack or who leads them. The navy admirals posit that a war between ocean-dwellers has spilled onto dry land. A spy claims a coven of ixitxachitls, the flying devil-rays, oppose a mad sea monster whose identity is not known. Or else they support him. It's all unclear. I came aboard this vessel in the Border Kingdoms when I heard the news. Calimshan needs me. Our homeland needs all its citizens, to fight. The land races must band together or else we'll be driven from the—"

A scream interrupted. Turning, more people screamed, and cried, and gibbered with fear.

Alongside the ship, rising, writhing, shedding seawater by the gallon, reared an octopus tentacle higher than the mast and thicker around than a hogshead barrel. The flesh was a mottled green and brown, the colors shimmering and shifting in the bright spring sunshine. The largest suckers on that gigantic arm were wide as a man's chest. As the watchers stepped back in fear, another tentacle arose alongside, then a third.

Heart of the Lion had sailed the seas for thirty years, as boy and man, and seen many fantastic sights, but nothing like this. He had time for only one chilling thought—octopuses had eight arms—so was not surprised to see three more tentacles rising from the depths alongside the dromond. Like loathsome, sea-spawned trees, the six arms formed an obscene cage that threatened to block the sun and trap the ships.

The tentacles toppled and crashed on the wooden decks. People scattered in all directions, some even jumping overboard. Severed rigging snapped and pinged. Loose sails flapped all which way. Barrels stacked around the hold flipped and rolled like dice, and several split to spill resinous liquid running in streams down the deck. Half a dozen pirates and sailors were killed outright, crushed by the massive tentacles. Two victims screamed as trapped, broken limbs were pulped further.

The marine lieutenant, her captors, and two other pirates were hemmed in with Heart of a Lion, trapped between living walls of slimy flesh as tall as hedgerows and stinking of the sulfurous sea bottom. The ships shuddered and groaned like over-laden donkeys—as Heart of a Lion knew they were. Another minute and both ships might shatter. Sucked into the depths, drowning, the crew would be minced like minnows by the yellow parrot's beak the giant octopus sported beneath its bulbous head.

Buoyant as a cork, the merchant vessel yet shuddered as the deck tilted alarmingly to starboard. Barrels skittered, timbers groaned, and planks popped. The pirate captain wondered frantically how to fend off an attack by a giant octopus. Strong men would need an hour to hack through these rubbery limbs.

More noises, odd ones. From beyond the fleshy prison Heart of a Lion heard shouts, curses, and the clank and ring of steel. Mixed in were guttural roars like the rush of surf and the hooting of seals. What where they? How could the ships suffer another attack? Could some fiendish master have ordered a giant octopus to enwrap the ships, then sent unseen soldiers of the sea swarming aboard?

"Don't stand there gawking like a sea bass—*fight!*" Lieutenant Destine shouted, then shook off her panicked captors and snatched her sword from one's belt.

143

Whipping it overhead, both hands on the pommel, Belinda Destine sank the sharp blade to the hilt in an octopus limb. Shearing flesh made a sucking sound ghastly to hear. Jumping high and hanging on the blade, she carved a furrow a cubit long that bled dark red. She called to the pirates, "Bestir yourselves! Wedge in your blades!"

Dazzled by rapid events, and wondering what else menaced his crew, Heart of a Lion attacked with what came to hand. The fire-casting wand. With no better plan, he jammed the tube against the giant, pulsing tentacle, then whisked his hand along the polished brass. *"As'tal rifa!"*

The flashback almost killed him.

Heart of a Lion was hurled backward as flame as big as a bonfire blossomed from the brass tube, filling his vision like a sun and blinding him. His head and shoulders thumped the opposite limb, and he sprawled on his broad rump. The huge limb didn't quiver now, but twisted and writhed. Rubbing his dazzled eyes, he discovered his shirt cuffs had been singed off.

A hole as big as a man's head was scorched in the octopus limb. Charred flesh rimmed a green hole that now gushed red blood like a hole in a dam. At the center of the wound glowed an inferno. The fireball, composed of mystical dweomer, continued to burn and bore into wet flesh.

All this damage he glimpsed for a second, then the limb was gone. Like a flying carpet, the never-ending arms ascended into the air. Evidently the octopus was bee-stung. It made sense, thought the dazzled pirate chief. An octopus was unlikely to feel fire on the sea bed.

One arm retreated so quickly the marine lieutenant

was hoisted into the sky, for she single-mindedly clung to her sword pommel. Only when her boots ticked a canted mast did she let go to thump on the deck. Quick as a mink, she grabbed a dropped scimitar and raced to the attack before the nature of her enemy was even certain.

Berserk as a northern bobcat, Heart of a Lion thought. The woman was battle mad. Crawling to his feet, feeling old and slow, he made a mental note to stay out of her way. What did they feed Imperial Marines anyway? Dragon's blood and wolf guts? Wiping his brow, making sure he retained his fireball wand, Heart of a Lion cast about to see what force attacked his ship and crew.

He wished he hadn't looked.

Green, weedy giants, a dozen or more, raged across both ships leaving chaos in their wake. Heart of a Lion recognized the creatures, having seen one dead, caught in a fisherman's net. Sea ogres, called merrow by mariners, loomed ten feet tall yet ran thin as barracudas, with elongated necks and bear-trap jaws. Naked, with flesh pale as a drowned corpse, the beasts were stippled with hair like seaweed. Every ogre was inscribed with twisted tattoos and hung with necklaces, bracelets, and anklets cobbled from sharks' teeth, swordfish swords, tarnished brass and silver, broken bottle necks, and other sea wrack. Teeth and nails black as chert were tough enough to rend humans in half, and the monsters reveled in an orgy of bloodlust.

As Heart of a Lion watched, an ogre drove a spear through a sailor's guts, hoisted the squirming woman by the haft and her hair, then bit out her throat so her head flopped against her spine. Two ogres swatted a pirate flat, then grabbed him by both arms and yanked.

The limbs dislocated, then tore from their sockets in gouts of blood. Many sailors and pirates didn't fight at all, just ran in terrified circles, and Heart of a Lion couldn't blame them. Others fought back. Harun swung a wicked boarding axe to slice a merrow across the waist and spill its guts, then swung the other way to hamstring another rampaging monster and bring it crashing to the deck.

Maddest of all was the berserk Belinda Destine. Since conditions changed rapidly and unexpectedly at sea, Imperial Marines were trained to improvise in battle, to attack with whatever came to hand. Bereft of her sword, Belinda hefted one of the many barrels that rolled and careened across the deck. Gargling her own battle cry, she smashed the barrel into the muzzle of a marauding merrow. Oak slats cracked and liquid gushed over both combatants. Oddly, the sharp reek set the merrow stumbling backward, clawing at its eyes, gasping and retching. Belinda merely shook her streaming blond bangs from her eyes, hefted the empty cask again, and walloped the merrow in the breast. When it fell, Belinda beat the cask to fragments on its hard head. Heart of a Lion grunted at her mindless ferocity, and reminded himself to sheer clear of Imperial Marines.

As humans struggled and died, Heart of a Lion was disheartened to see more merrow swarm over the sides, rapacious as rats. A pirate swung a scimitar to lop off a black-nailed hand against the gunwale, but another merrow seized his sash and yanked him overboard like a pike on a line. A tall and comical head reared suddenly alongside, with goggling eyes like lamps, a long nose like a flute, and raddled brown skin segmented like a scorpion's carapace. A seahorse, Heart of a Lion realized, fully as big as a land steed from the great plains of Amn. Two merrow had wrapped long arms around its neck, and now used the seahorse's curved back to vault onto the ship.

On this benighted day of strange sights, Heart of a Lion was astonished to see that Belinda had spoken true and he'd guessed right. This assault was controlled by a single mastermind.

By the cog's prow, farthest from the fighting, a single octopus tentacle remained suspended in the air, jigging and bobbing as the giant bottom-dweller writhed in pain. Poised on the tip of the tentacle, like a canary perched on a finger, squatted a sahuagin. Tall as a man, hunched like a pelican, with a head like a cod and the body of a frog, finned and spined, the sea devil waved a narwhal tusk as it exhorted its queer troops to attack. It croaked and squawked and waved both crooked arms wildly. Only the barbs of its froglike feet, clamped tight, kept it from toppling. A shaman invoking magic, thought Heart of a Lion, elsewise the pain-wracked octopus would flick it off. Perhaps it hurled more magic to goad the merrow in their attack, not that the bloodthirsty enemies of mankind needed much prodding.

Heart of a Lion's only magic trick was the fire wand, and he had no idea how much dweomer still charged the tube. He should conserve his shots, he thought, except the battle could end within minutes, with the merrow the victors.

"What shall we do, master?" wailed a sailor.

Heart of a Lion shook his head. Chaos whirled like a cyclone around him, and people died before he could think, let alone act. Up on the quarterdeck, three sailors were clubbed down by four merrow who flailed their spear butts again and again on the bloody

147

carcasses. At the prow, the sahuagin shaman made a tearing motion with green, scaly claws, and a pirate dropped dead, clutching his heart. The feisty Belinda's luck ran out, for as she belabored one merrow with a broken boarding pike, another dropped a fist like an anvil that hammered her to the deck, which was awash in the turpentine-reeking fluid.

All this Heart of a Lion glimpsed in seconds, then the attack stalled. Surviving sailors and pirates clustered around their captain. All hunkered at the starboard side of the cog, with the pirates' tethered dromond dipping and pitching alongside. More merrow rose to the attack, some climbing the sides of the dromond and tramping across the deck, trailing water. The defenders were surrounded—twenty weary fighters and their aging captain, who wanted only to go below and take a nap. Their future was bleak. Stand and die under bludgeoning fists and claws, or jump over the side to drown, or be crushed between the ships' hulls, or else be eaten by more denizens of the depths.

Unless . . .

"Grab that barrel!" barked Heart of a Lion. Half a dozen casks tumbled and rumbled along the deck. "And that one—broach the ends! The rest of you, strip your shirts or sashes."

Not comprehending, but glad to follow any orders that might save them, the knotty-armed seamen righted the barrels and stove in the ends with belaying pins. Ripe fumes of sap and sugar wafted around the survivors. As blood-spattered merrow closed on the humans like a wolf pack, Heart of a Lion ordered the shirts and sashes sopped in the liquid until it puddled around their feet. One man hissed as the fiery fluid stung in a long gash down his shin.

"Fling the juice in their faces—hurry!"

Bare-chested men and a few women hopped forward and whipped the wet clothing at the merrows' evil, elongated faces. Wincing, flinching, the sea ogres shielded their sea-green eyes from the spatters, and shied away, shoving back their bloodthirsty mates.

"They hate the stuff," crowed Heart of a Lion. "It offends their noses!"

"So what? It's their claws and teeth that'll kill us!" Always grumpy, Harun snapped a shirt at the monsters and drove them back, but had to soak his shirt while the creatures surged in. "We can't flick laundry at them all day. How do we stop them? Or escape?"

Heart of a Lion shook his head, black beard waggling. He hadn't planned that far ahead. Once the repugnant liquid ran out, or the merrow girded their courage, they'd be massacred. What to do? It didn't help his concentration that the leader of this murder spree, the fish-headed sahuagin, was still perched on its tentacle, raised higher now to observe them. The shaman croaked and rasped like a demented seagull, urging the merrow on with curses and charms.

"I don't know what else," growled Heart of a Lion, "but I'll fry that fish-fiend and bear it to the Nine Hells with us."

Sighting down his fire-casting wand, Heart of a Lion eyeballed the crooked sea devil as he stroked his fat hand down the polished brass. *"As'tal rifa!"*

Came a *VA-VOOMF!* like a volcano coughing, and the whole world exploded into flame.

Heart of a Lion hooted as the sahuagin shaman was smashed in the gut by a flaming fist. The foul creature bled red as it tumbled off the octopus tentacle and splashed in the sea. As he lowered the brass tube,

Heart of a Lion saw that his enemies, crew, and both ships were ablaze.

"Memnon immolate my soul! Who knew the stuff was flammable?"

Heart of a Lion goggled. Across two decks raged fire white-hot and glimmering blue. Flames scurried like rats across deck furniture and wreckage, soared up ratlines, rimmed the sails, and ran rings around the scuppers and gunwales. High above, rigging sparkled and winked like fireworks, and black jots of burning tar rained. Some pirates yelped as their clothing or hair burned, but cooler heads knocked them down and beat out the flames, or else hurled folds of canvas over them. Pirates and sailors leaned far over the side, braving the grinding hulls, to sop their clothing in seawater. They slapped the cool brine on sparks atop people and ships.

Mindless, the merrow suffered and died. Many were ablaze. Flames licked up their legs as if they waded through a grass fire. Some beat at the flames and only ignited their hands and seaweed hair. Many galloped, bellowing in pain, to the sides of the ships and dived headlong. One broke its neck ramming the brown armored hide of a giant seahorse. Another merrow hanged itself by snaring its long neck in rigging while jumping overboard. A few, unable to act for the searing pain, fell on the decks and rolled and writhed. Further saturating themselves in flammable liquid, they were incinerated. Evil, oily smoke wafting from charred corpses stank like burning garbage. Only a couple of merrow had yet to catch fire, and they ran in panicked circles below dripping ratlines and falling sails ripe with flame.

"To the dromond! Board *Shark's Fang!*" A true captain again, Heart of a Lion shoved people headlong up onto the gunwale, even picked up a few and lobbed them bodily into the low-built dromond. "Harun, make ready to set sail! Saida—no, she's dead—Kalil, pull a hatchet and cut the grappling ropes! Jassan, helm the rudder to haul us away from the cog! You sailors, beat out those flames!"

A slave to custom, Heart of a Lion refused to leave the deck until his crew was safe. Once all the living were aboard, he cast a last look around the cog to see if anyone remained.

The ship was a vision of hell. Smoke roiled and billowed across the deck like thunderclouds. Through dark curtains he glimpsed burning, dying merrow like ghosts condemned to torment, staggering or crawling or writhing in thrashing balls. Paint curled and burned in long, uneven stripes. All the rigging, dried by the fierce southern sun, blazed like tinder. Glancing aloft, the pirate chief saw that the standing and running rigging would soon collapse the burning sails and smother everything. Barrel after spilled barrel burned madly, and Heart of a Lion wondered if the sealed barrels would soon explode like the fire from his wand. If so, he needed to get many sea miles distant. Turning to mount the gunwale with a grunt—

—he paused.

Something had caught his eye. Movement where it shouldn't be. Whirling, he faced the billowing fire. The horrific heat dried his face and eyes, making him squint, but somewhere . . .

There!

"Shar shield her most shameful son!" prayed the pirate. Clutching his fire wand, he ducked his head and charged the flames.

What he'd seen was a huddled, crawling figure, not

a dying merrow, but the marine lieutenant Belinda Destine. She'd been hammered to the deck but not killed, too tough to die. Sweating buckets in fright, barely daring to breathe, he zigzagged past knee-high flame, skirted a rolling, burning barrel, stopped, dashed under a flaming flap of sail, then—his heart stopped cold—leaped over the open hatchway and crashed clumsily on one knee. An ankle popped like a old twig, and agony coursed up his leg.

Still, the fat pirate reached the lean lieutenant by skittering clumsily to her side. Dazed, she crawled aimlessly away from the nearest fires. Her pink silk shirt smoldered and her yellow sash was ablaze. With no breath to explain, Heart of a Lion ripped off his turban, beat out the fire, then dropped the greasy, burning folds. Kneeling, gasping, he hooked a meaty arm around her slim middle and rolled her to his broad shoulder. With a grunt, and a grimace of pain from his sprained ankle, the pirate chief squinted in smoke and fire and staggered toward the dromond, which seemed to lay a hundred leagues across a burning wasteland that would put all nine of the Nine Hells to shame.

Limping, cursing, praying, Heart of a Lion groped toward safety and cool, sweet air. His burden mashed his shoulder and his sprained ankle. He had to circumvent the mainmast, then the mizzen, because the entire starboard side of the cog seemed engulfed in flame. If he couldn't get past the fire at the prow, he'd have to risk the ocean—and he'd never learned to swim, an instance of laziness he regretted now, but perhaps not for long.

"Come—*uh!*—daughter of disaster! We can't—*oww!*—tarry here!" Heart of a Lion gabbled at the unconscious girl to keep up her courage, or his. "My, they must feed you marines—*uh!*—oats and hay! Come, this is no worse than a forest fire, or so I hear—what?"

Rearing from the smoke, tall as a flaming volcano, like a ghost from his haunted past, loomed a merrow scorched black along both its sides. Mad with pain, the monster lunged into the mizzenmast, bounced off, then saw the humans and roared a challenge.

Heart of a Lion had no weapon, neither scimitar or even dagger, and was saddled with an unconscious woman besides. Lacking anything else, he used what came to hand—the brass fireball wand.

"Begone!" Craning back one thick arm, Heart of a Lion slammed the tall merrow across the jaw with the brass tube. The sea ogre's mouth shut with a *clack!* as the creature was bowled sideways. The pirate wasn't sure, but guessed he'd broken the thing's neck, a feat more suited to his lusty youth than a middling age. Dropping the bent tube, he staggered on blistered feet for the dromond.

One last sheet of blue-white flame blocked his path to the dromond, and through it pirates turned and pointed, their images rippling in the heat above the fire. A roaring in his head wouldn't let him hear what they called. With no strength left, only heart, the pirate chieftain charged.

In five limping strides, he bulled into the cog's gunwale, pushed headlong, and dived.

Fire filled his vision, then blue sky, then green water—

—then he crashed on his shoulder against a pine deck.

At the last second he'd twisted away from the shoulder bearing Belinda Destine. Exhausted, pain throbbing in every part, roasted as if on a spit, he lay gasping while willing hands laid him flat. Blessed cool water was slapped on him and the lieutenant. A hand tilted his head and poured fresh, sweet water—truly the nectar of the gods!—down his parched throat, then the hero was left alone as pirates and sailors set sail.

Dimly, Heart of a Lion heard the thunk of axes. Under his back, he felt the dromond come alive and pull free of the burning cog. At more shouts, the decks canted slightly. The captain, thirty years at sea as boy and man, felt the dromond's rudder bite the waves as she gained headway. Squinting aloft, he saw sails billow, snap into place, and fill their tan bellies. His ship was safe, and he could rest, lying at ease and staring at the blue sky.

"You . . . saved my life."

"Eh?" Rolling his head, Heart of a Lion found the blue eyes of a northerner staring into his. Lieutenant Belinda Destine of the Caleph's Imperial Marines was scorched, smoke-grimed, half cooked, but alive. She croaked like a crow. "You waded through flames and . . . carried me out. You . . . coldcocked a merrow with . . . one punch. You truly do have . . . the heart of a lion."

"Oh, that was nothing. I did that every day when I was young. Even on holy days." Used to boasting about himself, Heart of a Lion was suddenly embarrassed, yet it was pleasant to see a pretty young woman smile. To show off, he pushed to his elbows and casually studied the sails.

"Still," he rubbed his running nose, "pirating has slipped into a lull as of late. Tell me, what do they pay captains in the Caleph's Navy?"

One Who Swims With Sekolah

Mel Odom

4 Flamerule, the Year of the Gauntle

"Stop this ship before we smash against the wall!"

The sahuagin prince—one of the surviving four of the recently destroyed Serôsian city, Vahaxtyl—lifted a hand bristling with thick, jagged claws and surged forward menacingly.

Laaqueel, High Priestess of the Claarteeros Sea sahuagin kingdom, crossed *Tarjana*'s wooden deck without hesitation, putting herself between the sahuagin prince and her king.

The prince stood over seven feet tall on splayed webbed feet, dwarfing Laaqueel's slight frame. The priestess knew the sahuagin were thought ugly and cruel in appearance by the surface dwellers, but to her they were perfection—something she'd never achieve.

Fins stood out from the prince's scaled body, jutting from forearms and legs. The anterior fins on the sides of his great-jawed head joined together on the dorsal fin down his back in the Serôsian way instead of remaining separate the way Laaqueel was accustomed to. His coloring wasn't the greens and blacks of the sahuagin of the outer sea. Instead, his scales shone teal, marked with splotches, the dominant colors in the world of Serôs.

The prince was broad and powerful, a predatory creature the harsh sea had bred to withstand the depths and combat. He wore only the sahuagin warrior's harness that provided carrying places for the few personal items he had as well as trophies he claimed in battle. The harness also bore the prince's insignia. He carried a royal trident chipped into shape from greenish-gray claw coral.

Little more than an arm's reach behind Laaqueel, Iakhovas stood unmoved and faced the angry prince. A small smile twisted Iakhovas's lips. "Maartaaugh, do not make the mistake of threatening me." He spoke in a low voice that traveled only to the nearest ears. "I've already killed one of Aleaxtis's princes. Though it wouldn't trouble me in the slightest to kill another and glut myself on your flesh and gnaw on your bones, I would see you live. If you remain intelligent enough."

Laaqueel knew she was the only one who saw Iakhovas as he truly was. He looked human, tall and broad now, with dark hair held back by bones with carved runes. A carefully groomed mustache ran down each side of his mouth then joined his sideburns, leaving his chin and cheeks clean-shaven. Runic tattoos covered his body. He wore black breeches and a silk shirt, black leather boots, and a heavy sea-green cloak that held magical secrets and weapons in its depths. He was missing an eye, but these days the empty socket somehow gleamed golden, as if something buried in its depths was beginning to surface.

Everyone but Laaqueel believed Iakhovas was a sahuagin. The magic spell he wove around himself prevented them from seeing anything else. Laaqueel had seen him at his weakest, and now she knew him at his strongest, but even she didn't know what he truly was.

Laaqueel seized Maartaaugh's wrist in her powerful grip, halting the movement. Surprise glinted in the prince's oily black eyes as he felt her strength. His great mouth snarled in warning, revealing proud fangs.

It was a face Laaqueel would have loved to wear.

"Stand back, malenti," Maartaaugh spat.

The word "malenti" slammed into Laaqueel, carrying all the savage disrespect and pain that she'd borne all of her years. The pain—the incompleteness and the stench of the outcast—remained sharp.

She was malenti—the unwanted offspring of true sahuagin caused by the nearness of the hated sea elves. Many priestesses thought the curse of the malenti-birth was one of the Shark God's gifts, a built-in warning that drove them to seek out their enemies and destroy them. Malenti were usually destroyed at birth, but a few of them were saved to serve as spies, masquerading as the hated sea elves.

Laaqueel was only a few inches short of six feet. She wore her long black hair tied back in a single braid. Rounded curves and full breasts that she knew attracted the eyes of sea elven males and surface dwellers made her body ugly to her. She preferred the harsh angularity of the sahuagin form. To further compound the curse she'd been given, her skin wasn't the greenish or bluish cast of the sea elves. Instead, it was the pale complexion of a surface dweller.

The priestess turned her voice to steel, using the pain that she felt but never letting it touch her words and make them weak. "Don't speak disrespectfully of me, Prince Maartaaugh. Sekolah has chosen me priestess of his faith. You may keep your opinions of me, and of my birth, but never of my calling. I live to serve Sekolah, and I will die in that service if I need to." With the merest thought, she flicked out the claws sheathed in her slender elflike fingers, baring sharp edges.

"Most Sacred One," Iakhovas addressed her.

Laaqueel kept her gaze locked on Maartaaugh. "Yes, Most Honored One." She watched the prince's guards over his shoulders. They were no problem. The sahuagin crew who worked under her had already surrounded them.

"Release him," Iakhovas ordered.

"As you command." Carefully, Laaqueel stepped back, setting free the wrist she'd captured so quickly and forcefully. She felt the currents flowing over *Tarjana*'s deck, wrapping around her, spinning warm and cool water together. She kept her eyes on Maartaaugh. "You will understand this, prince. No one may lift a hand against my king while I live."

Maartaaugh gazed at her angrily but didn't say anything. In the sahuagin culture, the females fought alongside the males with the same ferocious skill. However, the only positions of importance the females held within the sea devil society were as priestesses.

Laaqueel had often thought it was only that way because the males didn't like the idea of handling the hated magic that was contained even in Sekolah's gifts.

Maartaaugh threw his arm toward the wall growing ever larger as *Tarjana* hurtled forward. "Even if we survive the crash, you'll doom us to the untender mercies of the sea elves manning the garrison."

Iakhovas looked past the man and said, "We won't touch the wall."

"By Sekolah's unending hunger," Maartaaugh exploded, "we can't miss!"

Laaqueel stared at the wall, watching as it loomed over them. The Sharksbane Wall had been constructed thousands of years ago by the sea elves and mermen of Serôs. The sahuagin—true to their nature—had warred almost incessantly with the other underwater races. As a result, the sea elves of the Aryselmalyr Empire and other races joined to build the Sharksbane Wall.

The wall was one hundred and thirty-five miles long and stopped sixty feet short of the surface of the Sea of Fallen Stars. Sea elves and their comrades manned the garrisons strung along the top of the wall. It had been constructed to confine the Serôsian sahuagin to the Alamber Sea, the easternmost arm of the Inner Sea.

For thousands of years, the Sharksbane Wall had stood as proof against—and insult to—the Serôsian sahuagin. Now, Iakhovas had sworn to bring it down and free the sahuagin trapped behind it.

Laaqueel felt the steady strokes of the rowers as they powered the great galley beneath the sea. With sahuagin manning the oars, the big ship shot through the water. The wall was now less than two hundred yards distant. Even if the rowers worked at it, she didn't think they could keep *Tarjana* from breaking up against the barnacle- and coral-infested wall. She focused on Iakhovas's words, holding them as truths the way Sekolah had indicated she should.

Without another word, Maartaaugh turned to glare at the huge wall.

All of the prince's life, Laaqueel knew, Maartaaugh had lived in the shadow of the Sharksbane Wall, letting it define so much of his life. Personally, she found even the thought of that confinement horrible. Sahuagin were meant to be free, able to go where they wanted and kill what they pleased.

Her priestess training let her know Iakhovas was working powerful magic. She felt the rush of soundless noise vibrating in her ears.

Tarjana shot to within fifty yards of the Sharksbane Wall. The vessel contained magic, Laaqueel knew. Iakhovas put great store by the ship. It was a mudship, capable of traveling on or beneath the sea, and even across dry land. Precious little more than a handful had ever been created by magic all but forgotten.

Iakhovas had attacked Waterdeep, the stronghold of the surface dwellers on the Sword Coast, to get the talisman of diamond and pink coral that controlled the ship. He'd arranged the near destruction of Baldur's Gate to get the ship itself.

Despite her confidence in Iakhovas, Laaqueel's gills still froze, locked tight as they plunged to within ten yards of the Sharksbane Wall. She prayed, calling out to Sekolah though she knew those prayers fell on deaf ears. The Shark God had freed his chosen people into the currents of the seas, but he'd never intervened directly in sahuagin lives.

Maartaaugh stood resolute, his attention snapping back between the unforgiving wall towering over them and Iakhovas. His men stared at him as if awaiting his order to abandon ship.

The rhythm of the oars remained steady. The ship's crew had learned to obey Iakhovas during the wild ride through volcanic fissures from the Lake of Steam to the Sea of Fallen Stars. Perhaps that voyage had even caused the volcanic eruption of the mountain peak known as the Ship of the Gods when they'd arrived and destroyed Vahaxtyl in the process.

Without warning, Laaqueel felt the surge of magic washing over her, as sudden and as biting as heated slivers rammed under her nails. She struggled to bring in water through her gill slits.

Tarjana's prow suddenly pierced the Sharksbane Wall like a claw coral's edge through unprotected flesh. The magic galley sped through the wall unchecked, pulling her crew after. It took all of Laaqueel's willpower to stand on the deck as the rough wall rushed at her. She watched the sahuagin in front of her seem to melt into it, then she followed. A chill like none she'd ever known knotted her muscles and made her joints ache. In the blink of an eye clear ocean suddenly spread before her and she knew they were on the other side.

"Elves!" a lookout croaked.

Feeling her heart hammering inside her chest, Laaqueel glanced up. Limned against the lighter cast of the pale green sea above, the priestess spotted dozens of sea elves swimming through the water in pursuit. Like the sahuagin, the sea elves of Serôs had differently colored skins from the sea elves she was familiar with, most of them reflecting blue splotches as well. They swam, closing rapidly.

"Prepare to defend and repel boarders!" Iakhovas roared, racing back to the stern of the ship and up the stairs. "I don't want any of them who reach us to survive!"

Laaqueel followed her king but her eyes never left Maartaaugh. No matter what else happened during their quest, the priestess knew, she'd made a powerful enemy.

The sahuagin crew rushed to do Iakhovas's bidding. All of them had tridents and nets, but dozens of others carried crossbows made from whalebone. Less than a moment later, the royal guardsman in charge ordered them to fire.

The quarrels sped through the water. Several of them buried deep in sea elf bodies. Streamers of scarlet blood twisted through the water as the sea elves kicked out their lives.

More elves overtook *Tarjana*, locking onto the galley with their fingers as some of them tried to secure ropes to the railing. Sahuagin sawed the ropes in half with the sharp edges of their tridents. Others lopped off fingers and hands mercilessly. Still other sea elves were captured and torn apart, their flesh divided equally between every sahuagin within reach.

Come, little malenti, Iakhovas said into Laaqueel's mind. When she'd discovered him, he'd planted one of his eyelashes deep into her side. It had traveled by magic and lodged next to her heart. The quill also allowed them to talk unheard by anyone else. She still wasn't sure how much control it gave him over her, but he had used it to threaten her in the past when she'd still doubted him.

In the years before she'd risen to high priestess, her

faith had been all she had. She'd been strong in it because she'd had to be. In the end, that faith and refusal to accept anything less had led her to the prophecy of One Who Swims With Sekolah.

Yet when it seemed her faith would be strongest because she had found the truth in the prophecy, Iakhovas had stepped forward and assumed kingship of her people. Nothing but war had ensued. Now he was bringing it here to Serôs. He'd told her their journey to the Sea of Fallen Stars had been to free the Serôsian sahuagin.

And I will, priestess. Iakhovas's deep voice echoed inside Laaqueel's mind.

The malenti spun around and glanced at her king. He stood in the galley's stern and plucked a sea elf from the attackers swimming overhead as easily as harvesting a clam from the ocean bed. A thrown trident vibrated when it sank into the wooden deck. Laaqueel's lateral lines registered the discordant sensation even amid the other disturbances taking place in the water around her.

Between heartbeats Iakhovas's right arm blurred, becoming something edged and sharp, something that somehow looked more right on him. The razor edge sliced the captured sea elf's throat. Blood sprayed into the water, drifting into a fine mist.

Laaqueel drew in more water through her gills and tasted the coppery flavor of blood. The hunger that rose in her was the part of her that was most sahuagin. She took a trident from the railing near the steering section, then half walked and half swam to join Iakhovas.

Still having doubts, Most Sacred One? Iakhovas asked.

The battle raged around them. Sahuagin fought viciously, raking sea elf flesh to the bone with claws, fangs, and tridents. Even as savagely as the sahuagin fought, casualties floated away with spears and knives in them, yanked from *Tarjana* by the current.

Less, Laaqueel admitted, *than I've ever had.* And her words were true. The doubts were less. What bothered her was that they existed at all after everything Iakhovas had done.

Doubts are fear, little malenti, Iakhovas told her gently. He seized another sea elf that dared attack him and sliced off one of the elf's arms with hardly any effort at all. The amputated limb floated away, attacked almost immediately by a nearby barracuda that had joined the battle. *Not ever fearing doesn't test you. Having fear and conquering it, that's what makes you strong.*

Laaqueel knew what he said was true. Her studies had shown her that, but it was frustrating that prayer to the Shark God couldn't take those doubts from her completely. She whipped the sahuagin net from her side, spun it expertly, and threw it at a nearby sea elf.

The sea elf yelped in pain and surprise as the net wrapped around him and sank barbed hooks deep into his flesh. In the space of a drawn breath, he was tightly bound and bleeding from dozens of small wounds. Helplessly, the sea elf drifted toward the ocean bed. If one of his companions didn't free him, the smaller scavengers in the area would nibble him to death in hours or days.

Iakhovas spun again, sliding an arm over Laaqueel's shoulders and shoving her to the side. A trident slammed into the deck where she'd been standing.

The priestess kept her footing with difficulty. Even as she realized how inflexible and coarse Iakhovas's skin was in spite of his appearance, he took his arm back. No man or even sahuagin felt that tough.

Iakhovas ducked and ripped the arm-ridge across the front of a sea elf, disemboweling him. Glistening intestines spilled into the water in ropy snakes that wrapped around another sea elf guard.

Laaqueel spun, meeting a sea elf's swimming charge with a raised trident.

"Die, you traitorous bi—" The sea elf's scream ended abruptly as the trident tines crashed through his chest.

Laaqueel felt the man flopping like a fish at the end of the trident. She popped the claws of her left hand free and ripped them down the sea elf's face and across his throat, then she slung the trident and twisted it viciously, yanking it free of her opponent's chest.

In only a few moments, *Tarjana* cleared the attack zone. The last of the captured sea elves were put to death. With savage joy, the sahuagin crew ripped their enemies apart.

"Meat is meat!" they screamed as they dined on gobbets of flesh.

Even Prince Maartaaugh and his retinue joined in the post-combat festivities. The savage glee the Serôsian sahuagin exhibited mirrored that of the outer sea sahuagin.

"Will you eat, Most Sacred One?" Iakhovas held out a bloody chunk of flesh that had once been part of a sea elf's face.

"No," Laaqueel replied, feeling her stomach unsettled despite the hunger that gnawed at her. She didn't know what was causing the unaccustomed sensation, but she had noticed her diet changing over the past few days since their arrival in the Inner Sea. "Thank you, Most Honored One."

For a moment she thought she saw confusion travel across Iakhovas's face, but as quickly as it had arrived the expression was gone—if it had ever really been there.

Laaqueel's lateral lines picked up sudden motion coming from behind her, disrupting the flow of current over *Tarjana*'s deck. She turned, holding the trident before her.

"We passed through the wall," Maartaaugh cried out in unmistakable disbelief. The prince stared at Iakhovas. "What magic wrought this?"

Laaqueel's throat constricted in momentary panic. All sahuagin hated magic, and the Serôsians were no different. By revealing *Tarjana*'s nature as a mudship Iakhovas also risked igniting a mutiny.

"This is not magic," Iakhovas said simply. "This is Sekolah's will, a gift the Shark God gave to my people to free We Who Eat beneath the Sea of Fallen Stars."

Slowly, the dread and fear on Maartaaugh's face drained away, replaced by amazement. "The Sharksbane Wall can no longer hold us."

Iakhovas regarded the prince with his dark gaze. "The Sharksbane Wall cannot hold *me*. Soon it won't be able to hold you."

Maartaaugh gazed around the great galley with new appreciation. "This is how you traveled through the volcano and arrived at Vahaxtyl."

"Yes, but only because Sekolah willed it."

Laaqueel relaxed slightly, sensing that the prince offered no threat. She gazed behind *Tarjana*, barely able to make out the bodies of sahuagin and sea elves hanging in the water near the Sharksbane Wall. Ocean predators had already gathered, stripping flesh from bone.

"Where do we go now?" Maartaaugh asked. "You've never said."

"To Coryselmal," Iakhovas replied. He handed the prince the piece of meat he'd offered Laaqueel.

"The ruins of the elven capital?" Maartaaugh took the meat and chewed only briefly before swallowing it. Blood coated his fangs for a moment. "Why?"

"To do as Sekolah has directed," Iakhovas answered. "There can be no other reason."

"You'll find what you need to destroy the Sharksbane Wall there?"

Iakhovas nodded. "*We* will."

Maartaaugh gazed out at the sea around them. "Only twice, both times when I was much younger, have I ever been beyond the Sharksbane Wall."

"Soon," Iakhovas stated confidently, "you'll be living and slaying in these waters."

* * * * *

The headache pounded fiercely at Laaqueel's temples. Despite her prayers, the pain continued unabated, lasting for hours at a time. She swam easily, holding her arms at her sides and undulating her body. Not even the cool currents drifting in from the Vilhon Reach helped take the agony away.

The malenti priestess glided through the water less than twenty feet above the rock-strewn silt that covered the ocean floor. She only had to swim around coral reefs higher than that a handful of times in the last few hours. The older coral reefs had been crushed in

167

the gigantic upheaval that had smashed the elven city of Coryselmal nearly sixteen centuries ago.

According to the conversations she'd heard between Maartaaugh and Iakhovas, the earthquake that had reduced the once proud sea elf city to rubble had struck without warning. Seventy-five thousand sea elves had perished in the carnage that followed. An undersea plateau, shoved by the underground stress, broke through the eastern half of the city and buried the other half in rubble and mud. Few had survived. Like the coral colonies and other sea creatures, undersea vegetation in the area was sparse.

Only the Esahlbane Monolith remained standing. It sat on the westernmost edge of the sea bed at the mouth of the Vilhon Reach, forty feet tall and angled now to hang over the ridge where the continental shelf dropped suddenly away for hundreds of feet.

Laaqueel concentrated on the image Iakhovas had imprinted on her mind and felt another wave of torment slam through her head. For a moment, she faltered in the water, her smooth moves turned jerky. She flipped her feet, trying to stay in the same area until she could get past the searing anguish.

She called out Sekolah's name, but it was Iakhovas who answered.

What is it, Most Sacred One?

Nothing, Laaqueel assured him, but she gave up swimming for the moment, drifting down to sink inches-deep in the fine silt. A slight chill embraced her feet as they covered over. The headache remained, and she couldn't help wondering if it was coming to her from an outside source. Perhaps it was some warding against sahuagin that yet remained in the area from the time of the elf occupation of the region.

Perhaps it was something more. There were those who believed, she'd learned from Iakhovas's conversation with Maartaaugh, that no civilized races were supposed to live in the Selmal Basin, another name the Vilhon Reach was known by. Only merrow, koalinth, scrags, and sea hags were rumored to live there now.

Quietly, Laaqueel prayed to Sekolah, asking the Shark God for a sign that she followed the currents he'd put before her.

You're in pain, Iakhovas mused.

Yes.

You should have told me, little malenti. You don't have to suffer.

Even as she drew water in through her gill slits again, Laaqueel felt the quill next to her heart quiver. Almost immediately she started feeling the pain subside.

How do you feel now? Iakhovas asked.

Better.

Laaqueel peered across the distance to the northeast where *Tarjana* lay at anchor less than fifty feet above the ocean bed. Her vision wasn't good enough to pick Iakhovas out on the deck, but she knew he was there. He hadn't once left the great galley since they'd arrived at Coryselmal early the day before.

He had imprinted the image of the object he searched for on her mind and relied on the gifts Sekolah had given her to detect the lost article. He'd also drawn the area on maps and divided the search area into grids. Sahuagin scavenger parties shifted silt in various places, turning up scraps left over from the demise of the elf city.

Find the piece I sent you for, Iakhovas stated. *I am depending on you and your god-granted abilities, Most Sacred One.*

Though she wasn't feeling any pain, Laaqueel's head still felt too full. She wondered if Iakhovas had really dealt with the pain, or if he'd only masked it for her, enabling her to work even though the source of the agony continued unabated.

Still, she finned up from the silt and turned her attention back to the ocean floor. She wasn't sure what she searched for, but she was certain the image would never go away. The object was shaped like a scythe blade, no bigger than her open hand, and made of a distinctive yellow stone she had never seen before. The blade-shape contained rune markings in bright blue.

Even the image felt old, powerful.

Twenty feet above the ocean floor, she leveled off and tried to detect the object again. She'd used the ability granted by Sekolah to find magic items before—usually small things that she'd traded to surface dwellers while passing as a sea elf and serving Baron Huaanton as a spy for the sahuagin—but she'd never searched this long or this hard. She'd never been able to.

She glanced across the mile and more of scattered debris. Columns and pillars stabbed through the ocean floor in a number of places, the skeletal remains of Coryselmal. Half a dozen shipwrecks lay scattered across the seabed as well. Battles and storms had ravaged the ships, breaking them and burying them in the seabed. Experience told her that those remnants had been picked over by sea elves working salvage for surface dwellers.

The priestess watched the sahuagin crews traversing the ocean floor, prying into the silt with their tridents. She knew they felt more overwhelmed by the hunt than she did.

The bloated numbness stirred in her mind. Reluctantly, she turned her attention back to the quest laid before her. More than anything, she wanted to be alone, drawn into prayer and unmindful of anything else.

Minutes, or perhaps more than an hour later—she'd lost all track of time—Laaqueel felt the first vestigial pull of the object she searched for. As quickly as it came, the pull was gone.

Gazing down, spotting a pattern of shells across the sea floor, she marked her position in her mind. Surface dwellers or those not accustomed to living beneath the waves wouldn't have noticed the uniqueness of the shells. Carefully, the priestess stopped and turned. She finned back the way she'd come, going more slowly.

The sensation invaded her mind, grinding like a rot grub through flesh, slowly but inexorably. She waved a webbed hand in front of her face, halting her forward momentum without thought as she turned in the direction the pull came from. While turning, she locked onto the sensation. Her skin crawled at the object's power.

By Sekolah's hard-eyed gaze, the sensation thrilling through her mind could belong to nothing else. Could it? She pushed the doubt away, hating that it was there and blaming it on the bloated phantom numbness filling her skull.

She studied the sloping seabed below her as she swam closer. Broken coral and chunks of building so barnacled over it required a trained salvager's eye to know them for what they were jutted from the whorls of silt. None of the sahuagin crews worked nearby.

Closer still, the pull became intoxicating and seemed to empty her mind of the painful bloating. For the first time, she wondered if Iakhovas had instilled the pain in her, intentionally urging her to greater haste in the search.

Drawn by the release from the pain, Laaqueel searched the area carefully. The pull of the object was so strong there was no mistaking where it was. Every time she turned away from it the bloated numbness spilled back into her mind.

She dropped to the seabed near an outcrop of blaze coral standing out bright red against the blue of the depths. She'd learned the name from the Serôsian sahuagin. Blaze coral didn't grow in the outer seas, it only grew in the Alamber Sea and the Vilhon Reach in the Sea of Fallen Stars.

The blaze coral clustered in rounded clumps that looked like oval disks. The bright red clumps glowed with an inner incandescence. While in Vahaxtyl, the priestess had seen some of the harvested coral. Once torn free, it lost much of the bright red glow but still glowed pink.

Slowly, one hand holding onto a rough outcropping of coral to offset the pull of the currents that threatened to take her away from the area, Laaqueel slid forward and peered down the slope. Only a few feet distant, she made out the shadowy outline of a cave.

A cold wash of current spread across her shoulders and down her back when she saw the cave. Still, the pull of the object was too strong to ignore. The promise of relief from the numb pressure in her head drew her forward.

Laaqueel tightened her fist on her trident and glided down the slope. Only a few leg strokes later, she reached down and grabbed hold of the rough rock surrounding the cave mouth.

Darkness filled the cave's interior, cold and forbidding.

She thought briefly of calling out to Iakhovas, but the possibility that she was wrong eclipsed that thought almost as soon as it dawned.

Steeling herself, Laaqueel finned forward and pulled herself into the cave mouth, following the sharp tines of the trident. Her heart sped slightly as she twisted in the sea and righted herself to face the cave. The opening was nearly fifteen feet across.

She released air from her trachea and air bladder to lose the buoyancy that helped her swim at chosen depths within the sea. Gravity pulled her to the pebbled sea floor tracking into the cave.

Less than ten feet inside the tunnel, the cave became so dark she couldn't see. The cave drove even more deeply into the seabed's slope, angling down as well. The incline had turned sharply enough that she had difficulty maintaining her footing.

Halting, she reached into one of the several small pouches she carried on the sahuagin warrior's harness she wore. She took a finger-long chunk of lucent coral from the pouch and held it up.

The illumination provided by the coral drove the darkness back nearly five feet. The Serôsian sahuagin had brought large pieces of it onto *Tarjana* for the expedition, then chipped off chunks for the searchers. The large pieces maintained their incandescence for months even after being harvested, but the smaller pieces lost their glow within a tenday.

Laaqueel held the lucent coral up and started forward again. The tunnel walls ran nearly smooth, telling her it had been artificially constructed.

Already, her priestess's curiosity was aroused, seeking to find the answer to another mystery. That which couldn't be proven, yet was still revealed, was the tapestry of faith Sekolah had woven for his chosen people. That had been one of the first lessons Priestess Ghaataag had instilled in Laaqueel when she'd been taken into the temple at Baron Huaanton's command. It was a lesson Laaqueel had never forgotten.

She measured the distance she descended by her steps. Less than forty feet in, the cave ended without warning. Holding the lucent coral high, the priestess studied the blunt end to her search.

The coral's glow also illuminated the white and yellow of old and fresh bones mixed in a pile. Closer inspection revealed those bones to be a scattered collection of human and elf. Laaqueel thought the heap of bones might be as much as ten or fifteen feet deep.

Using the lessons Priestess Ghaataag had given her to remain in control of her fear, Laaqueel made herself take another step forward. Her foot splintered a cracked femur and the sound echoed, trapped within the cave and made even faster by the dense water.

Tooth marks marred the surfaces of all the bones.

She didn't hear the movement of the creature behind her, but she felt the displacement of water that movement created along her lateral lines.

Wheeling, Laaqueel brought the lucent coral chunk around and raised her trident.

The vodyanoi stood almost twenty feet tall even on stumpy, bowed legs. It was hard to tell because the predator stood humped over in the enclosure. Vaguely dwarflike in appearance, with a triangular head set squarely on massive shoulders half as wide as it was tall, the creature moved ponderously toward the malenti priestess. Thick arms hung to the floor, heavily corded with muscle, which ended in heavily clawed, blunt fingers capable of ripping open a ship's hull.

The sheen from the lucent coral revealed the cruel maw filled with triangular fangs. Mandibles nearly as long as Laaqueel's hand curved inward from the sides of the vodyanoi's jaws. Green slime clung to the thick, knobby hide. The cavernous mouth opened reflexively, showing the dark green gullet beyond.

Laaqueel knew vodyanoi were rumored to possess intelligence, but they were solitary creatures and didn't socialize. They dined on human flesh and only settled for other, lesser, creatures when their preferred prey couldn't be found.

Working quickly, a prayer already coming to her lips, Laaqueel slammed the chunk of lucent coral into the tunnel wall as far over her head as she could. The shadows inside the cave whirled and shifted as the angle of the light changed.

The vodyanoi lumbered forward, massive arms swinging as it closed on her. The malenti priestess threw a hand out, summoning up one of the gifts Sekolah had given her for the faith she'd shown. Immediately the pressure around the vodyanoi increased, doubling and tripling. Laaqueel felt the currents change as they slipped around her, altered by the spell she'd used.

The pressure beat the vodyanoi down to its knees. It roared in articulate rage and the basso cry filled the cave. Laaqueel looked desperately for a chance to slip by the beast, but the vodyanoi's bulk filled the tunnel in all directions. Incredibly, when the spell dissipated, the huge creature shoved itself to its feet again and lunged forward.

Laaqueel stepped back, lithely avoiding the charge. Bringing the trident up, she blocked a fistful of claws

175

that rammed deeply into the side of the tunnel. Huge clods of earth and rock ripped from the wall. The umber hulks, distant cousins of the vodyanoi, could dig through solid stone and soft earth almost as fast as a man could walk.

The creature swept out another arm. Relying on her skills, Laaqueel flipped backward through the water and took air into her bladder again to make herself buoyant. She rammed the trident into the vodyanoi's chest before it could defend itself. The tines bit deeply into the knobby hide but didn't appear to be more than an annoyance to the huge beast. Blood wept from the wound in thick, globby strings.

Still moving back, watching anxiously for any opening that might allow her to get through the vodyanoi's clutches, Laaqueel drew the power of Sekolah's gift into her and mouthed a prayer.

Before she could release the power, the vodyanoi surged forward, stepping ahead of the lucent crystal imbedded in the tunnel wall. The creature seemed to disappear, becoming a two-dimensional shadow that blocked out nearly all of the illumination behind it. A massive fist slashed out, connecting with Laaqueel's shoulder.

The priestess flew backward through the water, tumbling as the uneven currents resisted the burst of speed. Skipping like a stone across the ocean, she smashed into the knot of skeletons.

Laaqueel!

Iakhovas's startled scream ripped through Laaqueel's mind, re-igniting the headache. The intensity of the pain was almost blinding. Fear made her move, though, and she pushed her way free of the tangled bones of past victims, hearing their echoing *clacks* as they banged against each other.

The vodyanoi surged forward again, reaching for her.

Ducking under her attacker's arms, Laaqueel seized the trident haft sticking out from the creature's huge chest. She ripped the tines free, pulling a cloud of blood with it.

"Foul creature!" she shouted, half in fear and half in anger. "You're not getting a defenseless human or elf to feast on! My blood, my soul, is of We Who Eat! I am one of the greatest terrors in the seas. Set free by the Shark God, guided by Sekolah's merciless will that all his children might be strong and fierce. *I* will dine on *you!*"

Even though the vodyanoi gave no indication of understanding Laaqueel's words, it obviously understood her intent. It stood to most of its height, held back from full stature only by the cavern roof. Mouth gaping, the creature roared out a challenge of its own.

Laaqueel swam forward, following the trident's line. The tines sank deeply into the vodyanoi's stomach. The malenti had hoped that the area was less protected than the chitin-covered chest. The impact almost numbed her arms.

The vodyanoi snapped the trident in half with its claws. It bellowed angrily but didn't sound injured. It reached for her, claws snapping hollowly in its eagerness to get at her.

Dodging but unable to maneuver well in the tight quarters, Laaqueel couldn't avoid the blow that struck her head. She flew backward again, smacking up against the rear wall of the cave. For a moment she thought her air bladder had ruptured. Pain filled her head as blood eddied out from her flayed skin to muddy the water. She tasted the salt of her own blood as she drew in water through her gills.

Laaqueel!

The concern in Iakhovas's mental voice was readily apparent. Dazed, Laaqueel's thoughts chose that fact to center on rather than the hulking brute that moved toward her. In all their years together, in all the twisted webs of planning Iakhovas generated, she'd never thought he'd cared about her. The only one he'd ever seemed to care about was himself.

She struggled to move, watching as the vodyanoi reached for her, but her limbs wouldn't obey her, somehow couldn't hold her weight even in the water.

Hold on, little malenti. I am almost there.

Laaqueel knew Iakhovas would be too late. Nothing save Sekolah—who never directly interfered in any of the trials or tribulations of his chosen people—would prevent her death at the creature's hands.

The vodyanoi opened its claws expectantly until they were wide enough to encompass her head.

Fighting the nausea and miasma of pain that swirled within her, Laaqueel seized the creature's claws. Immediately, her hands were cut to the bone. Ligaments flayed, parting like the tender intestines of newborn squid that were considered a delicacy among the sahuagin. Numbness claimed her hands and took them from her. Still, she didn't give up. She fought as Sekolah would have her fight, intending to strike her opponent dead even as she drew her final breath if she had to.

Twisting away, trying not to look at the tattered remains of her hands, Laaqueel brought up her slim legs and popped the claws free of their sheaths in her toes. Still twisting, letting the currents do some of the work for her, she slashed at the vodyanoi's face, scoring wounds from ear to chin that left the flesh hanging open.

The great beast roared in hurt and anger this time, and the savage scream filled Laaqueel with pride.

Lashing out, the vodyanoi pinned her against the tunnel wall, its outspread claws wrapping around the malenti's upper body. It leaned in closer, opening its mouth.

With nothing else to do, Laaqueel prayed. She didn't pray for herself because that would have been selfish and sahuagin were trained from birth to think of their race first. She prayed instead for her people, for those who'd rejected her because of her physical deformity. She had no legacy to leave to anyone save them, and even then it was only prayer.

You're not dead yet, malenti. Iakhovas's voice burned through her mind. *Nor shall I allow* anyone *to take your life without my consent.*

Barely lit by the lucent coral, the shadows swam and twisted over the vodyanoi's massive shoulders. Iakhovas was there, hanging in the water just behind the creature.

Savage rage masked Iakhovas's face. The emotion pulled at the empty socket that held the gold gleams, at the scars and tattoos that ran in spidery lines across his features. Without hesitation, he wrapped his arms around the vodyanoi's head, barely avoiding the gaping mouth full of triangular teeth.

You will bend, loathsome abomination, Iakhovas snarled. *The uncaring hunger in your stomach will still your heart.*

Incredibly, Iakhovas pulled the creature back from Laaqueel. Less than half the vodyanoi's size, his strength was obvious. Iakhovas stood with his feet against the creature's back, using its own body to gain the leverage he needed to turn its head.

Released, Laaqueel stood shakily and tried to join in the battle.

Stand aside, little malenti, Iakhovas ordered. *I will show you the worth of a true warrior of the sea.* He yanked once more on the vodyanoi's head, jerking it back and off-balance again.

The beast roared and tried to scrape Iakhovas from its broad back. With its long arms, the reach was simple.

Only Iakhovas wasn't there when the claws closed. He kicked away from his opponent, throwing himself into the water. Even after everything she'd seen him do since they'd been together, Laaqueel stared at Iakhovas in disbelief. He fought like a thing possessed. In the uncertain light of the lucent coral, she thought she saw him change shape.

Long, ridged fins covered Iakhovas's arms and legs, ripping through his clothing. Another ridge of bone and cartilage rose from the top of his head and swept back. He grew to ten feet tall, then twelve.

The vodyanoi turned its full attention to Iakhovas. It swung its arms, hammering at its attacker. Still stunned, Laaqueel watched as every time Iakhovas touched the vodyanoi or the creature touched him, blood boiled out from a fresh wound on the beast. Pieces of the knobby skin peeled away.

Fins appeared along Iakhovas's cheeks, streamlining his features. He threw another blow filled with claws and sharp fins that landed on the inside of the vodyanoi's arm. Flesh and sinew parted in liquid rushes.

In that one blow, the battle turned. Protecting its wounded arm, the vodyanoi turned and tried to run. It clawed at the cave wall, rapidly tunneling into the packed earth.

"No!" Iakhovas shouted. "There will be no escape from my vengeance!"

Looking only remotely human, he dived after the vodyanoi. Nearly as large as the creature, Iakhovas wrapped an arm under his opponent's chin, then drove his other fist through the vodyanoi's back. Flesh split and blood spilled. Bone broke with high-pitched cracks. Iakhovas's fist smashed into the vodyanoi past the elbow. The great creature shivered all over, its antennae quivering spasmodically. Losing control over its muscles, the vodyanoi collapsed to its knees.

Screaming in savage triumph, Iakhovas withdrew his bloody arm. He held his opponent's heart in his hand.

"No one may take what is mine. No one!" He held the huge heart up and squeezed, bursting the flesh. With blood spreading from the ruined organ, he thrust the savaged meat into his mouth and swallowed.

Barely standing, Laaqueel tried to fathom what kind of being Iakhovas was. None of his lost legacy was mentioned in the prophecies she'd found and read. His identity was never revealed.

He turned to stare at her, his single eye flaming with passion. Blood dappled his mouth and face. The ridges along his cheeks, chin, and brows looked pronounced in the shadows. The fin on top of his head touched the cavern roof. The fins along his arms and legs looked like razor-edged bone.

"I am Iakhovas," he snarled, "and all who know me will tremble in fear of my name."

Laaqueel stared at him, knowing that of every creature that swam the currents of the sea, Iakhovas was the one to which Sekolah would give his highest approval. He was a natural-born killer, the merciless instincts of the predator honed to a perfect cutting edge.

But he was not sahuagin.

That she knew for sure.

Suddenly aware of the coldness that creeped through her, she sank. Only the buoyancy she kept in her air bladder kept her from dropping to the cave floor. Unable to move, certain that death was stealing over her, she floated loose-limbed in the current.

"Little malenti." Iakhovas stared at her in surprise.

Laaqueel tried to answer him. He'd been around so much death, she was surprised that he didn't recognize it when it was before him. Weakly, she reached up to her head, wishing the pain that plagued her would abate as easily as most sensations were leaving her. Working hard, she was able to touch the wound at the side of her head. At first she thought the rough object she found there was an embedded claw from the vodyanoi's blow. She pulled it away and turned it over in the uncertain light from the lucent coral to examine it.

It was bone—a piece of her own skull.

She knew she was dying.

"No," Iakhovas ordered in a tight voice. "No, little malenti, I'll not suffer you to die. My plans include you. Without you, they'll be much harder to attain. I won't have you leaving my side now. Not when we've come so far together."

She wanted to tell him there was nothing he could do. Death was the natural order of things. She only hoped that Iakhovas cared enough to order the other sahuagin to eat her as they did all their dead so that she would remain within the community. It was a sahuagin's final service to the race, to be a meal for the others.

"I am Iakhovas," he said as he strode toward her. "You don't know the depths of what I can do."

He stopped at her side, not even needing to bend over to reach her because she floated. As he stood there, the fins went away and he returned to his more familiar human shape.

Laaqueel knew she'd never seen his true self even then. There was more, and she couldn't even guess at it. Darkness started to span her vision, pulling her away. She watched, perplexed, as Iakhovas turned his head to the side then reached into his empty eye socket.

His finger emerged a moment later with a golden half-spheroid that gleamed in the pale light. He held it in one palm, spoke a word Laaqueel had never heard, and touched the half-spheroid with his forefinger. The mechanism scattered into pieces across his palm, sparkling with a dozen different bright colors, no longer only red and gold. He selected one of the pieces and turned toward her, the empty hole in his face holding the blackest shadows the malenti had ever seen.

"You can't go," he told her. "I won't let you."

Numb beyond fear, Laaqueel watched as the small item he'd selected turned into a black, full-sized humanoid skull with rubies mounted in its eye sockets.

Iakhovas held the black skull in both hands above her. He spoke a language the malenti had never heard before, the words coming in a definite cadence, rolling into a crescendo of thunder that couldn't have come from a humanoid throat. The quill next to Laaqueel's heart twisted painfully.

A blinding flash of virulent green flooded the cavern.

A voice sounded from far away, serene and pure, and undeniably feminine. "Go back. You are yet undone."

Soft and gentle resistance pushed against the malenti. The fragrance of clean salt sea and the pale green of the upper depths rolled over her.

Then there was nothing but blackness.

* * * * *

Laaqueel thought she had died, until her eyes blinked open.

"You're back," Iakhovas said gently. He still stood at her side though she couldn't tell how much time had passed.

"I was gone?" she asked.

He nodded gravely. "For a time."

His answer left Laaqueel cold. Sekolah's faith provided for no afterlife. The only thing the Shark God demanded from his chosen children was that they fight and die bravely. Where had she gone during that time? Whose voice had she heard? She was certain it didn't belong to Iakhovas, but perhaps it had belonged to the skull.

Miraculously, the pain that had quaked inside her head was gone. Hesitantly, she reached up to her temple, expecting to touch splintered bone and blood-slick, jagged flesh. Only smooth skin rewarded her touch.

"You healed me."

"I rescued you from the hand of Panzuriel himself. Don't underestimate what I have done, my priestess." Iakhovas looked at her for the first time with something as close to gentleness as she'd ever seen.

The emotion embarrassed and confused Laaqueel. She closed her eyes.

As if knowing what was going through her mind, Iakhovas turned away, the motion read by her lateral lines. "We must go. You've cost me enough time." His voice held a hard edge.

"My apologies, Most Honored One." Laaqueel fanned her arms out at her sides, catching the sea in her webbed hands. She opened her eyes and saw the half-eaten corpse of the vodyanoi slumped on the cave floor, evidence of Iakhovas's great hunger after healing her. Schools of small fish nibbled at it while crabs scuttled back and forth beneath it, tearing strips of flesh away in their pincers.

"The search for the object I seek has continued," he told her, "but the scavenger parties have only come back empty-handed."

The announcement surprised Laaqueel. She was used to Iakhovas knowing what she knew. How could he not know she'd found what they'd searched so diligently for? "I found the object, Most Honored One."

Slowly, Iakhovas turned to face her. His single eye narrowed in suspicion while golden highlights glinted in the empty socket behind the patch that he wore. "Where?"

"Here." Laaqueel pointed at the pile of bones at the back of the cave. "It lies somewhere below, buried in the silt and refuse from ruined Coryselmal."

"You're sure?"

"Yes."

"Then come." Iakhovas stepped into the sea and swam out of the cave. He followed the line of the slope upward until he reached the point above the cave. He landed on his booted feet.

For the first time, Laaqueel noticed that Iakhovas's clothing was no longer ripped where the fins had come through. He looked as human as he ever had, only one of the lies he wove so skillfully around himself.

185

"Swim away from here, Most Sacred One," he addressed her. "This is going to be very dangerous."

Remembering how he had fought for her, how he'd even stayed death's hand, Laaqueel hesitated. "Will it be dangerous for you?"

Iakhovas glanced at her, his single eye glowing with a feral light. "Do you care then?"

"Yes."

Deep laughter rolled from Iakhovas's throat. Laaqueel turned away and leaped up into the sea. Confusion swirled within her. She never knew for certain how to best handle Iakhovas. Any care on her part seemed to be perceived as weakness.

"Little malenti," he called out gently behind her.

She floated in the ocean above him, looking at how small he seemed against the great expanse of the sea floor. Yet his destruction had ravaged the Sword Coast, won him a savage kingdom, and that was only what she knew for certain about him. Even now there were other intrigues she knew he had underway with the pirates of the Nelanther Isles and their counterparts in the Inner Sea.

"I offer my apologies," Iakhovas whispered for her ears only. "I thank you for your kindness. It is truly something I've never become accustomed to. Now go farther."

Laaqueel swam higher. When she was more than a hundred yards away, she felt the thunderous ripple that started on the ocean floor below. She floated, adjusted the air in her bladder, and started downward.

Great sheets of silt-filled clouds roiled up from the seabed, all but obscuring Iakhovas. Around them, the other sahuagin immediately scattered, flitting through the water like a school of frightened fish.

Piles of coral smashed thousands of years ago, dozens of feet of accumulated silt from the mouth of the Vilhon Reach, debris from smashed buildings and homes, and shipwrecks all boiled up. In seconds, the area was forever changed.

Wanting to stay away from the clouds of silt so she wouldn't breathe them into her gills and irritate the membranes there, Laaqueel swam higher. She hung in the water above the edge of the contaminated sea.

Long minutes passed. The sahuagin search parties gathered close as the debris settled well enough to see the sea floor again. Where the slope had been, a deep hole plunged straight down into the earth. It resembled an anthill, the earth and other debris piled up concentrically around the opening.

Laaqueel wondered if Iakhovas had somehow gotten trapped in a landslide below the surface. Maybe he wasn't as infallible as she'd believed, or, perhaps, feared. She tried to sort through the confused knot of worry and relief that filled her, but had no success.

Only heartbeats later, Iakhovas emerged from the raw womb opened into the earth. The smile on his face told Laaqueel everything.

* * * * *

"That is the Akhageas Garrison," Maartaaugh declared. He stood in *Tarjana*'s bow, at Iakhovas's side. "It's one of the oldest garrisons the cursed sea elves built when they erected the wall."

Laaqueel stood on the other side of her master. Night had purpled the sea over the garrison atop of the Sharksbane Wall. Still, her vision was good enough for her to spot the sea elves patrolling the area in scout groups.

187

The garrison was constructed of coral, stone, and shells, the same building materials used in the construction of the wall. It stood two stories tall and had heavily shielded arms that branched out in each direction across the top of the wall. Huge nets lay in piles, ready to use against any sahuagin transgressors that dared try to cross the wall. The elf and merman guards wore silverweave armor and carried spears and tridents. Heavy wardings also protected the structure, complemented by the mages assigned there.

"It is one of the sea elves' most heavily fortified and manned garrisons," Maartaaugh continued. "We could choose another that isn't so well equipped and supplied."

"No," Iakhovas stated without hesitation. "This is the place. We do not have our choice in this matter."

Maartaaugh turned his black eyes to Iakhovas. "You suggest that Sekolah is not powerful enough to accomplish this?"

Iakhovas coldly met the man's gaze full measure. "This is the nature of the Shark God," he stated coldly. "Sekolah put this object in our hands to accomplish what we're setting out to do, but there is a blood price attached to that success that must be met. Only the strong shall survive, as Sekolah wills."

Maartaaugh scowled deeply, obviously not happy with the situation.

Laaqueel watched the two men, aware of the shift in power that had occurred between them. The Serôsian prince had been awed by the display of power at the mouth of the Vilhon Reach, but he hadn't given himself over entirely to Iakhovas's way of thinking.

"I can't guarantee the other princes will agree to this," Maartaaugh stated. "The last time We Who Eat attempted to overrun the Sharksbane Wall, the sea elves turned us back with their magic, then hunted my people mercilessly for more than a tenday. Thousands died. We had no place to run."

"Then we will persuade them," Iakhovas said confidently. He held up the scythe-shaped object. "This is their freedom. They'll fight for that."

"Only if they truly believe."

Iakhovas turned his single eye on the sahuagin prince and said, "They'll believe."

* * * * *

Despite the passage of days since the city's destruction, Vahaxtyl still resembled a war zone. Huge cracks ripped through the terrain, leaving shelves of rock and ridges overlapping each other. Huge coral stands lay tumbled and gnarled. Laaqueel searched the rubble as she stood at Iakhovas's side.

The sahuagin populace of the city and kingdom sat along the jumbled ruins and ridges. The city's amphitheater had been buried when the Ship of the Gods had exploded in volcanic fury. No true gathering place remained so they held their meeting among the ruins of the city. Some cleaning had been attempted, but the priestess knew the general consensus was that the city had been lost. With that loss, over the last few days, some of the sahuagin belief that Sekolah had made them strong enough to survive their present circumstances had begun to die.

Iakhovas's voice boomed out across the distance, carried by the currents. He stood at the makeshift table the four surviving princes had ordered built when they'd convened with him during his earlier meeting after the arrival in Serôs. It was also where

Iakhovas had killed and rended Toomaaek, one of the princes who'd stood against him.

Gravely, Iakhovas declared, "It is time that We Who Eat were once more set free."

Unease drifted through the sahuagin ranks. Laaqueel listened to the cautious clicks and whistles of the hesitant among the crowd. Fear gnawed at her stomach, afraid that, despite all the lengths they'd gone to, the Serôsian sahuagin wouldn't be able to rise to the challenge Iakhovas presented them with. It was one thing to dare to dream, but another to act. The Serôsian sahuagin had been penned up for thousands of years, exposed to a way of living that went against their very natures. How could they be touched by that and not be affected? She prayed silently to Sekolah, asking only that the true natures of these people assert itself.

"You won't be alone in your battle to take the wall," Iakhovas promised. "I will lead you, and I will teach you to be true warriors once more. There will be no more barriers to your destinies. This I swear. All of Serôs will tremble again at the knowledge that We Who Eat are free as Sekolah meant for us to be."

The hesitant clicks and whistles died away in the crowd, but Laaqueel knew the doubt still lingered. As priestess of the Shark God, she felt she needed to say something to shore up their belief. Before she could, Iakhovas raised the scythe blade he'd dug out in Coryselmal.

The strange metal caught the green light streaming down from the ocean's surface above, and the blue-cut runes flashed like lightning.

"I bring you power!" Iakhovas roared. "A gift from Sekolah himself. A fang in the throat of our enemies.

With this, I will bring down the Sharksbane Wall." He thrust the scythe blade up.

Without warning, crimson fire exploded from the twin tips of the scythe blade and shot a hundred feet and more upward. The crimson fire pooled above the meeting place, above the ruin that had been left of Vahaxtyl. The fire twisted and roiled, turning outward and inward at the same time, steadily growing larger even as it continued collapsing in on itself.

A chill spread over Laaqueel as she recognized the six sleek, brutal shapes that finned from the depths of the rolling underwater fire cloud. They looked like sharks, but her instinct told her they were much more than that.

"Look!" Iakhovas cried. "Let there be no more doubts. Sekolah sends us his blessings. Behold, his avatars!"

Laaqueel watched the six sharks as they pinwheeled through the water, creating a show of dazzling complexity and grace. Never in her life had she seen the avatars of Sekolah, though High Priestess Ghaataag had instructed her about them. The Shark God used the avatars to guide his people and to hone their battle lust during events Sekolah wished to influence.

Even as the sahuagin populace shoved themselves to their feet and pointed, the avatars began the deepsong that touched every sahuagin spirit. Laaqueel lifted her voice, joining in with the avatars, drawn in by the hypnotic effect. In seconds, the frenzy induced by the presence of the avatars and their deepsong took over the community. Total bliss and urgency combined in Laaqueel as Ghaataag had told her.

Iakhovas's basso booms joined in with the thousands of other sahuagin voices as he added to the deepsong that resonated through the ocean. In seconds, the deep resonance twisted through the sahuagin community, spinning all the individuals into one mind.

Abruptly, the avatars spun over the fallen city once more, then headed west. Laaqueel instinctively knew they were swimming for the Sharksbane Wall. As one entity, the sahuagin swam from Vahaxtyl, led by the avatars Sekolah had sent, drawn by the power the Shark God kept over his chosen people.

Most Sacred One.

Iakhovas's words burned through Laaqueel's mind. For a moment, she fought against them, obeying her nature to give herself over to the avatars' deepsong.

You will come with me, Iakhovas commanded.

The quill next to Laaqueel's heart quivered, bringing a sharp pain that filled her chest and made her air bladder feel as if it were about to burst. Her sahuagin nature and her tie to Iakhovas warred within her. Then her mind cleared from the fog induced by the hypnotic song sung by the Great Shark's avatars. She felt troubled and lost, angry that she wasn't allowed to fully experience the euphoria that came from riding as one with the avatars.

Now.

Reluctantly, Laaqueel turned from the crowd swimming after the avatars. She swam toward the outskirts of the city, following Iakhovas who swam easily before her. *Tarjana* lay anchored in that direction, but obeying Iakhovas went against her nature and that troubled her. Even though she believed him to be sent by Sekolah no matter what his own plans were, she didn't think she should be torn about her actions. It was confusing.

* * * * *

The defenders battled fiercely to hold the Akhageas garrison. They swam out to meet the oncoming tide of sahuagin, closing in battle with them. Even outnumbered as they were, the sea elves and mermen didn't lose ground readily. The spells and wardings that protected the Sharksbane Wall held the sahuagin back as well.

Laaqueel watched in horror as the sahuagin closest to the Sharksbane Wall suddenly burst into green and yellow flames, victims of the magic that guarded the structure. The blackened cinders of the corpses drifted toward the seabed or were pulled in orbits around nearby combatants. The priestess clung to the mudship's railing with one hand as the rowers propelled it through the midst of battle. She held her trident in the other.

"Save them," she pleaded, turning to Iakhovas who stood only a few feet away.

He didn't look at her, gazing intently at the wall they rapidly approached. "I can't, little malenti." He held his arms at his sides, the scythe blade in one fist. "This is Sekolah's way, the winnowing out of existence of those who are too weak to follow the currents he has set forth for his chosen."

Laaqueel held tightly to the railing, feeling *Tarjana*'s deck buck and twist beneath her as the mudship fought the torrential pull of the battle being fought along the Sharksbane Wall. Magic showered lightning throughout the depths as the sea elf mages gave vent to their power.

Still, the sahuagin horde closed in for the kill. Despite their losses, sahuagin claws, jaws, and tridents opened up sea elven flesh. Blood muddied the waters and carried the scent of salt and fear in every breath that flooded in through the malenti's gill slits.

In the next moment, *Tarjana* was in the whirling maelstrom of life and death. Gobbets of flesh, torn free or stripped by greedy sahuagin jaws caught in the full frenzy of the avatars' presence, swirled in the currents around Laaqueel. Some of them were still warm to the touch when they brushed up against her.

Hold steady, Most Sacred One, Iakhovas told her. *Within these next few moments, we weave a new future and new destiny for We Who Eat.*

Desperately, Laaqueel hung onto his words and to her belief that it would be true.

Tarjana knifed through the water toward the wall like a dorsal fin slicing through the shallow surface. A small cadre of sea elves on the backs of seahorses sped toward the mudship. Hoarse cries of alarm rang out around Laaqueel.

"Stand your ground!" the priestess ordered in a harsh voice. She held onto the railing with one hand while she spun around and brought up the whalebone crossbow that hung at her side. A quarrel was already notched in the groove. "Archers at the ready! Fire on my command!"

Quickly, the sahuagin warriors on *Tarjana*'s deck pulled themselves into formation. They raised their weapons.

The seahorse riders didn't flinch from their attack. Lances, powered by the arms of the elves and the speed of their mounts, arced through the water from less than thirty feet away. The coral tips slammed into the wooden deck, sending out vibrations that Laaqueel picked up through her lateral lines.

Hold them, Most Sacred One, Iakhovas encouraged. *Give me only the time that I need.* He spoke softly and smoothly in her mind.

For the moment, Laaqueel's fears and doubts faded from the front of her mind. She held the crossbow steady as the lead seahorse riders broke away to let the rest of the cavalry through. They moved like the currents themselves, suddenly there, then not there, gliding effortlessly.

The second wave of seahorses swam forward without hesitation, obeying the will of their riders. The sea elves had their spears and tridents lowered like lances, intending to bring the battle to a completely personal level aboard *Tarjana*.

"Fire!" Laaqueel ordered, squeezing the trigger of her crossbow. The quarrel leaped from the crossbow and sped across fifteen feet of distance to bury itself in the chest of the sea elf warrior directly in front of her.

Stricken through the heart, his silverweave armor no match for the shaved coral head of the quarrel, the sea elf released the reins of the seahorse. Instead of the smooth fluidity of rhythm exhibited by most underwater creatures Laaqueel knew, the sea elf jerked spasmodically as life left him and the troubled currents drew him away.

Riderless, the seahorse continued charging at Laaqueel. The malenti priestess swung aside, dropping the crossbow from the path of the seahorse. As the creature passed, Laaqueel flicked out her finger claws from their recessed areas and slit the seahorse's throat.

The sound of flesh striking flesh echoed across *Tarjana*'s deck as the line of seahorses struck the sahuagin groups. Seahorses and sahuagin ricocheted away, torn from the deck and from their path.

Laaqueel quickly reloaded, slipping her elvenshaped foot into the stirrup in front of the crossbow and drawing the string back. She hooked a foot under the railing so she wouldn't float free of the mudship. A corpse slammed against her unexpectedly, nearly tearing her from the precarious position she was in.

Pain filled her body from the impact. Still she brought the crossbow up and fired again, putting the quarrel through the open mouth of a yelling sea elf bearing down on her.

Unable to avoid the seahorse carrying the dead rider, Laaqueel dropped the crossbow and let herself go limp. The impact knocked the breath from her but she wrapped her arms around the creature's neck. It carried her toward the railing and she was certain it was going to sweep her over the side. At the speed *Tarjana* was making, she knew she'd never catch up again.

Then the seahorse and its dead rider were bathed in a greenish glow. In the next heartbeat, they were gone and a soft hand of force wrapped around Laaqueel and drew her back to the deck.

I'd rather you stayed, Most Sacred One.

Gasping for breath, steadying her trembling limbs, Laaqueel pulled herself along the railing and grabbed her trident from where she'd left it. She brought it into line and stabbed another sea elf from his mount. Before she had time to strip the struggling elf impaled at the end of her trident, *Tarjana* surged through the line of defenders.

A clear line of vision opened up to the Sharksbane Wall less than forty feet away.

Laaqueel felt the magic surge through the mudship a split second before the imminent impact. One moment she was aware of the deep blue of the sea around her. In the next there was only blackness as they slid through the Sharksbane Wall.

Now it begins, little malenti.

Expecting the deep blue of the sea to reappear on the other side of the wall, Laaqueel was totally unprepared for the sudden ruby flare that temporarily blinded her. Through eyes slitted against the pain of the light, she watched as the Sharksbane Wall came apart while they were still inside it.

Time seemed to move so slowly that she saw the fissures and fractures thread throughout the structure. Great chunks and blocks of the Sharksbane Wall blew away and the sea rushed in to replace the vacuum left behind.

A moment more and the blue of the sea surrounded her again.

Come, Most Sacred One.

With only a little hesitation, Laaqueel turned and followed Iakhovas up the stairs to the stern castle. She felt the mudship slowing beneath her. Standing at Iakhovas's side, she peered back at the wall.

The explosive force that Iakhovas had unleashed while within the Sharksbane Wall continued to rip through the structure. Huge pieces of it fell to the seabed below, leaving only ruins behind.

Ah, little malenti. Iakhovas held a savage grin on his face. *For a savior, I have come to be a most destructive one, have I not?*

Laaqueel didn't reply. She stared at the destruction, at the scores of dead sahuagin, sea elves, and mermen that had slowly started floating down to the sea floor. Battles still raged among the survivors, but not with as much vigor as before.

The Sharksbane Wall lay in fragments farther than Laaqueel could see. She didn't know how badly the structure had been damaged, but she knew it would never again be the same.

And it will never again hold We Who Eat penned like livestock, Iakhovas declared. *The time of this abomination is over. These sahuagin will be free.*

Roiling dust eddied around the broken pieces of the Sharksbane Wall. For a moment, Laaqueel thought no one had survived the destruction, then the avatars surged through the sand-clouded waters. Behind them, drawn by the irresistible force that filled Sekolah's representatives, came the sahuagin kingdom that had only known the Alamber Sea as home.

They flooded into the Sea of Fallen Stars, savage warriors whose destiny was going to be written in blood, sung about in song, who were going to create a new legacy for their descendants. Laaqueel watched them and a feral pride filled her, not held back by the quill so close to her heart.

It is done, Most Sacred One, Iakhovas said. *As I have promised.*

Yes, she replied. She didn't speak of the doubts that still filled her as she thought of the countless sacrifices made by the sahuagin. Iakhovas had lost nothing. Even as that thought struck her unbidden, she immediately felt guilty. He'd risked his life to save her, pulled her back from death itself, yet the doubts that plagued her wouldn't go away.

The Sharksbane Wall has fallen. Iakhovas threw the twisted and burned remnants of the scythe blade over the side of the ship. *The sea elves' precious Myth Nantar will fall next. As will all of the Sea of Fallen Stars.*

Laaqueel silently prayed, knowing Iakhovas meant what he said, and fearful of all the sahuagin lives that remained yet to be lost in those coming confrontations. She knew Iakhovas was out to win this war, no matter how many sahuagin had to die to do it.

A cold, bitter chill raced through the malenti priestess as she considered how much of a hand she herself had in the coming war. She remembered the words she'd heard while she was so close to death. "Go back. You are not yet undone." The chill turned even colder as she wondered whose voice that might have been.

Not undone. Not yet. But perhaps soon. She wrapped her arms around herself, feeling small and alone in the currents that swirled through her life now.

War had come to the Sea of Fallen Stars, and she stood near the eye of it all.

The Crystal Reef

Troy Denning

8 Flamerule, the Year of the Gauntlet

The isle lay well west of Tharsult. It was a tiny disk of palm-covered sand raked by hot subtropical breezes, barely a harpoon throw across and two hundred miles from the nearest shipping lane. Its single spring produced only one cask of fresh water a day. There were no fruit trees or meat animals to provide provisions on a long voyage, nor any sheltered bays or secret lagoons in which to hide pirate ships. The oyster beds never produced pearls. The island's sole treasure was a delicate ring of coral known as the Crystal Reef, a stony garden of twisted fingers and intertwined spikes whose entire value lay in the dazzling beauty of its thousand luminous colors.

So when the reef giant Tanetoa awoke one morning to find a fleet of war carracks anchored offshore, he did not know what to think. There were eight of them, with ballistae on their forecastles, catapults on their after-decks, and archers standing watch in their crow's nests. Their sails were furled and secure, their decks were crammed with landing skiffs and supply casks, and their hulls sat low in the water. Warriors stood fore and aft, armored in helmets and breastplates, staring at the Crystal Reef with eyes wide and mouths gaping.

Tanetoa called his wife to the hut window and asked, "Kani, what is that fleet doing here?"

Kani stared out the window for a long time. At just over two hundred years of age, she was still young for a reef giant, with a svelte figure, long ivory hair, and copper-colored skin. She was as beautiful as the Crystal Reef and as tranquil as the Shining Sea. Like Tanetoa himself, she much preferred the sound of the rolling surf to that of her own voice.

When Kani finally replied, her tone was mocking. "They must be pirates come to rob us of our treasure." She waved at the one room hut, which contained a palm-frond bed, a giant conch shell, a table, two sturdy chairs, and not much else. "I fear you must swim out and sink their ships, my courageous husband."

Tanetoa gave her a sidelong look. "You are sure you didn't call them to take you away?"

"From all this?" Kani gave a short laugh, then touched Tanetoa's elbow with genuine affection. "You know better. I'm afraid you'll just have to go out there and ask them what they want."

Tanetoa cast a wary glance at the carracks' ballistae. He was the type of giant who much preferred peaceful isolation to trafficking with humans, especially when those humans came heavily armed. Still, they appeared to have every intention of staying, and that meant he would have to deal with them sooner or later.

He sighed. "If I must."

"It's probably nothing." Kani patted him lightly on the shoulder. "Invite one back to have a look at the island. They'll leave soon enough after that."

"A good thought," agreed Tanetoa.

He stepped through the door into the golden sunlight. On the ships, warriors scurried along the gunwales, shouting to each other and pointing in Tanetoa's direction. Crewmen began to appear behind the ballistae, loading tree-sized harpoons into the weapons and ratcheting tension into the firing skeins.

"Wonderful." Tanetoa raised a hand and waved, hoping human eyes were acute enough to see his smile. "This is going well."

"Don't look frightened," Kani advised from the doorway. "Act like a giant, and you'll be fine."

"Right. I'll strike fear in their hearts if it kills me."

Tanetoa lowered his arm and stepped down to the beach, then waded out into the shallow lagoon between the shore and the Crystal Reef. Alarm bells began to clang on the ships, and the tall masts swayed back and forth as men rushed to their battle stations. Tanetoa wondered if it would be wiser to wait for the humans to send an envoy to him, but they would undoubtedly approach in boats, which would scrape long furrows into the reef and kill whole swaths of delicate coral.

When the water reached his chest, Tanetoa took a deep breath and dived. The lagoon floor was sandy and flat, littered with orange clams and rosy conches. A school of blue tang flashed past, herded along by the snapping jaws of a hungry barracuda, and a red-tinged jellyfish drifted by in a mass of fluttering membrane. As he neared the reef, thickets of jewel-colored staghorn coral rose from the bottom, filling the water with a luminous garden of tangled scarlet branches and sapphire starbursts. The giant swam closer to the surface now, so he would not brush any of the delicate formations and break them off. The coral was a living thing, and even the slightest damage could take centuries to repair.

Eventually, the luminous garden grew so tall and tangled it formed an impenetrable wall of color and motion. There were dozens of different corals: pink staghorn and golden elkhorn, diaphanous finger coral and tiger-striped fan, contorted spheres of brain coral, sweeping sheets of queen's lace, and more than even Tanetoa could name. Hiding among the corals were hundred-tentacled anemones, furtive clown fish, sponges of every shape and form—a profusion of different creatures that looked more like plants than animals.

Tanetoa swam along bare inches above the coral. Finally, he began to feel the rise and fall of the waves breaking over the reef. He entered a narrow, winding channel. Alongside him, the coral thickened into a solid mass, reaching the water's surface and forming a broad flat of dead, rocklike reef that served as a breakwater for the lagoon. It was the only ugly part of the reef, but one that teemed with crabs, starfish, and three-foot sea cucumbers.

Tanetoa reached the end of the channel and struck out into the open sea. The warships were anchored less than two hundred yards away. As he approached, the sound of alarm bells and screaming voices echoed across the water all the more loudly. He tried to take comfort in their fear, though he knew it was also their fear that made them swing their ballistae in his direction.

Tanetoa swam to the largest of the ships, stopping twenty yards off her starboard side so the sailors would not think he meant any harm.

"Ahoy, little people!" He waved his hand, which caused a great rustling among the men and prompted the flaunting of several dozen harpoons. Tanetoa scowled at the display of weapons. "There is no need to be frightened. I come in peace."

A bearded man in a white turban stepped forward and stood between two harpooners. "Then you declare for us?"

"Declare?"

"Declare your side." The man narrowed his eyes suspiciously, then motioned the ballistae crews to stand ready. "In the war. Surely, you know about the war?"

"I have heard the whales sing of it," Tanetoa answered, "but this is not my war."

"Of course it is," the man retorted. "This war is everybody's war. Now, where do you stand?"

Tanetoa considered this, then shrugged. "What are my choices?"

The man scowled. "You dare mock an officer of the caleph's fleet?"

Tanetoa started to apologize, then remembered he was a giant and clenched his jaw. He kicked his feet, raising himself high enough to display his mighty shoulders and chest. "Do you speak of the Caleph of Najron?"

The officer paled and could not help retreating a

step. "The very one, may the One grant him all bless-ings."

"And where does the caleph stand?"

"On the side of j-justice and honor, uh, of course," an-swered the officer.

"On the side of justice and honor," Tanetoa repeated, trying to disguise his disbelief. He had heard the whales sing of this Caleph of Najron and knew the man to be a Cyric-worshiping blackguard who thought nothing of pouring his city's filth into the sea. "Truly?"

"Truly," answered the officer.

Considering the ships and their ballistae, Tanetoa decided a diplomatic answer might be best. "I have always favored justice and honor."

The officer smiled, displaying a huge gold tooth, and spread his arms magnanimously. "Then we are allies!"

"If you stand on the side of justice and honor," Tane-toa answered carefully. He touched a hand to his breast. "I am Tanetoa of the Reef."

The crowd at the rail parted, and a new man in a golden turban stepped forward. Like the first, he had a long black beard, but his face was much more stern, more hawkish.

"And I am the emir Bahal yn Nadir, Admiral of the caleph's fleet." The newcomer gestured with a bejew-eled hand, and the harpooners lowered their weapons. "I have come to occupy your island in the name of the caleph."

"Occupy it?" Tanetoa glanced around at the eight carracks, trying to guess how many hundreds of men they held. "The island can barely sustain my wife and me."

"We have brought supplies," said the emir.

Tanetoa eyed the overburdened ships, trying to

imagine the humans ferrying tons of casks and chests through the winding channel into the lagoon. There would be accidents—and even if there were not, the mere presence of so many humans would poison the reef. Tanetoa shook his head vigorously.

"No. It will be bad for the reef."

"The reef?" The emir scowled, clearly confused. "What does a reef matter? We are at war!"

"This is the Crystal Reef," Tanetoa explained. "There is no other like it in the Shining Sea."

The emir looked unimpressed. "And?"

"And its death would be a great loss to the world." Tanetoa spoke in a stern voice. "I have sworn to protect it."

The emir surprised him with a broad smile. "Then you should be glad for our presence. That is the very reason the caleph sent us—to protect this island."

"Protect it from what?"

"From the Enemy Beneath, of course," the emir replied. "Already, the sahuagin and their allies have raided Waterdeep, Baldur's Gate, and many other places along the Sword Coast."

"But Waterdeep and Baldur's Gate are wealthy places," said Tanetoa. "So the whales tell me."

The emir's brow rose. "The *whales* tell you?"

"We sing to each other," Tanetoa explained. "They tell me the sahuagin are stealing human treasure."

"The whales tell you correctly." The emir and his officer exchanged meaningful glances. "What else do they tell you?"

"Only that the war is spreading," said Tanetoa. "But what could the sahuagin want from my island? Those other places have things worth stealing. My island is too poor to even have a name. Let me take you ashore, and you will see there is nothing here for them to steal."

The offer seemed to take the emir aback. He glanced at his officers nervously, then shook his head. "Your island's poverty is of no consequence. The caleph has commanded me to protect it."

"Yes, so you have said. But why?"

"It is not for me to question the caleph's wisdom," said the emir. "It is enough that he has commanded it. We will come ashore with the next high tide. Make ready for us."

"And if I do not?" asked Tanetoa.

"As the caleph's ally, you have no choice." The emir glanced at his ballistae, which remained trained on Tanetoa. "We must all sacrifice for the war."

Tanetoa swam forward, crossing the last twenty yards to the ship in three quick strokes. The ballistae crews cursed and scrambled to bring their weapons to bear, but Tanetoa pretended not to notice. He reached up and grabbed the gunwale, hauling himself up to stare at the emir eye-to-eye. The ship listed steeply in his direction, sweeping a handful of men off their feet and drawing several muffled booms from the cargo holds.

The emir gasped and stumbled back, motioning a dozen harpooners forward.

Tanetoa ignored the warriors. "We will talk again before the tide, but I warn you not to cross the reef without my consent. The rocks are very sharp, and the smell of blood in the water will attract hungry sharks."

The color returned to the emir's face, and he straightened his robe. "Of course. The caleph thanks you for your counsel."

"He is most welcome."

Tanetoa released the gunwale quickly, intentionally allowing the ship to rock back violently, then slipped beneath the waves and dived toward the bottom. It was not that he feared being harpooned; he simply wanted the emir to know he could come up beneath the fleet without exposing himself to attack. He swam deep underwater to the luminous, clifflike wall of the seaward reef, then slowly ascended toward the narrow channel that led into his lagoon.

As Tanetoa approached the surface, he was astonished to see a long stream of yellow figures gliding into the mouth of the passage. At first, he thought they might be a school of yellow-bellied snappers invading the lagoon in pursuit of a sumptuous meal, but he soon saw that could not be. The figures were far larger than most snappers, stretching to a uniform length just shy of that of a human. Moreover, they had fin-footed legs instead of tails and spindly arms instead of pectoral fins, and they were armed with a wide assortment of tridents, crossbows, and wickedly curved sea swords.

When the creatures noticed Tanetoa, a long file peeled off the main school and swirled down to meet him. Their faces were distinctly codlike, with heavy lips, deep glassy eyes, and a single pair of sensor tentacles dangling beneath their chins. They were locathah, a race of nomadic fishmen who sometimes hunted along the reef in pursuit of giant groupers or schools of red jack. Never before had they come in such great numbers.

Tanetoa stopped some twenty feet from the surface and hung alongside the reef in front of a beautiful elephant-ear sponge. The locathah encircled him and began to wave their arms and hand-fins in underwater Common, a complicated language of symbols and currents that allowed creatures with differing vocal capacities to communicate while submerged.

"Greetings, Reefmaster," the locathah said. "Have you hunger?"

Tanetoa spread his webbed fingers and waved his response. "I have fed," he answered. In a world where most species were both predator and prey, the question and reply were polite ways of saying *I come in peace*. "Greetings, Seawanderers. You come in great numbers. I fear the reef cannot provide for so many."

"We do not come on the hunt," replied the locathah. "Eadro sends us to defend your island from the Enemy Above."

"I have spoken with the Enemy Above," replied Tanetoa. "They have come to protect the island from the Enemy Below."

The locathah's glassy eyes widened. The creature glanced in the direction of the ships and signed, "Then you hunt for them?"

"I do not hunt at all."

"That cannot be," replied the locathah. "This is war. All must hunt."

"No," Tanetoa signed, shaking his head. "A great hunt would be bad for the reef. Humans have magic and the fire that burns in water."

"Have no fear," the locathah assured. "We have Eadro's favor, and we are here to defend the island."

"I do not wish you to defend the island," Tanetoa countered. "There is nothing here to defend, only to destroy."

"It is Eadro's will," the locathah answered.

"But why?" Tanetoa allowed his anger to show in the curtness of his gestures. "What does it matter if humans land on my island?"

"They come in great numbers," the locathah signed. "They will poison the reef."

"And a battle will destroy it," said Tanetoa. "If Eadro cares about the reef, you will leave and let me deal with the humans."

"I did not say Eadro cares about the reef," the locathah countered. "I said only that the humans will poison it, as they poison everything in the water. What Eadro cares about is the Enemy Above. If they want the island, then Eadro does not want them to have it."

"And if they go away?" asked Tanetoa.

"Then there will be no need to defend the island. Can you make the Enemy Above go away?" There was a certain buoyancy in the locathah's gestures that suggested he wanted this as badly as Tanetoa.

"I will try."

Tanetoa ascended to the surface and took a great breath, pausing to look back at the ships. They were just over two hundred yards away, close enough that had the sun been higher in the sky, the lookouts in their crow's nests might have seen the locathah slipping into the channel. As it was, the glare on the water prevented that—which was certainly the only reason the emir had not ordered his men into their skiffs already.

A tiny figure in the bow of the emir's ship waved to Tanetoa. The gesture seemed a nervous one, and the giant dared hope it meant the humans had taken the point of his little display. He returned the wave, then kicked into the channel and followed the great school of locathah into his lagoon.

Kani was waiting on the shore, and Tanetoa swam toward her, heart pounding with fear and anger. Only a few hours remained before high tide, and he could not bear the thought of what the coming battle would do to his reef. The clumsy skiffs would crash about madly, tearing the tops off the corals, and wizards would fire lightning bolts and magic rays at the locathah hiding in the thick cover deeper down. The stunning formations would shatter into luminous sprays of shrapnel or simply die of shock. The reef fish would perish from the explosive concussions and float to the surface in schools. The sponges would burst, the anemones would be blasted flat, and the destruction would not end there. The locathah would capsize the human boats, turning the lagoon into a frothing mass of thrashing blades and flailing tridents that would smash whole swaths of brittle coral. The water would turn scarlet with blood and entrails, and the sharks would come, smashing headlong through the delicate garden in a feeding frenzy that could well do more damage than the battle itself.

The reef would be destroyed, and Tanetoa could not permit that. He had to convince the humans to leave—but how?

As Tanetoa neared the shore, Kani waded out to meet him. "You have spoken with the locathah?"

Tanetoa stood and nodded. "They have come to defend the island."

Kani's gaze shot at once to the warships, and she said nothing.

"The humans are determined to occupy the island for its own protection," Tanetoa said glumly.

Kani furrowed her brow. "They will fight for *this* island?" She shook her head in amazement. "Why?"

Tanetoa shrugged. "Because their caleph ordered it."

Kani considered this for a moment, then said, "There must be more to it than that. Tell me what they said."

Tanetoa recounted the conversation, relating everything from "declaring sides" to warning the emir against trying to land his forces without Tanetoa's consent. Kani listened carefully, asking for clarification only twice, once regarding the emir's reaction to hearing that Tanetoa could sing with the whales, and the second time regarding the man's reluctance to come ashore alone.

When Tanetoa finished, Kani considered the account for a time, then said, "Whatever his master wants, the emir must be afraid we won't allow it. That's why he refuses to come ashore until he can bring his men."

Tanetoa's eyes went wide. "You think he means to attack us?"

"If we don't give him what he wants."

"How can we?" So overcome with frustration was Tanetoa that the question rumbled from his mouth like a peal of thunder. "He won't tell us what it is!"

Kani spread her palms in a gesture of helplessness. "We will find out at high tide."

Tanetoa remained silent for a moment, then shook his head. "No, we won't. The locathah will attack while the boats are still in the lagoon." He stared across the water at the war fleet. "I must stop the humans from coming."

"How?"

"I don't know. Maybe I can sink their ships."

Kani paled. "Tanetoa, I may not love your island, but I do love you. Attacking the humans is too dangerous."

"I could do it from underneath," he explained. "If I took a sharp boulder—"

"You might sink two or three, but what of their wizards? If it were that easy to destroy an entire fleet, the

Enemy Beneath would not let the humans venture onto the water at all."

"I could ask the locathah for help."

Kani rolled her eyes. "And how would that save the reef? Without their ships, the humans would have no place to go but our island." She paused, then took Tanetoa's hand. "There are other reefs, Tanetoa, on larger islands—with enough wood to build a proper house, and with oyster beds rich in pearls."

Tanetoa pulled his hand away. "But there is only one Crystal Reef. There are corals here that grow in no other part of the sea. If that is not wealth enough—"

"It is more than enough wealth, as long as we are together," said Kani. "But it means nothing without you."

Tanetoa instantly regretted his tone. Kani's sisters all lived on larger islands, in great mansions furnished with elaborate furniture and priceless treasures. But Kani had lived with him on this island, in near poverty, for more than seven decades. The mere fact that she stayed was proof enough of her loyalty.

Tanetoa took his wife's hand. "I'm sorry for speaking harshly. You are not the one who swore to protect this reef. Sometimes I don't know why you stay with me."

"I stay because I love you, and I love you because you are the kind who would guard an island with no pearls." Kani squeezed his hand. "Besides, the reef is the most beautiful one in the Shining Sea. Even my sisters say so."

Tanetoa raised his brow, for he had never heard them speak of anything beautiful except their mansions. "Truly?"

"Would I lie to my husband?" Kani's voice turned from playful to serious. "I don't want to lose you to this war. Promise me that if you cannot persuade the humans to go, you will not be foolish enough to attack them."

"But I must protect the reef."

"You cannot protect the reef if you are dead," Kani said. "Promise, and I will tell you how to stop this battle."

Tanetoa cocked his brow. "You will? Then I promise."

Kani smiled. "You must give them your whale horn."

"My whale horn?" The whale horn was the single treasure Tanetoa's reef had ever yielded, the magic conch shell that allowed him to sing with the whales. "Why would that make them leave?"

"Would not an alliance with the whales benefit the humans?" asked Kani. "You said yourself the emir and his officer exchanged looks when you told them of singing with the whales. Perhaps the horn is the real reason they have come."

"Of course," Tanetoa answered, beginning to feel hopeful. "But if they wanted the whale horn, why not ask for it?"

"Because humans are greedy and cunning," answered Kani. "They feared you would refuse to give it to them and hide the horn where they could not find it. Perhaps they think it is surer to come ashore and steal it before you know what they want."

Tanetoa nodded. "That sounds like the emir." He started toward the hut to retrieve the horn, then stopped short. "But what of the locathah? If the humans want the horn, the locathah will want them not to have it."

Kani considered this, then motioned Tanetoa back into the lagoon. "Swim out past the reef. I will throw the horn out, and you can take it to the ships before the locathah catch you."

Tanetoa eyed the reef. Like all giants, reef giants could hurl boulders a great distance—more than three hundred yards—and it was only two hundred yards to the far side of the reef. It would not be difficult for Kani to throw the conch shell to him.

"Wait until you see me wave," he said. "If you throw it before I'm ready, I'll have to dive for it, and the locathah might catch up."

"I'll wait." Kani kissed him, then turned to wade ashore. "Remember your promise."

"I remember."

Tanetoa waded into the lagoon, then swam back to the channel, where the locathah were continuing to arrive from the open sea. As he left the passage, several of the creatures stopped below him, and one waved its thin arms in greeting.

"Hail, Reefmaster. Do you go to the humans?"

Tanetoa dived under the water, where the conversation would be hidden from human eyes. "I do." Tanetoa could not tell whether he was speaking with the same locathah as earlier, for they all looked the same to him. "I go to make them leave."

"How can you do that? Humans are stupid creatures who never listen to reason."

"Nothing is truer," agreed Tanetoa, "but I am a giant."

"You will threaten them?"

"If I must," signed Tanetoa.

"Even a giant cannot stand alone against so many," said the locathah. "We will come with you."

Tanetoa shook his head. "No. If the humans do not leave, you will kill more if you attack by surprise."

The locathah considered this, then smacked its lips in the piscine equivalent of a nod. "Eadro's wisdom is

216

on you. We will ready ourselves for the hunt. May you eat and not be eaten."

It was a traditional good wish for anyone about to embark on a dangerous undertaking. Tanetoa responded with the less bellicose wish, "Swim with the currents."

Leaving the locathah to hover, Tanetoa returned to the surface and swam fifty yards toward the ships, then turned back to his island. Kani stood waist deep in the lagoon, holding the giant conch on her shoulder. A beautiful purple-striped shell with a crown of spines at the closed end, it was so large that even both of her large hands could not encircle it.

Tanetoa waved. Kani drew her arms back and hurled the conch. It arced over the reef ten yards in the air, then splashed into the water half a dozen strokes in front of Tanetoa. He swam after the shell, catching up to it as the last of the air left its chambers. He grabbed it by the flange of the opening, then stuck his head underwater and glanced back toward the channel mouth.

The locathah were continuing to stream into the lagoon, though a small party remained clustered just below the mouth of the channel. Their glassy eyes were fixed in his direction, but they showed no sign of being alarmed by the shell in his hand. Tanetoa did not know whether to be relieved or more worried than ever. He swam on the surface the rest of the way to the fleet.

The humans had already begun their landing preparations, having placed several skiffs in the water and started loading them with supplies. As before, they kept their ballistae trained on Tanetoa as he approached, but this time the emir showed himself at the rail as soon as the giant neared the largest carrack.

"Hail, Tanetoa!" said the emir. "I did not expect you to return so soon."

"I have come with a gift for the caleph." Tanetoa displayed the conch.

"Indeed?" The emir eyed the shell briefly, then feigned disinterest and looked back to Tanetoa. "Then you have decided to honor your duties as his ally?"

"There is nothing to be gained by denying him." Tanetoa grabbed the gunwale amidships, then gently pulled himself up and laid the conch on the deck. "This is the whale horn."

The emir and his humans seemed unimpressed. "The whale horn?"

"So you can sing with the whales," Tanetoa explained.

This drew a chorus of snickers from the crew, and the emir could not quite keep his lip from curling into a patronizing sneer. "I am sure the caleph will be most grateful. He has often spoken to me of longing to hear the whales sing."

"Then there is no need to stay." Still clinging to the side of the ship, Tanetoa had to crane his neck to see the emir's face. "I will show you how to blow it, then you can go."

The emir scowled. "Go? I thought I had made myself clear. The only place we are going is to your island."

Now it was Tanetoa's turn to frown. "What for? You have the whale horn. We have nothing else of value."

"Perhaps not—though you said the same thing before bringing us this, uh, magnificent whale horn."

"I said that only because I did not realize what you wanted," explained Tanetoa. "We have nothing else."

The emir gave him a silky smile. "If you say so."

"I do!" Tanetoa thundered. "You have what you came

for, and now you must leave!"

The crew drew back at Tanetoa's display of anger.

The emir glanced nervously at the ballistae on a nearby deck and raised his hand, then narrowed his eyes at the giant. "There is nothing I *must* do, save what the caleph orders. The caleph thanks you for your gift, but I am still here to protect your island."

Tanetoa's heart sank. "Then he did not send you for the whale horn?"

"The caleph's reasons are not for you to know," said the emir. "It is enough that you know what he wishes."

Tanetoa shook his head. "But with the whale horn, you can sing with the whales. You can ask them to fight with you against the Enemy Beneath."

"So you have said, but that changes nothing. We will come ashore with the high tide—and you will help us."

A sick feeling came over Tanetoa. He gently released the gunwale and sank into the water, allowing the ship to rock slowly back to center. Whatever the caleph's reason for sending his fleet to the island, it was not the whale horn. There would be a battle.

Tanetoa swam two strokes backward, then stopped to stare up at the emir. "No! You are not going to land. If you try, there will be a terrible battle with the locathah—"

"Locathah?" the emir gasped. His men peered into the water around the ships, and harpoons began to appear along the rails again. "The locathah are here?"

"They are already in the lagoon." Tanetoa was encouraged by the emir's alarm. Perhaps he would leave if he believed his humans to be outnumbered. "Thousands of them. They came to defend the island from you."

"And you let them?" The emir's face turned stormy.

"You're in alliance with them!"

"No, but I will—"

"Traitor!"

The emir brought his hand down sharply, and several deep pulses echoed across the water. Tanetoa ducked beneath the surface and saw a dark meshwork of giant harpoons dragging heavy lines through the sea around him. He dived for the bottom, but one of his legs went numb. When he tried to kick, there was something dragging in the water behind him. He emptied his lungs so his body would not be buoyed by a chest full of air, then spread his webbed fingers and pulled for the bottom.

A bolt of searing pain shot through Tanetoa's leg, and he was jerked to an abrupt halt. He glanced back to see a barbed hook tugging at the flesh of his thigh, the dark stripe of harpoon line stretched taut behind him. He began to slip toward the surface, being drawn up through the water by the humans at the other end of the cord.

Tanetoa swam one stroke toward the surface, then wrapped his hand into the thick rope and gave a mighty jerk. The line went slack, then something heavy splashed into the sea. When the wave circle cleared, he saw the crosslike shape of a wooden ballista floating at the other end of the harpoon line.

Human wizards began to unleash their spells, and the sea erupted into a storm of crackling flashes and ear-shattering blasts. Tanetoa's head exploded into a tempest of blinding lights and dizzying concussions, then he went limp and felt himself floating toward the surface. He shook his head clear and flailed his leaden arms through the water, slowly dragging himself into the depths and away from the ships.

A dozen strokes later, he came to the end of the harpoon line and felt the ballista dragging through the water behind him. He pulled his knife from its ankle sheath and turned to cut the line. A cluster of small hand-hurled harpoons came slicing down behind him, and he saw the oblong hulls of four skiffs plowing through the water alongside the heavy ballista. Without cutting the line, Tanetoa turned and swam for his reef. The humans were not yet close enough to hit him with their little harpoons, but if he paused to cut the thick rope, they would be.

No more spells came from the skiffs, but Tanetoa quickly began to tire and ran out of air. He came up for a breath and was rewarded with the prick of a hand-hurled harpoon lodging itself in his shoulder. He gulped down a lungful of air and dived again, but the new line stopped him less than thirty feet beneath the surface. The reef came into sight. Hoping to buy some time in the narrow confines of the channel, he turned toward the mouth of the passage—then recalled the locathah and realized what would follow if he led the humans into their midst. Praying that Kani would see what was happening and start hurling boulders, he turned parallel to the reef and swam away from the channel.

Another harpoon caught Tanetoa in the back, adding another skiff to his burden, and his pace slowed to a mere crawl. Having heard the whales sing of the "hauling death," he knew what lay in store for him if he did not cut the lines. He reversed directions, diving downward as the skiffs closed on him. Another flurry of harpoons came slicing through the water, and he felt two more of the barbed shafts lodge themselves in his back. There was the flash of another magic blast, but

Tanetoa's ears were still ringing from the earlier explosions and he barely noticed the concussion.

At last, the lines ran straight up from Tanetoa's back to the bows of the boats above. He sheathed his dagger, then gathered the ropes in his hands and swam upward, twisting the lines together as he rose. The skiffs turned toward each other and drifted together nose to nose, forming a tight little star above Tanetoa's head. A lightning bolt and a handful of harpoons slashed down through the water, but with the boats shielding him from above, none of the attacks came close. The sailors took up their oars and tried to move away from each other, but there was not enough room between the vessels to row. The humans began to hack at their harpoon lines in a panic.

It was too late. Tanetoa came up under the boats and began to sink them, capsizing some and using his bare fist to punch holes in others. The humans panicked and leaped overboard, tossing aside their heavy swords and unbuckling their steel breastplates as they sank toward the bottom. Tanetoa let them go, content to pull his knife and cut himself free.

The locathah had different ideas. They flashed past Tanetoa in a river of silver scales, overtaking the humans from below and opening them from gut to gullet. The water grew red and cloudy with gore, and the sound of garbled death screams came faintly to Tanetoa's ears. He cut himself free of the heavy ballista, then tried to pull the huge harpoon from his leg and managed only to lodge the barb deeper.

A locathah floated into view in front of him. "Does the Reefmaster wish help?"

When Tanetoa nodded, the locathah took its dagger and cut the flesh over the barb, then pulled the harpoon free and let it sink into the depths.

"Thank you," Tanetoa signed.

"This is no time for thanks."

The locathah gestured toward the human fleet, where twenty more skiffs were underway. In the bow of each boat stood a sorcerer, spells already crackling on his fingertips. Behind each sorcerer stood a dozen sailors armed with all manner of tridents, crossbows, and harpoons.

"We must return to the lagoon," said the locathah.

Tanetoa was about to despair when a boulder came sailing over his head and crashed through the hull of the lead ship. He looked back to see Kani kneeling on the reef flat, pulling another huge stone from a tidal pool, and Tanetoa realized that his wife had hit upon the only way to save the reef. If the humans and the locathah were determined to have their war, they could have it in the open sea.

Tanetoa turned back to the locathah. "You cannot return to the lagoon. That is what the humans want."

"Why?"

"Because you will be trapped." The pain of his wounds made it difficult for Tanetoa to think fast, but he hoped the explanation sounded reasonable. "We will kill more in the open water."

Without waiting for the locathah's answer, Tanetoa struck out toward the skiffs. Another boulder sailed over his head. This one splashed down harmlessly between two boats, but the resulting water spout knocked a wizard overboard. The skiff stopped to fish its sorcerer out of the sea.

Tanetoa came to the main school of locathah. Though the water was red with the blood of dying humans, many of the fishmen were turning to swim back toward the channel. He raised his hands, signaling them to stop.

"The giants will sink the human boats." He pointed at himself, then at Kani on the reef flat. "The locathah will hunt the humans."

Another boulder sailed overhead, lopping the stern out of a skiff. A pair of men fell into the water and screamed for help.

The locathah considered the scene for a moment, then one signed, "May you eat and not be eaten."

"And may your belly be filled a dozen times," Tanetoa responded.

He turned and dived deep, ignoring his pain and swimming toward the skiffs. The locathah raced along beside him in ever growing numbers, and it was not long before they saw the boats slicing through the water above them. The bottom of one vessel disintegrated into fragments as a boulder came crashing through the hull. Half a dozen humans suddenly appeared in the water, struggling to unbuckle their armor and sinking to the bottom.

As the locathah shot up to slaughter the humans, they were greeted by a cacophony of eruptions and concussions. A dozen fishmen dropped their weapons to grab for their ears. A like number simply went limp and floated toward the surface. The survivors swarmed the sailors still in the water, clouding the sea with swirling blood. Harpoons and crossbow bolts slashed down from above, piercing locathah chests and puncturing locathah skulls. Within moments, the water became an impenetrable red fog.

Tanetoa came up beneath a skiff and punched a dozen holes in the bottom, then reached out and capsized another. The water broke into a frothing mass of red foam as the locathah swam to the attack. A human grabbed one of the small harpoons still lodged in Tanetoa's back and began to hack at his collarbone with a sword. The giant dived beneath the surface, where a locathah rescued him by slitting the human's throat. A silver bolt of lightning crackled through the water and blasted a head-sized hole through the chest of Tanetoa's rescuer.

Tanetoa whirled toward the surface and ripped the prow off the attacking wizard's skiff. The boat went down in the space of two breaths, pouring humans into the sea like eggs from a spawning grouper. Kani kept up a constant rain of boulders, smashing gunwales and shattering hulls at an ever-increasing pace. Tanetoa grew dimly aware that the battle was drifting closer to the outer reef, but the human flotilla was sinking fast, and the pace of their attack was declining at a steady rate. He dared to believe he and the locathah might drive the emir's landing party back to the ships.

Then the sharks came.

There were only a few at first, slashing through the red water, snapping and chomping and devouring anything they touched. The battle continued until only three skiffs remained, their crews rowing madly for the relative safety of the outer reef. Tanetoa caught one boat from behind, ripping the transom off the stern. A large tiger shark wriggled into the sinking boat and chased the inhabitants into the arms of waiting locathah. Kani sank a second boat, smashing a skiff in two with a porpoise-sized boulder.

The sharks quickly outnumbered the combatants, rising up to bite off the leg or arm of a sinking human, or coming in from behind to snap a surprised locathah in two. A giant mako attacked Tanetoa, ripping a great

THE THREAT FROM THE SEA

circle out of the giant's hip before he could drive his dagger through the thing's snout. The locathah, what few there remained, dived for the deep and fled. The humans simply died before they could unbuckle their breastplates—sometimes even before they could drop their weapons. The sole surviving skiff sped toward the reef as fast as twelve men could row with only two oars.

The boat was still twenty yards from shore when Kani lobbed a boulder into the starboard side. The vessel began to take on water and slowed to a snail's pace. The warriors clambered out of their breastplates and leaped toward shore, desperate to reach safety before the sharks took them. Even the fastest managed only three strokes before a big hammerhead caught him by the foot, and dragged him to a watery death.

The skiff's wizard was not so foolish. He remained in the bow, glaring at Kani, yelling in some arcane language and weaving a spell with his fingers.

"No!" Tanetoa swam for the sinking skiff, but was delayed when a frenzied blacktip bit his foot. "Kani, duck!"

Kani's eyes widened, and she turned to hurl herself from the reef flat as a dozen bolts of magic streaked from the sorcerer's fingertips. The blast caught her in the back of the head and launched her into the lagoon.

Tanetoa kicked free of the blacktip and lunged into the sinking boat. He caught the wizard from behind, dragged him out of the bow, and growled, "Why?"

"It is war." The wizard's eyes were burning with hatred, and his fingers were rushing through the gestures of a cantrip. "People die in wars—even giants."

"And so do sorcerers."

Tanetoa tossed the wizard to the sharks, then swam

the last few yards to the reef. As he climbed onto the flat, the smell of blood and saltwater saturated his nostrils, and the air was filled with the clatter of waves hurling shattered boat hulls against the reef flat.

"Kani!"

"Tan . . . Tane . . ."

Her voice was full of pain, and too feeble to finish his name. Tanetoa rushed across the flat and saw his wife floating in the lagoon, surrounded by a roiling cloud of scarlet blood. Her eyes were open and glassy and staring into the sky with a vacant expression.

"Kani, I'm here!"

Tanetoa dived into the water and took her in his arms. Her breathing was shallow and her flesh cold, and he could feel a soft spot where the wizard's spell had shattered the back of her skull.

She grasped his wrist. "Your promise, Tanetoa. You didn't keep it."

"I . . . I tried." He started toward shore. "But when you started throwing boulders, I saw you had found the way to save the reef."

"Not the reef, Tanetoa." Kani's hand fell away. "You."

Her eyes closed, then her body went limp and her breathing grew too shallow to feel.

"Kani?"

She didn't answer. Tanetoa carried her up to their hut and laid her on their bed of palm fronds. He sat beside her all day and into the night, never looking out the window to see what had become of the emir's fleet, or thinking even once of the reef she had saved. He tended her wounds and held her hand and begged all the deities of the giants to save her, but there was a mighty war raging across the seas of Toril and the gods could not hear his prayers. In the heart of the night, a terrible stillness came to her, and Tanetoa sat weeping in the darkness.

At dawn, he carried her body outside. The fleet was gone and the Shining Sea lay as still as a mirror, but the war remained a close and black thing, like a hurricane roaring on the horizon. Tanetoa waded out into the lagoon and lay Kani in the warm water.

The locathah were streaming out through the channel, their silver-green backs flashing just beneath the surface. One circled away from the school and pushed its head out of the water so it could speak in the air-talk of humans.

"Greetings, Reefmaster." The locathah's voice seemed somehow both wispy and gurgling. "Your wife will be eaten?"

"Kani is dead," Tanetoa said, too sad and weary to take offense at what was to any sea creature the simple consequence of dying. "But she will not be eaten. I will build a tomb for her in the manner of a queen of my people."

The locathah's glassy eyes seemed puzzled for a moment, then it said, "Eadro praises her bravery. The humans have fled, and it was much her doing."

Tanetoa nodded, only half hearing the praise, then eyed the empty sea. "But why did they come at all? What did they want?"

"What do humans ever want?" The locathah opened its gills in the equivalent of a shrug. "No one knows."

The Patrol
Larry Hobbs

10 Flamerule, the Year of the Gauntlet

The summer sun blazed over Cimbar in a cloudless sky. The still air shimmered as waves of heat beat down on Riordan's face. The smell of rotting fish was heavy in the dockyard. Sweat burned in his eyes, but he couldn't take time to wipe it away. He stumbled backward as the Soorenar's blade flickered in front of him, nicking his arm and shoulder in rapid succession.

Shouts, screams, and the clash of weapons echoed in the distance as the Dragon Watch fought the rest of the Soorenar raiding party. A watch patrol had stumbled on the raiders climbing down the hawsers of a shabby merchant ship anchored near the end of the wharf. The watchmen were outnumbered and killed, but not before one had sounded the alarm. The Dragon Watch barracks were close by and the entire company had turned out at the alarm. Now it was the Soorenar who were outnumbered and fighting for their lives, abandoned by the ship that was clawing its way out to sea before Cimbar's navy could catch it.

Blood oozed down Riordan's arm, mixing with the sweat and making the sword slippery in his grip. He'd chased this man into a cul-de-sac of crates and boxes and they each knew there would be no escape except over the body of the other. Two other watchmen had followed him but they stood back and made no offer to help. Riordan realized they were waiting to see him killed before they'd step in and finish off the raider. For the first time, he realized just how much of an outcast he really was.

Muscles rippled across the Soorenar's tattooed chest as the man twirled the heavy sword in front of Riordan's eyes. Plumed serpents writhed across his arms and shoulders. The tattoos told Riordan the man was a slave trained in the fighting rings. The tiny silver skulls suspended from the hoop in the Soorenar's ear warned Riordan he was facing a veteran of many combats. He would be very lucky to live through this fight.

Surprisingly, the Soorenar stopped and stepped back, putting his hand on his hip and lowering the point of his sword. He looked at the guardsmen a moment, then smiled and saluted Riordan with the blade.

"It seems strange a man's comrades won't help him, but a man should die with honor for all of that. Defend yourself or I'll kill you where you stand."

One of the watchmen laughed and spat. "Go on,

milor', show him what those fancy fencing masters taught you."

"Milor' "—he hated the name, but ever since the other recruits found out he was the son of a noble, it had stuck. Thank the Gods they didn't know *which* noble.

Riordan was angry and frightened. After what had happened on his last patrol, his own comrades wouldn't help him. There was no hope for it. Taking a deep breath, Riordan moved into the guard position. He began his attack in a traditional style, hoping the ritual opening would lull the big man into complacency. The Soorenar parried in second and they sparred back and forth in the gritty street, neither able to gain an advantage. Sparkling motes of sand sprang up about their feet as they shuffled across the paving stones.

Riordan was not used to the heat. After several flurries his chest hammered and he was gasping for air. The Soorenar looked completely fresh. Riordan barely heard the jeers of the two spectators. His world had narrowed to the rasping sound of his feet on the street and the clash of steel. The Soorenar lunged and Riordan disengaged with a stop thrust that punctured the man's side, forcing the big man back.

The man put his hand to the wound and stared in disbelief at the blood that ran between his fingers, then he looked up and grinned, stepping forward to attack.

Riordan slowed and invited the attack in the first, exposing the outside low line and letting the other take the initiative. After a few feeble defensive moves, he decided it was time. Taking a tight grip on the hilt, he lunged, swinging down and under the Soorenar's blade, knocking the weapon to the side with a beat and reversing. The man laughed and continued the movement until his sword was back in position. Riordan pulled back at the last minute to avoid a riposte that would gut him like a fish.

"A pretty move, boy."

The big man's blade flickered and danced in front of him. Like a snake, it slithered under his guard and raked his chest, cutting a bloody furrow across his ribs and taking his breath away with a sudden, burning pain. The man kicked him in the stomach and Riordan gagged, falling to his knees in the street.

Riordan spat the sand from his mouth. He rolled away from a slashing cut that sent sparks up from the stone, and scrambled to his feet. One of the guardsmen laughed and Riordan glanced in his direction. Out of the corner of his eye, he saw the Soorenar's movement and cursed his inattention. He blocked, catching the man's blade and, without thinking, beat the other's sword out and swung under for a stroke that cut the big man across the thigh.

The Soorenar roared and charged in a series of lightning moves that Riordan could barely block. The invader's weapon caught Riordan's blade and spun the tips in the air in narrow circles. Before Riordan could disengage, the raider closed and slammed his shoulder into Riordan's chest, knocking him backward. He straightened reflexively and the man smashed the bell of his guard into Riordan's face. Riordan dropped his weapon and collapsed to the ground struggling to remain conscious. The Soorenar's foot caught him on the side of the head and sent him sprawling.

From the corner of his eye Riordan saw the man's sword come up.

The blow never came. There was a clash of steel above him and a groan as the body of the Soorenar sprawled beside him.

His eye was swelling shut and it was hard to see, but Riordan recognized the voice of Morka Kodolan, Swordmaster of the Watch, yelling at the two watchmen. "You may hate him, but by Tchazzar he's a member of the Dragon Watch and we stand together. I should teach you all a lesson for this."

Riordan rolled over and tried to stand up. He started to thank Morka but the swordmaster's face was dark with fury. Ropy veins stood out on his forehead and his broad nose flared. Morka was short, squat, and heavily muscled. His head was shaved except for a single long braid growing from the back of his head. Barracks rumors said only a southern sect of specially trained warriors wore their hair like that.

Everyone on the watch was afraid of Morka and for good reason. He was like a berserker when angered. Right now he was very angry. He pushed Riordan against a crate and waved a fist the size of a plate in Riordan's face.

"Shut up, recruit! You're more trouble than you're worth. The clerics tell me it will be at least another tenday before Kendrick gets the use of his arm back. Last tenday your foolishness cost me the use of a good man and could have gotten him killed. Now this . . ."

Morka nodded to someone behind Riordan and said, "Get him cleaned up. Get him out of my sight." He slammed his sword into his scabbard and stalked away.

Rough hands jerked Riordan to his feet and pulled him toward the barracks. His head was spinning and he couldn't see from his right eye.

It was dark and cool inside the barracks and someone shoved a wet rag in his hands as he collapsed on his bunk. The man cut his shirt away and began to clean the slashes on his chest and arm. Riordan bit back a scream. He felt something in his hand and tried to see what it was.

"The swelling will go away faster if you put this on your face."

Riordan couldn't make out the face of the speaker. The rag in his hand was sticky and smelled like rotten garbage. He grimaced and dropped it onto the floor.

"Easy, milor' . . ." The other bent down and picked it up again. "It's a special poultice."

Riordan tried to pull away, but the man put the rag over his eyes. He struggled for a minute, but the rag was cool and he relaxed as the pain went away.

"Thanks."

"Think nothing of it, mi—Riordan."

"I can't see you."

"It's Bashar."

Riordan was surprised. Bashar was Morka's corporal. Bashar, the barracks drunk. A burned-out husk of a warrior fit for nothing but to follow Morka around during drill and inspections. Yet the one man who'd decided to help.

"Thanks, Bashar."

There was a moment of silence, then the man spoke again. "Rumor says you're the son of Evern Marsh."

Riordan grunted. He wondered how anyone found that out, but decided it was best to say nothing.

Bashar waited, then finally nodded as if Riordan's silence had been an answer. "I knew your father."

Another rummy looking for a handout from the son of a hero, Riordan thought. He sighed, "Third son, not much left for the last. Father wanted me to become a cleric."

"And you knew better." Bashar laughed softly and handed him the wet rag again.

Riordan felt defensive. "There's a war coming with Soorenar. Everybody knows it. I'm needed here."

It was as if the old corporal hadn't heard him. "I remember you, but it was a long time ago. Your father made you a toy sword and used to drill you for hours. Wanted you to be a soldier, he did. Guess he must have changed his mind."

Memories came flooding back. Fragments of events that had been buried long ago. He propped himself up on the cot and stared at blurred image of the older man. "I'd forgotten that. You really did know my father?"

Images marched across his mind. Not of the sword, but of the studies. The faceless line of tutors that came and went under the stern and watchful eye of his crippled father. Memorizing endless books, but never meeting his father's expectations . . . who would believe him? Evern Marsh, not once, but twice a hero, forcing his son to become a cleric—until Riordan ran away and joined the Dragon Watch.

"Why are you doing this?" Riordan took the rag away and tried to make out Bashar's face. "It was my blunder that nearly got Kendrick killed."

"I know. You went charging into that alley and the Soorenar were waiting for you. Knocked you out and nearly killed Kendrick when he tried to protect you. Then they escaped. If you'd waited . . ."

In his excitement, he'd forgotten to sound the alarm. It was a stupid mistake and almost got his partner killed. He tried to explain. "I saw them run, I was right behind them. I could have gotten them all."

"Except for the rearguard they left behind in the cross alley." Bashar shook his head. "Oldest trick in the book, lad."

He hesitated a moment, then continued, "I heard you did the same thing today. The man you chased was a seasoned warrior. Morka told me he wore six skulls."

"Two guardsmen were with me, but they held back and let me fight alone."

"I heard that, too."

Bashar took the rag and dipped it in the bowl of green poultice. He wrung it out and handed it back to Riordan. The stench was terrible.

"You asked me why I'm doing this. Your father saved my life once. I owe him something."

Riordan took the poultice away from his eye. His vision cleared enough to make out the corporal. Riordan stared at him, really seeing him for the first time.

Bashar had a lined face, wrinkled like a prune, though he moved like someone much younger. Riordan realized that Bashar was probably not as old as he looked, it was just that the wars had burned away all the excess flesh. His muscles were thin and ropy like the gnarled roots of some tree. Two copper bracelets with strange runes encircled his upper arms. The top of his head was completely bald and he'd pulled the hair on the sides into a long queue.

Barracks talk said Bashar was once a great swordsman, but wine had taken his senses and now he was a drunk barely tolerated by Morka Kodolan.

Riordan looked at Bashar. "What was my father like when you knew him?"

"Lad, he was a great fighter and a proud man. I never saw anyone handle a sword like he did. You know, sometimes I see a little of him in you. He looked like you when he was your age."

Riordan shook his head, picturing the shriveled, bitter man his father had become. Wrapped in a faded red shawl and confined to a chair, Evern Marsh spent his last days staring endlessly at the distant mountains from the open window of his bedroom.

"No, lad. You can't deny it. You both have that lean and hungry look. You're taller than I remember him being, but you have the same darkness about you. Dark eyes, dark hair, and the same dark disposition. Evern was slender like you, but a hard man. When he was young, no man would mistake him for a—"

"Stupid recruit like me." Riordan interrupted. He rubbed his shoulder and inspected the bandages on his arms and ribs.

"Nay, lad. That's not true. The fight this afternoon, for instance. That raider was a seasoned warrior. Six victories in the ring. Few could have stood alone against him even that long, lad."

"Not much good it did me."

"You're too hard on yourself. You're tall and that gives you the reach over most men, but most important, you're quick and you have good moves."

"That Soorenar would've killed me. He had moves I'd never seen before."

"Ring fighter's tricks, lad." He hesitated a moment. "I could show you. They're not hard."

Riordan stared at him a moment. He could use a friend. Even an old drunk.

Bashar was as good as his word. They spent the next tenday doing drills and exercises that left Riordan exhausted. In spite of that, his skills improved faster than he would have thought possible. Several times he caught Morka Kodolan watching them with a frown on his face. Later, Riordan saw the swordmaster stop Bashar on the way to the Owl Inn where he drank every tenday leave.

He was too far away to hear what was said, but he knew they were arguing. Finally the swordmaster threw his hands up and stalked away. Bashar stared after him for a while until he saw Riordan watching, then he too turned and walked away. Riordan hurried after Bashar and found him at a table drinking by himself in a dim corner of the Owl. Morka sat nearby talking to a grizzled veteran and eating a bowl of stew.

Two big men staggered over, dressed in the green and gold of the Wyvern Watch. One put his foot on the bench next to the swordmaster and said, "Hey, Morka, I heard a couple of your recruits ran into an alley last tenday after some Soorenar that torched a ship. Let 'em go, I heard. Guess they must have decided the Soorenar were too much for 'em." The man nudged his partner and laughed, sloshing ale on the floor.

Morka tensed, gripping his knife and staring hard at the other man. The big man blanched and smiled. "Hey, don't take it out on me. Everybody's talking about it."

The two men backed away as Morka pushed his food away and stood up. Heavy muscles flexed as he moved, highlighting the pale scars that crisscrossed the dark skin of his chest and face. The two watchmen looked at each other and put their hands to the hilts of their swords, but Morka ignored them.

He walked past the table where Riordan sat with Bashar. "I'm going to the Griffin to drink. The stink of recruits is too strong here."

Morka looked directly at Riordan then shook his

head. "Bashar, I want to talk to you."

"I'll meet you there."

Morka stared at Riordan a moment longer, then walked away.

Riordan started to get up and follow, but Bashar put his hand on his sleeve. "Not now, lad. The Griffin is off limits to recruits."

"But what happened wasn't like that. It wasn't like they said."

"It doesn't matter, Morka's in no mood to listen. Didn't you learn anything last tenday?"

Riordan shook his head. "He has to listen."

"No, he doesn't. He doesn't have to believe you. He doesn't have to do anything at all. Don't you get it yet?"

Bashar waved his mug toward the door through which Morka had left. Ale slopped from the rim onto his shirt but he didn't seem to notice.

"Son, he's swordmaster. Things are the way he wants them to be. You're a recruit. There's nothing lower in this world than a recruit. Get used to it."

"He hates me. He thinks I'm the son of some useless noble. I've heard the stories about my father's fencing masters. The truth is, I paid for my own training and I had to sneak out every night to do it."

"He doesn't hate you lad, but he won't let you out of training till he thinks you're ready."

"I'll prove myself. He'll have to listen to me."

Bashar shook his head. "You already tried that once. Who're you really trying to prove yourself to?"

Riordan stared at him. "What are you talking about?"

"Unless you're blind, it's not hard to see. Third son of a famous warrior out to show everyone he's as good as his father . . ."

"Leave my father out of this. What do you know?"

"More than you might think." Bashar sighed and took a sip of his ale. "I served under him in three campaigns. Aye, a real firebrand he was. You're just like him."

Bashar put his mug on the table and motioned to the barmaid for another.

"That's what got you into trouble in the first place, lad."

He smiled at the maid and took the mug from her tray. He'd nursed a single ale tonight and Riordan noticed Bashar's hands were steady as he looked at him over the rim with sharp eyes.

"I guess you haven't learned anything. Maybe you're not like your father after all."

"My father again." Riordan started to get up.

"Wait, Riordan. There are things you should know about your father. Morka and I served with him in the last Flaming Spike uprising. We were with him at the Gap of Reth."

"The Gap of Reth?" Riordan stopped. It was his father's last campaign. He'd come home a crippled, bitter man after that battle. Riordan had heard stories, but his father would never talk about it.

"Aye, Evern had the rearguard. He held the Flaming Spike off until the Sceptanar's army got through. Those merchants were so grateful, Murzig Hekkatayn himself gave your father the hero's medal for that."

"He would never tell me what happened."

Bashar nodded. "Not surprising."

His voice dropped and his eyes took on a faraway look, remembering. "We lost too many companions in that action. Half the rearguard died on those slopes. Your father took terrible wounds. The clerics did their best, but couldn't save his legs."

Riordan nodded, remembering. "Mother was killed during one of the early raids of the war. Without her . . . when he came home he became different . . . He told me he wanted me to become a cleric."

Bashar sipped his ale and put his hand on Riordan's shoulder. "We all changed. It was a terrible, bloody battle. Perhaps your father had seen too much of what war could do. Maybe he wanted you to save lives rather than take them."

Bashar pushed away his ale and said, "Me . . . I became a drunk."

Riordan stared at him a moment. "My father . . . the wounds you described. How did he get out of the Pass?"

Bashar stood up and looked at Riordan a moment. His eyes softened, and he smiled. "Morka and I carried him, lad." Then he turned and walked out the door.

Riordan drank his ale and ordered another. He sat at the table and let his mind drift.

Riordan was groggy the next morning when the alarm clanged outside the barracks window. The recruits stumbled around the barracks in the dark, struggling to find their weapons and armor. There was a rush for the door and Riordan fell into line, panting and out of breath.

Morka stood there with his hands on his hips as he studied the line of recruits. Bashar stood beside him. The polished armor of the two men gleamed in the soft light of the dawn. Morka's expression took on a deep frown as they began to walk down the line of stiff recruits.

"You pissants probably think that was good." He shook his head. "I've never seen such a miserable performance."

He grabbed for the spear of the watchman in front of him. The weapon clattered to the ground. The recruit turned pale and tried to avoid the eye of the swordmaster.

"Release the weapon when I have it in my hand, not before. Twenty laps in the coliseum tonight."

He moved down the line and stopped in front of Riordan, inspecting his armor and harness. "Not bad. Someone taught you to hang your sword forward, I see."

From the corner of his eye, Riordan saw Morka glance at Bashar then move to the next recruit.

There was a clatter of hooves, and a column of horsemen entered the parade ground.

"Attention! Form up!" The two ranks of recruits snapped to attention on the swordmaster's command.

Khedra, Captain of the Dragon Watch, and one of his lieutenants rode up behind Morka and Bashar. Their polished armor cast blinding reflections in the sun. Two other men were with them. Riordan recognized Stilmus, leader of the Society of the Sword and one of the magistrates from the third section.

"Third section, Dragon Watch present and accounted for, sir!" Morka said.

"Stand at ease."

Khedra took a moment to look up and down the ranks of soldiers. Riordan could not tell if he was pleased with what he saw. His bronzed face looked weathered and tired, but his cold blue eyes seemed to miss nothing.

"Normally, you recruits would spend another month learning your drill, but things have changed. There are reports of raids along the western coast of the Sea of Fallen Stars. Yesterday, two triremes were cut loose and driven on the rocks in Airspur. Two others were torched a day later."

There was surprised muttering from the watchmen.

"All right men, settle down." Khedra paused and stared at the recruits.

"We know it's the Soorenar, stirring things up again and we have to be prepared. The raiders you caught last tenday are just one example. There have been several unexplained fires on merchant ships and even some rumors an assassin is loose. We believe there will be some attempt to cripple the fleet. I want these raiding parties stopped.

"Each of you recruits will be assigned to patrol with an experienced guardsman. You will find these raiders and you will call in the rest of the watch. Is that clear?"

"Clear, sir!" they shouted in unison

"By the way, Stilmus is looking for one or two outstanding recruits among the watch for the Society of the Sword. He will be observing you all in the next few days."

There was a buzz of excitement through the ranks.

"Good." Khedra looked over the ranks with a pleased expression. "Swordmaster, corporal, you know what to do." Khedra spun his horse and trotted away.

"You heard the captain. Fall out and suit up for patrol."

Riordan started to join the others when Morka held out his hand. "All except you, Riordan. You stay in the barracks."

Riordan jerked upright. His voice quivered with anger, but he couldn't help it. "I should be out on patrol, sir."

"Yes, you should, but you won't." He shook his head. "You're not ready. Your recklessness might kill the comrade you're with. The answer is no."

"But that's not fair!"

"Fair? The last time you were in an engagement the two watchmen with you would've let you be killed. Just who do you suppose I should pair you with?" Morka stared at him and started to turn away.

"Sir, perhaps he could patrol with me?"

"You, Bashar?"

"Aye, sir. You know we need every available man. We're stretched too thin as it is."

Morka frowned. "I . . ."

Bashar drew himself up. "I'd take it as a personal favor."

At that moment, there was something different about the corporal. He didn't seem like the stooped rummy that cleaned weapons for a silver and staggered into the barracks every night.

Morka frowned. He looked as if he would say something, but then he shrugged. "So be it. It's on your head, Bashar."

Bashar spent most of the day going over the route with Riordan. He pointed out the buildings that had to be checked and the layout of the streets they would patrol. Bashar warned him to be especially alert for fires. Cimbar had been hot and dry for over a month and there was still no sign of rain. By evening, Riordan felt ready.

The docks of Old Town were deserted. Moonlight filtered through the narrow streets threading between the overhanging buildings. In the distance, the peak of the Untheri pyramid was visible. Here and there, light reflected off iridescent puddles of water between the cobblestones. The smell of the sea and rotting fish lay heavy on the hot, still air.

The shops were closed and shuttered. Riordan and Bashar tested the locks and rattled the windows to make sure the buildings were secure for the night.

Bashar stopped by an apothecary. "Did you hear that?"

"It was just a cat."

"Then it was a cat with steel claws. I heard the sound of metal. Come on."

Riordan followed Bashar trying to move as quietly as the older man did. The corporal moved quickly down the street and hesitated. He held up his hand and gestured toward a narrow alley.

Riordan drew his sword and followed Bashar into the gloom. He tried to stay close to the wall, trailing his hand against the wet, mossy brick.

"In here." Bashar was right in front of him. Riordan noticed the deeper blackness of an open doorway beside him.

"Follow me and open your lantern when I call out." Bashar's voice was a whisper.

Riordan held the lantern up and followed Bashar into the room. Somewhere ahead came the sound of metal scraping on glass.

"Now!"

Riordan pulled open the door on the lantern and blinked as yellow light washed across the room. In the far corner, someone was bent over a cabinet. Papers lay scattered across a nearby table.

Bashar charged the man, but the intruder turned and drew his sword with incredible speed. There was a ringing clash of steel on steel and bright sparks scattered across the floor.

The two figures blurred together, and Bashar yelled as he was flung across the room. Riordan charged the thief, but it was like he'd hit a wall. The lantern was knocked from his hand and he was thrown to the floor.

A black shape blocked the moonlight in the open door frame, and the thief was out in the street. Riordan and Bashar stumbled over one another and followed him out the door. Bashar blew his whistle to draw the other teams.

"Come on. He's getting away "

Riordan ran after his partner, trying to keep up. They followed a dizzying series of twists and turns across Dock Street and into the merchant district. The thief was heading toward the university and the Sceptanar's palace.

Finally, Bashar stopped. He bent down and put his hands on his knees, taking deep, gasping breaths. "I'm getting too old for this."

"Why are we stopping?"

"Because the alley he ran into is a dead end. I want you to stay here and signal for the rest of the watch."

"What about you?"

"I'm going in after him. You wait till you hear the others, then come in and back me up."

"You're doing just what I did!"

"This is different. Riordan, this is no ordinary thief. I caught a glimpse of him just before he ran out the door. We're not chasing a Soorenar, this is a malenti."

"A malenti?" Riordan couldn't make the connection. He tried to remember the stories he'd heard about the creatures. "What's a sahuagin assassin doing on land?"

"Exactly. Why would a malenti be working with the Soorenar?" Bashar looked down the alley and spoke quietly. "This is important, lad. One of us has to signal, you heard the commander. Now do as I say!"

Bashar stared at him until Riordan nodded. The

older man smiled and clapped him on the shoulders. "You're learning. Your father would be proud of you."

Riordan stared into the gloom and blew his whistle as the corporal crept into the alley. If the stories Riordan had heard were true, Bashar had just sentenced himself to death. There was no way Bashar could overcome a malenti and he knew it. Even together it was unlikely they would kill the creature.

He blew his whistle again and again until he heard an answering cry in the distance. In the alley behind him there was the brief sound of swords clashing and a sudden groan. He blew the whistle one more time and heard shouts and answering whistles approaching. Hardly thinking, he set his lantern on a barrel where it could not be missed, drew his sword, and ran into the alley.

Bashar lay curled on the stones. Riordan knelt and felt the weak pulse at his neck, relieved that the old man was still alive. Several yards away, the malenti stood in the alley. Riordan stood up and crept toward it. He drew his sword and the creature turned and faced him at the sound.

"Throw down your weapon," Riordan commanded. "The watch is right behind me."

The creature laughed. It was a harsh, barking sound. "Should I throw myself on your human mercy? Will it be any better than these?"

For the first time Riordan noticed the movement in the darkness at the other end of the alley. Two figures stepped forward, then more emerged. Moonlight glittered on dark scales and polished black harnesses. His heart sank. It was a sahuagin raiding party, come to the aid of the malenti.

A flickering light came from the window of the

building behind the sahuagin and Riordan thought of crying out for the people inside. Then he saw the black smoke billow out a broken window and heard the crackle of the flames. The sahuagin were going to burn the docks.

More of the creatures stepped forward and Riordan realized the sahuagin raiding party carried torches and tools used for sinking ships. He remembered Khedra's stories of ships destroyed and burned.

There was a groan from Bashar and one of the sahuagin glanced at the corporal. Its ears twitched and it looked at the sahuagin leader. The leader of the raiders grunted something, raised a greenish-black arm, and pointed to Bashar and Riordan. The smaller sahuagin gripped its trident and stepped toward Bashar. Riordan moved in front of it to protect his comrade. There would be no escape from this, but perhaps he could hold them off until the guard arrived.

The leader of the sea devils snarled something and the malenti shook his head. Riordan couldn't understand what was said, but the meaning was clear enough. The sahuagin wanted something the malenti wouldn't give them.

The creature turned to look at him as the moon came out from the clouds and illuminated the scene in the alley. The malenti was manlike except for silver-green skin. The hair that Riordan thought was black was really a dark blue. Dark eyes studied him and gill slits on the sides of its neck quivered when he spoke. "It seems you will not capture me after all, human. These scum . . ." he nodded toward the sahuagin, "have decided they have first claim."

Riordan smiled and shifted his sword to a two-handed grip. "I see. Between malenti and sahuagin there is no honor among thieves."

The malenti drew himself up and hissed. "I am not one of them. I am a sea elf."

Riordan's head was spinning. What was going on here? "So you say. No matter—they'll have to wait their turn. You're my prisoner first."

The elf raised an eyebrow and laughed. "You are either a fool or the best swordsman in Chessenta. However, I believe you and I will have to kill them first before we can determine that."

The leader of the sahuagin signaled with its trident and stepped into the light. The rest of the band moved with it. Moonlight glittered on scales that ranged from green to black and their claws scraped the stones as they moved into position. The narrow alley filled with the scent of their musk and the sea.

Riordan took a step alongside the elf, who stared at him with a strange expression, but only for a moment. He nodded as if a question had been answered, then lowered his spear and faced the sahuagin raiders.

The sahuagin circled the two until they were completely surrounded. Back to back, Riordan and the elf stood over Bashar and watched the creatures advance.

There was a shout and two of the sahuagin charged Riordan. He moved back, blocking the thrust of the spear with the flat of his sword and maneuvering the creature in front of its companion. Snarling, the creature tried to get a clear opening to thrust. Finally, Riordan saw his chance. He caught the shaft of the first one on the edge of his sword and felt the vibration up his arm. Twisting, he parried the weapon to the side, into the path of the other creature. Before it could react, he kicked the legs from under the first sahuagin and stabbed it through the throat as it fell. There was a bubbling scream and warm blood spurted across his arm.

The second sahuagin snarled and leaped across the body of the first. Riordan ducked under its swing and stabbed upward, slashing into the soft underbelly of the creature. The sahuagin screamed and staggered backward, holding its stomach. The sea elf buried his spear in the sahuagin's heart.

The elf spun away from the creature just in time to block the slash of another sahuagin that leaped from the shadows. The sea devil slammed into the elf and knocked him against Riordan. Two more sahuagin attempted to close with Riordan when he fell, but he rolled under the thrust of one and slashed at the leg of the other. Dark blood spurted from the wound and the creature screamed in pain as it clutched its thigh and scrabbled back against the wall.

Using a move Bashar had taught him, Riordan slammed the bell of his sword against the knee of the second sahuagin. He heard the bone snap and the creature collapsed with a moan in a pool of filthy water.

Wary now, the remaining sahuagin thrust and lunged, hoping to break through their guard. The stone walls of the alley echoed with the sharp clash of steel on steel.

In the distance, Riordan heard the horns of the approaching guard. The sahuagin grew desperate. The beast in front of Riordan charged, but slipped on the blood in the alley. Riordan jumped back from the desperate thrust it made as it fell. The creature threw a torch at Riordan as he prepared to lunge. There was a crash of glass as the burning torch went through a window. Behind him Riordan felt a sudden blast of heat as the building caught fire.

The blaze momentarily blinded the sahuagin and it blinked and turned its face away from the flames. Riordan slashed at the creature's wrist and it shrieked and dropped its spear. Riordan continued his thrust and the blade sank into the creatures' stomach.

The elf was fighting the leader of the sahuagin. The sahuagin was fast, but if anything, the elf was faster. The sahuagin swung its trident at the elf, but the creature was no longer there. All Riordan could see was a blur of movement and a dark ribbon of blood appeared across the sahuagin's chest. The creature roared and lunged again and this time Riordan heard the meaty sound of the weapon hitting flesh.

The elf grunted and staggered back. With a roar, the sahuagin charged the elf, holding the blades of the trident out and low. The next thing Riordan saw was the tines striking a blank wall and the elf appearing behind the sahuagin as if by magic. The shaft of the elf's spear slammed across the throat of the surprised sahuagin leader. Twirling the weapon, the elf spun and buried the spear in the sea devil's chest. The creature moaned and its claws scrabbled at the shaft as if it would escape, but the elf twisted the blade with a jerk and the sahuagin collapsed.

Reacting without thinking, Riordan spun and knocked the elf back. The elf tried to go after his spear, but Riordan pressed the point of his sword into the elf's throat, forcing him up and back from the weapon. He noticed the sea elf was bleeding from a deep gash in his side.

"Our truce is over."

The elf stared at him, ignoring the blade at his throat. "Our fight meant as little to you as that?"

"This fight meant nothing. You have no interest in helping us."

The sea elf shook his head and sneered at Riordan. "They will kill you all, you know."

The elf started to move, but Riordan pressed the tip of the sword harder against his throat. A thin stream of blood sprang from the tip and ran down the sea elf's neck.

"You're right, human. You and your kind mean nothing to us. For months I've been spying on the sahuagin, pretending to be one of their assassins. They've breached the Sharksbane Wall now, and already flood the Inner Sea. My people are prepared, but the war will be long and costly."

"That means nothing to me. You're my prisoner." Riordan tried to sound sure of himself, but what the elf was telling him made him worried. He needed Morka to listen to this.

"Foolish words. Don't you know that you and everyone here in Cimbar will be next?"

There was a shout nearby, and Riordan answered. Before he knew what happened, the elf had knocked his sword aside and was sprinting down the alley. Without breaking stride, he jumped on top of a stack of several crates and sprang to the top of a low roof. Flames burst from a building nearby and outlined the elf clearly.

The sea elf hesitated for a moment and Riordan heard him say, "Tell them what you saw here, human. It is the sahuagin who are burning your fleets." He turned and Riordan saw his outline vanish over the roofline.

There was a groan and Riordan bent down to check on Bashar.

"Are you all right?"

"Other than a cut and a knot on the head. I'm lucky to be alive. Funny, it seemed like the malenti was holding back."

"He wasn't a malenti, Bashar." Riordan explained what happened.

The corporal nodded, then grimaced in pain. Riordan realized Bashar's wounds were more serious than he let on. "I've got to get you out of here."

"No . . . wait." Bashar groaned and grabbed his arm. "When the watch gets here . . ." Bashar coughed. "Don't say anything about the sea elf. Khedra would never believe you. Tell Morka."

"But—"

"That's an order, Riordan. Tell Morka." Riordan agreed and the corporal nodded and collapsed.

There was a clatter of hooves and Khedra and Stilmus rode into the alley with a dozen guardsmen behind them.

Khedra took immediate command. "Seal off both ends of the alley. Now! No one comes in. Get the fire crews in here immediately."

"Aye, m'lord."

Khedra dismounted and strode through the bodies to where Riordan stood.

"These are sahuagin!"

"Yes, sir. They had torches and had already set one building on fire when Bashar and I got here. They had cutting tools as well. I believe they were going to destroy the ships next."

Khedra stopped and stared at him a moment. "Were you responsible for this, watchman?"

"Yes, sir. Bashar and I . . ." How much could he tell them? "Sir, it's important you know—the sahuagin are behind the recent attacks on the fleet, not the Soore-nar."

"Hmm . . . at least this attack. This is important news." Khedra smiled and put away his sword. "Well done, watchman."

Morka Kodolan had arrived and was kneeling and talking to Bashar. From time to time he looked up at Riordan, but Riordan could not read his expression. He motioned to two guardsmen who helped Bashar onto a litter.

The swordmaster came up to Riordan and clapped him on the shoulder. "You've accounted well for your-self, Riordan."

Khedra stared at Riordan intently. "Riordan . . . aren't you the one that . . . ?"

Morka stepped forward. "A minor error in judgment, sir. Riordan is one of my finest recruits. Bashar also speaks very highly of him."

Khedra stared a moment at Morka, then turned to Riordan. "I'm certain he does. Perhaps Riordan can join us later?"

"That's right." Morka clapped Riordan on the shoul-der. "The Dragon Watch will be gathering tonight at the Griffin. It's somewhat of a tradition after an action."

Riordan felt a lump in his throat and mumbled, "I . . . I'd be honored."

Khedra nodded. "Good. That's settled, then."

Morka pointed to Bashar's litter that was being car-ried from of the alley. "You'd better hurry. No knock on the head will keep Bashar from a party for long."

On the way out of the alley, Stilmus stopped Rior-dan.

"I have need of good men, son. I could find a place for

you in the Society of Swords. What do you say?"

Riordan looked first at Morka, then up the street at Bashar's disappearing litter. "Thank you, sir, but I think I've found my place right here."

Star of Tethyr

Thomas M. Reid

3 Eleasias, the Year of the Gauntlet

Merrick sighed in frustration as he once again dragged his damp sleeve across his brow to wipe away the dripping sweat. No matter how many times he scrubbed at his forehead with his arm, the perspiration still trickled down into his eyes and along the bridge of his nose, tickling him as it went. The hot stench of the pitch in the bucket in front of him did little to improve his mood, and he finally shoved it away from himself in disgust and sat back, squinting from the glare of the scorching sun bouncing off the water of the bay of Thordentor Island. What breeze blew in did little to disturb its glimmering surface, nor did it offer much relief from the muggy heat of the day.

"Oh, the sea," he grumbled to himself sarcastically. "A life of adventure in the good queen's navy, that's for me," he spat, not really caring if anyone else heard him. He scrubbed his hands absently across the knees of his pants, trying unsuccessfully to wipe away the blobs of half-dried pitch that made his palms sticky. He knew without looking in a reflecting glass that there was pitch on his face, in his hair, and certainly on his clothes.

Merrick turned his eyes back toward the water, to the *Star*. He stared longingly at the magnificent vessel several piers over, dreaming of sailing aboard her someday. *Star of Tethyr,* named for the newly crowned monarch herself, was fresh out of dry-dock and hadn't even taken her maiden voyage yet. At nearly fifty paces along her keel and a beam of fifteen paces, she was the largest the queen's navy had ever built. Her four masts stood proudly straight, but her crisp, white sails had yet to be unfurled. Atop the highest mast, Merrick spotted the Tethyrian standard, two green sea lions bearing a golden star, fluttering lazily. A few carpenters moved about her, finishing their work and readying her for the sea. She would make a fine flagship in the queen's growing navy.

"Merrick!" roared a voice behind the youth, making him jump. "The blessed queen doesn't pay you good silver to sit and stare at the water all day, boy!"

"N-no, Cap'n," Merrick answered guiltily, grabbing for the pitch bucket and brush without turning to face Captain Hoke.

"Finish up with that skiff, then report to Gullah. There's cargo to unload."

"Aye, Cap'n," Merrick responded glumly, shivering

despite the warmth. Gullah, *Lancer*'s first mate, had taken a disliking to Merrick the very first day they met, and the bulbous-eyed, beak-nosed man's mood had not improved in the two months since.

Merrick took one last peek at the *Star* and imagined what it would feel like to stand in the very bow, leaning into the head wind, as the magnificent ship cut through the swells of the open sea. Thinking of the fresh breeze on his face only reminded Merrick of how hot and muggy it was.

The queen can keep her silver, the youth thought, if I never have to look at another bucket of pitch again.

A shout arose from behind him. It was followed quickly by another, and Merrick heard "Sound the alarm!" and "Attack!" as the commotion quickly reached a crescendo. Merrick looked up and saw a couple of sailors pointing into the bay, but from where he was standing, *Lancer* blocked his view. A dozen or so others were scrambling madly about the decks or in the rigging, unfurling sails and pulling on halyards.

The entire quay was a mass of confusion. Merrick heard men and women shouting, and there were screams, too. People were running everywhere, from sailors to laborers to soldiers, all scurrying or just dashing madly past him.

What in creation is going on? he thought, still watching the sailors climbing above him.

Captain Hoke was yelling, "Keep them out of the bloody rigging!" when Merrick finally saw one. A lithe, green-scaled creature that stood like a man but was obviously built for the sea came tumbling over the side of *Lancer*'s gunwale, landing with a wet splat at Merrick's feet, a javelin protruding through both its chest and back. A wide death grin was spread across its face, showing too many razor-sharp teeth. It was covered in fins with sharp spines, and the hands that still clutched at the wooden shaft of the javelin were webbed. A cold, salty odor wafted from the creature, as of the deep sea, but what made Merrick gasp were the unblinking, soulless eyes that were all silver and pupil-less. Cold, dead eyes that stared at nothing sent a shiver down his spine.

"Damnation, Merrick!" yelled Hoke from overhead. "Quit standing there like a tart on her favorite corner and move, boy! Release those bloody lines and get up here!"

Merrick blinked, forcing himself to tear free of the death gaze of the creature, and lurched forward to loosen the rope entwined around the bollards. As it came free in his hands, he saw that the gangway was already being pulled up by a pair of sailors. The frigate began inching slowly away from the pier as the sweeps dipped into the water.

Two more of the creatures appeared suddenly on the quay, not ten paces from Merrick. They had shot up out of the water like quarrels fired from a crossbow, dropping to their feet smoothly, water cascading down their glistening, scaly skin. Each held a dangerous-looking trident and was crouched, scanning for prey. When they spotted Merrick, they turned and made for him, their webbed feet slapping wetly on the stones.

Desperately, Merrick shouted for help as he drew up the slack in the coarse mooring line and leaped up, swinging out over the water and bracing his feet against the hull of the frigate. He grunted as he slammed against *Lancer*'s side and slipped downward a few feet, feeling the rough hemp of the line chaffing his hands raw. Pulling hand over fist as hard as he could, he began climbing, dragging himself up and away from the vicious creatures. Two other sailors who had been hauling the mooring lines saw the danger behind him and launched javelins at the beasts. The two creatures easily avoided the missiles, but it was enough of a delay. Grabbing Merrick by an arm each, the sailors hauled him the rest of the way up. He scrambled over the gunwale and landed with a thud, his heart beating madly as nervous sweat drenched his back.

Bloody sea devils, he thought. They're attacking in the middle of the bloody day!

All around Merrick, *Lancer*'s deck was a scene of frantic chaos. More of the sea devils—sahuagin as they called themselves—had boarded the ship, and sailors fought desperately against them. One of the beasts broke through, gutting a man with the fin along its arm and leaving him screaming, then made for the rigging and clambered up it easily, slicing ropes and sails to ribbons as it went.

"Damnation!" thundered Hoke. "Keep them away from the bloody rigging! We're all sleeping with the fish if we can't get underway!"

Someone fired a crossbow at the sahuagin and caught it squarely in the chest. It spasmed once then went limp, tumbling partially down until it was hung up in the ropes, fouling them further. Hoke had already turned and was running a wounded sea devil through with a spear by the time the one in the rigging stopped moving.

Merrick gaped in awe at the savage battle being waged around him until a tough, leather-skinned sailor who was running by paused and grabbed him by his collar.

261

"Move, lad!" the snaggle-toothed woman yelled in the youth's face, her breath stinking of fish. "The bloody dragon turtles'll get us!"

The sailor was gone.

Merrick shuddered, remembering the tales sailors told as they gathered in the evenings in the lone taproom on the island, telling grisly stories of ships going down, their decks swarming with sea devils and their hulls punched full of holes from the fierce dragon turtles. Great, snapping jaws that could crush a man in half, or the scalding hot breath that warped wood and boiled a man's skin from his body were the hallmarks of these sea monsters. If they didn't get *Lancer* away from the docks and out into the bay where she could outrun the beasts, she'd go to the bottom for certain. He shook his head and peered out past the side of the ship toward the rest of the harbor.

Everywhere there was turmoil. Knots of men, women, and sahuagin fought while ships milled about, some listing to the side and half sunk already, others floating aimlessly, their now-tattered sails flapping crazily in the breeze and their rigging a tangled mess. The attack was thorough and complete. Few ships would make it out of the harbor.

Lancer might not make it, either, Merrick told himself sternly, unless we get into open water.

The youth darted toward the stern of the ship where four ballistae, huge crossbows that launched barbed wooden spears nearly as thick as Merrick's leg, sat upon the sterncastle. Before he had taken three steps he was nearly run down by a sailor tugging a halyard tight. The sailor cursed at him but never stopped, and Merrick had to duck to escape getting entangled in the rope. He started forward again, this time being careful to weave around the sailors who crossed his path.

Most of the fighting had subsided. There were only one or two sea devils still on the deck of the ship, and most of the sails were hoisted now. Merrick could feel the ship beginning to gain some speed as the sails unfurled fully into the breeze.

The youth breathed a small sigh of relief as he reached his artillery unit. *Lancer*'ll make it! he grinned despite himself, thrilling at the fresh, salty breeze that drove the frigate forward and cooled his skin. We're going to make it!

Lancer was a fine enough ship, a fast frigate built for war, but this was the first time she had put to sea since Merrick had come aboard two months ago. He and the rest of her crew had been working long days, building the new shipyards on Thordentor. The youth's gaze swept across the deck of the frigate and past the water of the bay to the sad little shanty town that was being built a little back from the beach. So far, they had little to show for their efforts.

Too much time spent building the ships to give much thought to decent homes, thought Merrick with a disdainful sniff. At least it was better than what the soldiers had been living in before. He glanced beyond the buildings to the old and crumbling watch tower, a fading remnant of some ancient civilization. He hated even imagining what it must have been like for the company of Tethyrian guardsmen before the shipyards sprang up. Nothing at all to do but wait for the next supply ship to arrive from the mainland, nothing to look at but white sand and low, scrubby bushes, as far as the eye could see.

And now, thought Merrick, there's still nothing much to see at all.

"Merrick! Get over here and get ready to handle reload." It was Retny, the chief gunner for the unit. The man was standing at the rear of a starboard ballista, already making adjustments for aiming at targets low in the water.

"Aye, sir," Merrick replied, taking his place near the stockpile of the huge, barbed missiles designed to be fired from the giant weapon. "What will we be shooting at today, sir?" he asked, a grin on his face. He grabbed up the crossbow that was sitting there, holding it easily in the crook of his arm. It was also his job to watch the unit's back between reloads.

"Nothing, if we're half lucky," Retny replied. "If we have to start shooting at dragon turtles, then we've already let them get too—"

His words cut off suddenly in a strange, strangled squawk and he lurched backward, a long, slender shaft protruding from his chest. The artillerist stumbled into the youth and knocked him off-balance, then fell to the deck and was still, lying across Merrick's legs. Merrick stared up in horror as a sahuagin hanging from the side of the ship tossed the crossbow it had just fired back into the water and began to clamber up over the gunwale. In one webbed hand, it held a jagged-bladed dagger. Merrick could see two more of the creatures pulling themselves into view from the side of the ship even as the first beast took a threatening step toward him.

"Look out!" Merrick croaked, his throat constricted in terror, even as one of the other artillerists, holding a huge bolt, swung it in a wide arc like a great sword.

The blow caught the scaly attacker full in the chest and knocked it backward against the gunwale. Merrick fired his own weapon, the bolt catching the beast squarely under the jaw. It lost its balance and dropped from view. Other men were there now, blades in hand, trying to drive the remaining two back over the side.

Merrick scrambled out from under Retny—still lying across the youth's legs, soaking the deck with his blood—and leaped back, staring in horror. The man's face was twisted in a sick scream that wouldn't make a sound, his hand feebly opening and closing around the shaft of the quarrel in his chest. He turned and looked at Merrick, trying to speak, but nothing emerged, and with a final spasm, Retny's eyes went blank and his head rolled to the side, staring at nothing.

Merrick wanted to retch. If he'd been paying more attention, if he'd been a moment quicker, he might have seen the creature before it fired, but he had been too late to save Retny.

The two other sea devils that had come aboard had been driven back over the side again, but others had mounted attacks elsewhere on the frigate. Once more, sailors grimly dueled with the hated beasts, driving them all off again at the last, but not before several more men had gone down.

Merrick groaned. Without Retny, the ballista was all but useless. Cocking and loading it shorthanded would be difficult enough, but Retny was the only one among them who had any experience firing the weapon.

"Come about, you dogs!" Captain Hoke roared. "*Centaur* and *Ram* have broken free and are running for open water!" A small cheer erupted from the crew. "We'll run with them, and send these devilfish back to hell! Now, move, you bloody fools!"

The angle of the sun changed as the ship turned in the water. Merrick glanced over his shoulder, looking back toward the harbor, and saw that two other frigates had separated from the destruction at the docks and were under full sail. Behind them, the rest of the ships burned or sat half beneath the surface. The attack had been successful, the small fleet at Thordentor was all but annihilated. Merrick swallowed hard and looked to see what *Star of Tethyr*'s fate had been. When he did, he gasped in surprise.

The ship had somehow managed to escape the docks, but in the fury of the battle it had strayed off course, near to the dangerous shoals along one side of the bay. Her sails were only half up, and she didn't seem to be tacking properly. From this distance it was hard to tell, but there seemed to Merrick's eyes to be a great deal of fighting going on.

"Cap'n!" Merrick called out, noting that his voice rang clearly. Most of the crew worked in grim silence now, ready to go where their captain demanded, even if it meant taking the battle back to the hated sea devils. "Cap'n, it's the *Star*." He pointed.

Hoke swore softly to himself and drew out his spyglass, gazing toward the struggling ship for a long moment.

"Bloody hells," he growled. "Gullah has her underway, but without near enough crew to sail and fight, too."

"Cap'n!" came a cry from the crow's nest high overhead. Merrick looked up to see a lone sailor aloft, studying the *Star* with another spyglass. "Three dragon turtles, closing with the *Star!*"

Hoke swore again, louder this time. "Blast! They'll never make it. She's weaponless, too. No ballistae aboard her, yet."

A rumble of anger and sorrow arose from the crew. Without ballistae, Merrick knew, the ship didn't have a prayer of warding off the dragon turtles. Hoke watched the *Star* for a moment longer as the crew seemed to hold its collective breath, wondering what orders the captain would give.

Finally, Hoke slammed his glass into the pouch at his belt. "Blast!" he roared again. "I'll not let them take her without a fight!" A cheer rose up from the crew, Merrick's voice as loud as the rest. "Signal *Centaur* and *Ram* to follow!" Hoke ordered, "We're coming about! Helmsman, set your heading for *Star of Tethyr!*"

A thrill ran through Merrick as *Lancer* began to come about, her sails billowing and flapping as her crew madly trimmed them for the new heading. She caught the stiff breeze more directly now, and seemed to leap ahead, eager to engage the enemy. Aft, both *Centaur* and *Ram* pushed through *Lancer's* wash in an effort to keep up.

"Listen up!" bellowed Captain Hoke. "When we reach the *Star,* we rake the thrice-bedamned dragon turtles with artillery, *Centaur* and *Ram* following our lead. The rest of you make bloody sure nothing gets aboard this ship. Don't make me sorry we came back. I want those bloody beasts to look like sea urchins!"

Merrick groaned softly to himself. Without Retny, his unit was crippled. He looked around desperately at the other three ballistae mounted on the sterncastle. Each of them still had a full complement of men, primed and ready to fire when needed. He moved to the artillerist of the other starboard weapon and said, "We lost our gunner, sir. We're shorthanded and have no one to fire the weapon."

The man eyed him critically for a moment, then nodded toward the crossbow in Merrick's hands. "You know how to fire that thing?"

Merrick nodded. "Aye, sir. I practiced with my pa's growing up. He was in the militia back home."

The man nodded. "Then you're the new gunner." He turned to one of his own crew. "Thurin—we can manage shorthanded here. You cover for the boy."

Thurin eyed Merrick uncertainly, but nodded curtly and moved across to the other ballista, reaching for the crossbow in Merrick's hand to assume his responsibilities.

Merrick himself stood there, staring in bewilderment at the artillerist who had just promoted him. He opened his mouth to speak, but closed it again without saying a word. He turned back to the ballista, shaking.

Me? he thought. I've never fired one of these in my life!

Suddenly, Merrick was remembering with clarity the day he had enlisted in the navy. Gullah was there, at the dockside tavern in Zazesspur, sitting at one of the crude wooden tables, coarse parchment spread out, glaring sourly as Merrick came looking to join the queen's navy.

"You're nothing but a farm boy," Gullah spat. "And a runt at that. Go back home to your cows, boy, and leave the sea to the men."

But Merrick wouldn't be cowed so easily. He argued with the frowning man, insisting he could be of use, until another sailor, overhearing the argument, came over and stood in front of Merrick. The sailor towered over the boy, appraising him with a critical eye. Merrick stared at the floor then, for the youth sensed that this sailor was someone of authority, used to giving orders.

The man's stance was easy, his coat a bit faded but the buttons still shiny. His boots were high and soft, and he wore a wide belt from which hung an open pouch holding a spyglass. The man smelled slightly of spiced fish and sea spray.

"What's your name, lad?" The sailor had asked.

"M-Merrick, sir."

"And why do you want to join the good queen's navy, Merrick?"

"To sail on a ship and see the world," the youth answered. "And because I want to do right by the queen, long may her reign be. I reckon she's put a lot into this realm, and it's the least I can do to give a little back again."

The looming sailor laughed, a big, hearty, booming laugh. "Well, lad, you'll see the world, all right. All the dirtiest, most foul, stinking parts of it, to be sure, but you'll see it." He turned to the sour man behind the table. "Enlist him, Gullah. I have a notion his spunk will serve *Lancer* well."

"Aye, Cap'n Hoke," Gullah answered, looking even more disgruntled, if that was possible, as Captain Hoke stomped back to his table.

"Well, runt, you've become a sailor," Gullah growled. "I doubt you'll amount to much, regardless what the captain says. Pray you stay out of my way, boy." And with that, Merrick had joined the navy of Tethyr.

Now, Gullah's words echoed in Merrick's ears, seeming to haunt him. Thurin and the others eyed the youth expectantly, waiting for him to assume command of the ballista. Still shaking his head, he looked down at the body of Retny, where someone had tugged the man's cloak over his head out of respect. He felt the shame of failing to protect the man, but set his jaw.

I will make up for it, Merrick swore to himself. *I'll prove Gullah wrong.*

The youth took his place at the rear of the weapon and begin to adjust it, like he'd seen Retny do during drills, trying to get a feel for the thing. Surprisingly, it was mounted well and felt more like a crossbow than he had expected. He balanced the thing and tried aiming it a few times, hoping he was getting a true feel for it.

For the first time since the attack, Merrick realized that he was no longer sweating. The sun was still hot and clear overhead, but the salty breeze and the fear of the coming battle seemed to leave him feeling cold rather than hot and damp. His mouth felt like wool and he longingly eyed the water barrel nearby. It wouldn't do to leave his station, so he tried to ignore his thirst. He turned his attention back to the water rushing by, waiting for a target and an opportunity to fire.

"The dragon turtles are closing fast on the *Star*, Cap'n," called the lookout in the crow's nest. "It's gonna be close."

Hoke nodded, peering through his glass at the besieged ship once more. "Ready with those tree shooters," he growled. "We'll be on top of them fast at this speed."

Lancer was almost in range of the dragon turtles when the first wave of sea devil attacks hit it. Groups of sahuagin launched themselves out of the water, landing in tight groups on deck and fighting with daggers and tridents. Merrick eyed them nervously but stood fast, keeping an eye on the water and waiting for targets to come into view. At one point, a sea devil made it to the sterncastle, and it was all Merrick could do to keep from cowering away, but Thurin wounded the beast with a shot from the crossbow and other sailors ganged up on it and drove it back into the water. *Lancer*'s crew fought furiously, driving more than one wave back off into the bay. Combatants went down on both sides, but the sea devils never gained a good foothold on the ship.

"Steady," Captain Hoke called at last, "Artillery, prepare to fire." Merrick tried to swallow and tightened his grip on the ballista. "Helmsman, port seven degrees. We're going right between the bloody beasts!"

Merrick caught sight of the first dragon turtle and nearly fell to his knees in fright. The beast was huge, its deep green shell alone ten paces long and covered with sharp, silvery ridges that could easily shatter the planks of most hulls. Its lighter green head loomed out of the water, jutting forward as the creature swam easily, but unlike any turtle Merrick had ever seen. The beast looked for all the world like a great, vicious sea serpent, one of the fearsome illustrations that decorated some of Captain Hoke's maps. He gaped at the dragon turtle's giant hooked mouth and golden, razor-sharp spines running down the back of its neck, remembering the tales the other sailors had told, shuddering.

The beast growled menacingly, a deep rumble that sounded like strange words to Merrick, and glared balefully at *Lancer* as the frigate churned past it. Merrick swallowed thickly, wondering if the cold gleam in the creature's eye was meant for him alone.

The other ballista on the starboard side fired immediately, and Merrick blinked as he watched the missile bounce harmlessly off the creature's shell.

I've got to hit the head, he thought, and brought the ballista to bear. He steadied his aim, holding his breath, and fired. The bow twanged sharply and

Merrick felt the weapon kick as the bolt knifed into the water five paces from where he had targeted. Merrick groaned. He hadn't anticipated the speed of the ship. The beast began to submerge, retreating temporarily from the sudden attack.

"Reload!" the youth yelled, desperate for another try before the beast was out of sight.

The men were instantly in motion, cocking and re-arming the ballista amazingly fast and yet agonizingly slowly. It was no good. By the time he was armed for another shot, only the tip of the shell still glided on the surface, and the angle was already awkward. *Lancer* had run by too quickly.

"Second target ahead," called the artillerist for the other ballista. "Leave that one for the other ships."

Merrick turned and saw that there was, indeed, a second dragon turtle, this one busily swimming toward *Star of Tethyr.*

Around him, Merrick was dimly aware that more sahuagin had boarded *Lancer* and that a furious fight was taking place for control of the ship. He could hear Captain Hoke screaming orders to the men and women, but he ignored it, concentrating solely on finding the right aim for the ballista. At one point, Thurin fired the crossbow at something behind Merrick, but he nervously ignored it too and waited, lining up the weapon.

This time, when he thought the angle was good enough, Merrick didn't hesitate, wanting to leave himself time for a second shot. He aimed a little behind the target, trying to compensate for *Lancer*'s speed. He fired the ballista and was rewarded with a direct hit— a little back of the dragon turtle's head, on the tip of its shell. The bolt stuck there, jutting out like a crooked

272

mast, but the dragon turtle didn't seem phased by the intrusion. The sister weapon fired, and its missile grazed the creature's neck, causing it to whip its head around and growl at them furiously.

"Reload!" Merrick yelled, but his crew was already in action.

As the bow was cocked again and the bolt laid into place, the dragon turtle swerved slightly closer to the side of the ship. It reared upward, staring coldly at the men manning the other ballista, and opened its huge mouth.

"Look out! It's going to blow!" one of the sailors shouted, but it was too late. A great gout of steam blasted from the beast's mouth, and Merrick stumbled back away from the scalding vapors as others were caught full in its heat, screaming and lurching away in agony. Merrick crouched as the super-heated cloud of water billowed across the deck of the ship, feeling his clothing suddenly drenched in warm, foul-smelling moisture.

When the cloud dissipated a bit, Merrick blanched. Men lay unmoving, their skin boiled and red, visages frozen in pain and horror. He turned away and saw his own crew unharmed, and his ballista armed and ready. He darted forward, praying that the hated dragon turtle was still in sight. He peered over the edge of the gunwale and saw it, still swimming alongside *Lancer,* but slipping back as the swifter ship passed it by.

Merrick quickly swung the ballista around and took aim, his hands shaking in fear and revulsion. He sighted down the length of the bolt, picking a spot a little behind the beast's head, and took a deep breath. He fired. His eyes stayed focused directly on the spot he had targeted, and the missile flew true. As it closed, the dragon turtle's head slid into the line of sight, and the barbed head of the bolt sank deeply into the creature's flesh, a little behind one eye. It roared in pain and fury and immediately dived, swimming at an awkward angle, thick, dark blood streaming behind it. Merrick's heart leaped into his throat.

I hit it! He crowed to himself. I did it! He glanced around and saw Thurin grinning at him, as well as the other members of the unit.

"Reload!" he called, a grin wide on his face.

The sailors around him obeyed. He'd issued an order, and seasoned seamen hopped to. He glanced back at a pitch bucket sitting idle on the deck, waiting for the swabby who'd left it to return to his drudgery. Merrick knew that when the battle was over he might have to go back to his own pitch bucket, but he would go back to it a sailor. He'd go back to it a man.

He was set to fire again in no time at all, but *Lancer* had already shot past the fight. As she came about, Merrick began scanning the water, waiting for the chance to fire another shot, but the chance never came.

Cheers rose up from everywhere, and Merrick turned to see why. As quickly as it had started, the battle was over. The sahuagin were abandoning the attack on *Star of Tethyr* and departing in droves, leaping over the side to escape the deadly cloud of missiles being fired from *Centaur* and *Ram*. Two of the dragon turtles had been killed and the other two wounded, and those two were in full retreat. The *Star* herself was a sorry sight, her once fine sails ruined and her rigging a tangled, shredded mess, but she was intact. The remainder of her crew, led by First Mate Gullah, cheered the three smaller vessels as they came about once more.

Merrick smiled and sagged down, relief draining the remaining strength from his knees.

We did it, he thought. We saved *Star of Tethyr*. The price had been high, he realized, as he saw the numerous bodies on the decks of both *Lancer* and *Star*, but they had saved the pride of the queen's navy.

Thurin slapped Merrick on the back, grinning from ear to ear. Hoke was roaring at his crew to come along side the *Star* and secure her for boarding, kicking a man in the rear who didn't move fast enough for his liking, but Merrick could see a twinkle in his eye. The captain was proud of his crew, a crew Merrick was finally really a part of.

"Long live the queen!" a seaman shouted from the rigging.

"Long live the queen!" the crew exclaimed, and they broke into song, a victory chantey. Merrick sang along, smiling to himself.

Long live the queen, he thought, long live *Star of Tethyr*.

Persana's Blade

Steven E. Schend

10 Eleasias, the Year of the Gauntlet

Here before him was the life he hoped for—the exciting life outside the walls of the Tower of Numos amid all the excitement of war and magic. The battle lay spread out before him, the great triton priest Numos and his warrior comrade Balas facing off against First Arcane Xynakt of the Morkoth Arcanum. He saw it all—the deaths caused by the rampaging morkoths, the savagery of their kraken allies, and the resolution of the triton that all the death and pain would end here that day.

He saw everything save the many carved coral heads of tritons and hippocampi in the army. The smaller figures often became blurred when covered by the detritus and marine snow that drifted into the chambers from the upwaters. Keros buffed the mural clean with a rag of sharkskin, returning the Founders' Battle to cleanliness and clarity. All around him were murals of heroism and faith, and Keros had the distasteful job of polishing all the mosaics before evening prayers.

"If you don't start applying yourself to your studies, Keros, you'll never amount to anything. Feh," Keros muttered aloud, sarcastically mimicking his father's tone and shaking his finger emphatically against the current.

He quickly glanced around to see if anyone heard him. Finding himself alone, he dived in a quick spiral to shake off his unease. The young triton still smarted from the argument he'd had with his father a few hours previous. Keros had been reprimanded for abandoning his morning prayers to see the armies massing and heading upwater to investigate the mourning songs of the whales and the other sounds of conflict there. He'd been caught swimming back to his chambers. His father was sitting where Keros should have been, reading what he was to know for the next day's service. As punishment, First Priest Moras sent his youngest son to the antechambers of the Great Vault to polish the mosaics—a practically endless task as they spanned the nearly thirteen fathom-deep walls from floor to ceiling on both sides of the corridor leading to the vault.

Getting back to his task, Keros swam easily across the hall to the uppermost mosaic, momentarily catching a glimpse of himself reflected in the crystalline doors to the Great Vault. He had almost reached his full growth, his shoulders and frame having filled in with strong muscles. His skin had lost the lighter blue of his youth and now its deeper color signified his entry into adulthood. While a contrast from the norm, Keros had long since stopped wondering why his hair was a kelp green rather than the usual blue, and accepted it. Though he shaved it off more than once, it had grown back to a full mane of hair trailing just past his shoulders now. He looked like an adult—why couldn't they treat him like one?

Keros knew that many expected him to become a priest like his mother and father both, though the closer he got to his indoctrination from acolyte to the ranks of the clergy, the more pensive and sullen he became.

They never ask me what I want, he began the argument in his head for the thousandth time, because they're still mad at Nalos for rejecting the church and joining the army. I don't want to do that—by Persana's mane, I don't know what I want to do—but they've never given me a choice. They just assume I'll become a priest like them, and they don't listen when I tell them I don't hear Persana's voice in me.

Keros began buffing the mosaic depicting the capture of the Arsenal of Xynakt, binding the unholy items in solid ice, but his anger put more force behind his hand, and he heard a crackle beneath the rag.

Panic brought Keros out of his reverie, and he brought the rag away from the mural. Coral chips over a thousand years old glistened in the rag, and many more now tumbled off the wall. He sank as quickly as his heart did, scooping up the fragments before they drifted too far in the waters. A roaring began in his ears as he began to imagine the punishments his father would dole out for such sacrilege. Far worse would be the disappointment in his mother's eyes, for she loved these murals with a passion. In one second, Keros had ruined a priceless treasure. Having caught what appeared to be all of the fragments, Keros swam up the wall again to look at the damage, though the small pile of coral in his cupped hands seemed more terrifying than a horde of koalinth descending out of the gloom.

Returning to the mural, Keros gasped in horror. He had totally crushed and eradicated the mosaic of Numos casting the ice around the artifacts taken from the morkoth. While Numos's figure still remained on the wall, there now loomed a jagged blank spot between him and the figure of the wounded Balas. Keros shifted the coral fragments into his right hand and touched the blank area with his left. The stone wall felt rough from the missing coral pieces, but it too crumbled at his touch. Pushing himself away from the wall in another wave of fear, Keros gasped as cracks appeared in the very spot he'd last touched. They grew wider with each passing beat of his heart. The coral chips drifted out of his right hand and down through the water to the floor, forgotten as Keros watched an entire section of the wall crack and split from where he touched it.

Distracted by his rising panic and the roaring in his ears, Keros had ignored the sounds before now. Fearing the worst punishments, the triton boy imagined the loud booms to be cell doors slamming behind him as he mentally threw himself into the dungeons beneath Vuuvax, city of the Wrathful. He finally recognized them to be real sounds as the cracks widened, and the wall exploded inward. Thrown back by the force of the blast, Keros barely registered the chunk of coral carved to represent Xynakt the Arcane flying toward his head by the time the blackness closed around him.

* * * * *

Keros swam fitfully through the seas, as he had seemed to be swimming for days. No matter how quickly he swam, the sharks kept to the waters around him. His heart racing, Keros wondered why they didn't close in for the kill. He was tired and wounded, with blood clouding the water around him, and they proved more than a match for his speed. One shark lunged at him and Keros dived frantically, leaving the shark with only a mouthful of green hair and Keros with a sharp pain in his head. The other shark closed in and Keros found himself too tired to avoid this one's attack. He blinked once, then opened his eyes to see his death coming—as his father would want him to do. The jagged teeth of the shark seemed innumerable and—

—the shark veered upward and thumped him on the chest with its tail.

Keros blinked in shock, then woke up to his little sister Charan pounding on his chest in terror.

"Wakeupwakeupwakeupwakeup! Keros! Getupgetupgetup," she screamed.

She kept her eyes firmly shut in desperation as she clung to the only thing she wanted right now—her brother to wake up and make things better for her. She almost looked comical perched there, flailing her little four-year-old arms against his chest as hard as she could, but he could hear the fear in her wails.

"All right, all right, Char, I'm awake. What's . . . ?"

Keros grabbed her hands and held them as he woke

up more fully, and his senses came back to him. All around him was rubble, the coppery smell of blood, and the sharp tang of fear. His head pounded, but he didn't seem to have any wounds on him. Keros almost believed he was still hallucinating, as the Founders' Battle erupted once more all around him. Where the broken mosaic once was there now gaped a massive hole in the wall, which had also knocked out the supports and archway for the doors into the Great Vault. The doors lay in massive fragments on the hall's floor. Keros and Charan huddled among them in an impromptu lean-to of stone. While the lucent coral globes still provided light to the hall, more light streamed out of the Great Vault, as did the shadows of fighting figures made large in shadow on the shattered wall.

All about Keros and Charan lay the shards of the Great Vault's doors and the broken bodies of triton priests who'd died defending home and honor. Each time she saw another dead body—often a family friend whom they both knew—Charan grew wide-eyed and silent, her tiny grip nearly puncturing the webbing between Keros's fingers. Keros lifted her onto one of his arms and looked toward the former exit. "Let's get out of here, Char," he said.

She nodded silently, one hand around his neck and the other firmly planted thumb first in her mouth. Her gills and nostrils flared wildly, and he knew she was terrified. Keros began to hum Charan's favorite lullaby, the melody audible to her via her touch on his throat. As she relaxed slightly, Keros began swimming toward the far end of the hall, using the rubble for cover. He didn't know what brought the morkoths here, but he knew he couldn't face them while he had charge of his sister.

Charan began to whimper, the high sobs resonating through the water. Keros heard someone swimming swiftly in pursuit of them, and exhaled in relief as Second Priest Naran flashed through the waters far above them, her glowing trident preceding her out of the Vault. She appeared tense and ready for battle, but she heard her children beneath her and swam to meet them.

"Thank Persana you're alive, Mother," Keros said in a relieved exhale as he swam up to meet her. When she turned to him, Keros saw a look he'd never seen before—a look of despair.

"Keros, listen very carefully to me—no arguments." Locking eyes with him, Naran shook her mane of sapphire hair back as she glanced at the Vault. "Arcount Axar Xyrl and his morkoths have invaded Abydos. Though their efforts concentrated first on the tower your father guessed correctly that they're after the Armory of Xynakt."

As she talked, she undid the strange belt at her waist and handed Keros a strange shaped item. A bright golden loop shone atop a long, flat, hide-covered sheath, all of which was hooked to the belt by golden loops.

"The morkoths have broken out a number of the artifacts once held by Xynakt, and we must keep them from claiming them. Take this—and your sister—and get out of here. Head up to the sunlit water and find your brother. Until you hear otherwise, it's not safe here."

Charan embraced Naran with the fierceness of a child in need, and Naran hugged her back just as intensely. Naran pried her daughter loose and handed her to Keros when she heard the sounds of more tritons dying behind her in the Great Vault, which lay open and exposed to the outer waters. Naran cupped her hands around Charan's chin and kissed her forehead.

Gripping her son's forearm in a sign of respect that showed she considered him an adult triton, Naran nodded seriously and said, "Go, my son, and keep yourselves and that sword safe from our enemies. Persana's grace shall lead you to calm waters." Her eyes shining, she kissed him on the forehead, then turned sharply and said, "We'll meet again when we can."

She turned and swam up to intercept a warrior morkoth swimming down toward them. While he longed to be of help, Keros still had to see to Charan's safety.

Swimming as fast as he could, Keros arced through the tunnels of the Tower of Numos despite Charan's screaming. The girl desperately wanted her mother now that she realized she wasn't following them. Ignoring her cries but holding her all the more tightly in one arm, Keros swam up into a corridor that attached the tower to the stables. If he could reach the stables, they could get away quickly and keep this "sword"—whatever that was—away from the Ollethan dark ones.

Making another turn, Keros's hopes plummeted as a dark shape moved to block his path far ahead of them. Its tentacles undulated beneath it, and its silvery-black hide glistened in the arcane purple light of the rod it held.

"Give that to Duupax, you should, and allow you to live Duupax shall. Oppose Duupax you cannot, young triton." The morkoth clacked its beak and laughed mirthlessly at his prey.

Keros found himself smiling as all of his rage, fear,

and confusion drained away. The sword was emitting a blinding energy through its pommel that gave him a plan. Barely by conscious thought, he doubled his speed in the long corridor rather than slow and stop. He brought the glowing sword out ahead of him, gripping it near the top of the scabbard without touching the metal grip. Before Duupax could finish the spell he was weaving against them, Keros had closed the distance and slammed fully into the morkoth with the sword grip preceding him. Keros was braced for the impact, and he held onto Charan easily, but he was not expecting what happened next.

Intending to slam into and force his way past the morkoth, Keros yelled as the sword hilt's glow increased to blinding brightness, and the smell of seared flesh filled the water around Duupax's head. Duupax screamed a shrill grating noise that drowned out Keros's yell and the bubbling noise of the point of contact. The bowed grip and pommel burned its shape into the morkoth's face, encircling its right eye and part of its cheek. The light burned directly into Duupax's purple eyes, causing the morkoth even more pain.

Keros lowered his arm to get the light out of his face, but did not slow his pace or loosen his grip on the sword. Duupax, who'd been carried nearly two dozen feet from the point of impact, fell off the weapon and dropped to the ground, clutching his face. Keros wondered for a second about going back and making sure the morkoth was unable to harm them, but the stables and their safety were close at hand.

"You can't fight until Charan is out of danger, fool," he chastised himself. "Get her and this thing away from them, then you can prove you're adult enough to return to battle."

Swimming into the stables, Keros finally pulled to a halt at the nearest stall, his legs burning from overexertion. The stall belonged to Wavestar, their father's hippocampus companion, who nickered at Keros's brusque entrance and backed away from the two tritons. Keros swam toward the proud beast, his palms out before him to calm the beast as he spoke. "Wavestar, I have to ask a favor of you. We are overrun by mor—"

The hippocampus thumped its powerful tail indignantly against the ground, his sign for wishing to enter battle, and the action was mirrored by other hippocampi looking to their herd leader for direction.

"No!" Keros shouted, the hippocampi and his little sister a bit stunned by the force in his voice. Collecting himself, he placed Charan on Wavestar's back despite much fussing on her part, and strapped her in with a kelp frond rope. "Mother wants us safely out of here with this—" he showed Wavestar the golden sword and belt before looping it around his powerful neck "—so the blasted morkoths can't use it against us or some upwater folk. I need you to find our brother Nalos, Moras's eldest son. He's gone upwater and that's the only safe place for us right now. Can you take us to him? Can you keep Charan safe from all harm until Father can come for us all?"

The hippocampus cocked his head at Keros, as if to mull over what he'd been told, and after using his head fins to tickle his small rider, Wavestar nodded his head, and began cantering toward the stable exits.

With a snort and a whinny, Wavestar directed two other hippocampi to join him in protecting Charan, while a third—Keros's own companion and mount, Swiftide—moved over to the young triton. Keros grabbed a small trident off the wall as well as a net, which he draped in a loop around one shoulder. He wished he'd worn his harness or a belt, but now he'd have to take only what he could drape across his unclad body or carry. As he thought about more weapons and some food for the trip, a tremulous voice whined for his attention.

"Keros! Don't leave me! I'm scared!" cried Charan, as she tried to wriggle out of the straps that held her safely on Wavestar's back.

Wavestar nickered and looked back at him. As he swung up onto Swiftide's back, Keros spoke softly to her, though he kept a sharp eye on the doors leading from the tower.

"Don't worry, Charan, you'll be safe as a bedded pearl with Wavestar. Remember how long he's kept Father safe?" He and Swiftide swam alongside, and he readjusted the straps she'd worked loose. "Why don't you try and teach Wavestar one of your songs? I'm sure he'd love that. Just lean in close and whisper it to him as we travel." Keros caught the indignant look and snort from the powerful beast, but they both understood that Charan needed the distraction for them to get away safely. "Now get ready, and hang on tight. By your command, Wavestar."

The quartet of hippocampi and their two riders swiftly swam out of the stables and headed due north. Just as they cleared the courtyard of the Tower of Numos, Keros heard his mother scream her mate's name—and he immediately urged Swiftide up and around, back toward the tower.

"Take Charan upwater to Nalos, Wavestar, and protect her and the sword. We'll follow when we can, but I've got to go help, and keep anything else from following you," Keros called back to the trio, which stayed on its course despite the protests of its young charge. "Good currents, friend."

While it hurt tremendously to do so, he had to leave Charan to check on his parents. She was safe—he knew that—but he had to be certain their parents were safe as well, even though the rage in his mother's scream left that outcome in serious doubt. Keros shrugged off his fears and headed for the huge opening torn in the side of the Tower of Numos. He got some grave satisfaction at seeing the kraken that created the entry dying under a score of military tridents. He just hoped the battle inside fared as well as the one outside.

Even before he reached the central Great Vault, Keros heard the screams of the wounded and the moans of the dying. Swiftide reluctantly swam into the building despite the smells of fear and death, due to his loyalty to and trust of Keros. They followed the path torn open through numerous walls and defenses to breach the Great Vault. Keros had never been inside it, and his first view showed him his first war.

The room was over seventy feet high and round on all sides save the wall where the doors once stood. Gleaming white coral lined all surfaces, and numerous holes were smashed into the walls, revealing hidden caches of items, books, and sundries swiftly looted by morkoth invaders.

The great Armory of Xynakt should have floated on the currents at the heart of the chamber, trapped in magical ice that never melted. Keros knew the armory had already been violated, since Naran had given him one of the artifacts—that strange surface-worlder weapon called a "sun sword"—that now swung around Wavestar's neck, heading for safety in the upwaters.

A cloud of blood, shards of ice, and flotsam swirled where the artifacts once bobbed. Only the largest of the pieces remained intact, though it held the most malefic treasure of them all, the desiccated Claw of Xynakt—or, more properly, Xynakt's entire left arm, with the powerful gem set in its palm. The ice held it for now, but the red glowing tentacle cast by a large morkoth who hovered near the ceiling was wrapped around it. As Keros watched, cracks were forming on the ice sheath around the claw.

Keros looked down to see hundreds of ice fragments floating in the chamber, along with the broken bodies of priests who died defending their faith and their stronghold. Blood clung in the water, causing Swiftide to begin to panic slightly.

Still, the pair moved forward, and Keros called out, "Mother! Father! I've come to help!"

Instantly reacting to Keros's shout, a morkoth slid into his path, clicking its beak and menacing them with its claws, only to be met by a fierce head butt by Swiftide. Keros followed that with his small trident, skewering the creature's heart, but the attack cost him his weapon as it remained lodged in the chest of its victim.

Keros dropped the trident just as he spotted both his parents in the lower parts of the chamber. He recognized Naran by her strong, clear voice as she cast a spell paralyzing the foes facing her, though Keros saw another trio of morkoths close around her. Despite her own danger, she seemed intent on another part of the room. He followed her eyes and found his father, pinned at the midpoint of one wall by a trident through his leg and trunk, blood clouding thick around his slumped figure.

"No!" Keros yelled, and spurred his steed forward. "Help my mother, Swiftide. I've got to save my father."

Keros dived off Swiftide's back, diving sharply down, dodging ice shards that now acted as obstacles rather than defenses. Keros swam in search of a weapon conspicuously absent from his father's hands for the first time in years. Behind and above him, Keros heard the loud cracking of the ice and his mother yelling, "Keros—get out of here *now!*"

Naran's voice intermingled with the loud neighs of Swiftide, as the hippocampus lent his hooves and fins to battling the morkoth. Keros wanted to explain why he was here, but he couldn't even explain it to himself. His father seemed dead, but his legacy would not be abandoned to these scavengers.

Keros kept a sharp ear out for incoming attacks, but surprisingly none came as he tore through the rubble on the chamber floor. A glint of dark metal revealed what he sought: an ancient tapal that had been in the family for seventeen generations. It had been Moras's weapon for Keros's entire life, and its deadly beauty was apparent to the young triton as he picked it up. Razor sharp on the external edge, the metal arc wrapped along the outside of his forearm and up around his knuckles, coming to a point on the thumb side of the grip with another deadly point near his elbow. Settling the bladed weapon on his right arm and straightening his arm out with the tapal forward, Keros started up toward his father, but a voice inside his head stopped him short, a spell of his father's, no doubt. Moras spoke quickly, but with more emotion and strength than Keros had personally heard in years.

Keros, my son. I know you mean well, but you must ignore us. Our fates are in Persana's hands. Naran and

I know for what we fight—to prevent Axar Xyrl from claiming the magics of this place. Hurry, for he nearly has the prize he seeks. Thwart him there, then we can look to our own survival.

The spell did not allow Keros to communicate back, and to speak would draw more attention to himself. Silently, he swam away from his father and began weaving among the larger ice fragments nearer the floor. Keros soon noticed that few morkoths bothered to look for him during their moment of triumph. A resounding *crack* sounded like a death knell in the Great Vault as the ice sheath shattered under the pressure of the magical tentacle.

Keros saw his mother's face contort in horror, though numerous morkoths hemmed her and Swiftide in. Keros swam around toward the back wall, and he followed the silver-beaked leader of the morkoths with his eyes. The large morkoth moved forward and out of Keros's sight atop the hovering iceberg. Within moments, the light in the room took on an greenish tint. The remainder of the ice shattered with a blast of green. Keros heard the sound he learned to hate earlier that day: the grating beak-clicking of morkoth laughter.

Looking upward again, he saw the larger morkoth— the Axar Xyrl his father named—waving the petrified tentacle of a long dead morkoth leader, a green gem glowing brightly in its palm. Keros grinned as he heard his mother finish a spell, and saw arcane energies immediately come into play. Naran transformed her trident into pure energy and launched at Xyrl— only to watch the magic dissipate harmlessly.

While everyone's attention was focused on Naran and Xyrl, Keros leaped upward from almost directly beneath the claw, intent more than ever to heed his father's words and keep the Claw of Xynakt out of morkoth hands.

They might have it for the moment, he thought, but they can't hold it if Persana aids me now.

"Whole lives can take place between heartbeats," was a church teaching Keros never believed until now. In the short seconds it took him to close the space between himself and Axar Xyrl, he watched in dread as the morkoth took notice of Naran and trained the claw at her. His hands only feet away from the morkoth's tentacles, Keros screamed as the claw coruscated with green energy that enveloped Naran. Keros watched in horror as he saw the flesh burned from his mother's skeleton, then her bones were blasted to ashes. During it all, Axar Xyrl's clicking laughter continued, though it seemed to slow to a crawl.

"Mother!"

Grief-stricken and angry beyond belief, Keros continued swimming upward with his shout. Appearing instantly after the attack, not even Axar Xyrl could defend against the sudden assault. Keros kept his arm straight as he swam past the morkoth. The tapal's cutting edge effortlessly scored a long wound across the morkoth's chest and the outstretched arm that held the Claw of Xynakt. While the tapal damaged the arcount, Keros used the element of surprise and his anger-driven strength to wrest the mummified tentacle from Axar Xyrl's grasp with his left hand. He then continued swimming up toward the ceiling and over to the gaping doorway, maneuvering out of range of some spells and using the debris they caused to gain cover from morkoth attacks. Keros had reached the ceiling by the time the whole attack even fully registered to Axar

Xyrl, who screeched in pain at his wounds and in frustration at realizing he had lost the Claw of Xynakt so swiftly.

In those moments, Keros could have swum out of the Great Vault and headed out toward open water, away from those who wished to use the artifact he now held. His concern for his parents and friends slowed him as he wondered how to get to them safely. He whistled for Swiftide to join him, though the fearful whinny he heard in response told him his trusted mount was still trapped. He heard the grating, sibilant voice of Axar Xyrl address him then.

"Escape Axar you shall not. Return the claw, you must, or watch more die you will. The high priest father is—die will he unless Xynakt's Claw to Axar is returned."

As if to punctuate the threat, the morkoth cast a spell and Keros heard the sound of electrical magic arcing in the water, mixed with his father's screams of pain.

Keros no longer saw or thought or consciously swam through the dark depths. He was nothing more than a swimming rage intent on sharing his pain with the being who slew his mother and now threatened his father as well. As he flipped over amidcurrent and swam back toward the heart of the now ruined Great Vault, Keros felt only his anger—at the morkoths and at himself for not being strong enough to obey his parents' commands. He failed to notice the glow of the claw clutched in his left hand and the related glow of his own right hand within the grip of the tapal. He didn't feel anything more than the rush of water over his body, but arcane scales writhed across his skin, crawling within him as if moved by an intelligent hand. He ignored the fact that he was swimming faster than he ever had, and he no longer felt the fatigue that plagued him earlier. He was now far angrier than he'd ever been, and all that anger was focused at Arcount Axar Xyrl.

Keros swam with the sole intention of adding the Head of Axar Xyrl to the tower's collection of relics. His fury kept him from avoiding the spell attacks or even caring about their existence. Magic flared at him from all sides as the morkoths all sought to slay him, but he ignored it all. Each spell impact increased the greenish glow around Keros, which grew brighter while all the young triton felt was a growing warmth in his arms and his own rage. He wanted to use the claw's power to free his father and force the retreat of the morkoths, but part of him now thought of killing them all. Slowing his dive, Keros looked toward his father. He froze when he noticed the green glowing scales on his arms in front of him. In that instant of hesitation, Keros found himself snared by a massive spell tentacle, its arcane energies tracing back to Axar Xyrl.

"Give to Axar the claw, you must, and crush you quickly like sea slug Axar can," the bloodied arcount exclaimed, "or else make death take forever Axar can."

The silver-and-black morkoth with the silver beak descended from his higher vantage point in the chamber down to where Moras is pinned to the wall. He wrapped two of his lower tentacles into Moras's long mane to maintain his immediate threat.

"Close to death the father is, young one. To end his life Axar does not wish, but kill Axar will to gain the claw's power."

Other morkoths surrounded Keros while Xyrl spoke to him, and Xyrl manipulated the coils of his spell

tentacle, allowing his minions to seize the claw. Keros
struggled to hold the artifact, but with two morkoths
pulling it loose and another choking him, Keros felt it
tear from his grasp.

Keros felt defeated, but his rage continued to rise.
He watched as the morkoths relayed the claw down to
Axar Xyrl, who held a black, glowing tentacle over
Moras's heart, which he moved to grasp the claw. Keros
watched the arcount turn the mummified tentacle over
and over, as if looking for something. He wondered why
the claw no longer glowed green, as apparently did
Xyrl, then he thought about the confusing green scales
along his arms. Only after the morkoth screamed in
frustration and gazed directly at him did Keros know
the secret. The power of the Claw of Xynakt had moved
into him.

His mind awhirl with the turmoil of events, Keros
still meant to save his father, and he now had the
means to do so. The triton summoned all his emotion
and roared as he flexed his muscles, trying to slash his
way out of the tentacle with the many-times-blessed
tapal he still carried. The world went red in his eyes,
and magic shattered in the face of his anger, the back-
lash separating three morkoths from their limbs and
heads. Axar Xyrl shrank before this unexpected power,
as Keros stepped free of his dissolving spell and advanced on the arcount. The tapal in his right hand now
glistened with emerald energy, and he leveled it at the
silver-beaked villain, his eyes devoid of any emotion
save fury.

Visibly shaking with hostility in his defeat, Axar
Xyrl said in a voice far more chilling for its calm,
"Taken my prize, little triton has, or take you did it?
Know the powers of the claw, Axar Xyrl does, and tell

you I will not. Gains the little triton only sorrow and revenge everlasting, your victory does."

Swiftide reared up quickly behind the morkoths to attack and Keros rushed forward, but Axar completed a spell with a few quick gestures and disappeared in a swirl of water.

Keros screamed in protest, the frustration of losing his foe so easily boiling out of him with all of the fury that gripped him during the battle. His eyes tightly shut in his scream of rage, Keros didn't see the tapal glow the brightest green, but he noticed as the weight on his arm lightened. Opening his eyes, he watched as the blade shimmered and dissolved into nothingness. While shocked by that, he saw beyond himself to the wounded body of his father still pinned to the wall. Moras locked eyes with Keros, though not with the expected disapproval.

Keros swam over to his father, suddenly immensely grateful that he high priest still lived. He didn't notice that Swiftide floated apart from them. The hippocampus was silent for a moment, as if wondering who this person was who had raised him from a foal. Though his body was angry with scars and fresh wounds, Moras ignored them and looked at his son with new eyes.

"Of all the currents open for you, Keros," the priest said, "this one I never expected. I have awaited Persana's Blade for many tides, and I never expected it to be you, my son."

"What do you mean, Father?" Keros asked. "I did what you asked and kept the claw away from the morkoths. Now I just hope you know of some spells that can get this thing out of me and back into the ice."

Keros allowed his father to lean over his shoulders, and both men grunted as Keros pulled the trident loose from the wall. Keros carried Moras down to a level slab of rubble at the floor of the chamber, the trident still in him until they could find another healer to aid him.

"He must have passed out from the pain," Keros told himself. "That's why he isn't answering me." Settling his father as best he could, Keros looked at his face, to find him awake and looking at him with compassion.

Taking his son's right hand, Moras turned it palm up, and Keros gasped—a great green jewel now glinted at the center of his palm.

"The tapal will come to you when you need it—that it shall remain in the family's service is a good thing to know," Moras said. "The only magic that can separate it and the claw from you now, son, is that magic that awaits us all at currents' end. You carry this burden for the rest of your days, but you are strong enough to bear it. I have seen this, at least." Moras breathed in, and a hacking cough shook his body, blood clouding the water near his mouth and gill slits.

"Father!" Keros cried, his confusion turning to alarm as the older triton's wounds now seemed more serious with the rush of battle behind them. "Father . . ."

Moras stopped coughing and opened his eyes. "You are my son. A cold current lies before you, but do not shirk it. You know your duty to Pumanath, to Serôs, to Persana. Protect and keep this power from anyone who would steal or abuse it. Do this, and know that we are proud—" Moras began to cough again, more blood flowing from his gills.

Keros was so focused on his father's last words he didn't hear the entrance of the triton military forces above him. Swiftide's sharp whinny warned him of an attack from behind and Keros brought his right arm up to block the stabbing tines of a trident, and gasped as it glanced off his arm, striking sparks where the metal trident grated on the tattooed scales. Both tritons gasped at that, but the attacker now redoubled her efforts.

Turning away from his fallen father, Keros saw eight more tritons all bearing down on him from all sides and above. These were tritons he had known his whole life, all looking at him as if they did not know him and as if he were their worst enemy.

"What's going on?" Keros pleaded. "Why are you attacking me?"

The only answer he got was a flurry of nets thrown over him. Swiftide came to his defense, knocking aside two tritons to rise under Keros and bear him and the fight away from the wounded high priest. Keros found himself seething with wrath over the loss of his mother, the near death of his father, the unexplained attack on him, and the confusion of his newfound power. He wanted to lash out at the tritons, and in response, his right arm glowed and the tapal appeared on his right arm, gleaming emerald bright. Slashing away the nets that surrounded him, Keros saw more tritons entering the Tower of Numos, and all of them reacted to him with fear and revulsion. As he rose through the water on Swiftide's back, he called to them, though his hopes of explanation were lost in a flurry of tridents and expletives. Despite the fury that seemed to rise uncontrollably in him now, Keros hardly wanted to fight his own people, regardless of why they attacked him. Settling onto Swiftide more readily, Keros turned his back on his attackers and swam off into the depths.

From the chamber floor, Moras called out weakly to the tritons above him. "Leave him for now. We have suffered grievously today, and we shall not slay our own, regardless of what magics now possess him."

Two centurions swam down to where Moras lay, hardly believing what their superior ordered them to do. As the centurions removed the trident from Moras's leg and torso, two minor priests administered some much needed healing magic, and the high priest regained consciousness.

"Keros?" Moras muttered. "Centurion Barys, did my boy make it away?"

Barys seemed puzzled, but answered, "Yes, your holiness. What happened here? What happened to him? We thought him another of those *tathak*."

Moras looked at the centurion in surprise. The harsh expletive was often used to refer to morkoths, but never within the temple grounds. The high priest eased himself to a sitting position with some aid, and he spoke loudly, his voice resonating in the water for all in the chamber to hear.

"Many of you saw an enemy leave here just now astride one of our own hippocampi. Whatever you think you saw, know that you have witnessed the coming of Persana's Blade. My son Keros is triton no longer, but I pray that he will forever remain safe, and that he find his destiny among the waters of Serôs."

* * * * *

It had taken Moras over a tenday to recover, and during that time he thought about how the claw could have bonded to Keros during the fight. He found his answers among some lore about the Armory.

Of all the things of power in Serôs, Xynakt's Claw provided the greatest power but extracted the greatest price of one's soul. It was drawn to emotions, and while it fueled them and gave them more power, the touch of that talisman ultimately only brought corruption. In hopes of finding some hope of redemption for his son, Moras traveled to the Library at Coman in eastern Pumanath. There he finally found the ancient coral tablet that held the Prophecy of Persana's Blade.

As he read the ancient tablet, he felt both compassion for the currents on which Keros must now swim, and sorrow for the loss of his son. The tablet lay before him and he committed its words to memory once again. Moras vowed to watch and listen and wait. He would be the chronicler of the deeds of Persana's Blade, the gods be willing. He read the words aloud, a vow to Persana in honor of and in petition for Keros, his son.

"Crafted by Darkness, Persana's Blade shall come to the guardians from an enemy.

"Forged in Anger, Persana's Blade shall become light from darkness.

"Tempered by Sorrow, Persana's Blade shall protect all save one.

"Wielded in Fear, Persana's Blade shall fight darkness within and without.

"Guarded by Duty, Persana's Blade shall be forever on guard, but never a guardian."

And the Dark Tide Rises

Keith Francis Strohm

7 Eleint, the Year of the Gauntlet

The last rays of the setting sun spun out over the waters of the Inner Sea, transforming its rippled surface into shimmering gold. Umberlee's Fire, the sailors called it, and considered it a good omen, a sign that the Sea Queen had blessed their work. Morgan Kevlynson stood on the bow of the sea-worn fishing dory that had served his family for years and ignored the spectacular display. Absently, he pushed a strand of coal-black hair from his face, blown there by the swirling, salt-flecked fingers of the wind, and let his thoughts wander beneath the fiery skin of the sea.

Darkness surrounding, like a cocoon, the wild impulses of the deep; blue-green presences where sunlight caresses sea-halls.

There were mysteries here. He knew that as surely as he knew his own name. The sea held an ancient wisdom—wild and untamed; carried dark promises upon its broad back. And sometimes, when he sailed the waters in silence, they called to him.

Today was such a time.

Morgan closed his eyes, absorbed in the dance of wind and wave and foam. He felt a familiar emptying, as if some inner tide receded; his heartbeat pulsed to the rhythm of the sea, slow and insistent, like the whitecaps that struck the side of the dory, until everything became that rhythm—heart, boat, sky—the world defined in a single liquid moment.

That's when he saw her: eyes the color of rich kohl, skin as green-tinted as the finest chrysoberyl, and blue-green hair that flowed more freely than water itself. Yet, there was a sadness, a vulnerability about this creature that set an ache upon him more fierce than any he had ever felt. He was about to ask what he could do to set a smile back upon her face when she opened her mouth and—

"*Tchh*, laddie! Lay off yer sea-dreamin' and give us a hand." The voice was deep, resonant, and rough as coral, worn smooth only by the companionable lilt of the fishermen of the Alamber coastline.

Morgan opened his eyes and spun quickly to face the sound, only just catching himself as his sudden movement set the dory rocking. Angus, his grandfather, sat athwart the starboard gunwale stowing line with the ease of long practice. The old man's sun-burnished skin covered his face and hands like cracked leather. A

302

thick shock of silver hair crowned the ancient fisherman's bowed head, and his rough woolen clothes were worn thin and dusted with dried salt. Despite the weathering of years, Angus showed no signs of slowing down. His wits and his grasp remained firm, as was the way of those who spent their entire lives fishing the rough shores and islands of Alamber.

Despite himself, Morgan smiled at the thought of his grandfather ever needing anyone's assistance. "But Granda, I was just—"

" 'Tis sure I knew what you were about, lad," the old man interrupted. "Moonin' over the water. 'Tis not natural. The sea'd just as soon swallow you up as leave you be. Never doubt the right of that, boyo. She's a fickle lover, she is, and a man cannot hope to understand her."

Morgan sighed, moved to the small wooden mast at the center of the boat, and carefully folded up the coarse cloth that made up the dory's only sail. He had heard this same lecture at least three hundred times. His grandfather would never tire of it. The old man's voice droned on as the young fisherman gathered up the now-thick bundle of sailcloth. It was difficult to keep the irritation out of his movements. Morgan was sure that he felt his grandfather's disapproving stare when he dropped the cloth a bit too forcefully into its storage area beneath the prow.

Still, the old fisherman continued his lecturing. It was not fair, really. Morgan had lived nearly eighteen summers—and had sailed for most of those. He was no land-bred lackaday, ill-prepared for work upon a fishing boat, nor was he a pampered merchant's son come to the Alamber coast on holiday. He was a fisherman, born into one of the oldest fishing families on the Inner

Sea. Yet his fascination with the sea seemed to frighten his grandfather—and the close-knit inhabitants of Mourktar.

Thinking back, he knew the reason why. The superstitious villagers had never really accepted him. His mother dead from the strain of childbirth, his father lost in grief so deep that he sailed out into the Inner Sea one winter night, never to return, Morgan had grown up wild, spending many a sunset running across the rocks and cliffs that jutted out over the water, listening to the song of the waves and breathing in the salty musk of the wind. "Sea-touched," they had called him. Changeling. Pointing to his black hair and fair skin, so different from the sun-golden complexion and reddish hair of Mourktar's natives, as outward proof of the very thing they whispered softly to each other in the deep of night, when the wind blew hard across the shore. Even now, Morgan knew that many still made the sign of Hathor behind his back if he gazed too long out at sea or sat on Mourktar's weathered quay in deep thought.

He searched for signs of bitterness, for some resentment of his reputation, but found none. He had grown up with the simple reality that no one understood him. He had friends, conspirators who were happy to while away the time between childhood and manhood by stealing a mug or two of frothy ale from old Borric's tavern or playing at war amid the scrub-choked dunes, and there were evenings enough of stolen kisses beneath the docks. But no one truly knew what went on in his deepest core, that silent part of him that heard the measured beat of the sea's heart, that felt its inexorable pull like a vast undertow of need. No one could know these things—except perhaps his father.

Morgan shuddered at that thought and shook himself free of his reverie. His frustration and resentment drained out of him, leaving behind only emptiness and a numbing chill. The sun had nearly fallen beneath the horizon, and he looked up to find his grandfather staring expectantly at him in the purplish haze of twilight, his discourse apparently finished.

"I said, 'tis a fierce storm'll blow tonight, and we'd best be finishing soon." The old man shook his head and muttered something else under his breath before opening the waterproof tarp they used to cover the boat.

Morgan hmmphed guiltily and moved to help his grandfather, threading a thin rope through the small holes around the tarp's edge and running it around the metal ringlets attached to the sides of the boat. In truth, not a single cloud floated anywhere in the twilit sky, but the coastal breeze had picked up, bringing with it a sharpening chill. He had long ago stopped doubting his grandfather's ability to guess the weather.

Once he'd finished securing the tarp, the old man spat and walked down the quay toward Mourktar. "Come lad, we've a fair catch to bring home, and there's a dark tide running in. Besides, I've a yearning for some of yer gran's fish stew."

Morgan bent and hefted the sack of freshly caught fish over his shoulder, thanking the gods that they had sold the rest of the day's catch to the merchants earlier. As he turned to look one last time at the dory, rising and falling to the swelling of the waves, he caught sight of a furtive movement near the boat. He was about to call to his grandfather, fearing the mischievous vandalizing of a sea lion, when he caught sight of a head bobbing just above the surface of the water. Morgan couldn't make out any more of this strange creature, but that didn't matter. Staring at him in the fading light, he saw the face of his dream.

In a moment, she was gone, and he turned back to his grandfather. Though the two walked back to the village in silence, Morgan's mind was a jumble of confusion and disbelief.

* * * * *

The storm raged throughout the night, battering the rough thatch of the simple hut. Morgan tossed fitfully under his thick quilt while the wind howled like a wolf through the dirt lanes and footpaths of Mourktar. His grandparents slept deeply in the main room. He could hear their throaty snores, a rough counterpoint to the storm's fury. Sleep, however, refused to grant Morgan similar relief. Instead, he lay there curled up into a ball, feeling lost and alone, and very small against the night.

It had been like that the entire evening. When he and Angus had arrived at their family's hut for supper, storm clouds had already blotted out the newly shining stars. Morgan had barely noticed. The vision of the sea woman's face had flared brightly in his mind since he'd left the docks, and his thoughts burned with her unearthly beauty. Everything else seemed dull in comparison, hollow and worn as the cast off shell of a hermit crab.

He had sat through supper mostly in silence, distracted by the rising song of the wind. Several times he had almost gasped in horror, for he heard in that mournful susurrus the slow exhalation of his name ushering forth from the liquid throat of the sea. His grandparents had borne this mood for as long as they could. Morgan's muttered responses to his gran's questions, however, had finally earned him a cuff from Angus. Though even that blow had felt more like an echo of his granda's anger, a memory of some past punishment. Frustrated, the old fisherman stormed away from the driftwood table, cursing. Morgan mumbled some excuse soon after and staggered to his cot, seeking relief in the cool release of sleep.

He failed.

Thoughts of *her* consumed him, and his skin burned with the promise of her touch. She wanted him, called to him in a voice full of moonlight and foam and the soft, subtle urging of the sea. He lay there for hours, trying to hide from her, trying to retreat into the hidden places of his mind. But she followed, uttering his name, holding it forth like a lamp.

Morgan, come!

Come, my heart-home!

Come!

Briefly, irrationally, he wondered if his father had heard the same voice on the night he stole a boat and, broken by grief, sailed out to his death on the winter sea. Perhaps, Morgan thought wildly, this madness was hereditary.

Come!

The voice. Stronger this time, driving away all thought except obedience. With a cry, he flung himself out of the cot, no longer able to resist the siren call. The compulsion took a hold of him now, drove him out of the hut into the gray stillness of false dawn. The storm had spent itself. Wind and rain no longer lashed the shore. The world held its breath, waiting.

Waiting for what? Morgan thought.

In an instant he knew. It waited for him. Rubbing his arms briskly to ward off the predawn chill, he followed the dirt road down to the docks. Every step brought Morgan closer to *her*. He ignored the downed branches, shattered trunks, and other detritus that littered the road, and began to run. He had no choice.

And yet, there was a sense of promise to this call, a hint of mystery unveiled. If he was going to end his life sea-mad like his father, he would at least receive something in return, a gift from the dark waters that had been his true home these past eighteen seasons more truly than the insular huts and close-minded folk of Mourktar. He understood that now, and the notion filled him with equal parts terror and fascination.

At last, he reached the end of the dock, sweat soaked and gasping for breath. He cast about desperately, hoping to catch some glimpse of the mysterious creature that haunted both his waking and dreaming, proof that he had not simply lost his wits. *She* was there, floating idly to the left of his family's dory.

Even from this distance her beauty stung him with its purity. The skin of her green-tinted face was creamy and smooth as marble, and her delicate features set his fingers twitching, so much did Morgan long to trace the curve of chin, nose, and throat. Long blue-green hair, though matted with moisture above the water, floated tenderly over the outline of her body.

Morgan would have dived into the chill sea that very moment to be with her, had she not opened her full-lipped mouth and spoken.

"Greetings, Man-child, son of Kevlyn. I feared that you would not come in time." Her voice was sweet and clear, her intonation fluid, making it sound to Morgan as if she sang every phrase.

Questions filled his head to bursting. Who was she? How did she know him? Why did she call him here? As he hurriedly tried to decide which one to speak aloud, he realized that the compulsion was gone. His thoughts were his own.

He looked at the mysterious creature again, noting for the first time the thick webbing splayed between the fingers of her hands as she easily tread water. She tilted her head slightly to the side, obviously waiting for his response.

Morgan said nothing, letting the moment stretch between them, letting the rhythmic slap of water against dock, the wail of early rising gulls, and the faint rustling of the coastal wind fill the void her compulsion had left inside of him.

He was angry, and not a little frightened. This creature had used him, manipulated him, and when at last he spoke, his voice was full of bitterness. "Of course I came. You gave me no choice."

She laughed at that, though he heard no humor in it, only a tight quaver that sounded suspiciously to his untrained ear like sadness. "There's little choice any of us have now, lad," the creature said softly, almost too softly to be heard. Then louder, "But you must forgive me, Morgan. These are desperate times. I sent out the Call; you came. And a truer Son of Eldath never walked or swam upon the face of Toril."

Now it was her turn to stare, deep-colored eyes locking on to his. Morgan felt his anger drain away, only to be replaced by he-didn't-know-what—embarrassment? Shame? He felt like an ungainly boy under the weight of that otherworldly gaze.

"H-how do y-you know my—my name?" he stuttered quickly, trying to focus the creature's attention elsewhere.

The sea woman chuckled, her amusement plain to hear. "You mortals wear your names as plainly as a selkie does her skin. It is child's play to pluck it from you—if you know how to look for it." Her smile faded. "Ahh, but I see that I am being rude. Forgive me, again, for it has been a long time since I have spoken with a mortal. I am Avadrieliaenvorulandral. You may call me Avadriel. I am Alu'Tel'Quessir, those folk your ancestors called 'sea elves,' and I need your help."

Morgan sat on the dock, stunned. Alu'Tel'Quessir. Sea elves. Morgan had only dreamed of ever seeing such a creature, and here he stood, talking to one in the flesh.

"You need *my* help?" he asked incredulously. "But lady—"

"Avadriel," the creature interrupted. "I gave up such formalities centuries ago."

"Avadriel," he continued, choosing to ignore the implications of the sea elf's last statement. "I'm but a fisherman."

Clearly, Morgan thought, this beautiful creature who floated up out of the depths was mistaken. Soon, she would realize this and return to her watery realm, leaving him alone and feeling the fool. At this moment, he did not know which would be worse.

"A fisherman," Avadriel scoffed. "You are far more than that, Morgan. You are one of the few mortals left who can hear the Old Song.

"Yes," she continued, noticing his look of confusion, "the sea has set its mark upon you, even if others of your kind fear and distrust you because of it. That is why I have come."

Here were words straight out of a bard's fancy, the young man thought, but could he laugh them away, dismiss them as so much nonsense, when they came from the mouth of such a creature? Morgan's world had spun out of control since he first saw her. He felt caught in the grip of some implacable tide, carrying him to the depths of a black abyss. Yet, Avadriel's words rang with the truth, and her presence gave him something to hold on to, an anchor in an otherwise tumultuous sea. Gravely, he nodded his head, too afraid to speak.

Avadriel shot him a half smile. "It is good to see that the children of the sun are still brave—though I fear even bravery may not be enough to save us. You see, Morgan, a great evil has awakened deep within the blackest abyss of the sea, leading an army of its dark minions. Already this force has destroyed Avarnoth. Many of my people . . ."

The sea elf faltered, and Morgan saw the pain she had been hiding burst forth, marring her beautiful features. He looked away, not wishing to intrude. After a few moments, she continued—her voice a tremulous whisper.

"Many of my people made the journey to Sashelas's halls, but it will not stop there. This evil grows daily, and it will sweep across the lands of Faerûn like a tidal wave, destroying everything in its path."

Something in her voice made Morgan look up. Avadriel looked pale, her face drained of color. He was about to ask her what was wrong, when a large wave pushed her hair aside, revealing a deep gash across her right shoulder. Flesh, muscle, and vein were ripped apart, exposing thin white bone.

Morgan cursed softly. "Lady—Avadriel, you are wounded!" He was angry; at himself for not noticing sooner, and at her for concealing such a thing.

How she had managed to carry on with such a grievous injury was beyond him. Hurriedly, he searched about the wooden wharf for one of the small dinghies used to ferry fishermen to boats anchored away from the limited space of the docks. He soon found one tied off near a set of rusting crab traps. Adroitly climbing down a rickety rope ladder, the young fisherman cast off and rowed the battered dinghy toward the wounded creature.

"Do not concern yourself with my well being, Morgan," Avadriel protested weakly, as he neared. "My message is far more important than my life."

Ignoring the sea elf's instructions, for he had already concluded that her life was far more important than his own, the young man drew close to Avadriel and gently pulled her into the rude craft, careful not to further damage her wounded shoulder. The sea elf was surprisingly light, and, despite her initial protest, offered Morgan no resistance. Carefully, he laid her down, folding his sweater under her head for a pillow and covering her naked body with a weather-worn tarp.

Avadriel's skin was cold to the touch, and her once bright eyes began to glaze over. Even so, she reached out to him with her webbed hands, turning her head to reveal three gill slits running through either side of her delicate throat. He bent down to her, fascinated as the slits sucked noisily in the air.

"Morgan . . . you . . . must listen," she whispered unevenly. "There is something you must . . . do . . . something . . ." Her voice trailed off into silence.

At first, he thought she must have died, for her gill slits had stopped opening, but his fears were allayed when her chest began to rise and fall shallowly. Avadriel was sorely wounded, but by the gods, Morgan thought, she was alive.

Quietly, he sat down in the small boat. The early morning wind raked his now bare arms and neck. His thin, short-sleeved undertunic offered him little protection against the seasonal cold. Morgan ignored the chill, however, and began to row. There were several shallow sea caves not far from the docks. He would take Avadriel there, away from the prying eyes and fearful minds of Mourktar's inhabitants. He would tend to her wounds, and when she awakened, he would travel to the ends of Toril for her. He remembered her impassioned plea. He was needed.

* * * * *

Blood. The scent of it filled the water, thick, heavy, and rich. T'lakk floated idly amid the waving kelp strands, savoring the heady aroma, sucking it in with each flap of his gill slits. It stirred something deep within his hunter's heart, an ancient hunger, older than the sea itself. He waited, letting it grow, letting it build, until the hunger sang within him—tooth and claw and rending flesh, a savage, primal tune.

Quickly, he shook his green-scaled head, refusing to go into the Place of Madness. Though it cost him great effort, the creature focused his senses back on the hunt. He still had work to do, and the master would be displeased if he failed in this task. Three long clicks summoned the other hunters from their search along the rocky sea floor. Balefully, he eyed each one as they arrived, satisfied that they approached with the proper humility. He would brook no challenges now. Not when their quarry lay so close.

He smiled grimly, revealing several rows of needle-sharp teeth, as the assembled hunters scented the blood. A quick signal sent them arrowing through the water to follow the trail. Soon, T'lakk thought gleefully as he swam after his companions. Soon the Hunt would be over.

* * * * *

Morgan sat in the damp cave, watching the measured rise and fall of Avadriel's chest as she slept. A battered lantern lay at his feet, perched precariously between two slime-covered stalagmites. Its rude light licked the jagged rocks of the cavern, revealing several twisted stone shelves surrounding a small tidal pool.

He had arrived at the bank of sea caves just as the morning sun crested the horizon, grateful that he was able to reach shelter before most of the village boats sailed through the area in search of their day's fishing. Once he had maneuvered his small craft deep enough into one of the caves to shield it from sight, Morgan had gently lifted Avadriel out of the dinghy, placed her on a low, relatively flat lip of stone overhanging the tidal pool, and set about binding her wound as best he could.

Now he sat stiff-necked and attentive, anxiously waiting for the sea elf to awaken. The silence of his vigil was broken only by the slow drip of water echoing hollowly in the enclosed space. His grandparents would be frantic by now—though Morgan knew that his granda would no doubt have sailed the boat out to sea, not willing to miss the day's fishing, thinking all the while of ways to box his grandson's lazy head. Still, he thought in the foreboding chill of the cavern, he would gladly suffer a great deal more than his grand-father's wrath for Avadriel's sake.

As Morgan kept a cold, damp watch over the sleeping sea elf, he marveled at how much his life had changed in such a short time. Yesterday, he had given no thought to the world beyond the coastal waters of Mourktar. Today, he found himself hiding in a cave with a wounded sea elf, ready to leave behind everything for the beauty of a creature he'd never thought he would actually see.

When Avadriel finally awoke, several hours later, the water level in the tidal pool had risen, lapping gently around her body. She sat up with a start, looking rather confused and frightened, until her eyes met Morgan's. He smiled, hoping he didn't look as foolish as he felt, and approached her carefully, determined not to turn his ankle on the slippery rocks in his eagerness.

If he had expected a long litany of thanks and gratefulness, he would have been disappointed. Though there was a softness about the sea elf's face, a gentle hint of a smile in answer to his own, her words were abrupt and as hard as steel.

"You must leave at once," she said. "Before it is too late."

Morgan stared at Avadriel once again. He didn't understand—didn't want to understand. He only knew that his place was by her side.

"Leave?" he asked incredulously. "But Avadriel, you're still hurt. Perhaps once you have healed a bit we could travel together." He tried to keep the wistfulness out of his voice, failing miserably.

"If only that were possible, Morgan, but we don't have that much time. You must go to Firestorm Isle and tell the wizard Dhavrim that Avarnoth has fallen.

An ancient evil is free once again. Its black army is even now poised to strike at Faerûn, and the wizards must be warned." She paused, then added, "Please, Morgan. I need your help."

Silently, he cursed the luck that separated him from his heart's desire the moment he had discovered it. It would be difficult to leave, but Morgan knew that he would do it. Too much was at stake.

Avadriel smiled then, as if reading the young man's thoughts, and drew herself closer. "Thank you," she said simply, and brushed her lips lightly over his.

Morgan closed his eyes at her touch. Avadriel's scent surrounded him, intoxicating in its subtlety. Their lips met each other's again, firmer this time. A wave of desire crested through him, wild and strong as a riptide. The world faded away in the wake of that desire, leaving only the ebb and flow of bodies.

After a time, Avadriel pulled away. "Morgan," she whispered softly, sadly into the shadows of the cave.

He nodded once, and wiped a blossoming tear from her eye. "I know . . . it's time." With that, he stood and climbed into the waiting boat. "I shall return as soon as I can."

Slowly, he rowed out into harsh light of day.

* * * * *

With a grunt of effort, Morgan let the rhythmic slap of oar on water carry him through another hour of rowing. The sea surged and foamed around him, threatening to turn aside the small force of his craft. Spume sprayed his face as the boat's bow bounced hard against the trough of a rolling black wave. Insistent burn of chest and arm muscles long-since spent,

316

harsh gasp of salted air into lungs, sting of wood chafing raw skin—these were his offerings, sacrificial prayers to the gods of his people.

They ignored him.

Slowly, he made his way across the churning water, more by force of will than anything else. When his energy flagged and the oars seemed to weigh as much as an iron anchor, he summoned a picture of Avadriel's face. The memory of her lips on his, the salted taste of her tongue, renewed his determination. Too much lay at stake, for his heart and his home. He would not fail.

By mid afternoon, the heat of the sun had dried the sweat from his body, and his tongue felt thick and swollen, like a piece of boiled leather. With a deep sigh, he pulled up the oars and gave his knotted muscles a brief rest. Shielding his eyes from the sun's glare, he scanned the horizon.

Several years before, he had stolen out with a few friends and sailed to the wizard's island on a dare. Though none of the intrepid band of explorers had set foot on the island, Morgan alone sailed his ship around the rocky shore of that forbidden place.

Even now, amid the burning heat of the sun, he shivered with the memory. Dhavrim's tower had stood stark and terrifying, thrusting up from the coral of the island like the tooth of some giant whale. As Morgan had guided his craft around the island, he couldn't help but wonder if the wizard would send some deadly spell arcing out from his demesne to punish the trespassing boat.

The upsurge of a wave snapped Morgan out of his reverie. He still had a fair distance to row before he reached the island, and he felt as if time were running out.

By late afternoon, when the sun began its lazy descent, a calm fell over the waters. Morgan quickly wiped his brow and surveyed the silent scene. The sea lay placid and serene, its gently stippled surface resembling nothing so much as the facet of a blue-green gem in the sunlight. In the distance, he could make out a small shadow, a black pimple on the horizon that could only be Dhavrim's tower. Before Morgan could even celebrate his good fortune, he caught sight of something that tore an oath out of his parched throat. There in the distance, dark and ominous, a roiling wall of haze bore down on him.

Terrified, Morgan renewed his efforts, hoping that he could reach his destination before the line of fog enveloped him. The sailors of his village called such unnatural weather the Breath of Umberlee. It often lured unsuspecting boats to a watery grave. Even the beacon fires set upon the cliff walls of the Alamber coast were often not enough to save the doomed vessels.

With a determined grunt, Morgan bent his back to the task once again. Whipcord muscles already pushed beyond their limit protested mightily, but he pressed on. Time seemed to slow in that silent moment, until he felt as if he were trapped in some artist's sketch. He continued to row, of that he was sure, but the island did not seem to draw any closer. At first he thought himself dreaming, until the first patchy cloud of fog rolled across the bow of his craft, followed soon after by more until the fog drew close around him like a thick blanket. Desperately, he cast about for sign of the island, for any landmark in the sea of gray that surrounded him, but to no avail. Even the sun, which had lashed at his skin with its fierce rays, hung muted and dim, a hidden jewel in the murky sky.

Filled with frustration and not a fair bit of rage at the unfairness of it all, Morgan shouted fiercely at the blanket of fog. "Damn it all! I will not fail. I can not!"

Savagely, he beat his fist against the oarlock and continued to hurl invectives at the fog, at the gods, at the wizard in his thrice-damned castle, but most of all at himself, for agreeing to this fool's errand in the first place.

The answering cry of a gull surprised him so much that he stopped his railing in midsentence. Again, its wail cut through the fog, echoing in the gray murk, followed by a white streak and a light thump as the creature landed on the bow of his craft. Startled by the gull's appearance, white-crested and intent, Morgan didn't even wonder why such a creature should fly out so far from shore.

"Heya, silly bird," the young man said pitifully. "Fly away before you become stuck like a poor fisherman's son in a fog bank."

The large gull simply cocked its head slightly and regarded the young man with a serious gaze.

"Go!" he shouted finally at the stupid creature, letting frustration and anger creep into his voice.

The bird ignored his command and continued to stare at him. Finally, with a soft chirrup, the gull flapped its wings and hovered gently a few feet from his craft. It was then that Morgan noticed a small crystal clutched in the bird's grasp. The jewel began to pulse slightly as he stared at it, softly illuminating the gloom around him.

The bird landed again on the boat, casting a knowing glance at Morgan, before it lifted off once more, now flying a few feet in front of the craft. Surprisingly, the light from the crystal pushed some of the fog away, allowing him the opportunity to see a few paces on all sides.

Confused, but unwilling to pass up this odd gift, Morgan dipped oars to water and followed the gull and its gleaming treasure. Hours passed—or minutes—it was difficult to measure the passing of time in the gray waste that surrounded him, and still the young man rowed after the witchlight. Without warning, he burst through the spidery maze of fog into the fading evening sunlight. In front of Morgan loomed the great white stretch of Dhavrim's tower, set only fifty feet or so from the shore. A few more quick strokes brought him scraping onto the rock-strewn beach.

Offering a quick prayer to any god within earshot, he gratefully stumbled out of the boat, stretched knotted muscles, and pulled his craft safely onto the shore. Now that he had arrived on the wizard's island, fulfilled part of Avadriel's wish, he felt hopeful. Perhaps the sea elf had chosen correctly, he thought, as he basked in the pleasurable warmth of sun-baked sand. The simple fisherman, braving wind, wave, and fog to deliver a desperate message. He liked the sound of that, and despite the all-too-real urgency of the situation, he could not help but think himself a hero.

The crash of surf on shore reminded him of the reason for this journey. Anxiously, he studied the stone structure, searching for some entryway. In the fading light of day, the wizard's tower looked more weathered than forbidding. Thick lichen and moss covered parts of the cracked stone structure in mottled patches, and even from this distance he could make out the long, thin stalks of hardy scrub vines twining up the tower's base. Gone were the mystical guardians and arcane wards that had populated his adolescent imaginings, replaced by the mundane reality of sand, rock, and sea-blown wind. Smiling ruefully at his fancies, Morgan the fisherman headed up the path toward the black tower.

And found himself face-to-face with death.

He had little warning, just a slight scrape of sand and the span of a heartbeat in which to react, before he was struck by a powerful blow. He hit the ground hard, felt the air explode out of his lungs. Gasping and dazed, he struggled to his knees, only to find himself staring into the heart of a nightmare. It stood nearly six feet, covered in thick green scales that glistened wetly in the dying light. Deep scars pitted its humanoid face, nearly closing one large eye completely. The other eye fixed Morgan with a baleful stare, its cold black orb seemed to pull what little light remained into its depths.

The creature took a step forward, opened its slightly protruding jaw. Still kneeling on the ground, Morgan could make out row upon row of needle-sharp teeth, no doubt eager to rend the flesh from his bones. He wanted to scream, but the wind was still knocked from him. Instead, he forced himself to his feet and stumbled desperately toward the wizard's tower. If he could just make it from the sandy footing of the beach to the tower's path, he would have a chance to outrun the creature.

Morgan felt the beast's claws rip through his shirt, scoring the flesh underneath, just as the path came into sight. He twisted to the side, avoiding the creature's next strike—and tripped. The last thing he saw before his head exploded into light was the outline of claws against the sky.

* * * * *

By the time the world resolved itself back into color, the sun had set. A pale half moon bathed the island in gentle illumination. By its light, Morgan could see a figure standing over the smoking corpse of the nightmare creature. The figure, obviously a man by the suggestion of a beard visible from this distance, prodded the ruined body with the end of a long staff. The smell of burnt flesh wafted off the corpse, fouling the sea air.

"Ho, I see our visitor has come back to us," the strange man called out, ending his grisly examination.

Morgan's voice caught in his throat as he tried to reply. Dhavrim Starson—for who else, he reasoned, would he find standing on the shore of the wizard's island—resembled nothing of the legendary mage. Short and fat, with a deep-jowled, ruddy face and scratchy salt-and-pepper beard, he looked like nothing so much as a drunken wastrel whose appetites had long since consumed him.

The wizard wheezed heavily as he lumbered toward the fallen fisherman. Morgan watched in morbid fascination as the man's prodigious girth stretched the fabric of his generous blue robe with each step. Only Dhavrim's white staff, inlaid with spidery runes that flowed like molten silver down its length, betrayed the wizard's true power.

That, and his eyes.

Cold and gray, charged with the promise of a hundred storms, they held the young man frozen beneath their ancient gaze. Morgan felt himself pulled within their depths, felt the weight of the wizard's gaze as it measured him, searched him, then cast him aside.

"Can you stand?"

A voice. Calm. Reassuring.

Release.

He felt his body once again, reached for the pudgy hand extended before his face.

"Y-yes, th-thank you," Morgan stammered. He looked once more at the corpse lying in the sand. "What . . . what manner of beast was that?" he asked unsteadily, not really sure if he wanted to know the answer.

Dhavrim followed the young man's gaze. "Those who wish to appear learned call it a sahuagin. Those who truly understand it, simply call it death." The wizard paused for a moment and turned to look at Morgan once again, one silvered eyebrow arched expressively. "The real question, however, is why it followed you here."

Morgan hesitated before answering. Wizards, he knew from the old stories, were unpredictable and quick to anger—this one most of all. For a moment, he was once more that headstrong youth who sailed a small boat around the mage's isle, fearfully waiting for the wizard's wrath to fall.

I don't belong here!

The moment passed, and Morgan mustered his courage enough to speak—he owed that much to Avadriel. "I bear a message from the sea elf Avadriel," he said in what he hoped was a firm tone.

Dhavrim's expression grew grave. "Go on," he replied simply.

The wizard stood in silence as Morgan finished recounting his message.

The young man wondered what the wizard could be thinking, but was loath to interrupt the mage's rumination. The silence grew, charging the air with its intensity like the moments before a lightning storm. Morgan's skin prickled as he watched Dhavrim grip his staff tighter.

Abruptly, the wizard spun and began to march back to his stone tower. "Come!" he barked commandingly, "there is much to be done this night."

"Wait!" Morgan called to the retreating figure. "What of Avadriel? If these . . . sa-sahuagin . . ." Morgan stumbled over the unfamiliar word before continuing, "followed me, then they must surely know where she is. We have to help her."

"Avadriel is a warrior and daughter of a noble house, she can take care of herself," Dhavrim replied, not stopping. "But if what she reported is true, then all of Faerûn is in danger. A great war is coming, and we must be prepared!"

Morgan ran after the heavyset wizard, the thought of Avadriel being torn apart by sahuagin driving everything else from his mind.

"She may be a warrior," he shouted at Dhavrim, "but right now she's gravely wounded and alone, while those creatures are out there ready to tear her apart."

He watched in disbelief as the wizard, only a few steps ahead of him now, ignored his plea. Avadriel would be killed and this fat coward refused to do anything about it. Wizard or no wizard, he thought acidly, I will make him come with me.

Increasing his pace, Morgan caught up to Dhavrim and jerked hard on the wizard's meaty shoulder. "Listen to me!" he shouted.

And instantly regretted his decision.

The wizard rounded on Morgan, his eyes flashing dangerously in the moonlit sky. Horrified, Morgan took a step back as Dhavrim pointed the glowing tip of his staff right at him—and began to laugh.

"By the gods, boy," Dhavrim managed to wheeze in between chortles, "you've great heart, you do. There are few warriors who would dare brave the wrath of Dhavrim Starson." Another wave of laughter racked the wizard's frame. Seeing the young man's obviously confused expression, Dhavrim sucked in a huge gulp of air and tried to calm himself. "You've wisdom, too," he continued, "though I doubt you know it. Avadriel is perhaps the only witness to the strength of the enemy. Such information is undoubtedly critical."

Morgan stood in stunned disbelief as the wizard, still quietly chuckling, raised his arm and called out a name. A few moments later, a familiar white form hurtled out of the night to settle upon Dhavrim's pudgy arm. The wizard whispered something to the gull, then Morgan watched the night reclaim it as it flew away.

"It is time we were off, boy," Dhavrim said softly, and started down the path toward the beach. Leaving Morgan to wonder briefly at the quicksilver nature of wizards.

* * * * *

Dhavrim stood at the stern of the boat and whispered a word into the deepening night. To Morgan, sitting anxiously in the small craft, it sounded like the dark hiss of sea foam—ancient and redolent with power. The boat surged forward and cut across the waves, eventually piercing the thick wall of fog. Another word brought light, pale and ghostly, pulsing forth from the silver-shod tip of the wizard's staff. The mage-light shredded both fog and night. In its path, Morgan watched Dhavrim scan the horizon, grim and rigid as the unyielding stone of his tower.

Despite himself, he could not suppress a shiver of fear. The wizard's words had frightened him. War. It was coming, and the tides would run dark with blood before it was over. Damn it all, he thought, everything and everyone he knew was threatened by a danger he could scarcely comprehend, let alone fight.

Especially Avadriel.

That's what frightened him the most. The sea elf wounded and alone, while a host of Umberlee's darkest creatures hungered for her flesh. If she should die, he knew that the world would seem empty. Geas or not, he loved her.

This was madness, he thought bitterly. Perhaps his father had it right, sailing into the moonless arms of the sea, silent and alone. Perhaps some forms of madness were better than others.

Lost in the darkness of his thoughts, Morgan was surprised to hear Dhavrim's voice cut through the night. "We're close now, lad. Keep watch." With that, he extinguished the light from his staff.

They had traveled through the thick bank of fog, and the moon shone once more in the sky. By its light, he could make out the ghostly silhouette of the sea caves just ahead.

As they drew nearer, Morgan's blood ran cold. In the pale light, he saw several figures creeping around the rocks near Avadriel's cave. Their movements seemed stiff and awkward, but even at this distance he could identify them as kin to the creature that had attacked him on Dhavrim's island. He reported this to the wizard.

"Aye, lad, I see them," Dhavrim replied. "Wait until I give you the signal, then cover your eyes."

Morgan nodded silently and waited as the dinghy drew closer to the sea cave. His heart pounded heavily in his chest. The names of several gods came to his lips, but he was too scared to utter a prayer. What am I doing here? he thought.

"Now!" shouted Dhavrim.

Hastily, Morgan drew both arms over his eyes. Even with this protection, his vision flooded with light. Just as suddenly, it disappeared. The boat rocked and he heard a splash, followed by the wizard's voice.

"Row hard for the cave and bring Avadriel out. I'll keep the foul creatures occupied."

All thought stopped as Morgan struggled to obey the voice. Quickly, he set the oars to water and rowed toward the cave. Off to his side he could hear the sibilant hiss of sahuagin and the fierce cries of Dhavrim, but he forced them out of his mind. When he reached the sea cave he called out for Avadriel.

A small voice answered, "Morgan? What are you doing here?"

"Quick, Avadriel, you must get in. I've brought Dhavrim, but the gods-cursed sahuagin are everywhere."

She jumped into the boat. Morgan found it difficult not to crush her to his chest. Avadriel was alive, he thought, though their survival depended on his strength and the power of an inscrutable wizard. Desperately, he turned around and rowed back out toward the wizard. In the wan moonlight, he could see the evil creatures lying in crumpled heaps upon the rocks. Dhavrim leaned heavily against his glowing staff, a beacon of hope amid the broken sahuagin bodies.

Relief flooded through Morgan. They were safe. Steadily, he propelled the boat back toward the wizard, thinking all the while of what his life with Avadriel would be like. He couldn't help but smile as she drew her body closer to his. He turned toward her, ready to speak his heart, when the water in front of the boat began to froth.

Suddenly, the last sahuagin slavered out of the churning water into the boat. With a cry, Morgan pushed Avadriel back, drew one of the oars out of the lock, and swung it at the beast.

It glanced off the creature's thick hide with a dull thud.

The sahuagin hissed loudly and brought its scaled arm down upon the oar, snapping it in half. Morgan watched helplessly as the beast made a grab for Avadriel. Desperately, he took the splintered haft of the oar and jammed it into the creature's chest. This time the wood pierced the beast's scales, sliding past muscle and bone. The sahuagin roared in pain and lashed out wildly, raking Morgan across his throat, before the boat overturned.

As Morgan struggled feebly to the surface, his throat a corona of agony, he cast about for signs of Avadriel. In the distance, he could still see the glowing tip of the wizard's staff, obscured now and then by the crest of a black wave. His limbs grew heavy, as if they were weighted anchors, threatening to pull him down, and his head spun from loss of blood. Disoriented and in pain, it took him a few moments to realize that he no longer needed to keep himself afloat. Silently, Avadriel had come up from behind to support him.

Morgan tried to turn and see her, but his sluggish limbs would not respond. Instead, Avadriel gently laid him on his back, and carefully held his head above the water. He watched her in silence for a few moments, marveling at the way her eyes absorbed the crystalline light of the moon, before speaking.

"The sahuagin?" he gurgled from the ruined strip of flesh and cartilage that remained of his throat.

Avadriel touched a webbed finger to his lips. "Hush, Morgan. The beasts will trouble us no more." She paused before saying, "Twice now, I owe you my life."

He tried to protest, to profess his love before the darkness that danced at the edge of his vision claimed him forever, but a spasm of pain racked his body. All he could do was let out a single, frustrated gasp.

The sea elf gently stroked his forehead, and, as if reading his mind, spoke gently into the night. "Do not worry, my love, I, too, hear the calling of my heart." She looked away, but not before Morgan caught the look of pain and sadness that creased her face. "Come, the wizard has recovered the boat. It's time to go."

As she turned her face back toward him, Morgan stared deeply into her eyes. He nodded his head slightly, understanding flooding his awareness.

"May Deep Sashelas bless you until we meet again," Avadriel whispered before touching her lips to his.

At that contact, Morgan felt his pain flow out of him, leaving only a steady, measured sense of peace. Water enfolded him, circling him gently like the protective arms of a lover. They had succeeded, he thought dully, as his body slid through the depths. The wizards knew of the sahuagin invasion, and Avadriel was safe. Smiling, Morgan floated down into the dark waters of oblivion.

And beyond.

Appendix

The Calendar of Harptos

The calendar used throughout the realms of Faerûn consists of twelve months, each with an even thirty days. With the addition of five "special days," the Faerûnian year is three hundred and sixty-five days long. Months are further divided into three tendays each.

The new year begins on the first of the month of Hammer, and ends on the thirtieth of Nightal. Years are numbered using Dalereckoning, based on the year that humans were first permitted by the Elven Court to settle in the forests. Concurrently, years are given names in the Roll of Years. These year names were drawn from the prophesies of the Lost Sage, Augathra the Mad, and her student, the great seer Alaundo. The

Year of the Gauntlet, during which all of the preceding stories are set, is 1369 Dalereckoning.

Order	Month	Colloquial Description
1	Hammer	Deepwinter
	—Midwinter—	
2	Alturiak	The Claw of Winter, or the Claws of the Cold
3	Ches	Month of the Sunsets
4	Tarsakh	Month of the Storms
	—Greengrass—	
5	Mirtul	The Melting
6	Kythorn	The Time of Flowers
7	Flamerule	Summertide
	—Midsummer—	
8	Eleasias	Highsun
9	Eleint	The Fading
	—Higharvestide—	
10	Marpenoth	Leafall
11	Uktar	The Rotting
	—The Feast of the Moon—	
12	Nightal	The Drawing Down

About the Authors

I'm **Lynn Abbey**, ex-New Yorker, ex-Michigander and ex-Oklahoman. I moved to Florida in 1997. It's nice, but I prefer snow. My first novel, *Daughter of the Bright Moon,* was published in 1978. I've kept busy since then with nearly twenty published novels, including *Siege of Shadows* (ACE Books) and *Jerlayne* (DAW, 1999), and a ten-year stint as co-creator of Thieves' World. In the early '90s, TSR invited me to play in their DARK SUN® and FORGOTTEN REALMS® sandboxes where I get to write about people who think they're gods (little do they know. . . .). It's been a blast. I can hardly wait to see what the editors come up with next and how I can confound them!

When he's not being beaten and abused by editors, **Peter Archer** lives in the Pacific Northwest with his wife, daughter, and a mentally unbalanced cat, who is under the illusion that she's descended from Attila the Hun. He's the managing editor of Wizards of the Coast Book Publishing, author of several short stories, and under the patient tutelage of his wife hopes someday to learn to balance a bank statement.

Richard Lee Byers is the author of *X-Men: Soul Killer, Dark Kingdoms*, and many other novels. His short fiction appears in numerous anthologies, including *Realms of Mystery, The Colors of Magic,* and *Tales from the Eternal Archives: Legends.*

Elaine Cunningham is the author of a dozen or so fantasy novels, most of them set in the FORGOTTEN

REALMS. Prompted by her latest story, *The Magehound*, she is venturing out of Waterdeep for an extended visit to the magic-rich lands of Halruaa.

Though prone to sea sickness on the big water, **Troy Denning** enjoys boating and water-skiing on the relatively secure confines of Lake Geneva, Wisconsin. He is the author of seventeen novels and a handful of short stories. To learn more about Troy, visit the Alliterates homepage at alliterates.com.

Clayton Emery has written a dozen fantasy-adventure novels and several historical mystery shorts. He lives in New Hampshire and spends his time restoring a Colonial house and gardens and a World War II Jeep, and dashing around in a kilt reenacting the American Revolution.

Ed Greenwood is a Canadian librarian, the creator of the FORGOTTEN REALMS, the author of a dozen novels and over fifty game products set therein—and, by Mystra, he's even starting to *look* like Elminster.

Larry Hobbs was born and raised in Ohio, where his daughter Jennifer still lives. He and his wife, Sharon, now live in Minneapolis with their two sons, Matt and Dan. He just turned in his first fantasy novel, *Sword of Brittany*, to his agent and has started work on an alternative history set in the sixteenth century.

Mel Odom is diligently working on something of a bardship in the FORGOTTEN REALMS. Now where's that hat he's supposed to pass?

Having grown up in central Texas, **Thomas M. Reid** readily admits that the majority of his own waterborne adventures have been limited to swimming pools and the occasional trip to South Padre Island.

Though this is his first foray into fiction, **Steven E. Schend** has called the Realms home, having worked in it as a designer and editor since 1990, far longer than he's lived in the state of Washington. While he can find his way around Waterdeep's Trades Ward much easier than Pike Place Market, Steven lives in Seattle and vastly appreciates two factors it provides for keeping writers at their craft: wonderful coffee and far too much rain.

Despite turning in his editor's pen to run the RPG business at Wizards of the Coast, **Keith Francis Strohm** still finds time to exercise his creativity. When not writing short stories, he enjoys performing opera and singing choral music with Seattle Pro Musica. He lives in Washington with his wife, Marlo, and a stubborn, far-too-clever-for-its-own-good Akita named Osen.

The Magehound

Counselors and Kings, Book I

Elaine Cunningham

Available April 2000

An Excerpt

"Come," the little girl's mother gasped as she stumbled toward a rounded, freestanding tower.

Though the tower appeared utterly smooth from even a pace or two away, a narrow flight of stairs had been carved into the pink stone. They stumbled up the stairs, frantic now, all pretense of adventure forgotten. When they reached the top, her mother bent over, struggling for breath and speech. The girl barely made out a request for light.

She had been schooled in which light to conjure during just such a "game," and she quickly cast the unique little cantrip that summoned a moonmaid's tear. Softer than moonlight and shaped like a giant teardrop, the globe was visible only to her eyes. It illuminated not the natural or the material world but the created magic that embellished both.

The faint light revealed a glassy, translucent path that stretched from the tower to a nearby villa, one on the very shores of the lake, but this was not how she remembered the path. She sent a questioning look at her mother. The woman nodded. Without further hesitation the child stepped out into the seemingly empty air. Her mother followed closely, trusting her daughter to see what she herself could not.

No moon shone that night, but suddenly the two of them were silhouetted against a large, softly glowing orb. The girl muttered a phrase she'd overheard from an impatient merchant who'd cursed the fickleness of Selune and her inconvenient tides. For once her mother did not reprove her for her inelegant speech.

They scrambled over the wall of the strange villa and down a flight of stairs toward the courtyard. There a small pool with a fountain bubbled and beckoned—and possibly offered a tunnel into Lake Halruaa. The girl had encountered such things before on their "adventures," and usually such tunnels were short, safe, and smooth, with no surprises more unpleasant than the magic that tickled her skin like sparkling wine and the brush of the occasional fish that the magic summoned for the wizard-lord's table and his children's sport.

The descent took far longer than it should have. Down the stairs they ran, eyes frantic on the mosaic floor below. The girl noticed, suddenly, that the floor's pattern seemed to be shifting. The color turned from its intricate inlay of deep reds and rich yellow to a uniform hue of darkest sapphire. Small lights began to twinkle in the glossy tile.

Puzzled, she came to a stop on the first landing. Her mother bumped heavily into her. The child glanced back the way they'd come.

"Look," she said grimly, pointing up. Or possibly down. The fountain bubbled overhead, and below them was the unmistakable void of the night sky. Inexplicably the two had changed places.

"A puzzle palace," her mother said in a faint, despairing voice. "Mystra save us."

The child's trained gaze darted around. Several flights of stairs led from the landing, some going up, some down, and some leading nowhere at all. There were four levels of balconies surrounding the courtyard, and all levels seemed to be split into several parts. Some had elaborately carved or tiled or painted ceilings, others were roofed or floored by the night sky. It was as if some crazed wizard had inserted this small section of the city into a gigantic kaleidoscope, fracturing and fragmenting reality beyond logic or recognition.

"This way," she guessed and darted toward a waterfall that disappeared into the air, only to resume its fall a hundred paces to the south.

It proved to be a good choice. In moments they stood before a door—a real door, one that opened with a latch and led into the stolid, staid reality of the villa beyond.

As the door swung open, her mother's amulet started to glow. Never had this happened before, and the fearsome novelty of it froze the child where she stood. In the span of a heartbeat the shining bit of electrum turned rosy with heat. Her mother tore off the amulet, breaking the slender chain.

Instantly the courtyard was alive with verdant magic. The questing vine, fragmented into an impossible maze, writhed and twisted like a titanic snake that had been many times severed, and floundered violently about in death throes.

But apparently someone could make sense of the path. A shout came from beyond the villa's walls. A door crashed open, and footsteps thundered through the building toward them.

The child turned to dart back into the insane courtyard, plucking at her mother's skirt to indicate her intent rather than risk speech and discovery. The woman gently pried the small fingers loose.

"Go," she said quietly. "My magic is nearly gone. They will find me soon whether I run or stay."

"I won't leave you," the child said stubbornly.

"You must. It is you they seek."

She only nodded. Somehow that was another thing she had always known. But knowing was not the same as doing, and she could not bear to leave.

A figure appeared suddenly in the open door, though the sound of footsteps was still many paces away. The child stared with mingled awe and horror at the most beautiful creature she had ever beheld.

In the doorway stood an elf woman of rare and exotic beauty. Her skin was the coppery hue of a desert sunset, and her elaborately curled and braided hair was the deep green of jungle moss. Rich displays of gold and emeralds and malachite glittered at her throat and on her hands. Over her yellow silk dress she wore an overtunic of dark green, much embroidered with golden thread. A little smile curved her painted lips but did not quite touch her eyes, which were as golden and merciless as a hunting cat's. She was beautiful and terrible all at once.

"Greetings, Tekurah," the elf said to the child's mother. "You have led us on a merry chase. I Almost admire you for it. And this, of course, is your accursed little bastard."

Her voice was as sweet and clear as temple bells, but the child was not fooled. "Bastard" was the worst epithet a Halruaan could hurl. Suddenly, the child understood that it was not just an insult, but the truth.

The crescendo of footsteps came to a sudden stop just beyond the door, and the elf woman glanced back over her shoulder. "Take them both," she said with cold satisfaction.

Tekurah leaped forward and braced her hands on either side of the lintel. She cast a desperate glance back at her daughter. "Run," she pleaded.

The child hesitated. Green light began to encircle her mother, twining about her like choking vines. The woman tottered and went down to her knees, her hands clawing frantically at her throat.

Terror urged the child to flee, but guilt held her in place. She had begged her mother to summon a fierce creature. Was this what had come of her wish?

The elf woman shouldered past the faltering wizard and lunged for her small quarry, but the child dropped to the ground. The sudden shift of her weight made her slip like a trout through the slender copper hands. She rolled aside and darted out into the courtyard.

Her mother's voice followed her, urging her to flee. She ran to the waterfall and dived in, not sure whether she would crack her head on tile or soar out toward the bright shards that followed Selune. She fell smoothly and splashed down into the pool. And yes, her flailing hands found a tunnel opening in the tiled wall.

She came up for air, breathing in as deeply as she could, then diving deep. Her mother's last words followed her as she swam.

"Forget me!"

Never, the child thought grimly as she paddled toward the lake. She would find her mother, and if that was not to be, she would see their mysterious pursuer dead at her small feet.

Her flailing hands touched something slim and smooth. A small pulse of power skittered across her skin. An eel, perhaps?

She frowned, puzzled. This had not happened to the child she had been, nor had it ever been part of her dream. A second jolt struck, dragging her swiftly upward.

Tzigone awoke suddenly, gasping for air as if she had indeed been underwater too long. A startled, almost panicked moment passed before she remembered where she was.

Her resting place this night was unusually secure. Earlier in the day she had trailed a starsnake to this tree—the enormous bilboa tree that shaded and dominated the public garden known as the Glade—and climbed until she found its perch. The snake was sleeping still, its gossamer wings folded and the blue and white scales of its long, coiled body glittering like moonstone in the cool light of Selune.

Tzigone pushed herself up into a sitting position on the broad limb and shoved a hand through her short, sweat-soaked hair. The rope that lashed her to the tree had pulled tight around her waist, giving testimony to a restless sleep. She'd probably touched the snake while she was thrashing about.

Had she been almost anyone else, she would now be swinging from her rope, smoking like an overcooked haunch of rothe. The slumber of starsnakes was guarded by powerful magical defenses. A wandering sage had once informed her that creatures changed over the centuries in response to their surroundings and in particular to thwart the threats offered by their enemies. In Halruaa, wizards were the most dangerous beings, potential enemies of anything that slithered, flew, or walked about on two legs or more. The starsnake developed defenses that were more ingenious than most. No wizard had been able to negate their shield, though from time to time there was tavern talk of yet another attempt—or darkly humorous tales of those who had tried and failed. No one in full possession of their senses would approach, much less touch, the sleeping creatures. That made this limb one of the safest spots in all Halruaa—provided that Tzigone left before the sun rose and the creature awakened. This arrangement suited her just fine. She and starsnakes were frequent bedfellows.

The winds rustled slightly as if touched by a night breeze. Tzigone brought her legs under her and crouched like a wary cat, one hand on the hilt of her knife. Sometimes the reptiles were roused by the release of their own killing magic, especially if they were hungry. . . .

From under the waves of the FORGOTTEN REALMS® world's mightiest oceans comes a rising tide of war, hatred, and death—and the face of Faerûn will never be the same again.

THE THREAT FROM THE SEA

The beginning of the first must-read series since Avatar—*Rising Tide* begins the epic story of the Threat from the Sea, a story that continues in:

Featuring stories set against the backdrop of the sea invasion by Ed Greenwood, Elaine Cunningham, Troy Denning, Lynn Abbey, Mel Odom, and a host of your favorite FORGOTTEN REALMS authors!

The epic tale concludes in:

Iakhovas invades the Inner Sea!

May, 2000

You'll never look at the blue spaces on your maps the same way again. . . .

Lost Empires

In nooks and crannies of the FORGOTTEN REALMS® setting, explorers search out hidden secrets of long-dead civilizations, secrets that bear promises and perils for present-day Faerûn.

The Lost Library of Cormanthyr
Mel Odom

Is it just a myth? Or does it still stand somewhere in the most ancient corners of Faerûn? An intrepid human explorer sets out to find the truth and encounters an undying avenger, determined to protect the secrets of the ancient elven empire of Cormanthyr.

Faces of Deception
Troy Denning

Hidden from his powerful family's enemies behind the hideous mask of his own face, Atreus of Erlkazar seeks his salvation on an impossible mission. Driven by the goddess of beauty to find a way past his own flesh, he must travel to the ancient valleys of the enigmatic Utter East.

Star of Cursrah
Clayton Emery

The Protector crawls forth, the shade of a dead city whose rulers refuse to die, and young companions in two distant epochs learn of a dreadful destiny they cannot escape.

GREYHAWK

Novelizations of the best-selling game modules

Against the Giants
Ru Emerson

A village burns while its attackers flee into the night. Enraged, the King of Keoland orders an aging warrior to lead a band of adventurers on a retaliatory strike. As they prepare to enter the heart of the monsters' lair, each knows only the bravest will survive. Against the odds. Against the giants.

White Plume Mountain
Paul Kidd

Three companions find themselves trapped in a city filled with warring priestly factions, devious machinations, and an angry fiend. To save the city they must find three weapons of power that lie in the most trap-laden, monster-infested place this side of Acererak's tomb: White Plume Mountain.

GAME OF THE YEAR

"Baldur's Gate delivers everything you could ask for in a computer game."

Computer Games Strategy Plus